THE TOM-WALKER

Books by Mari Sandoz published by the UNP

THE

TOM-WALKER

A NOVEL BY

MARI SANDOZ

University of Nebraska Press
Lincoln and London

First Bison Book printing: August 1984
Most recent printing indicated by the first digit below:
1   2   3   4   5   6   7   8   9   10

Library of Congress Cataloging in Publication Data
Sandoz, Mari, 1896–1966.
  The Tom-Walker.
  "Bison."
  Reprint. Originally published: New York : Dial Press,
1947.
  I. Title.
PS3537.A667T6 1984   813'.52   84-5221
ISBN 0-8032-4150-X
ISBN 0-8032-9147-7 (pbk.)

Reprinted by arrangement with the Mari Sandoz Corporation,
represented by McIntosh and Otis, Inc.

CONTENTS

"But none can escape the Paphlagonian, his eye is everywhere. And what a stride! He has one leg on Pylos and the other in the Assembly; his rump is exactly over the land of the Chaonians, his hands are with the Aetolians and his mind with the Clopidians."

—DEMOSTHENES

THE KNIGHTS: ARISTOPHANES

BOOK ONE

—*If you surpass him in impudence
the cake is ours.*

CHORUS

1 — *Skyuglers*

In the spring sun, the Ohio lay like a gleaming sickle against the wooded hills above Cincinnati. There was only a scattering of larger craft on the river now: a white-galleried boat or two moving slowly against a reluctant scarf of water, an occasional packet, and a few old stern-wheelers and heavy freighters; but the flatboats, rafts, dugouts and other stragglers were thick as waterbugs, the biggest run since the stampede for the frontier at Lincoln's first call for men five years ago. Mostly these were heading West too, and lead-loaded; some carrying covered wagons and oxen for the overlanding, many with returned soldiers going homeseeking, perhaps to the gold fields or to swing a pick and spike maul against the micks and the Chinee on the Pacific railroad. There was a deal of singing and carousing to pass the time, one string of rafts flying a pair of worn blue britches from a pole at its head, and as the new war-built Cincinnati Cannonball came snorting along the wooded bench, somebody blew a Mike Fink blast on a cowhorn at the high-toned skyuglers. But the fast train passed the river traffic like a coachwhip snake on a creek bank passing a clutch of ducks. Then everything was quiet again, only on the river the movement seemed even slower than before, and among the trees the stench of engine smoke hung long after the last blueness was gone.

At the little station of Martins Park a couple of hound-dogs lifted their ribs from the quaking rails and padded off to the hitchracks a while. The Cannonball never stopped except for some important personage; perhaps Secretary of War Stanton, Treasurer Chase, or Senator Tolley and Congressman Hayes come visiting friends and kinfolks at the large country places on the Cincinnati hills. With all such in yesterday, the depot loafers were dozing over on the shady side and not noticing the pretty ash-blonde girl who came hurrying up the back path behind the row of blooming lilacs as the train neared. Lifting the hoops of her white dress high she ran, but the path was steep as a goat trail and her new stays so elegantly laced that she had to pause to catch a breath even though the train was slowing. A young soldier appeared in a doorway, his face tallow-pale above the soft smudging of beard, his blue kepi set back on his dark, curly hair, and the girl gathered up her skirts again. Then she saw that the soldier was leaning on a crutch and that one britches leg was folded over high above the knee. She stopped, let her hands fall, and with a little crying in her throat she turned and ran back down the path, tripping over her white flounces billowing in the dust.

From the train door the young soldier looked uneasily around his little home station, as deserted as any he had seen through all the Rebel country, even where the rails had been uprooted and twisted hot from the bivouac fires. But the engine was whistling and so he reached a crutch stick down ahead of him like a tom-walker and swung off to the cinders, balancing himself awkwardly, a flat red calico sack hanging from his hand as the train pulled away in a skift of white smoke. As he stood there, one of the hounds lifted an ear, came over to sniff hopefully at the sack, and then trotted off down the slope, his tail in a listless, swaying bow, leaving the returned soldier alone on his crutch, looking down the empty track.

When the whistle of the Cannonball was gone toward Cincinnati, and the spring flies settled back to the horse droppings, an old Negro came uncertainly from the hitchracks. "Is that you, Mister Milton . . . ?" he asked. "I didn't rightly catch it was you to first. I guess I was forgetting about the . . . the laig."

At that the young soldier swung around on his crutch, feeling mean as a tromped-on cottonmouth. But it was only an old colored man got up like one of those fancy show bills, tailcoat and all. "Godamighty!" he defended, "didn't nobody need to know about the leg! No sense sending the stink home ahead of the carcass, was they?"

"Oh, no suh, no suh," the old man agreed, wiping his tall hat apologetically. He was Uncle Joseph, sent to fetch young Mister Milton. No, there wasn't nothing wrong with the folks. Fine as swamp hair; just busy getting up a little party for the homecoming.

At that young Milton Stone let his hand ease up on the smooth wood of his crutch and laughed a little, a pleased, remembering laugh. "Party! Well, I be a long-haired pup in a bur patch!" In his three years away he had forgotten his mother's habit of getting the blood kin together every whipstitch, whether funeral or kittening; to grub together, talk, maybe with a smidgin of singing and if there was hard cider or white mule, maybe she'd lift her skirts and dance them a jig with one of her no-good cousins, Moneymusk or The Irish Washerwoman—and he'd forgot!

But he was such a young 'un when he left, barely fourteen the day he and Johnny Stanger skinned off across the river to Sherman's army gathering in Tennessee. Now he was back, a man, a veteran, hobbling after a dyked-out old hacker to a mighty tony rig, an open carriage like the ones Cincinnati ladies used to ride out in, along Fourth Street or through the park of a Sunday, showing off their satins and plumes, the horses stepping high and farting.

With the red calico sack safe under his hand, and the crutch braced to take the jolts from the travel-sore stump of his leg, Milton rode along fine as any fancy lady, but when he sneaked a look back to the station one of the loafers was slouching off toward town, and a little wind was shaking the lilacs behind the weathered depot. Otherwise there was nothing; even the hounds were flat between the rails again.

But an uneasiness was eating at the boy like a weevil working in hard tack. "Spanking team a bays Bill Blaxton's got there," he said loudly. "A jim-dandy layout for high-toned buryings and such. . . ."

Old Joseph didn't turn his head. "This here ain't no hired rig," he said, talking high as any Georgia house nigger to a poor white. "It you pa's, and the horses belongs to you pa too."

His pa's! Hell's buzzards, now wasn't that sticking gold shoulder scrubbers on a straw foot for certain! Hiram Stone, the old Indian pain oil man, with such a layout! Not that anybody except Sarah ever called him a pain oil man and she only when she was black-guarding him. Hiram was a regular apothecary, even if his place was a hole in the wall down among the rivermen, and him so steady it must have taken a tubful of his bitters to get him up to buying such a thunder buggy. And somebody full of more than bitters to let him have it on tick.

Then it occurred to Milton that perhaps his folks had bogged themselves so deep in this war spending he had heard about that they couldn't help him. Maybe when the two hundred dollars in his pocket was gone he would be begging the streets like old Crutch

Williams, selling dirty pictures on the sly and mumbling dirty words to the women passing. Godamighty, it made a man's belly crawl like a mess of blacksnakes in a sack just to think on it.

Seemed, too, that this fancy rig might be tied in with his father not coming to the depot, if his mother was so busy rustling grub for the shindig. And Lucinda, little Lucinda who wrote him the stiff young lady letters, with pressed reseda or heartsease tucked inside, and always signed "Ever Yours" since he was home that time. Folks had made fuss enough over his returning then, young ones following at his heels and women gathering around him like hens clucking over a chick pulled out of a swill bucket because his arm was tied up from the minié ball, and the boy-fur just coming out on his cheek. Maybe it was like old Clyde Winston, who fought under old Fuss and Feathers against Santa Anna, used to tell them: "You'll hafta run home like the devil beatin' tan bar' the minit the shootin' stops if you want any flags flyin' for you, and folks not actin' like you been doin' a stretch in the pen."

Well, the old sarge sure knew a few things besides slashing Rebs with that Arkansaw toothpick of his. Not that Milton wanted the band playings and lady kissings Johnny wrote about last year, and the Grand Review in Washington, soldiers marching six abreast for two whole days, the greatest army in the world, like the papers said, buttons shining, brass cannon flashing, and people going crazy when Sherman's army came along, yelling, crying, children singing "Marching Through Georgia," girls falling down on the ground for any bummer. But that was last year. All Milton had hoped for today was that Lucinda would be at the depot so he could tell her right off he wasn't holding her to a crutch-cripple, a one-legger, and give her back the little prayer book he carried down to the sea and around. Now the loafers would spread the bad news like a pup tearing home from a skunk killing. He should have written about the leg himself when he found out the hospital hadn't, with so much of the help kiting off for home the minute the war was over. But the pain and misery was such a long dark cave, his handwrite almighty awkward to carry bad tidings, and his spelling, too.

Travel-worn and low-down, Milton shifted his crutch wearily against the seat. Better to have gone straight out West like the raftsman blowing his cowhorn at the biggety train today. Better even to have stayed back with the other hospital crips than be sitting alone in this tony carriage that was flinging up dust like a marching column, powdering the wild rose bushes and the lower branches of trees that had never been ripped by cannon fire, settling like mold on his faded blue uniform and on his sick-man hands.

He remembered how deep and fur-soft the dust used to feel when he and Johnny ran barefoot behind the wagons along this road, maybe falling when the wheels spun too fast, but getting up again, good as new, maybe even doing handstands and cartwheels to prove it. Now the road was deserted as a plantation run, with only the sporty George Shefton out—Yeller Weskit George exercising a trotter. Old Joseph gathered up his lines to pass, giving not an extra inch to the flying road cart, although he would have fetched himself a whip cut from the copperhead for it three, four years ago. Milton looked back and spit off into the dust. A Knight of the Golden Circle, one of that dirty outfit that helped draft dodgers, got tens of thousands to desert and maybe get caught and shot, putting off the peace for months, getting a lot more killed in the fighting, killed and crippled. . . .

But a man couldn't let himself think down that road, as Andy Burke, an old soldier who'd got shot in the neck with the Russians in the Crimea used to say. Andy was from Lincoln's home county and knew all about the Knights and their kind, plotting the Northwest Conspiracy to grab off a chunk of the Union clear through to Chicago for the Rebs while the fighting men were gone, trying to carve up the country like an old goat hide; one of them, that John Wilkes Booth, even shooting old Abe in the play show at Washington. A mess of polecats that folks hadn't ought to take up with, although some of the women seemed to, lollygagging around Booth, almost pulling his britches off when he came to Cincinnati that last time. Maybe it was his play acting, or his fancy dude's clothes. And George Shefton not much better, with the rivermen saying his fast horses, his bounty man and the perfumed brandy breath he carried all paid for by Beecher's Bibles—powder and ball smuggled over the Ohio to the Rebs instead of the Abolitionists. But it looked like any pig could whistle nowadays, with the ladies making sweet mouths for George Shefton too, even Lucinda writing that the girls thought him quite flash, and an elegant dancer.

"But not so good as you will be . . . " she added loyally. And although that was months after the leg, Milton rolled his wheel chair back among the dispensary shelves at the hospital and bawled like a calf with a foraging Federal on his tail.

Even Milton's mother wrote about George's elegant ways, saying he had gallantly carried Lucinda home from the Sherman's Christmas party, since her fiancé preferred flunky work in one of Andy Johnson's hospitals to returning to her side. "The party was very fashionable. The most elegant gowns and jewels were present . . . " Sarah had written, sounding like the old snips she saved from the *Inquirer* about the Longworth receptions, back when she and her brother were mud-paddling young 'uns looking across the river to the big double-pillared house on the hill, maybe all lit up for a duke or a prince. Seemed to Milton that the chickens sure were roosting high these days for Sarah Stone of the Ohio bottoms. It used to be only Lucinda's mother who went in and out everywhere, even in her plain cloaks, because the Martins once had a town house too, and a big country place called Martins Park—a hill-top mansion and a game preserve, with buffaloes that a German prince stopped off to see. But in the panic of 1837 everything went down the buzzard's gullet except the keeper's lodge, where the family lived now.

Maybe it was because Sarah's brother got to be a shyster lawyer and was appointed to a Senate vacancy that she made it to the Sherman's party; that and the family of her son's intended, as she called Lucinda. Or maybe it was the war, mixing and miggling bricks and straw like a tornado in a tub. A lot of things were miggled when Yeller Weskit George was loose, and his blackleg friend, Eph Dix, an ass-sitting colonel right here in Cincinnati. They helped get a lot of good boys shoveled under on the way to the sea with the arms they shipped south by the boatload, while a poor meachin little man like Preacher Goodwin, paddling his dugout over the river to a night-dying, got shot as a gun runner.

Uneasily Milton shifted the stump of his leg on the seat as the carriage topped a rise that overlooked the broad, shining river. It seemed a monstrous long time since Lucinda came down there that last day he was home. Three years, she fourteen, him not a year older but over a foot taller and a man, a powder-burnt, fighting man, with a wounded arm in a sling, and her just a sliver of a girl child without a hoop in her skirts, her pretty little face pinched together like from cold, her gray eyes dark as a storm coming up the Ohio against a morning sun.

With a soldier's loneliness on furlough, Milton had gone to a stand beside the stream where he and Johnny used to loaf and fish on Sundays, they not being of religious folks. Several times the boys found runaway slaves hiding under the bank, breathing through reeds, like strange, black sea monsters through the water. Once on a flatboat tied to a stump they saw a man dance a queer slow shuffle to his own fiddling, and while he fried catfish for the boys he told about the gold and the Indians out West. He even taught them some new steps, fine ones, only no good for a crutch-cripple, a one-legger. . . .

But it was there, standing beside the cold winter river, that Lucinda came up beside Milton. She was in her church cloak and slipped the little white prayer book of her confirmation into his hand.

"To keep you safe," she had said, her voice so low a man couldn't be expected to hear, her cheeks red with the shame of her boldness. So he had taken an apple from his pocket and naming it between them, split it in two, awkwardly, because of his arm. Afterward he counted the seeds into her little white mitten, beginning with "One, I love," to "nine, he comes, ten, he tarries," laughing loudly at Lucinda's disappointed face that there were ten.

"Maybe I can get the General to send Johnny home," he teased.

But the girl shook her head. Johnny wasn't her naming and so Milton dropped two more seeds into her hand. "Eleven, he comes, twelve, he marries," and closing his fingers over the seeds he held the mitten tight as he went beside her up to where her folks tried to run a little orchard on the hill acres around the lodge. When he went away he kissed her good-by, for they were promised.

Milton moved himself on the jiggling carriage seat as though he were resting a marching foot. Lucinda would be at his mother's shindig today, have to find out about his crippling before a lot of strangers . . . after she had waited, not throwing him over like in the letters a lot of them got. "We think you should know," they mostly started, telling that a wife or a sweetheart wasn't rightly waiting. Turned out it was mostly another copperhead trick getting the letters written, and no telling how much trouble it made or how many got killed reckless, or deserted and got irons and the firing squad. Desertions jumped by tens of thousands the weeks the letters came thickest, he heard say. He knew a dozen from old G Company that skun out.

But Lucinda had waited. Yet she was a girl; some dudey yeller weskit who was an elegant dancer with a pair of legs would make her forget soon enough. In a week Milton would be off for the gold fields in Idaho or at least Colorado, where nobody who knew him needed to turn his face from the pinned-up britches. He had seen crips come crawling back to the hospital to hide from the eyes at home. That was why he stuck as long as the place stayed open, learning about dosings and splints and dressings to use on the miners. "We done well, with your Uncle Steven's kind assistance in the Senate," his mother wrote once, and while Milton looked on this as her usual big talk, he hoped there might be enough of his bounty money left in her shuck tick to get him West. But seeing Uncle Joseph and the carriage made him uneasy as a hog in a smokehouse.

Nor had Milton realized how it would be to look down on the old Ohio again, so broad and pretty in the sun, a great shining band around the dark hills, the church-steepled city of Cincinnati like a narrow brown rug tucked around the bottom, with smaller, darker scatterings on the Kentucky side that were towns too, and not a shell-torn wall anywhere, nothing like in Atlanta, or Charleston.

Seeing the town and the river again brought back the old shaking in his belly and all down his arms. Godamighty, he could blubber like a sugar-tit recruit, right before Uncle Joe. But he was a soldier, and so he held himself together, and looked away. Then he noticed they had left the old road for the turnpike, and unless he had forgotten too much in the months of pain and morphine, this was the way to the big Rickert place on the hill.

"Yas suh, this the Rickert drive," Joseph admitted, "but the old copperhead Reb he gone. Chased out in the night, and you pa and ma move they stuff in."

"My folks moved in?" young Milton exclaimed, feeling he ought to laugh at this story as at some big joke, some great bull alligator tale told in the dark of the moon. Flipping his kepi off he pounded the dust from it and set it back on his dark hair. Hell's buzzards! the Stones wouldn't be more than squatters with their sticks of furniture in that Rickert place—thirty rooms, an iron deer on the lawn, guest houses on the slope, the grounds big and fine as a park. They'd fit better in the servant quarters down the back hollow, about as good as the slave shacks he saw from Kentucky to the sea. It was laughing funny—and as disturbing as the dreams of those long months of sickness, disturbing and frightening.

Then it occurred to him that his folks really must be working there, the little drug store gone and times as hard as the vets who came back to the hospital said. But old Joseph was already swinging the bays up the front way, up the curved drive to the double-towered house that topped the high point like an eroded butte of brown sandstone. Now the time for the bad news faced Milton like a Reb position to be taken by naked steel, and a bad time for it too, with the place full of visitors, traps and carriages lining the drive clear around the back, thirty, forty at least, and pretty music and talk and laughing coming from the wide windows. To Milton it seemed he was in some strange, far-off country, or in a morphine dream of homecoming, with nothing familiar and known—outside of Yeller Weskit George not even a known face.

Then Hiram Stone came hurrying through the porte-cochere, his belly buttoned up tight in a genuine banker's coat, his hair and beard trimmed like a banker's too, and his hand held out. But seeing the crutch, he stopped, his purpled face darkening above the grizzled beard.

"Why, you damn clamp-mouth young scalawag! Coming home a legless cripple!—sneaking in like a whipped cur!" he roared. "Or did your mother encourage this fraud, this breech of filial duty?" Making a noise like old Chet Tidwell all right, the son thought, or maybe a senator, throwing his shoulders back and his belly out so there was nothing you could say to him.

But the sight of his crippled son really caught the father anti-godlin, for all his puffing. He rubbed a hand miserably over his beard and shook his head. "Son, I'm damned grieved to see your misfortune," he said, and taking Milton by the arm, led him away into the carriage house before the boy could get his calico sack in hand. On a bench beside him, Hiram listened to the story of that last engagement, with everybody holding off because it was known Lee had surrendered, most of the Rebs skedaddling. But there was some scattered musketry and Milton got a flesh wound in the calf, as was reported home; not enough to stop him, not half as bad as the minié ball in his arm. But it got poisoned so they had to saw the leg off below the knee and then above, and finally most of the rest before they got the rotting stopped.

"And your story of being cured and staying on to work at the hospital was all a lie, a damned, barefaced lie to your mother!"

Seeing that his father was swelling up again, the boy tried to explain that with the hospital staff stripped down like a molting hen, he helped roll pills and fold powders, later dressing wounds and changing drain tubes from his wheel chair or crutches, and glad of the chance to learn enough so he could make a living out in the mines.

But Hiram, not listening, was already off on his own plannings. "If that damned Johnson wasn't such a goddamned Reb himself, or if the war could have lasted another year, been stretched out even six months——"

"Stretched out?" the boy's face was white as suet under the dark curling of beard. "Stretched out—Godamighty! and more crips like me coming home!"

"Oh, damnit, we'll take care of you son, give you a good position. Business has been shot to hell by the peace and the Rebel-lovers, but we're still getting around ten thousand a month profit from the government on those old wharfs and warehouses of Stilson's, just standing empty now, and not a cent invested. And we got other pots coming to a boil. . . ."

Holding tight as a clamp to his familiar crutch, Milton looked away from this big-talking father who used to be tickled to pick up ten dollars here and there outfitting a train of Overlanders with pills and potions against cholera and bloody flux. Now he was running on about ten thousand a month from a row of water-front shacks, sheds empty as long as Milton could remember, since back when the railroads first cut into river shipping. Him a strong Lincoln man and talking against Johnson and against peace because he made money out of the war. Godamighty, it was like having a bluecoat, like having Johnny himself putting his Barlow knife in your ribs.

But before Milton could fetch up a reply for his father, the doors of the carriage house were flung open and half a dozen girls in billowing dresses of pink and blue, with ribbons and curls flying, trooped in, a pack of young fellows in dude clothes blocking the doors behind them. Then one of the girls saw the pinned up trouser leg and with a pretty little cry she fell back among the others, and together they shrank away from the crippled soldier, while through them pushed a black-eyed, high-bosomed, graying woman, lifting the hoops of her yellow brocade sideways to let her pass.

"So—Mr. Stone!" she exclaimed, making it half in fun before these guests, "Already I catch you keeping my darling son from me!" But when she saw Milton struggling to his crutch, her face was suddenly winter-swept. Then she ran forward and standing beside the boy, she turned quietly to the others.

"Leave us be together a minute," she said, and so the young people had to go, but looking back as they went, and letting their voices rise as soon as they were outdoors. Then they ran off toward the house, the excitement of their news sweeping them together like saplings in a windstorm or leaves skittering over a meadow.

Sullen and helpless as a suckerfish on a spear, Milton hobbled after his mother to the doorway of the biggest room he had ever seen in a house, crystal chandeliers glittering and sweet music playing off somewhere behind the bankings of greenery and flowers; the place packed to stinking with people dressed up wedding-fancy—silks and satins and hard shirts and all kinds of monkey uniforms, even Zouaves and bearskin shakos. When the faces all turned toward him the boy wanted to run as he did from his first Rebel charge, yet all he could do was brace his shaking against the stout wood of his crutch and glance quickly down his clothes with the soldier's uneasiness about his fly.

But Sarah's brother, Senator Tolley, had seen them too, and the opportunity for oration. Rallying the company and sucking his belly up inside him like a medicine wagon man, he roared out: "We bid you welcome, O heroic son of Ohio . . . " making Milton's tired young face burn with a shame that was like the scalding of a wound. Godamighty, why hadn't he hired river passage straight through to Independence, taking a chance on getting through to the mines somehow before he starved. Better to have failed it; better to jump in the river with a mud hook tied to a man's neck than to come home from a war.

But the Senator used to be a protracted preacher and so the boy had time to quiet down and see that none of the faces seemed turned toward him in friendliness. Some looked polite as Sunday, some gawking, some even laughing sly as magpies among themselves, but nowhere was there anybody of the old days, not even his mother's relations still living on the bottoms. Besides, it looked like his folks had gone churchy and not Holiness either, for there stood Reverend Johnson of St. Matthew's. Milton remembered pushing his boy into the canal long ago and then having to haul him out because the ninny-tit couldn't even dog paddle.

Nor was Lucinda anywhere, and uneasily Milton decided that even the solid figure of his father beside him must be something from the old hospital dreams, something that would fade when the pain of awakening came again. Then suddenly the girl was there, Sarah Stone bringing her into the room. "Our dear daughter was detained," she said. "A maidenly headache . . . " and kissed the girl's cheek while the men passed their knowing looks among themselves, and the women made syrupy mouths. But Milton saw she was very pale and so unsurprised by his leg gone that he was certain they had told her, and was dog-thankful. He saw, too, that she had grown up while he was away—taller, and beautiful in the wide-hooped dress that was white and soft as folds of mist over the Ohio in the spring.

Behind Lucinda were her parents, Nellie Martin like a Dominique hen, so neat and plain, the father awkward and red faced from his visits to the brandy keg since his daughter came whipping her pony home in a slow, fat gallop not two hours ago and flung herself from the cart into his arms, sobbing, "He has a leg gone! Oh, father— almost a whole leg gone, cut off!"

"Who, child, who?"

Oh, it was Milton! She had gone down to the depot. It seemed too cruel to do as his mother wanted, only the carriage meeting him, and so she had seen that his leg was off.

"On crutches?" the father demanded, unwilling to believe this thing.

"Yes."

"The devil!" David Martin snorted. "I will not have my daughter the wife of a peg leg!" And when the girl started to cry again, "Oh, father, I promised . . . " he took her to the house, to her mother.

But Nellie Martin's concern was for the girl's silly sneaking off in her wedding gown. The match she wouldn't consider breaking off. The plans were all made, the guests waiting, probably Sol Chase and even Secretary Stanton, with Steve Tolley working so thick with the Radicals. Besides, the time had come when the Martins of Martins Park couldn't be choosers, now that even their little peach crop was gone through the frosting. As a Stone, Lucinda would have both family station and the means to its proper maintenance, besides helping to make suitable marriages for her sisters. These reasons Nellie Strathorn, the schoolmaster's daughter found proper to tell her husband; another she kept for herself: Sarah Stone had a new green moire costume from that place in New York where Mrs. Lincoln was said to owe seventy thousand dollars.

To the girl's fear that maybe Milton wouldn't want it that way now, she was also firm. "Fiddle-faddle! He's only a boy; how would he know what is best?"

So David Martin slipped down to his keg of peach brandy in the cellar while the mother bathed Lucinda's face and cleaned her dust-soiled ruffles. Now the girl was standing in the great crowded ball-room of the Stones before the returned soldier, holding out her strong little hand shyly, her gray eyes dark and agitated, her soft lips trembling. Milton wanted to stoop over her to whisper, "You ain't tied to me, Lucie, not to a cripple. . . ." He wanted to shout it aloud to the angels on the painted ceiling, yell it against all these stuffed, dressed-up, whole-bodied people. But he couldn't, and so it was never said, unless trying to give the girl her worn little prayer book back a while later counted for words. She wouldn't take it; perhaps she didn't understand.

Within two hours of his return, the seventeen-year-old Milton Stone was married to Lucinda Martin. When the boy finally saw that this was more than a homecoming that his managing mother had got together, he dug out the little prayer book and smoothing it tenderly against his blue sleeve, said, "You can have it back, Lucinda. You can take it right now and no hard feelings. . . ."

But the girl just shook her head, her eyes flooding. The orchestra behind the palms started the wedding march and Milton found himself up before the Reverend Johnson at the flower-banked fire-place, and Lucinda coming up with her father. Even now there would have been time, when someone noticed the satin kneeling pillows and ran to take them away because kneeling is very awkward for a one-legged man.

It was a gay and colorful wedding, everyone said, with Milton confused and embarrassed, as was becoming in a groom, and very handsome in his romantic darkening of beard and the new uniform of good blue cloth Sarah Stone had made for the day. He was attended by his cousin Sumner Tolley who used to be named Mike in the old days on the bottoms and had lost no leg in the war, although the bounty man hired to go in his place fell at Vicksburg. Beside Lucinda stood her younger sister Malinda looking lovely in rose-garland mull, and behind them the six girls in pinks and blues with rose-trimmed bonnets, a city dude for each. There was color in the crowd too, and the clatter of sabers, the Guthrie Grays, Zouaves and Turners in parade dress, as Sarah had requested. She managed to get some of the Ohio Fifths too, in their red flannel Garibaldi shirts, and even a couple of Rover Guards in scarlet coats, their great bearskin shakos on their arms. Against this fine showing the bride was shy and lovely, her hair with the sheen of silver maple leaves before a rain, her skin soft in the first bloom of womanhood, although she was turning seventeen, an age when many about her were already mothers.

"She sure picked her a tongue-tied bog-jumper!" one of the young Zouaves said, seeing the red of embarrassment and long illness gather about the sockets of Milton's sunken eyes until the warm glow of oysters, creamed chicken in patty shells, ices, wedding cake and champagne spread through his veins. Then his flushing spread too, and he began to talk. "Not much like picking skippers out a the sowbelly, is it, Colonel?" he demanded, breaking in on Sam Boolton's story of his suffering in Libby prison, leaning over the officer's shoulder, spilling champagne on his brass.

Later Milton sang a little, songs of the camps and the marches, mostly soldier parodies that reddened maidenly cheeks and brought amused glances and whisperings behind the busy fans. But when he bawled out, "Lift your skirts, maw, and pat it down . . . " and then started out to the carriage house to find the calico sack with his fiddle when the orchestra wouldn't play for him, Sarah stepped in, and with Lucinda beside her, led him to the library to see the gifts. The Martins Park constable was at the door, with two detectives from Cincinnati, and inside, under a brilliant chandelier, stood a long table piled with linen and damask, cut-glass and crystal, porcelain and silver and mother of pearl. And in the foreground was a new embossed wallet containing tickets for Niagara Falls, which Sarah slipped under her fan and away.

But Milton wasn't noticing. "Is—is all this plunder yours?" he whispered thickly to Lucinda.

"Mine?" she said in confusion. "Why, it's ours."

"Ours?" Milton echoed foolishly, reaching out for the card propped against a cake stand. "Huh, old John Sherman himself! You know, it's funny, two brothers from right around here, both big men, one a great general, t'other a schemin' bastard!" And when Sarah tried to shush him, he waved her aside and reached an uncertain hand for the elaborate crystal stand. But its heaviness surprised him so he let it slip from his fingers to hit the edge of a marble bench with a mighty crash, the flying pieces reflecting light like a cannonball bursting in the black of night.

Long after dark, when the moonsickle was near setting, two wagons full of old acquaintances from around the little water-front drug store, a few workers at the warehouses and some vets of old Company G like Clyde Winston gathered to charivari the new couple before the wedding tour up to Niagara Falls that the newspaper told about. They took a jug of Kentucky corn along just in case, and had lowered it a gallon before they got near the Rickert place, as they still called it, even though Hiram Stone had taken everything over as it stood, help and all, down to the last dish rag, and farther, some said—to that high yellow down near the river— old Hiram fancying a little tomcatting, too.

At the edge of the grounds Clyde and some of the others pulled back, wondering if it was proper to come making a noise and joking around a crip like young Milton.

"Hell, he's married, ain't he?" others protested. "He ain't lost nothing besides that leg, has he?"

No, Clyde guessed not, and they didn't want him feeling bad that his old cronies didn't come shivareeing; but banging tubs and shooting guns somehow didn't seem the right thing, even with old Jacob Sturmer along to play *Ich liebe dich* on his accordion. Standing together at the wagons in the fading moonlight, they looked up the long, empty slope to the dark butte of the house and tipped the jug around once more. Then they climbed back into the wagons and went down to Gottfried's for a beer or two, singing loudly over the accordion to show that their fun wasn't spoiled. In the dusky beer cellar their talk turned to the Stones, and the Tolleys from the bottoms south of the river, and to the sudden money some could make if they took to running with the Radicals, the anti-Lincolnites. ". . . The greasy bones of war sure makes the buzzards fat and biggety. . . ."

"Well, by God, they sure did shut that old ape of a Lincoln up in the backhouse and run off with the knob," one of the men said admiringly as he stripped his long blond mustaches of their foam.

"Yeh, they took over like that bunch of bushwhackers what caught a general with his pants down in a briar patch," Clyde Winston agreed, his campaign-weathered face sour. "Been running everything to suit 'emselves since. Pieced the war out long's they could, and 're still stirrin' up trouble."

"Stirrin' up trouble, hell!—workin' to keep the damned Reb traitors from taking the country over!" the man with the horsetail mustaches complained, elbowing aside a mild little shoemaker who tried soothing words.

But one of the vets in faded blue wasn't for smoothing anything over. "You can yell damn loud now, Ben," he said, "but we know you done your fightin' under a torch in the peace parade down Main Street, hanging that pair a pants full of straw for Jeff Davis to a lamp post. I say them Radicals off in Washington and their skull-duggin' hired hands around here's a bunch a war-graftin' sons a bitches!"

"By grabs, a blowin' outfit a pension hounds!"

"An' I ain't sayin' we ain't," another blue coat put in. "Nor that Milty Stone ain't 's good a young 'un in a joke or a fight as you could ask for, but it ain't no more'n fair that one a the graftin' outfit's got a dose a the lead too, when the war should a been done long before . . ."

"Why, you goddamn trampoosin' bummer—crazy as loony old Sherman hisself! But you better learn to talk like you shot, or there'll be more blood lettin'."

"Gentlemen, gentlemen," old Jacob coaxed, pulling a little at his accordion. "Is not money where one can find it this bad time? It does no good to lay down blame for the soldier's unluck. . . ."

"Igonnies, no," one of Hiram's war-time hands agreed, "you can't be heavin' rocks at the contractors no more than you could hold a man in a powder factory responsible for them's gets their guts shot through, or a gravedigger for 'em that he shovels under."

Clyde Winston pushed himself back from the table. "You musta got fat wages outa Stone and Tolley. A man don't curry no horse as long as that one for nothin' . . ."

"Anyhow, you ain't hearin' me yell for the government to feed me, an' I ain't robbin' and stealin' like you bummers what thinks you're still out raidin' on the Rebs!" the old man roared out against them.

When he got no answer and the silence drew out, he looked up, his bloodshot, watery old eyes shifting from one to another around him. Then slowly he stumbled from the table and backed toward the door, for the veterans among the shivareers seemed to have drawn close together—mostly still in their army blue, or poorly hidden under the dirty gray-brown of walnut hull stain—drawn close as battle.

Up at the Stone house the travel-worn young soldier was asleep. Hours earlier he had been taken to his room by some of the guests after he broke into an angry, drunken quarrel in the smoking room with his cousin Sumner, whom he kept calling Mike as in the old days.

"I tell you my name is not Mike," the Senator's son corrected stiffly, drawing himself away. "Furthermore, I do not care to bandy words with an uncouth, inebriated bluecoat cripple!"

But Milton stomped his crutch after him, grabbing the beflowered lapel of his plump best man. "Oh, so you don't bandy words with a bluecoat crip? No, by God, but you took good care to see you stopped no bullets, you goddamn bounty puke!" he said, and knocked his fist in his cousin's mouth, short, neat and quick, as he learned in the army, leaving Sumner gap-mouthed, spitting bloody teeth.

"Now you can't never bite hardtack nor the cartridges for fighting, you draft-dodging——" He added a name he had learned in the camps and the long marches, a name for the male hangers-on who fought with the prostitutes for the soldiers' pay. He roared it out, and in the silence that followed somebody laughed, and then everybody began to talk fast, and to whip out fine linen handkerchiefs to wipe the blood from Sumner's face while Milton was led away to his chamber to protect the ladies from hearing his loud, vulgar doughboy tongue.

Sprawled across the silken bridal bed without undressing, Milton dropped into sleep, groaning a little now and then, his hand moving vaguely to the stump of his leg. He did not hear the door open and close or see Lucinda standing with her back against the oaken panels, a blurring of pale white in the duskiness of the night lamp. After a long time the girl slipped out of the dress that she had stitched so lovingly herself, and out of the rack of hoops. Timidly she crept into the far side of the wide bed and lay there very still, crying softly into her palms.

2 — Tall as Any Tree

The May sun was high outside the dusky, velour-draped room when Milton awoke. In his long hospitalization he had learned to hold himself together until the sleep drained out of him and he could stake out the boundaries of movement possible this side of pain. So he lay still, only his eyes moving, going carefully over the strange room as though he were scouting a Rebel position through the grass of a hummock, but here the walls were paneled in cloth he didn't know was damask, heavy rose and blue draperies at the windows, deep carpeting, dressing-tables, mirrors and satin chairs and at the foot of the silken bed a settee with the white billowing of a hoop-skirt dress slung across it. That brought him up on his elbow. There, beside him, was Lucinda, her hair like tangled skeins of pale silk over the pillow, her cheeks shiny with dried tears.

At sight of the girl, Milton's champagne bust-head began to pound and his first movement toward her brought back the pain in the stump of his leg, brought the whole recollection of yesterday boiling over him like the fog of another morphine dream, and he pushed his face into the pillow to choke his crying in the feathers. When he calmed he went over himself for more amputation, but he seemed all there except the leg; still in his coat and britches like on campaign bivouac, so he pulled himself cautiously from the bed and dragging his crutch along, crawled over the store-bought carpet that was soft as some strange, deep fur. At the door he looked back to the sleeping girl in the quiet duskiness. Then he got himself up on the crutch and stumped away to find his mother for an explanation and a reckoning.

But first he had to find a place to relieve himself. Hell's buzzards, even fancy livers like the Stones were pretending to be, had to squat now and then, he thought, remembering how his mother used to come for the pot under his bed on cold nights. He finally managed to make the woman dusting the stairs understand his need, and was shamed by it, and that the place should be in a living house, him a grown man, and not hospital sick.

Then when he finally found Sarah she was lying back on a wine-red lounge in her boudoir, a robe of lace and gold satin trailing around her, a little maid chattering in French and broken English as she ran back and forth with ice bag and cologne and smelling salts. To Sarah it was like something from her *Godey's Lady's Book,* but to Milton it brought back the stories of high-toned sporting houses around Atlanta, only here, there was that maid chattering like a magpie will around a shell-gutted horse.

But Milton had man's work to do and so he pushed in as he would have down at the old home place, and got the tears and complainings turned on him. Who was this raggletail barging so bold into a lady's chamber, his hair tousled, goose mush in his eyes and his new uniform already like a mud-flatter's castoffs! It did seem she had enough to bear today, with his father roaring in here before a body could have her morning tea, waving a telegram saying the bank in Washington had failed.

"In—Washington?" the son asked, shifting his weight on his crutch with a soldier's uneasiness about things of the capital. "But, ma——"

"Ma, ma!" the woman cried, turning her black eyes upward, her voice taking on the thin, high-lady tone that was as new to Milton as the diamonds on her fingers. "Oh, the vulgar, degrading army!"

"Godamighty, ma——" the boy began, and bulled it through over his mother's interruptions, "there's been lots of bank failings lately, ain't there, and closer around than Washington?"

"Listen to our buckshot hero! Of course there's been bank failings but your Uncle Steven had special interests in this one—him and your pa—your father, had a hundred thousand dollars laying there."

"A hundred thousand?" Milton asked, holding to his crutch-stick like to a tree in a water flood—him in a fret for months about a hundred dollars more to get to the mines and his father with a thousand times that much loose in a bank 'way off in Washington!

When she had the maid, Marie, shooed out for tea, Sarah Stone from the bottoms settled back into something her son could recognize in spite of the trailing robe and the diamonds. Yes, his pa had a hundred thousand in that bank, just stashed there until Steven could use it to make connections, connections for a little business, like you had to, with Andy Johnson swinging the broad-ax against them all. But it was all they could manage to scrape together just now, and so Hiram came stomping in like a liquored-up flatboater, laying blame, and then hurrying off to toll the money out the back door if he could, leaving an important political dinner spoilin' in her lap, and with her still nervous as a hawk-struck pullet from yesterday's experience.

"Yesterday's most humiliating experience," Sarah Stone repeated, her neck reddening up dark under its fresh coat of whiting. "My son come dragging in with a leg chopped off and his own mother not knowing! Slapped smash in the face with it before the company of expensive guests I scrabbled together like a cat scratching gravel. And then you have to go shoot off your dirty, insulting mouth. . . ."

So Sarah put Milton in the wrong as if the leg were a thing of his own scheming, and when the maid brought the silver breakfast tray she went into another fit of hypo, of lady-weeping, dabbing her eyes with a lace handkerchief but careful not to spot her whiting. Oh, it all came from having that drunken whelp of a chambermaid in the White House, she complained, noticing the bold eyes of Marie on the son of the house, not unhandsome, even with his hair standing up like a stable broom, and green as a jake about such hussies.

But young Milton wasn't noticing. Leaning on his crutch he squeezed his head between his palms, to clear away the ache and the confusion. This was worse than the fighting around Atlanta or even his first Reb charge. Here he was alone as he was the day he awoke with the sheet sagging down, and a good leg gone.

Yesterday he was scared that helping him to the gold fields might rob the bread from his mother's kitchen safe. Instead he found this big-buggery, a brownstone house with rooms high as a church and spilling over with fancy people, this talk of a great wad of money lost, while upstairs in a bed soft as cotton in the boll was a pretty girl signed in marriage to him, a gold ring on her finger. But nowhere was there anything of the old days.

Seeing he had no more chance than a dawbug of making his mother listen today, Milton slipped out to the terrace to look for old Joseph. Then he turned his back upon the house that was like a butte on the hilltop and struck off down the road toward the place where he was born, the red sack swinging against the crutch at every hobbling step, the fine dust spurting under his slow, heavy foot.

The road along the hills was almost as empty as yesterday, a boy riding behind the hames of a flea-bit work mare, a dog following, then a couple of men walking, one getting clear out into the weeds to pass the crippled bluecoat, and when he answered the road greeting, he showed a gap mouth, the two front teeth, the cartridge biters, missing.

By the time Milton had gone a mile his underarm was sore from the crutch, and the stump throbbed, so he dropped down at one of the great oaks and started a little chew from the plug in his fiddle sack, just a smidgin, so Sarah wouldn't spy out this dirty army habit.

When his jaw was juicing he leaned back and looked off over Cincinnati stretched out in the old way, but quieter now, with less smoke, the churches and the Trollope bazaar plainer than in the old days, or maybe it was just fresh and new to his eyes. Beyond the city and the levee lay the river, shining in the sun, but quiet too, not like the hell-roaring Mike Fink river some of the boys used to sing about on their marches. "The snortin', rantin', roarin' O-hi-o!" There were fewer craft on it than before the war, and not one that was sizable or fast and white-waked, not even a horn-blower among the raftsmen like yesterday. Something had been lost here at home, too.

Once he stripped the sack from the fiddle and played a few camp songs that old Billy Field taught him before he gave Milton the fiddle the morning he went back to Nebraska with a hand off at the wrist.

"She ain't gonna be much good to me no more, Milty boy, with only this iron grab-hook I got for the fingerin' " he had said slowly as he held the fiddle sack gentle as a sleeping baby in his arms beside Milton's cot. "Not that a hook like that wouldn't a come in handy liftin' coffee pots and toastin' weevils out a the hardtack in old Company G, eh?"

Today, Milton had no plan beyond finding something familiar, some one thing that was recognizable, even if it was only his old coondog Feller or the leaning tree where he used to wait for Johnny Stanger and watch Lucinda and her sister come by on the way to school. As he hobbled past the stick fence of the Stanger yard, the one the boys used to vault with their stilts, their good old tom-walkers, he heard the mocking bird in the lilacs, smelled the fine baking smell from the open door, and old Mollie there calling him in for coffee cake. Heavy-footed, she wiped a chair, turning her broad face from his crippling, and asking heartily how his mother was. "We miss neighboring with your folks since they moved away . . ." meaning since they came up in the world; were skyugling it so big.

But she couldn't hold in long. "You poor boy!" she cried, throwing her thick, sweaty arms around Milton from behind his chair. "Why, you're puny and blue-skinned as a starving rooster cock. Here you and my Johnny run off to Sherman together, and him home almost a year ago, lively as a skillet a snakes and gone off to the gold fields."

But she was as fussed as Milton, and wiping her eyes on the ruffle of her apron she scolded at herself. "Ain't I the old fool though, and forgetting entirely that you was married yesterday! Lucindy's a fine girl. That's one time you shure beat my Johnny," not letting on that it had been a big wedding, with everybody except old neighbors like the Stangers invited. It made Milton feel mean and lowdown and so he got away, promising to come again, when Johnny's father was home.

"Keeps pa humping—" old Mollie was saying, "with my medicine an' all. Poor box wages, 's all they is, and the Freedmen coming over the river black as a scourge of crickets all the last year. They'll do anything for a handful of hog corn to parch. Our cows's gone for doctor bills, and carpenters, young, handy men, is walking the streets. Dollars sure is big as mill wheels these days and as hard to come by. . . ."

Milton felt a little better that Johnny's mother was still the same, still fighting her skillet, complaining. It reminded him of the time the boys found the big eel cat stranded after a flood. He looked bigger than a brindle calf and took a lot of donnicking before he was dead enough to tie to a pole and lug proudly home. But Mollie made the boys take him off again; wouldn't even let the hogs have him.

"Just notional," old John comforted, tipping his cherrywood pipe sideways as he set the teeth of a saw, one by one. "Some days women is plain notional."

Then there was the night they stole old Dolan's dugout to paddle around the point where a couple of steamboats had rammed in a high wind and were burning. The fire was snapping and roaring, shaking red on the waves, the smoke boiling off into the black night, and dudey folks jumping into the water with burning brands falling all around until the boilers blew up. The wind upset the boys and they had to be picked up with the rest and got a good strapping on their wet britches from Mollie and no end of complaining. Lucky Sarah was away, helping Spencer, Milton's brother, older by five years, out of a scrape down in Louisville. Hiram hadn't said much, but Milton remembered running old Dolan's fish lines until fall to pay for the dugout.

Now all that time was goners, and so was the old leaning tree, only a stump-mushroom left, and a piece of slate, and suddenly Milton remembered everything of the day he broke that slate over Johnny's head in a fight about a bluey, a blue glassy that they got from big Val Porter, dead outside of Vicksburg all of three years now. But that afternoon was clear in his mind as yesterday, clearer, with its smell of spring from the ground, warm to their knees as they smoothed off the circle for the scattering of mibbies.

"Godamighty" Milton said slowly as the piece of slate chipped into gray slivers under the touch of his crutch stick. "God-amighty. . . ."

Nor was there any comfort in the old home place, no bigger than a stave shack, and with washtubs and a broken cart wheel against the porch that his mother used to keep so pretty with her painted rockers and the trumpet vine. There was still a dog, not Milton's old lop-eared brindle Feller but a broken-jawed mutt who came growling with slobbering fangs, a woman at the well curb sicking him on, calling out to Milton that they wouldn't have tramps and peddlers on the place.

And it was no good coming in soldier clothes. That dodge was long wore out.

To Milton the first few weeks at home were like swimming under water in some mossy, sunlit August hole, the water so soft and warm around him it seemed he need never come up, that maybe he had already drowned and was seeing everything the way the dead see. It was a little like the drugged stretches between the times of pain from the leg, maybe because the dull ache was coming back on him nights sleeping on the floor, as he did since that first one home, or even when he sat in the daytime with nothing in his hands or head—as though he would be waking up soon to all the old misery and pain.

But gradually from the newspapers and the talk around Hiram's empty warehouses Milton got a squinch at some things to think about. He hadn't made it to the mines but thousands of others were going this spring, gold or homeseeking, many in faded blue, with times so hard and women hanging to their jobs, working cheaper than a man could live. The Jeff Davis trial for treason was on too, and the accomplices to Lincoln's murder still loose, with a new story every week that John Booth was here or there, alive; that the U. S. Secret Service had burnt up a ghoul-body to collect the fifty thousand reward. Probably got paid too, for letting him get away, some said, if not in gold then in a currency dearer to those who wanted Lincoln out of the road, like those who celebrated over in Union County, Illinois, the day after he died, with beer and hurrah and gunfire, Andy Burke said, the paraders yelling, "He had it coming, the crazy loon!" Then there were the Fenians, Irishmen, planning to grab Canada from England, and the rioting going on in cities like New Orleans and Memphis, Freedmen and their families killed wholesale, their homes and churches burned, just about the time many were putting flowers on the graves of the Federals through the South.

"Dead niggers won't be taking the bread out a our mouths" some of the job-hunting soldiers told each other.

The old wharfmen spoke their minds even with Milton Stone squatting among them. "The massacrees down there's stirred up by them Radical Republicans like old Steve Tolley himself. Wants to keep a standing army through the South so long's there's a penny around loose—keep 'em stomped down so's they can't get to votin'. . . ."

But at the warehouses and at home he heard that the Radicals were working to preserve the nation from the traitor Democrats, men from Jeff Davis' cabinet already elected to Congress, and the Lincoln Republicans, including that secesh-lover in the White House, as bad.

"Throwing away the glorious victory our boys bled and died for!" Milton heard his mother tell the political guests around her shining dinner table, talking big like her senator brother, covering up her fidgets by looking fondly toward her son, making Milton feel meachin small in his father's place at the head of the shimmering table, forgetting all he had been told to remember, wishing he were back on his hunkers at some bivouac fire.

But there was agreement enough for Sarah from the visiting legislators, mostly hunting support for reelection and maybe a speech or two from Senator Tolley, if the Radical chances looked good enough in August. With the Senator's fill-in term expiring, and his own election coming up before the Legislature next session, it was mostly a game of put and take, a vendue, a raffle. With the out-state pepper-haired Alton Brewer seated next to Sarah, it was a plain offer to sell himself to the Radicals for a seat in Congress.

From these men and their wives the sister of Senator Tolley got soft sawder by the bucket, and a toast from Brewer in a glass of the golden Catawba of the Longworth wineries: "To a lady of infinite wit and fascination, the most charming mother of our son who sacrificed his limb!" shaming Milton so he looked down into his plate, feeling Lucinda's eyes on him, sad that he had to stand this pointing out, this pitying. Godamighty, he better be spearing his vittles with a Barlow knife, like his mother said, when, with the butler's help, she tried to drill him for his father's place. Yes, better even salt horse roasted over the coals on some fool recruit's bayonet that would bend from the heating the first time he fetched it up against the britches button of a Reb. Godamighty, talking about heroes, when no telling how many hid the stink of their pants behind the smell of powder their first fight, or even the second.

Milton had never heard of a dinner so fancy as his mother got together, not even in the whoppers told on the hungriest marches. But Sarah had her plans. "They's not many such folks can watch fancy table manners, their wine glasses, and their tongues for long. . . ."

So Milton waited with doughboy patience his mother's maneuvers, reminding him of the time she brought three pigs and a couple of cows home from the river, herding the hogs up the road together to a patch of Indian artichokes or a mudhole, then hurrying to fetch up the cows before they were off into the bush scraping the flies off their rumps. By the time the critters found out they weren't roaming free the pen gate had slammed behind them.

Before the dessert, Sarah was almost through the lighter topics she had copied to the ivory ribs of her fan from *Harper's Weekly* and reached the current Queen Victoria joke: Why is the old girl like a deef lady? Because she's 'avin' trouble with 'er Erin. That brought up the Fenians, somebody wondering why so many of the guns for the attack on Canada were falling into the hands of the government. Must be spies.

Alton Brewer had been silent since the game course, too many glasses, maybe, or he had been putting Sarah's apologies for Hiram's absence and the Washington bank failure together. Anyway, he spoke up sudden and independent as a jaybird on a rock. "The problem isn't why some of the Fenian guns are intercepted but that some must be getting through, constituting an act of war against England, while our country is already bled white. Besides, one might wonder who is furnishing the money and the contraband, if one may confess to such mundane thoughts with our hostess so entertaining, so completely charming." He said this teasingly, drawing his brows like clipped black mustaches together and turning his shoulder deliberately against his wife's anxious signaling.

But Sarah Stone ignored his playfulness, yet managing some concern over a crumb caught on her lace-shadowed bosom, flicking at it with her napkin. "There's no law against selling guns, is there?" she asked, "or to make the dealer inquire where they go to?"

"Ah, no, dear lady, no law compelling inquiry of their ultimate destination, not even if the arms plunge us into a foreign war, or bring a Sioux uprising against the settlers. Besides, it's all equitable and golly even, with both the Indians and·the soldiers getting guns that blow up in their faces."

There was the clatter of a fork dropped, the tines ringing in the silence and a choking little sound from Lucinda. But Milton didn't notice. He was remembering something out of his sickest time—the face of a soldier in the next cot, the lower jaw blown off by an exploding gun, the tongue gone too, the man trying to feed himself through a tube, making gurgling, crow-cawing noises when he tried to talk, or to keep his crying quiet, until the night he wadded his undershirt into the horrible hole, choking himself to death. God-amighty, putting guns like that into the hands of the poor devils a purpose!

When the butler touched Milton's shoulder he looked in confusion around the table, and to his mother, ready to rise, saying in her lady voice, "Dear Mis' Brewer, I'm sure your husband will be most invaluable in Congress. . . ."

The man smiled and bowed as to a fine compliment. Then he dropped back to walk beside his wife, smiling into her white, miserable face, and matched his step to Milton's slow stomping on the polished floor.

"Don't forget to make application for your pension when the time comes, my boy," he said. "You can never tell who'll need a few dollars steady income."

The newspapers were full of the Rose Arbor murder in Clifton among the Johnny come latelys pushing in where the Southerners used to live, and the woman-raping out near the old Longworth vineyards, with a stern warning to the Freedmen. There were a few lines too about an attack on Chile by the Spanish fleet and that the cholera epidemic in New York was spreading southward. "Our Hiram right in the middle of it!" Sarah complained, when she wasn't decrying the loose morals of Washington, with its painted harlots enticing the animal appetites of man. Besides, Hiram ought to be remembering the horrible epidemic the year Milton was born, around eight thousand people dying, his own brothers and five of the Tolleys, including Steven's wife. Still no telegram, not a word about the closed bank.

But Sarah found time for other things. The day that Milton hobbled off to the old place she had sent Joseph to fetch him home. Worn and hungry and without hope he was brought back like a runaway young 'un. The tailor was waiting.

"Even with a leg off you got to run around in the heat and dust lugging that calico sack like any trampooser on the road," Sarah scolded as she sent him away to clean up. "We will repair to my sitting-room. . . ."

There, over teacups, the son was studied and measured, and the needs of one in his position discussed as though he were a stick in the corner. Lucinda, on a low stool at Sarah's feet, made a pretty picture in her soft, blue gown as she held up samples and style books for the woman's farsighted eyes, and turned a troubled face toward her husband of a day whenever she dared, her cheeks turning pink in her boldness.

"Ah, Mrs. Stone, you have indeed found a jewel of modesty for your son in these froward times," the old tailor said as he tugged at the tape measure hung around his neck. No one made polite denial that the wedding was her scheming, for wasn't she the sister of the Senator who made all this possible, and nobody seemed to notice the young soldier's silence, his going to the window between measurings—looking out, his crutch turned from those in the room, his hand tight on the strong wood.

Two weeks later they went into town for a day of shopping and to pick up the finished garments, get Milton out of the despised bluecoat. Lucinda begged to stay at home but Sarah would not have it. A wife should learn about her husband's clothing and, besides, there might be time to pick up a new bonnet fitting for a new bride. There was—a leghorn straw pale as Lucinda's hair, with a wreath of velvet forget-me-nots over the top and velvet ties under her chin. But best were Milton's suits, particularly the muffin-brown one, with a low-crowned hard hat the color of coffee, his hair curling up dark around the back. There was an assortment of waistcoats too, one as gay as any of George Shefton's and it brought the first free smile to Lucinda's serious little face since the day she came running up the back way at Martins Park to welcome her soldier boy home.

"You look elegant" she said softly, clasping her hands together to keep them from going out to touch Milton. But he wasn't noticing. Standing before the sloping, full-length glass, with its bearded young cripple, handsome, tall and so dudey his identity was lost like a penny in the dust, his whole justification. "You want to shuck your blue britches fast as you get home," Clyde Winston had warned, but now with them went everything Milton knew of himself. And later there was further humiliation in the consultation about the artificial leg, limb as Sarah called it, complaining that nothing had been done at the hospital. But with the government allowance only seventy-five dollars and the stump still painful. . . .

"Ah, yes, the government . . ." the man said, nodding knowingly, giving Sarah a ready promise that Milton would be walking on two feet in a few weeks. But even in this there was no joy, only shame that he was less than whole.

Afterward they sat for a tintype, Milton standing, hiding his mutilation behind Lucinda, and low-down as mud over it. Then Sarah took them to a matinee, Milton's first play, and as good as a sham battle where even with blanks a few heads got busted and eyes gouged out. At the end he found himself stiff with leaning forward, the dull ache in his leg unnoticed as he sat stupid and migglin' among a lot of crying women helplessly watching a soft-eyed, trusting maiden betrayed to the sound of far thunder. He came to himself as he stepped into the storm-threatened daylight and roared out laughing at the way he had been honeyfugled, laughed so people looked back at him, Sarah shushing, Lucinda fussing her handkerchief. But, hell's buzzards, that was good as an evening with new recruits in camp, old Clyde and Pete Dutchly telling about the swamp serpent thick as a pot-bellied stove, with jaws so wide a sharp-witted Federal once saved himself by sticking his bayoneted musket upright in the open mouth.

They made the porte cochere in a great clattering of hoofs, the first rush of the river storm sweeping up behind them out of the early darkness, the lightning white on the slope of lawn. The servants ran out to fetch the bundles and boxes and to exclaim at Milton. "Oh, isn't he the elegant young gentleman, ma'am!" the housekeeper cried, while Marie, the little maid, looked with her bold eyes from the stairs.

At the supper table Sarah Stone announced that it had been a most entertaining day. A real satisfaction to drive along Fourth Street with such youth and beauty in the carriage. "The admiring looks! I declare, I think George Shefton clean forgot his lady friend over our Lucinda, and Mrs. Mitchell saying 'Such a handsome pair!'—her who's connected with the Grants and very well-to-do, but her own son ugly as a hog in a wallow for all that."

To this, Lucinda made the stiff little replies taught her at Miss Farnsworth's where she was sent the last two years learning lady ways, to walk with a glass of water on her head, paint violets on hair receivers, use embroidery hoops, play the piano a little and, of course, roll bandages and scrape lint from old linen for the wounded while practicing genteel conversation, also offered in French for an additional fee. Listening to her, Milton looked down into his plate and remembered the little girl-woman she had been, sober with the responsibility of her three younger sisters, but free too, and like a flying shadow over the ground in her busy-ness.

Then he noticed his mother talking to him, calling his attention to the blue dinner plate he had been staring into. It was the picture of Uncle Steven, the Senator mighty puffed up and important, the dome of the Capitol in paler blue behind him.

When the storm cleared and the lightning was no more than the flash and rumble of far cannonading, Milton slipped away from the whist table to the servant's quarters and caught a ride with the young folks going into Cincinnati for a dance.

"Sneakin' off to see some of the boys from the river . . ." he mumbled in explanation. They laughed a little among themselves; the maid Marie making room in the back of the spring wagon beside her and putting her arm around behind his stiff back, the others shut-mouthed before the son of the big house. He looked over the lights of the town and the gleaming bend of the Ohio—a sickle a man might lash to a pole for a skyhook to pull down a thunderhead. But he was a man now.

In town Milton hobbled to a side alley where he and Johnny used to spy in excitement and itching uneasiness on the women in their lighted windows. The place seemed half deserted now, with a dull quarreling sound from somewhere, and the smell of an old privy hole after a rain. Finally a woman coming home found Milton leaning in her dark doorway and made it easy for him to follow her inside. She helped him in other ways too, and afterward, when he was ready to go, she reached under the bed for a couple of pillows. "Don't be a hurryin' to yank your britches on, honey. Ain't no rush a customers along here no more and I likes me somebody clean to sleep with. . . ."

The thunder was starting again, and the rain, and so Milton lay down for a little and went to sleep with the woman's hand over his shoulder, as quiet and dreamless as when he was a shirt-tail young one. It was morning when he awoke and found out the woman was probably as old as his mother.

"In the warring?" she asked matter of factly about the leg, speaking around the bone pins in her broad mouth as she combed at her tangle of greenish brown hair.

So he told her about it, easily, as the winter wagon moves when it has once broken from the frozen ground, and as openly as he might have about a shin barked in a scuffle, or a black eye, if it happened to change a whole life. He felt no tightening inside and no need to pretend courage and gallantry. It was plain hand-hammered hell to come home only part a man.

"Yeh, particular the son of a old studhorse like Hiram Stone," the woman said. "But you ain't got no call to worry. You can make 'em hang out their tongues with the best, son, only you better scout around for some pill shooter right away and tell him where you been. . . ."

Milton was stumping along Main Street before the woman's meaning hit him. It made his insides shake as he remembered the soldiers he saw around Memphis, and Atlanta and Charleston too, dropping out at the first march, walking spraddle-legged and howling worse than scalded pups when they made water.

So he hunted up Dr. Powell, who had been with Sherman too, and wrote a round robin letter once a month to the hospital boys after he got home. Maybe he was lonesome, anyway he was aged and sour because his wife ran off West with a bounty jumper, some said; others claiming it was the things that were done at home by Congress and by everybody. But then he was a Lincoln man, one of the delegation that escorted the President through Cincinnati in an open victoria with six white horses on his inaugural tour to Washington.

Charley Powell got the whole story from Milton, even about the pain in the leg that was off, and the new bride. Pulling at his foxtail mustaches he said he remembered Lucinda as a pantaletted young 'un, passable enough as females went, her folks probably good as Milton's even if she had no uncle on the Joint Committee for the Conduct of the War to hogtie Lincoln, rant against him until they got a poor lunatic worked up to killing him.

Milton moved uncomfortably, rubbing his beard. "Yeh," he finally said, "I guess Uncle Steve is a great man, all right. . . ."

The doctor looked over his steel-rimmed glasses to aim at the spittoon. "I hope you always manage to see the Honorable Senator so," he said, and turned to talk of old Milton Stone, Hiram's father. There was a man to think on when the general cussedness of the human race wore one down to the knucklebone. Old Milt had come to Cincinnati when it was just a peppering of log huts along the Ohio bank, bringing his drugs and herbs and his mortar and pill slab in a covered wagon drawn by a couple of cows. Believed in milk as food and physic so the cows not only carried his carcass along but helped keep it fed and healthy. He grew a brush of hair in his ears and a magnificent Ohio belly that pushed up to part his flowing whiskers. Did a good bit of doctoring too, mind and body. Always was poor as Johnny Appleseed, of course, while folks like the Martins built big businesses and big houses, but old Milton could spit the devil square in the eye and had no call to rosin any man's bow.

But his grandson and namesake here had at least inherited old Milton's good straight nose along with the hair of the black Irish that the Tolley's were. Exposure to venereal disease with immediate treatment was less serious than the persistent pain of the amputated leg. That called for a hospital specializing in stump cases and limb fittings. "Your folks oughtn't to mind spending a little on a war casualty, particularly in their own household," Charley Powell said sourly.

"Oh, the folks always done all they could for me," Milton defended. "Mother's had me to the Kellers to see about a leg."

"Kellers, huh?" the doctor said absently as he examined the puckered scarring of the stump. "Hacked off, by God—a chunk of hambone hacked off with a penknife and then pulled together like a hole in a sock!"

Still, with a good fitting a fellow young as Milton ought to get around on a cane, limping, of course, but with two pant legs and two shoes to show. The real cat in the meal tub was the marital situation, particularly considering the widowing effect of war's violence on some soldiers, a sort of emasculation, a temporary unmanning, a sort of hypo to be busted up as soon as possible. Besides, as a doctor, Charley Powell believed in a sound bedding of the bride the first night. None of this catering to maidenly modesty urged by the bewailers of gross male appetites. But with the wedding night lost, wasted like good whisky spilt on sand, Milton ought to be arranging a substitute. After an appropriate check on any possible dose, they ought to go for an afternoon drive to some place of childhood memories.

". . . Take along a picnic basket for a late supper and plan to talk about yourself," the doctor said. "Telling a woman the story of your life, it's called. That fetches 'em. And remember, a light moon for sparking; a dark one for planting. And don't forget the robe. The buffalo buggy robe is the greatest single contributor to the phenomenon of prematurity in the first born. . . ."

Milton laughed, foolish as a shirt-tailer. "You're a great codder,

Doctor," he said, as Powell held the boy's coat for him, and then stood off sizing him up. "Say—why don't you go in for doctoring? You could make up the educational deficiencies easy and squeeze in a little literature and philosophy on the side. Handy as a hacksaw, you'd find. In the meantime you can be learning a little more about pill rolling by helping me here and then finish up in some good medical school, not a quack outfit like in the old Trollope bazaar here but a good one, Philadelphia, maybe."

"It would take a lot of money, and time. . . ."

"Well, yes, but a lean horse for a long race, and a short-bodied woman for children, as old Milt used to say. Your folks seem to have been in the money and judging by the Memphis riots and other inspired hell-raisings, the Radicals intend to keep it rolling in." He leaned toward the spittoon again and wiped his long mustaches. "To a doctor of your connections a rubber leg won't be a drawback at all. No more than a leg off was to old Santa Anna, or old Dan Sickles. Fact is, a distinguished limp and a dark, curly beard are the two best assets a young medico can have," Charley Powell, who had neither, said.

So young Milton Stone went out into the sunshine, feeling better than any time since he got off the train at the deserted station of Martins Park. He swung on his crutch as on a vaulting pole, stepping along like on the great tom-walkers he and Johnny once made, taller than anybody, tall as any tree.

3 — The Buffalo Robe

By the time young Milton got home it was evening and his great news was dulled like a day's victory by a foot slog through a night of sleet and mud, or by pain and the bitter white powder of the hospital. Even his far-swinging gait on his crutch had slowed down, become awkward as a whopper-legged skater bug on a pond, so when he tried to sneak up the back stairs, he got caught. The cook, little Marie, and even the stiff-backed butler had tried to help him but there was a grayish mist over everything, and when something slipped and clattered to the bare floor beside him, Milton went down with it. Before they got him up and moving again his mother was in the doorway, her hoops filling its width.

"So my son's brought home drunk as a flatboater nowadays! Comes dumped off the grocery wagon 'round back like a sack of grits!" She roared it out so loud that Lucinda, watching at her upstairs window, heard, and came running down the broad curve of stairs, her blue flounces lifted from her hurrying feet. At the bottom she stopped in confusion, letting her hands fall as she saw the wavering, unsteady boy brought in from the back. Her eyes were swollen with sleeplessness and tears, her cheeks pale, but the evening sun from the window above shone golden all about her.

At sight of Lucinda, Milton pushed his sleeve uncertainly over his blurring eyes and started forward to tell her the fine things that were spinning in his head. But his mother pushed her broad hoops between them. "No," she commanded, "not in your condition. I must insist you show your bride some respect if you have none for your mother!" speaking in her angry, high-lady voice for all the back of the house to hear.

To Milton this fancy talk, this barrier to his progress was an outrage, but the fog was like a swarming of gnats before his eyes and his foot felt peculiar too, numbish, almost as though it wasn't there and he was walking on hickory blocks, one much taller than the other. Besides, it seemed that he really had been dumped off by the grocery wagon, although he didn't remember much after he left Charley Powell's, except that he felt better than any time since that last blue pill, that last bullet, struck him almost fourteen months ago. He had hummed a little as he stumped along, mostly the Battle Hymn of the Republic, its thump-rhythm fitting his mind so he almost forgot his crutch in the plans sour-faced Charley had laid before him: work to be a doctor, make his own living like any man.

That was when he saw old Joe come backing out of an alley, a woman shaking her broom at him, at Joe Deaver who used to teach Sabbath school and often took the boys to the ruins of old Fort Ancient; Milton and Johnny invited along because they were good campers and could do a lot of things like flip-flops and cartwheels that ended standing up, just like in the circuses. Joe always was a meachin little man but now he looked thin and scrawny as a molting buzzard in his old neckband shirt, his bleary, frog-egg eyes. When he recognized Milton he pulled the boy into the Hound's Tooth.

". . . Get in out of the sun, visit a little and maybe have a beer for old times—hah?"

The taproom was dark after the bright sun, with a humming of talk and a sour smell. Joe threw his first beer down like a soldier in from a twenty-mile hike on a dry canteen. For the next two steins he fetched rye bread with cheese, sausage and bloaters piled high on his palm from the free lunch. Finally he wiped his stained beard and began to talk.

No, he hadn't done much camping; got his fill of sleeping in the mud with Grant to last him. Anyway, he wasn't going to church any more. Nobody but the shouters would take him now, looking the bummer that he did. Back in the old days he used to do all right in carriage making, but when he got home from the war his job was gone and his savings too, with the state banks taxed into bankruptcy. So after pinching the pennies for twenty years he was on the town, scouring the streets like a Freedman, ready to gouge and fight all comers, black or white, for a chance at a job or a garbage bucket, even if the women chased him with brooms and sinful words. Sometimes he wished he were eligible for one of those forty acre and mule places the Freedmen were promised, or even the nag Grant let Lee's Rebs take home to work their shirt-tail patches. He had thought some of tramping out beyond the Missouri for a homestead but where was a man to get the fifteen, twenty dollars for a filing, or the horses to bust the sod? His bounty money was gone, swallowed up while he hung around hoping to get back into his trade. Even offered money, twenty-five and then fifty dollars for a job, like a lot of others did. Ought to started denying they were soldiers right at the beginning, when they first noticed folks looking at them as shiftless, criminal.

"I guess I don't remind you much of Sabbath school any more, with my beer swilling and all, hah?" he said apologetically.

Milton was put out with himself but he was caught like a Reb up a chimbley. By now he could see that the men at the bar were the plug-hatted George Shefton and Ephraim Dix and their outfit. Eph was a river gambler before his military start as a slab officer under General Lew Wallace the couple of weeks Kirby Smith threatened Cincinnati; and mighty careful to stay away from the smell of exploding Reb powder and ball. Probably some of their shady business brought them here today, for all those around the tables playing euchre, twenty-one or just sitting were day laborers or job-hunting soldiers like old Joe and drawn toward him by his talk.

"Yes, here I am, forty," he was saying, "as handy and willing a workman as you'll find, and I have to cadge drinks off a poor unlucky lad like you for the free lunch, and fill my hide to busting because no telling when I'll get another chance. But hundreds right here in town's worse off than me, their wives and children not stowed away safe in the graveyard like mine, so they have to sit by, watching 'em starve."

"Aw, hell's buzzards, the salt pork'll come in tomorrow sure—" Milton comforted, with the soldier's way. "You just out-marched the pie wagon. . . ."

"You kin talk, with your pockets jinglin'—" one started to say, but others cut in. "Yeh, yeh," they said, quick enough, yet without much bottom. "Better time's coming. . . ."

But a bull-necked man called Mack spoke up against this hope. "Sure, better times'll come, and so'll the gravediggers," until there was a protesting from the bar.

"You better shut up them blasted bellyaching pension hounds," Eph Dix warned as he poured himself another brandy, the bartender mumbling something as he wiped his hands and fussed over the men, making conciliatory noises, like a pup caught in a meat-house, or a man who owes too much money.

But Mack wasn't shutting up. "Hear them slick-fingered gents giving orders! Making money slippin' guns and corn likker to the niggers and poor whites off South, keep 'em stirred up, keep hell a-poppin'.—So them gentlemen don't like bellyachin' pension hounds, eh?" he said, his voice coming up. "Hell, no! But they liked us good enough when we was fightin' the war for 'em, gettin' shot like suck-egg dogs by the guns them soft asses here to home was runnin' to the Rebs. And graftin' off the government on the side all the while, electin' them crooked politicians that's sellin' us for hide and taller this minit!"

"Oh, don't go bein' so feisty, Mack. You're just letting wind in a barrel, to hear yourself——"

"Hear myself, hell!" Mack roared, picking his chair back and rolling his sleeves up his thick, red arms. "I'm ready to help string up every damned one a the graftin' rascals, and their pimps and stump-suckers in Congress along with 'em!"

It was then that Milton, who had had several beers, decided his Uncle Steven and his father were being blackguarded, and so he reached for his crutch and clipped Mack alongside the ear, sending him off balance, bringing a loud laughing from the bar.

"Why, you goddamn grafter's crip!" Mack yelled, lunging at the youth, but the others caught him, dragged him away. "Tarnation, now, Mack, he's only a lad," one argued. "He can't remedy his folks no more'n you can your skirt-liftin' old Aunt Hat—" while Mack kept bawling, "Let me at him! Let me throw that drunken deadbeat Tolley in his teeth!"

It all happened fast as slashing a picket, and when Mack and his friends were gone the dark saloon was quiet, very quiet, and lonesome, with everybody except Joe moving away from him. Like he had the pest or something.

But mostly Milton thought about what his crutch had done—knocked a husky pie biter sideways easy as a tattooed keelboater swinging on a midget. For a moment power ran in his arms like a flood current in the Ohio, like he were one of the old river men, maybe steel-fisted old Mike Fink himself. But at the bar the men were laughing over their own toad-stickings now that they had caused their trouble, and even Joe had nothing to say any more, his eyes watering down the furrows of his stubbly cheeks. So Milton dropped the three dollar gold piece from his pocket on the wet table for Joe and went out, promising himself to keep away from what Sarah called the undesirable elements—whining beggars like Joe and people like that Mack, who were dangerous; their tongues mean as hedge thorns to stir up strife and such. But Milton couldn't put Joe Deaver out of his head. Maybe the seat of old Joe's pants was never very far from the ground but he was a good worker. And maybe the army did make tramps and bummers of them all. To think this over Milton turned in at the next place and sat alone with another beer—with several, and when he finally started home the ground was almighty uneven so he was glad to be picked up by the grocery boy.

Now Milton found himself teetering on his crutch, alone in the middle of a great room that seemed to be lit by clusters of winter icicles overhead sparkling in a white fog. Somewhere, far off, he could see that his father was there too, back from his trip East. With his plump hand stuck into the breast of his frockcoat, his beard jutting out, Hiram Stone was marching up and down, pompous as a jack-leg lawyer with his hair parted behind, or an exhorting preacher warming up. There were certain duties a son owed his people, he was saying. Furthermore, drink was an evil when taken in excess—beyond purposes strictly medicinal, although nothing better was known than a little bourbon for colic. Seemed to relieve cholera too, made the dying easier.

"You are wandering, Mr. Stone," his wife reminded him in stiff, lady talk, still not letting on that the boy had sneaked off without her knowing, and was gone all night.

The words got Hiram's back up. Wandering was he? Then he would draw bead on the real target. They had planned to make a place for the son in the business but now there was no business left, not with the Honorable Senator Tolley drunk all the time, going to hell in a handbasket like all the Tolleys before him. When Sarah tried to cut in, Hiram just raised his voice as though hallooing over the river for the ferry, and so she had to mind the listening ears in back and save her anger for a club to whip a handier dog.

Certain matters, Hiram was saying, that old Steve should have looked after months ago had been grossly neglected. Now the bank was clamped tight shut on the money they needed to turn supply contracts for the soldiers in the South their way, get government arms and ammunition condemned for sale to them. Hiram had warned the old whisky bloat there would be a big demand for fire-arms this summer, with the Fenian troubles and the Indians up and swarming. Now Carrington's army was headed out into Sioux country without one wagonload of Stone and Company goods in the whole expedition, while on the upper Missouri the Indians were tripling their offers of robes for guns and Hiram didn't have a single one on hand, when he had done so well there last year.

"You done well? You mean you sold guns to the Indians to shoot soldiers with?" the boy demanded, his face suddenly like salt-rising dough under the dark beard, all the redness of the beer gone. "And probably them blow-up guns to the government too! Why, that Mack was right! I am a goddamn grafter's crip!"

But his mother stopped that kind of talk fast enough, glad to turn some of her anger at the insult to the Tolleys where she could. "We've had about enough of your big mouth! What do you know about business, with your backside barely dry?"

"Hell, yes, son," Hiram said grandly, hauling out his snuff box, "If we don't supply the Indians or the Fenians they'll just go else-where. When you're older you'll understand that. As for the profit, the tail goes with the hide, don't it?"

So Sarah Stone made one of her syrupy mouths and putting off her revenge against Hiram, led the son away for a talk alone, to find out where he was all night. Milton couldn't seem to manage his crutch, the feeling of power it had given him when he sideswiped Mack all gone; so he went, without looking toward Lucinda stand-ing with her hands helpless at her side, his head feeling light and fuzzy as a cotton boll.

Three weeks later there was a scurrying around at the Stones' to get a picnic basket packed—a carpetbag and a few other things into the top buggy for Milton and Lucinda. Today they were taking a little excursion; not the honeymoon trip Sarah had planned to Niagara Falls, the tickets turned in long ago without Milton's knowing about it, but his own idea, his and Charley Powell's—an outing along the Ohio, with a picnic supper somewhere toward Buf-fington Island; a drive, after the moon rose, to an old inn, and an easy jaunt home tomorrow.

They had been on short drives before, Lucinda home once to visit with her sisters and not hurrying back. "I don't know what things are coming to, with so many war marriages breaking up" Sarah complained, and so she went for Lucinda in the carriage, making Madam Cheret's recital the excuse; Camille Cheret of Miss Farnsworth's. Milton let her go, even was dragged along, like the shamed and limping booby that he was.

For him this outing was the first night away since the one with the woman near the wharves; tomcatting around, his mother had called it, complaining even more about his explanation: that he went to hunt up Charley Powell for a talk about the war, and Atlanta.

"Why do you have to do everything secret, sneaking around like a grave robber in a thunderstorm? If you got to keep harking back on war and bloodshed, cultivate them that's nearer to your station, like Colonel Boolton and Major Johns."

Milton couldn't tell his mother that these men were what old soldiers like Clyde Winston called the Ass Kissers—officers appointed to chair jobs by the pull of the Radicals, and paying for the favor by helping with the graft, dragging out the war. Besides, what potatoes could these men have to roast at the fire of a sloony foot-slogger, a powder-burnt, crippled doughboy? So he told his mother it was the amputated leg, still hurting bad sometimes.

"The limb that is—ah, laid away?" she had demanded skeptically. "What new folly you thinking up now?" But she admitted she had heard of cases where the amputated member was buried crooked, maybe with a toe cramped under. Wasn't that just like Andy Johnson's stupid army doctors? she asked of Clarice Boolton and Mrs. Matthews at the literary society tea. And the dear boy so sensitive and high strung!

Between Milton and Lucinda his night away was never brought up, or anything else much, with Milton still sleeping on the floor and Lucinda silent, and sneaking a quilt over him on chilly nights.

Now, today, there was to be the new beginning Charley Powell had planned, and a fine July afternoon for it, too, with half a dozen fair-weather clouds riding the horizon like a row of white showboats rounding a bend. Young Milton looked well enough to give the lie to the crutch at his elbow, his hair thick and grackle-shining, his cheeks sun-reddened above the growing beard that would soon hide the softness of his mouth.

Beside his darkness, Lucinda seemed fair as a new loomed flaxen cloth spread to the sun. Her pale curls were looped up inside her blue shaker bonnet hanging at her back, her maiden slimness as free of bulking hoops as in the days before she went to Miss Farnsworth's at rates the Martins could manage because one of the teachers was Lucinda's cousin. It was this finishing, and the family standing, that hurried Sarah Stone when a war senator and the war profits didn't open the expected doors to her, that got her scheming to marry the son safely into the Martins before they knew how much of a Stone he was, with no more sharpness or git-up than a turtle sunning on a rock. Yet for all the big show she managed, everything went anti-godlin as a sapling caught in a mill race, and so now the connection was doubly important.

With Lucinda beside him Milton quieted the spirited little gray mare until the fly net swayed gently to her even gait. Together they looked down upon the smoky brown city and beyond it to the new suspension bridge over the river.

". . . Standing there with one foot on each side of the old Ohio easy as a boy straddling a spring runnel!"

"Oh, Milton, you soldiers are always exaggerating!" Lucinda complained, impatient as Sarah Stone, then suddenly turning very red and trying to laugh, make it seem codding. But Milton gripped the lines so they cut his palm and looked off down the river, the way to the West, to the mines. He wanted to grab the whip from its socket, bring it down on the mare a dozen times, whip her until she went wild, battle-shot, crazy wild, and then pull out West.

But he held himself, and after a while he began to talk. The river really did look like a man might vault it if he had a long cr . . .—a long pair of tom-walkers, like out of those southern pines. Yet how unconquerable it used to seem—wide as the blue oceans in their geography books, its traffic thick as skater bugs on a mossy pond, particularly downriver—dugouts, rafts, everything, to the big steamboats that were like the great galleried southern houses floating along, with thousands of flatboats around them, each probably holding enough goods to set up a farm complete from cow brutes to parlor organ, or a whole store somewhere.

As children they had seen war come to the border city that had so many Southerners, most of its commerce with the South; its wharves, warehouses, foundries and machine shops hanging like ripe plums ready for the Reb raiders. As far back as Milton and Lucinda could remember there was loud talk of conflicting loyalties, with underground stations like Rankin's, where Eliza of the Uncle Tom's Cabin book crossed the ice, within whooping distance of Fourth Street. While thousands of slaves got away to Canada, Abolitionist speakers were ridden out of town on fence rails or tarred and feathered, once from a pillow stolen off Sarah Stone's own clothesline. Sometimes there was rioting in the Negro quarters, with torches spreading flames among the wooden shacks, and guns, even cannons, roaring, and the next day the smell of death and battle over the town.

They had seen families split like oaks riven by lightning, Lucinda crying herself to sleep when one of her twin uncles rode away South with the thousands of ferryboat Rebs, the other one glumly joining up with the Federals at the booth on Main Street. Holding a younger sister's hand tightly in hers, Lucinda had watched him march off with the Guthrie Grays and the Turners and the Rover Guards, all fine in their bright uniforms, bands playing, flags flying, women fluttering moist, romantic handkerchiefs. But not Lucinda. Her father had reminded her that a Martin woman never made a display in public. Yet that day it seemed to Lucinda she was all Strathorn.

". . . I howled right out, like a deserted pup," Milton admitted cheerfully. "I was halfway up a tree, yelling and bawling so hard to go along my foot slipped and I fell and cut my lip."

"Oh!" Lucinda cried, lifting her eyes for a second.

"Hell's b— Oh, it wasn't nothing," he said, letting out the little mare, not even a scar now, as she could see. But the waiting to grow up was hard, particularly that next year, with Rebel cavalry grabbing off Lexington, and some detachments reported just beyond the breaks south of the river, General Wallace putting Cincinnati under martial law and ordering even copperheads like Cal Rickerts out to drill while folks scrabbled out of town like scared rabbits from a burning brush patch.

"Oh, Milton, don't say rabbits!" Lucinda objected. "Why, mother gathered us up too, and started out for Aunt Betsy Horner's in the cart. But it took us days to get there, the roads were so full. . . ."

Godamighty, sticking long tails on rabbits don't make foxes out a them, Milton was thinking, but he agreed that the roads must have been full, with all that flee-fleeing, and a raft of men coming in too, the Squirrel Hunters gathering from the farms and the backwoods of Ohio and clear over in Indiana to help defend the town. With Johnny he had watched them throw the pontoon bridge across the river and saw it settle under the double line of men marching south; sweating, sunburnt men with tobacco in their gaunt whiskered jaws, coats hooked to shoulders and guns slung to their backs, all kinds of guns, with here and there an officer riding, or a covered wagon carrying powder and ammunition and bandages. Hour after hour the pontoon rumbled under the tramp of cowhide boots, the girls cheering them on, not as elegant as those out for the Grays but louder.

The boys couldn't hold out against the boiling of excitement, so they sneaked in with the rag tag and bobtail end, Milton with his father's old flintlock and Johnny with only a shovel, but it came in mighty handy throwing up entrenchments against a Reb cavalry charge that never came closer than a horse galloping in the night that scared that fancy George Shefton to bawling. Before long they were back with discharge papers and thirteen dollars apiece like the rest, except that instead of carousing they buried the money and the papers in a tin can. And at home their mothers made them scrub with ash lye soap because they were crawling with graybacks.

"Lice!" Lucinda shuddered. "Miss Farnsworth says those neglectful of bodily cleanliness are unworthy of the slightest consideration."

Unworthy? Godamighty!—the lousy soldiers were good enough to fight for the likes of her! Milton wanted to throw this into the girl's face, but he was trying hard to remember Charley Powell's advice, to hold his tongue, and keep his hand from the accusing crutch at his side. Nor did he say anything at all about the camp-followers who were out even the first night, tolling the men into the bushes, and not all water-front whores but a lot of pretty girls, some maybe no older than Lucinda, like that Maidie Clark, from Miss Farnsworth's, too, and acting just as feisty. Nothing was too good for the boys when the war was still to be fit.

But, as the doctor had ordered him to talk of himself, so Milton told what a bodacious waiting it was to grow up. The fighting would all be over before they could even grow a whisker, although they slept with pigeon droppings plastered on their chins, said to be used by all the bearded ladies. But old Mollie found out.

". . . It was around then that I began to think about you," Lucinda said softly, looking down at the ring on her finger, her cheeks pink. ". . . Canceled our names out, the *m's,* the *i's* and all, but I never thought mine would come true . . ." waiting for him to ask so she could tell it came out in marriage.

But Milton was too busy getting the shying gray mare down to a little bridge. "Steady, Floss, steady," he commanded, holding her firmly to the road with line and whip until her black hoofs hit the planking in a spatter like a grafter's cannonball, and Lucinda clutched at her bonnet with one hand and Milton's arm with the other, laughing in relief when they were across.

And just beyond, in the cool shade of the woods, a bay horse was tied beside a flashy single-seater that they both recognized as George Shefton's, Lucinda stealing a look around for the man who bowed so elegantly over her hand, and over Sarah's, too, lately. While Milton spoke angrily of bounty givers and arms running and the story that George was working up a gang of night riders south of the river and selling them guns, Lucinda thought about the beautiful woman sure to be in the woods somewhere with him—usually somebody's young wife, it was said, because married women were much safer.

But Milton had no real mind for Yeller Weskit today. Stopping the mare on a high place that overlooked miles of the broad, wooded hills of the Ohio he pointed his whip around the way that Morgan circled Cincinnati the year after that first scare, and wound up at Buffington Island. They captured seven hundred of his raiders there, cut them off with Union gunboats in the flooded Ohio.

"I remember when they took Aunt Betsy Horner's silver tureen and her canary, with her running after them down the road waving the old squirrel gun and crying because it wasn't loaded!"

Well, Aunt Betsy would have liked seeing Morgan's officers dumped off at the wharves and marched up Main Street to the jail, beat out, their grays ragged and dusty, some with clean Yankee bandages. People gathered like flies along a streak of sorghum to hoot, throwing eggs and other stuff, shaming them for the raiders they were, instead of honorable prisoners of war. So Milton and Johnny dug up their discharge papers and money, and crossing the river, cut off south towards the Federals on the Tennessee, where Sherman was coming from Vicksburg.

"Oh, I missed seeing the Reb prisoners. Mother wouldn't let me come to town. Too much raggle-tail out, she said."

There was raggle-tail, all right, Milton agreed, laughing, beginning to enjoy this talking about himself, even to a woman-piece, a girl. And every hound-dog bellerin' loud as old John Brown when the copperheads helped Morgan escape and get away right past Cincinnati. But by then the two boys were sleeping in the great camp with veterans of Vicksburg all around them, and feeling like veterans too, with discharge papers to prove it. Of course they got the whey scared out of them the first hour of fighting at Missionary Ridge; tried to dig in like badgers, an old campaigner told on them later, laughing fit to bust. But they were lucky as a couple of brindle pups until the minié ball got Milton his furlough home while Johnny had to stay and help make camp for a winter of drilling and recuperation along the Tennessee.

Lucinda sighed. "All the girls thought you were so romantic, with your cap back on your curly hair that soldier way and your arm in a sling."

Godamighty, he didn't have to be told an arm in a sling was romantic, but not a leg off, and didn't want it throwed up to him like a handful of cold mud in the snoot. Yet Charley Powell had warned him against being hen-skinned, and so he held his tongue and took it out on the little mare, whipping her into a rolling sweat, Lucinda holding to the side of the buggy and afraid.

After a while Milton started to talk again, of Sherman's preparations that winter, the General looking beat out, gaunt as a stick, his red beard a ragged brush broom. Seemed his small boy had died of typhoid at Memphis and he was blaming himself for having him along. "Named for his pa, the lad was," the older men said over their evening pipes, maybe thinking about other young 'uns named for their soldier pa's.

In the spring they moved against Buzzard's Roost and nothing finer to see than a rested army marching out in the sun, muskets and cannon shining, gold braid galloping up and down, the men singing a little, and the dust starting up in a slow cloud. But it wasn't so fine sieging Atlanta, crawling through mud made redder with the fighting, and buzzards there too, fat as holiday geese. The installations of military value made a blazing that even old-time soldiers admitted was no fox fire a passing varmint might leave smoking behind him in the snow. Then the Federals struck out again, Johnny staying, but Milton off with the long march, everybody about stripped down to ammunition. "Travel light if yer's goin' fur," an old campaigner chuckled and predicted they were headed clear to the sea. They made it, with scarcely a bean hole cooking or a weevily hardtack roasted, living off the country as they went, sending back no news. For a month not even the government knew where Sherman was.

"Oh, we were so worried," Lucinda said. "More even than other times. The copperhead press was full of the most dreadful stories about the lost army, surely captured and destroyed."

Milton laughed with the soldier's contempt for civilian confusion. People ought to know their loony lunatic Sherman, as so many at home called him, was all right. They had started out foraging or destroying only by command but after a while things got like berry-pickers on a holiday, with thousands of stragglers and smugglers and other trash tolling up, including Freedmen and a lot of soldiers away from their regiments. None of those outfits took orders, and long before they got to the sea the bummers were rampaging the whole country. They found plenty of depredations ahead of them, too, where Wheeler's Reb cavalry had passed, some said, but the Yankees getting the blame. Pretty bad things.

"Oh, Uncle Dell says there were dreadful things done. . . ."

"Bad enough," Milton admitted, moving the stump of his leg uncomfortably. "But seems they happen in war. You got to win and the quicker the better for both sides. Seems even if you start out polite as preachers, it lasts so long everybody goes hog-wild and hornet-mad. Besides, there's too many chances for deviltry for them that's so minded."

"I still think those things were wrong," Lucinda said, not certain what she meant, but stubborn as a Georgia mule, her chin set white.

"And it's right—your own man losing his leg?" Milton wanted to yell in her face, mad to ager-shaking again. But Doc Powell had warned he wasn't to expect much from civilians; learn to look on his mutilation like a natural handicap—a hare-lip, maybe, or a hunchback—keep its tanbark bitterness from his tongue, never use his crutch to club others to his way.

"We got blamed for a lot," Milton finally said, "like the burning of Charleston. I'd been shifted, and so was there from the start, and all I know is that the Rebs skedaddling ahead of us fired the cotton stores and that night a lot of the town burned down. Maybe from the cotton, maybe set by the niggers or the starved Union prisoners. Anyway, liquor was like a cloudburst in the streets, everybody celebrating that the war was 'bout done. . . ."

Turned out Lee did surrender right afterward, the Rebs scattering into the brush and for home to put in the spring crops, but Milton still had the little hole in his leg coming, no bone or gristle touched but puffing up dark as blood pudding. Peace came, great bonfires were built by Sherman's horn-foots, Lincoln was shot and laid away, but all Milton knew was the delirium and the fog of drugging.

". . . Sometimes at night it comes back . . ." he admitted, shamed, eating dirt as for a faulting.

"Oh, Milton! I didn't know," Lucinda said softly, her hand creeping shyly under his elbow, almost without her knowledge. Milton pressed his arm against it, too embarrassed to see the red sweep up the girl's face at this first gesture of softness toward her since he was back.

But he still couldn't tell her about the long months in the hospital, although the whole story had come spouting like a gully washer for the woman down near the wharves. It was a hard thing for a man to admit about his bride, even to himself, but it was so.

Milton's evening fire burned slowly, making a pile of red coals that would live far into the gloom, as a soldier's campfire should, its lighted circle his clubhouse and saloon, billiard hall and home. It was good to sit by tonight, play a few old tunes on his fiddle, a thick buffalo robe spread against the damp, chilling earth, with Lucinda beside him. Together they watched the last glow of the sky disappear from the river far below, the fireflies lacing the shadows of the bottoms, the gray mare snorting sleepily beyond the firelight.

Then Milton started to talk of the future and the things planned with Charley Powell. The red of the dying coals played along the bridge of his nose and on his young beard, the mutilated leg lost in the shadows, the crutch too. He felt bigger than any flatboater talking about the gold out in Idaho as he told of the plans for school, and for work and study in Powell's office, followed by medical school and a doctor's shingle of his own.

"Oh, Milton!" Lucinda cried, "isn't that flash!" Then suddenly she became serious, her voice concerned, shaking a little. "But, your mother—she dislikes Doctor Powell so. . . ."

"Yeh, because he laughs at the lady hypos, says the cure is a little honest work, and respect for their husbands," Milton laughed easily. "It's only a puff of wind in a barrel."

"Oh, no—she says he's a renegade to his class!"

"To his class?" Milton roared out, pulling back from his mother's big-talking words on the girl's tongue, pulling back into himself, all his weeks of hope and planning suddenly empty as a turtle shell in an antheap. Godamighty, what was he doing with these lady-talkers, these skyuglers! He was a doughfoot, a bummer. He had to get away now, with nobody here who could stop him, slip off into the dark brush this minute, be his own man like the galoot on the raft who tootled his cowhorn at the engine whistle—anything, just so he could get away.

But as he reached around for his crutch, he saw that Lucinda had turned from him, her face hidden in her hands, the fading light a sheen over her hair. Feeling scurvy-mean about going without a say why, or anything, he turned the girl toward him, lifting her face to tell her as gently as he could. But her cheek was wet in the firelight, a bit of the red caught in each tear, and so he wiped his fingers gently over them and kissed them away, shyly at first, ashamed, and then her eyelids too, and her lips, her throat, until his months of pain and misery seemed forgotten, all the confusion, the humiliation of his return melted away, and something grew great within him until he felt powerful and gigantic, a tom-walker to stride the world.

4—A Lean Horse

A lean horse for a long race and a short-bodied woman for children, Charley Powell always said, and spoken true, it seemed. Almost a year had passed since Lucinda slipped away through the row of blooming lilacs from the sight of her soldier boy coming home with an empty britches leg. Some things had changed in this time; many were more the same. On the river the shipping moved steadily westward with the current, hoping to leave the hard-time country behind, but Milton Stone was still not among them, and still on his crutch. As Dr. Powell had predicted, the Kellers took Sarah's money and after a lot of briar-tongue talk, finally produced an India rubber leg that was clumsy and awkward as the butt of an oak.

"Like the butt of an oak that's been soaking in Ohio mud for years," Milton said bitterly, feeling a curried-down fool as he tried to strap the heavy leg in place, to stand on it, move around, fretting himself with it to please his mother. And when the Kellers finally patched the top to hold on, it still made his walking awkward as a string-halted mule, even with the crutch. At home he went down the back slope where the trees hid him from the house and the grounds, working at it like a pie biter, ten times harder than to learn the whirling cartwheels when he was a young 'un. But the stump got raw to festering; all the old pain of the malahacked leg came back, and when Lucinda tried to help she turned fainty-white and had to run through the door with her hands over her mouth. When he went to Charley Powell he got sour words.

Foolishly, young Milton told his mother. Her heavy face darkened to the color of her port under the whitening. "You ungrateful cur-hound!" she cried, in her old river bottom voice, "going around blabbing our business among your scalawag friends, letting them egg you against us! Even Lucinda at it too, spiting me. . . ."

So Milton was put to defending his wife, and soon the rubber leg stood catching dust in a closet along with Hiram's mortar and pestles and the old dress form Sarah used when she was forty pounds lighter and did her own sewing. The leg slumped, knee-sprung and done for too.

Milton had a tutor most of the summer, some poor relation of Mrs. Matthews, who kept flattening down his toupee and saying "Master Milton, Master Milton . . ." like to a milk-tit young 'un. Lucinda helped encourage the penmanship practice with her own lady-like tracery, and ciphered against Milton as far as cube root. His spelling and memorizing she heard while she worked at the silken floral embroidery pieces, like delicate little oil paintings, that every proper Farnsworth girl had framed on her boudoir wall—or played softly at the little folding organ her father left at the back door one day.

"It has come down through the eldest daughter in her mother's people for a long time," David Martin explained as he unloaded it from his fruit wagon on the way to market. "Such things no money or prominence can provide. . . ."

Sarah had the organ taken to the young people's room and set it before the rose drapes, where the battered old case looked so mean and poor it brought tears to Lucinda's eyes.

"Your father ought to realize we'd have a new Steinway grand piano, the best on the market," Sarah complained, "even if he wasn't in shape to notice it at the wedding."

So Lucinda had to apologize for him. "We're a little foolish about old things in our family," she said, admitting it was as well, with no prospects for new.

During the summer, Sarah planned Milton's time full-up to keep him from his common army acquaintances. His *Soldier's Friend* she threw into the fire when she got her hands on it. "Takes longer to rid my son of such vermin than from the graybacks he brought home in his britches when he was out with General Lew," she said to her ladies literary. Toward fall she started him to school with those as much as four, five years younger; years that meant the difference between a milk-sprout and an old soldier. In the games like pum-pum-pullaway or fox and geese he learned to vault after his classmates fast as some great tom-walking giant so that the bigger boys ran whooping and laughing before him. It was wondrous fun to see, particularly for the smaller ones.

Mostly the talk was of Indian fighting, running away to the gold fields or maybe finding a girl who would let them do what they wanted, like Milton and Johnny did years ago about Smeggie, one of the Deeker girls' brush fillies. Finally they had managed to toll the seven-year-old Smeggie into a hollow with a stick of Hiram's licorice. Sucking at the black stick in the corner of her dirty mouth she flopped down on the ground and pulled her dress up, but when they saw how skinny she was, with nothing more than a rabbit's, and pink-like, even when she pulled herself apart, they got scared and ran.

Sometimes the boys at the academy remembered that the cripple among them had a wife and then they would gather around him, swaggering to cover their greenness. "Bet you have a time—with only one leg," making motions among themselves like old Crutch Williams selling his dirty pictures, and almost getting clubbed down with the crutch, like so many Rebs with a gunstock. But they had never seen a starving, proud-mouth woman offer the hated Yankees anything for a fistful of corn grits or a sliver of salt horse to feed some ailing kin. Nor had they seen a man die, or learned how long he can take to it with his entrails dragged out over the ground, his eyes turning flinty, his mouth round and terrible as it let out the yells he had to get shut of.

To hide the shame of this knowing, Milton began to tell the boys great stories of slaughter and other gostratious doings, tales that were really of a fighting with broomsticks and mud balls instead of cannon, the blood like the wash water from Sarah's old turkey red quilt. And sometimes he would hand one of the others the crutch and practice his cartwheels, awkward as a wheelbarrow in a cloudburst at first, but his one leg getting stronger, until he got so he could almost make it over and to a standing.

Away from the school Milton felt awkward as a handrake too, whether in the double-towered brown house on the hill or in the little flat down in Cincinnati that Sarah rented for them near the school. It was only one room with a couch bed, a kitty bender stove and bedbug specks along the wall cracks—not what her son should have, yet she had to grumble about the rent. Without the hundred thousand dollars at hand Steve Tolley hadn't been able to hold the War Department to the lease on the empty warehouses, so the ten thousand a month went up the flue. Nor could he get anything else, with credit tight as Mary Todd's stays, and things looking almighty rocky for his return to the Senate unless he could lay hands on enough important money to honeyfugle the Legislature. But even with a bill collector behind every bush, it was a comfort to know that the old Lincoln haters among the Democrats in Congress would keep voting with the Radicals. Maybe something could still be hatched for Steven.

"The damned politicians got high-toned notions of the value of a vote during the war! They forget the boom days are past," Hiram complained over his snuff box.

Sarah still couldn't talk about it without switching her petticoats. After poor Steven had worked so hard at organizing the joint committee to take the war out of the hands of that jackleg Lincoln! Set fire under Andy Johnson to move him out of the White House! Drive out shoddy money. Raise the tariff. Put the army into the South to keep the traitors down.

"—Uncle Steve sure's a cowalloper." Milton interrupted.

Yes, and now that everything was safe they drummed him out! Like a common rascal out of the army!

"Hell's buzzards, not drummed out," Milton said, uneasily, remembering the first time he saw a man given this public shaming.

Well, that's what it made up to, no matter how it was fetched and hauled, and no home left. Young Sumner was coming here to look around. "He'll be a comfort; such a gentleman, even with his mother dead and everything—growed up gallant as George Shefton, if you can remember from your drunken wedding. . . ."

Milton remembered what he had called Sumner, and that his front teeth were out since—like any common draft dodger's.

Milton's flat was close to Dr. Derringer's office, where Sarah decided he should assist, as she called it. "Paulson Derringer serves a high-class patient, not like that hurrah's nest over to Charley Powell's."

It was true there was raspberry-colored carpeting in Derringer's office, a cut-glass bowl for the leeches, but to Milton the doctor looked like the Ohio River suckers he used to catch with Johnny, the same pale, blank eyes, the round-lipped, colorless fish mouth, his hair baby-white, his mustache sparse and pale as wild cucumber spines. He insisted that Milton shave off his dark beard, leaving his soft red lips naked, making him look like a milk-sop stripling with a smudgy jaw.

At the flat Lucinda was miserable as from a wood's colt, mornings, the sickness growing with her girth, until Dr. Derringer complained to Sarah that she was taking this as hard as a woman of gentle breeding, not a fruit peddler's daughter. And it was unreasonable of Lucinda to stay so gaunt and yellow; dauncy as an ailing pullet, her Grandmother Strathorn called it, and recommended fresh game: wild turkey, venison and squirrel, best broiled with the animal heat still in. Cured her when she was that way with her first, but then her man was a hunter, not a crutch cripple.

Finally Nellie Martin came for the girl and while Lucinda worried that all the old household responsibilities might settle back upon her as the eldest daughter, she went. Milton had no word to say against it. He could see nothing of the slim, lovely girl he married in this heavy, wide-standing woman who leaned back so dully from her burden, her gray, sad face a constant blaming before his eyes. Out at the surrey he couldn't even help her to the step.

But the mother had brought Malinda and a stout box. When the girl was safely in the seat, she turned her wet eyes down upon her husband, but the sickness came over her again and with her face in her mother's lap they drove away.

Milton's studies went no better alone, or his work. The baby-skinned Dr. Paulson Derringer, with his fancy eclectic and hydropathic rigamarole, was coming up in the world while some thought that the Stones had hit a sink.

"Up like a rocket, down like a Stone!" the doctor said behind the back of his bottle washer, letting his patients in on something: flattering the new ones, amusing the dull time of those soaking in their hydropathic sheets. When they praised the doctor, he made a face of modesty and patience, admitting a crutch cripple was depressing for people of class, no matter how romantic some might find curly black hair, and those high-boned, shiftless faces. ". . . Stone's particular disability makes him—ah—valueless with those cases in which a dashing young assistant could prove most—ah—most therapeutically efficacious," he said, his mouth working like a sucker breathing.

So when Steve Tolley went back to his jackleg law practice Dr.

Derringer came right out to say he must have more money for Milton's training.

It was like a stray shell hitting the only kettle of stew at bivouac. "More m-money?" Milton asked foolishly, looking up from the spatula he was polishing. "You mean you been taking money for me working?—Godamighty, Dr. Powell offered me a chance to learn a little about doctoring at his place, and for nothing!"

"Ah, yes—Charley Powell!" Derringer said, with the expression Milton had seen on his face when an overripe boil splattered corruption over his white linen. "The pension-claim faker. . . ."

Slowly Milton stumped through the rest of the cleaning and then home to the empty flat, with the wedding silver in the commode, and beside it the marble bench that shattered a cakestand of sparkling crystal from Milton's clumsy hand. Tonight there wasn't even one of the notes Lucinda sometimes wrote when she felt better on the goat milk and thick dark beer Grandmother Strathorn brewed in the Martin cellar. But when Milton tried to answer he could only remember Lucinda like a sick cat the last few months, even when he looked at the wedding tintype with her sitting slender and serious before him, hiding the leg that was gone. So he hobbled out to lean against the billiard saloon with Lee Redding, rheumatic from Andersonville prison, and maybe a hurdy-gurdy war crip collecting tobacco tags to get a wooden leg and old Mat, the palsy shaker. Sunning themselves they watched the girls from dancing school pass, pretty and slim in the March wind. If it was night and not even the fiddle from the calico sack helped, Milton went along the shadowy street to the Hound's Tooth and sat with a half dozen other vets: sometimes a befuddled boy from the Wilderness tootling softly on his bent fife, and a bald old cavalryman, his blue coat as flittered as Sherman's battleflags. Their talk was comforting as a rail fence at bivouac time, even when their grievances came up: the girls who didn't wait, the hard times, business and jobs gone; maybe some poor devil hanging himself the night before or another carcass come floating to the top in the river.

Usually some outsider, some pinch-pants civilian, horned in on their talk to do a little blackguarding. Why didn't they go West? get off the doorstep where folks didn't have to see their worthlessness. Or join the army again? those of them still man enough.

Yeh, join up, take the place of the Galvanized Yankees, the Reb prisoners who had enlisted to fight Indians rather than lay around in prison. Join up and get massacreed like old Morrie Rosen sitting right over here amongst them last spring. After chasing Mexies to hell an' gone, and four years after the Rebs, he reenlisted and got himself ordered out onto a frozen ridge off there in Wyoming territory by a greenhorn West Pointer and lost his scalp to a Sioux. "Yeh," Andy Burke said, spitting into the sandbox, "Join up and get off the doorstep. . . ." He'd done it enough, got as far off as Crimea, but his pockets were still holes.

If somebody had a *Soldier's Friend,* it was spread over a table with maybe Mel Daniels, who could do it as natural as walking, to read them the pension news, the warning for job hunters to stay away from the big cities, and complaints that soldiers couldn't get work because they were considered criminals.

"Tarnation, a lot of them are! Look at the times you see 'ex-soldier' after the name of a thief or a woman raper. . . ."

"Like that bank robber up to Elyria," an old teamster from Company G snorted. "He claimed he'd been in the army, but happened it was Sing Sing."

"Yeh, mebby, but you wouldn't likely trust a man who has been whoring around, foraging and thieving, making killing his business," Mel Daniels admitted reasonably.

"Now don't you go gettin' hard nosed too. You didn't hafta do any killin', not you, belly-robbin' your way through the war, and then home to a hash house set up by your pa-in-law!"

So it went, and sometimes when there were western emigrants or other newcomers around, the vets turned to stories of outfighting and outmarching any other outfit that came down the pike. "Prove it to 'em, Milt," someone would roar out. "Stand up!—See!—Marched clean off to the hip!"

And if the outlander was befuddled enough to scoff: "How about the other leg?" Milton would answer with a shamed look, "Had a game knee, favored it a little. . . ."

It was a poor joke, nothing like the old campaign days, but it helped pass the time and maybe got them a round of drinks and sometimes Milton would turn a cartwheel or two for a little more, maybe dance a one-footed jig, balancing his crutch by its tip on his chin, until he had to be helped home afterward, to a sleeping that was heavy as a winter badger's.

Finally Sarah Stone came to see why the carriage was returning empty, and ran into her maid, Marie—let go when times first got hard. The girl was face down on the couch, crying, with Milton standing beside her, balanced in embarrassment on his crutch.

"Ha! So I find another Stone who'll follow his nose after any dirty petticoat!" she cried as the girl fled past her. Milton tried to explain that she was begging for something from the doctor, now that the Stone's gardener had gone to the gold fields and left her in a fix.

Milton's mother snapped him off short. "That hussy? She's too knowing!"

But there were more important britches to patch. Sitting rigid in her stays, Sarah Stone folded her arms and spoke her mind. The place was a boar's nest; plainly Lucinda hadn't returned from her visit home, wanting to be run after again. Besides, Dr. Derringer was displeased with Milton's work and the academy reported he hadn't been in attendance for weeks, while here he sat like a common army bummer, dirty, unshaven, his hinder out bad as the rest of the loafers around the Hound's Tooth. Fine thanks she was getting for all her plans and schemes to give him a big wedding, bring important people from as far as Washington. Wouldn't even try to wear the expensive limb she bought. Satisfied to be a crutch pauper all his life.

"But the leg was like a stump washed down by a flood; you saw yourself I couldn't——"

"Oh, no, but you can cut the fool with your cartwheels, you can bring me a daughter-in-law that pukes up everything excepting what's wrong with her—her that's such a feisty red wagon she gets caught spite of all the remedies I give her, and when I tries to help her out, she big-eyes me and says, 'Why, Mother Stone, that would be wick-ed!'"

While his mother threw all this up to him, Milton sat with a hand clenched on the crosspiece of his crutch, shamed and low-down that he couldn't do what his mother expected of him, not understanding that her bitterness was because her handsome young couple could make no dashing picture at receptions and balls, particularly the governor's inaugural, or even riding in the park and playing in the croquet tournaments. Nor were there the invitations she had schemed for. Many who came to the wedding with gifts had been uppity as a goat on a shake roof since, although some might have collected on their gifts through marryings among their own.

Milton kissed his mother at the carriage but he wouldn't go with her, not even if Sumner Tolley hadn't been there. He would bide here until Lucinda was over her time, then they would see what must be done. The next day Sarah sent Hiram. He came, looking much older than even a few weeks ago, his beard almost white, and wearing no banker's frockcoat now, or anything of a banker's way. He was more like a Southern planter come down to riding the double-trees, war-widowed of everything he owned.

What's eatin' on you, pa, you used to be a good apothecary? Milton wanted to ask of the man sitting heavily on the flat, hard couch and talking about the foolishness of a young fellow throwing away the chance of a lifetime. This duty done he took Milton to the old beer cellar near the warehouses to heist a couple. The old-timers greeted Hiram as in the apothecary days. "Well, well, Doc, how you find your liver?" and "What're ye and the boy drinkin', Doc?" But when Hiram asked how things were with them, they hesitated until a hardware man spoke right out.

"We're about down to giving away anvils as premiums with a pound of nails, most of us," he said over the beer Hiram ordered. "Not so much's a brad nail or a mouse trap moving, and nothing of the big stuff. Even the farmer, who's always been itching to order all the implements he could get on tick, is suddenly leery as a scalded hound. And you can't blame him, with his debts for war price land and tools, and grain down so $1.25 wheat's hardly worth the gunny sacking."

"Money's tight as hick'ry bark," a newcomer admitted.

"Yeh, it's them bums a soldiers, gettin' pensions, takin' the jobs. . . ." But it was a gap-tooth talking, and so the others gave him no mind. Hank Gibbs, the freetrader, speaking his say: "If we could get the tariff claws a the big boys out a our vitals. . . ."

Some nodded, some protested, while a gentle-voiced old keelboater with a tattooed cheek talked about the ways of forty years ago. ". . . You didn't got to have money then. Why, a man mightn't see so much as a shinplaster in months on the river, but credit kept tonnage rafting. Now credit's as innadekate as a shirttail young 'un taking a leak in the Ohio in a dry spell."

"And not no watermelon-eatin' young 'un neither!"

"Well, dealing with that Wall Street outfit's always been like licking the devil 'round a stump," Hank said. "Now they choke off our banks and our credit, boost the price of manufactures to home and kill our foreign trade so's the little fellow, farmer nor nobody, can't buy. Then factories got to shut down, and more folks can't buy. Soon everybody's starved naked because the market's glutted with goods."

"Still slashing around like a broken-back coachwhip, Hank," Hiram Stone laughed, nudging Milton in friendly partnership. "We don't see any buzzards sitting waiting. . . ."

"I mind me the lad there beside you ain't so sure," the flatboater said quietly.

"Yeh, and maybe Doc ain't tried to get a job or the borry of a dollar. It's hell, with our banks taxed shut and legal tender called in, claimin' it's to save the credit of the country, keep the guyas-cutus* from gettin' loose. Now the holders a government bonds is hollering for gold, and getting it too, hundred cents on the dollar, when all they paid was forty-nine."

Hiram wiped his beard and, nodding to Milton, pushed back from the little table. "Forty-nine cents?" he asked. "Lots of the bonds went for far less, if you count in the war inflation."

"Tarnation—admittin' it baldfaced!"

"He might's well. The rich can't go on without us buying no more than that river out there can keep running without the cricks and springs and runnels to fill her up."

"Seems to me you got the wrong pig by the tail, if you're count-ing me in with the rich," Hiram said wearily as he started away, on Milton's good side. He admitted that the grumblers back there were at least half right in complaining. Times were hard. Sarah would be losing her big house on the hill soon, the payments already months behind. "Your mother could use you to cheer her up Saturday, with Uncle Joseph and the bays going——"

"Godamighty! That bad?"

Yes, Hiram admitted. And worse. A woman from the East was blackmailing him, threatening to bring the child she was bearing here, to Cincinnati, if he didn't come across handsomely.

* A fictitious animal used to draw trade to shows and circuses. When the customers get insistent for a sight of the monster a great commotion and a cry that the guyascutus was loose always cleared the tents.

Godamighty! Godamighty! The old man with another woman, and got her full!

It was a cold, rainy night when David Martin rode in for the doctor. But Derringer said it was too early; just a hysterical girl's notion, nor was there any telling where the unreliable Milton might be entertaining himself. So David went to Charley Powell's. The doctor came out in oilskins, yawning open-mouthed, his big old satchel case in one hand, a flickering storm lantern for the dashboard in the other. "Derringer's tony patients may shell out by the calendar," he said ruefully, "but for me, horse or human, they seem to pick times of extreme inclemency or downright catastrophe."

David Martin watched the buggy draw away into the rain, black and top-heavy against the glow at the dash, and understood why young Milton liked this mean-tongued man.

But the young whippersnapper was still to be found, and when the messenger came back from the Stones without news, Lucinda's father began to search the town, leaving the policemen grinning under the wavering gaslights. "Them young rascals! Always around when there's a chance for the planting, and harder to find than a flea in your undershirt come shelling out time!"

But Milton was spending the night with the woman of the greenish hair, and so it was the bartender at the Hound's Tooth who first saw him, and not until around noon. "Son," he said, "they been all but shooting cannon over the river to fetch up your carcass."

"Why? Something happened?" thinking of the house on the hill going, and his mother maybe finding out about Hiram's woman and her catch-colt.

"Something happened, he asks? Ain't he the innocent one?— Your wife's poppin'."

"Popping?" Milton asked blankly, but the laughing that started struck him like a Barlow knife between the ribs. Quickly he looked from one face to another in the dark bar. "It's too early!"

"What you mean, too early? It ain't never too early if you beat the whelping to the preacher. Besides, you been back almost a year," the bartender laughed, the dirty apron over his belly shaking.

Milton hired a rig and drove out, the wheels throwing water and mud at every chock-hole. The sun shone overhead, redbirds sang, and in the Martin orchard butterflies swarmed around the white clouding of the plum trees, but Milton didn't notice. He left the buggy in swinging leaps using his crutch as a vaulting pole. At the door Lucinda's mother kissed him and turning her wet face away, took him to the girl.

She lay in a great canopied bed looking so white and still that Milton thought she must be dead, and something balled up in him like a fist against the horn of his crutch. But as he stood there the girl's eyelids lifted slowly, heavily, her face changing without seeming to, and with a groaning in his throat as at a new wounding, Milton dropped to his one knee beside the bed, the forgotten crutch clattering to the floor.

"Lucie, Lucie," he whispered.

She didn't speak or move, just lay there looking down at him, and finally Milton found himself talking to her, saying all the things that had accumulated within himself, all the sorrow and regret over the foolish, hurtful things that had been done the last year because he had neglected to let her know of his crippling. She had had a right to know, to make her choosing without the hullabaloo and the crowding around.

Oh, but he was the one who had no chance at choosing, the girl said, her voice low and sorrowful. She knew. She couldn't bear it that nobody would meet him the day he came home, and so she had seen him from behind the lilacs at the depot.

"You mean you outright picked half a man?"

A clouding came over the girl's face. "I—the babies, they died."

Died?—Godamighty!

She made a little moving with her hand on the coverlid. Twins, both dead, and there were to be no more. So now she was the half one, only half a woman. Her white lips seemed steady as she said it, but her gray eyes were yellowed as with old age, or a long, long sickness, and when Milton kissed her she began to cry, shaking like a young birch in a williwaw. He held her tight, afraid she would tear herself.

Two weeks later they came back to the little flat that looked lost and forgotten as an old mitten in a gutter: Lucinda to rest; Milton like so many the last two years, to try another shot at a new start. Not at school; that was smoke in the wind, but to study lancing and dosing with Charley Powell.

"I warned you, you won't be making the proper social contacts here, and that my layout's not up to the recent Stone tradition," the doctor said every day or so.

To this Milton learned to laugh a little, and swing casually on his crutch as he muddled powders and ointments, folded filters, or rolled pills. He even learned to overlook it when the doctor said, "My God, boy, did you have all your brains stashed away in that leg they hacked off?" or "Hello, Crip!" like caustic on wild flesh, searing but healing. Mostly old Charley and the cronies hanging around his office chewed over national affairs like other men talked about their business and their sons, quarreling like tomcats tied in a pillowslip over the Molly Maguires or the purchase of Alaska—Seward's Folly, as some called it, and whether the Indian troubles out West were a fracas cooked up by contractors and their tools in the Senate. Neb Collings, with a son stationed out in Kansas, said the agency Indians complained they were starving, stole blind by the hirelings of the Great White Father.

Hell, who wasn't being stole blind, even using the army to collect down South, the Radicals making the occupation lawful with the Reconstruction Act. And after Sherman promised them their own government, and was charged with taking Reb gold for it.

"And who's to say he didn't?" old Jim Kelly, with two sons in Libby graves, demanded. Charley Powell nodded. No good telling Jim he was believing a lie; a man who viewed events emotionally lied to himself. ". . . Anyway, the Act gives those carpetbagging buzzards legal status—and keeps us from voting the Radicals into the ashcan."

Sometimes they talked hopefully of a new outfit among the farmers called Grangers, or quarreled over the usurpation of executive powers by the Senate, men not elected by the voters but by the state legislators, who could be bought up with a pocketful of buckeyes or a handful of railroad passes. Milton wondered if this was the same office-buying that Hiram and Uncle Steven found so expensive. Maybe these loafers were troublemakers like that Mack at the Hound's Tooth; maybe they were like camp-weary soldiers counting weevils in the hardtack, but barely skimming them off the dunking coffee when the fighting picked up.

"Still looking at everything like a soldier—" Charley Powell called it, a soldier too young by three years to vote on the issues they discussed here, and yet with much of old age already behind him; its pain and misery and long familiarity with death, and beyond that the larger dying of a sheet flat and empty where a good leg had been.

Wiping the stem of his pipe over his long mustache Charley Powell watched Milton sight along the broken edge of a scalpel blade he was honing down patiently. The steel was good; he would make a useful instrument of it yet, if a shorter.

Somehow Lucinda didn't pick up as she should, staying listless and pale as a tree stripped of its leaves in midsummer. Sarah Stone had washed her hands of them both, and when she said "my son" nowadays she meant the first-born Spencer, who had run off to Chicago years ago, and then got the western fever a jump ahead of Lincoln's draft. But she still gave Milton a small allowance, explaining its penury quite reasonably: "It don't take so much money to be a Martin like it did when you was a Stone," while Hiram walked up and down, a hand on his beard, not opening his mouth.

One day a boy came hurrying to the doctor's office with a note, calling him around to Jimson Baker's law office. "Your respected pa's mixed up with a real shyster this time," old Charley whispered to Milton, and grabbing his big black satchel he left his pill roller to finish bandaging Katie O'Shea's ulcered legs. She grumbled about it, but the old sores really were healing, either from the doctor's salve or from the poultices of moldy bread recommended by a swamp-doctoring river woman.

"Old Katie comes to me now and then like she goes to Mass of a Sunday, after raising hell with her Jim and the young ones all week," Powell once said. "A sort of insurance. . . ."

By the time the legs were bandaged, Charley Powell was back, setting his half-open satchel on the laboratory table and hustling Katie out. When the place was empty he returned to the little laboratory, pulling at his long mustache as he came. "Young man— as I suspected, Hiram Stone's sure got himself up a sour gum tree this time. Why should a healthy man like your pa be calling a doctor, and Charley Powell at that? Well, there's the reason," he said, opening the satchel wider, showing a sleeping infant inside. "You have been presented with a new brother."

"A new brother?" Milton asked, rubbing a palm over his bearding chin.

"Oh, he's your brother all right, a little sleepy from soothing syrup, probably, to keep him quiet, but a sound young fellow," the doctor said as he laid the dark-haired baby out on the table next to the pill slab, the long white dress trailing over the edge. "His mother's just fell from Baker's window, so they got the young 'un out the back door while the police were pulling down the skirts of the remains on the sidewalk out front. The mother, and a right handsome, upstanding brunette she must have been, has tried to hugger-mugger the old stud horse to set aside a good portion for the boy, as seems customary with these war-rich, their position not solid enough for much public dirty linen. Either she jumped from the window or carried her bluff too far, leaving the little booger there behind with the lawyer and your pa. Because the Stone name must be kept sweet and pure, I have the chee-ild."

"My brother . . ." Milton said, still unbelieving. And the mother dead!

"Oh, she's dead all right, and no witness except that shyster Jimson Baker. With a little more money at stake he might make it his word against your father's whether she fell or was pushed."

"Pushed?—Murder?" Milton gripped the crosspiece of his crutch.

Charley Powell snorted through his mustache. "Oh, I doubt if Hiram still ranks such a shakedown. The woman smuggled the baby in under a fur cloak on her arm, so probably nobody else in the Queen City knows about it."

"But what will become of the young 'un, the baby?"

"My efficient young helper, one of the important duties, and privileges, of a doctor in these froward, unsettled times is the happy and inconspicuous disposal of just such little bastards."

Leaning on his crutch, Milton looked down upon the sleeping child, a pink fist hardly bigger than a pigeon egg clenched tight as a knuckle fighter's. He was small, the size of the little wart Company G found in a brush patch outside Atlanta, dirty and squalling like a pig caught under a fence. But this one was plump, and pretty as a poppet. Poor devil, probably be locked up in an orphanage and then farmed out to some old flogger who was bound to get a man's work for a boy's keep.

Milton was still hanging around the baby when Lucinda came by to walk home with him. She stopped in the doorway, not seeing the men at all, only the long white baby dress that fell over the edge of the laboratory table in a cascade of fine embroidery.

"Oh—adorable!" she cried, standing over him, her hands held tightly to her sides and when the sour-faced doctor put the baby into her arms, she sank into a chair, her young face shining as Milton had seen it only once before, the evening he came stumbling home after he had been down to the woman near the wharfs, the first time away all night.

Finally Lucinda looked up. "Whose—whose is it?" she asked.

"Yours, if you want him, dear lady," the doctor replied, putting on the beauing way he had for the girl. But she was not to be teased now, and so Charley Powell set to filling his pipe. "I mean it," he was saying, when the waiting-room bell rang and there were steel fragments to take from a foundry man's eye, with Milton needed to help. When they were done with the magnet and instruments and bandaging, the doctor had something to say quietly to his helper.

"You know, we've gormed into something in there," nodding toward the laboratory. "If you can stomach having your father's bastard around. . . ."

A moment Milton hesitated. Then he clenched himself together as he would to a surprise bayonet charge, or a Reb cavalry with saber and yell. A quick breath, a tensing of his muscles, and he was ready.

"Me?—I can stomach anything," he said, and swung himself over onto his crutch stick. It went well, and so he pulled his leg up and whirled clear around, like a top on a spindle shank.

5—Gold Eagle Warm in the Palm

The spring the boy Stevie was seven, Milton Stone swung himself up over the wheel of his covered wagon and headed West with his family, on that road that had become one great extension of man's footstep, his wagon tongue, the sight-span of his hand-shaded eyes. He went much as a hundred thousand others, driven out by the break-bone winter that followed the panic of 1873, when Hank Gibbs' prediction of people starving naked while the market was glutted with goods had come certain true. Many more would have gone West if the money could have been scraped together, for out there the land was free and a man could build up his own community, make his own laws, get a plumb new start.

Milton had talked some about it before his soldier bounty was gone, like a hobbled mule looking over a corn patch fence, and more since, whenever the railroad come-on pamphlets showed up around the Hound's Tooth. Then Hank Gibbs or old Joe Deaver would stand under the flickering gas light of the old bar to read the fine print aloud. Each time more were minded to listen, their card games, their arguments and broodings put aside. It seemed the ground really was rich as suet out there along the Platte River and down through Kansas; ground where a man could tromp a kernel of corn into the sod of May, snap out roastings in August and shuck ears long as his arm in November—fifty, sixty bushel to the acre, for the breaking and planting.

"Hell's buzzards, they're wanting to sell the land they got free-gratis from the government." Milton had scoffed the first few times. "Just railroad flapdoodle!"

"Maybe," Hank admitted, "but if you was to dock both head and tail off a them stories they's still a lot that's meat to a hungry man's stommik. Besides, there's plenty of the land out there free for the taking."

It did sound good, good as a gold eagle warm in the palm of a

Saturday night, but still Milton protested. "Honeyfugle!" he roared, as sour as Charley Powell. "Liars spout honeyfugle at the sight of a blank sheet of paper like flatboaters around a tub of Kentucky moonshine." So, noisily, he covered up his realization that a one-legger had no business with free land and a walking plow, doing it even at home before Lucinda and the boy, who was growing fast by then and bearing the good Tolley name of Steven. Sarah had decided on that, since they wouldn't ever have a son of their own for the name. Milton flushed hot as mustard plaster but there had been nothing he could say to his mother, particularly with her big house up for sale by the mortgage holder, and snoopers streaming through like ants in a cupboard, diving into every cranny, rubbing wet fingers over her sealskin sacque to see if it was genuine. So he tried to get help on the naming from Hiram.

"The ointment's blue enough now, without my muddling it more," his father said wearily.

It was true Hiram didn't stand just right to mix in, not on this catch-colt. By the time the boy was a year old it was plain there would not be enough Stone money to set up a cripple in a medical practice. So one desperate day Lucinda went to Hiram, still with an office in the warehouses; kept the rats away, the owner said. There was no one to leave Stevie with so she took the boy along, carrying him first on one thin hip, then on the other. He grew heavier and heavier, waving his rattle around, pushing her hat sideways, disordering her hair, crying to every dog and horse, including the bay pacer that was to George Shefton's rig. But the man pretended not to see Lucinda and no wonder, she thought, her eyes stinging, an aching in her heart as she caught a sight of herself in a window —a dowdy, drab young woman with a crying baby on her arm.

But the boy helped her get the promise of a little drug store for Milton, one aimed at the working man and the ex-soldier.

". . . Most of those fellows are poor pay, deadbeats," Hiram had argued, still managing to talk like the owner of the big house on the hill.

Lucinda admitted that the profits would be small, but there was Milton's pension that Uncle Steven had managed for him, fifteen dollars a month now, and perhaps she could learn to use her needle for something besides punching it idly through what Dr. Powell called that prime instrument of flirtation, the embroidery hoop. She didn't tell Hiram that the night before Milton had come crawling home through the filth and horse apples of the street, and that it was morning before she got him scrubbed and to bed so she could slip out to find his crutch. Hiram, suddenly so aged by the last few months, watched the dark-eyed young Stevie toddle from one dusty chair to another and back to Lucinda, clapping his fat hands in delight at his new game of walking. Pulling out a bandanna, Hiram agreed to do what he could. It wasn't much; enough to get a start of stock in a little place hardly wider than the length of a broomstick, but it was a lot, considering that within three months everything Hiram owned was hauled away.

To Milton the whole difficult time since he left the hospital, all the misery and confusion everywhere, seemed somehow tied in with the loss of his leg. Everything done blind and foolish: the expensive rubber leg Sarah sold for five dollars; the soldiers faunching around to get started again, keep alive; the thousands pulling out West— all makeshifts, awkward as his peg leg. Like his tom-walker, as those who saw him vault puddles and picket fences called it.

In Charley Powell's laboratory Milton had managed with the crutch, propping it within reach as he worked at the laboratory table, but in the little store he had to get around with his hands free, and so he whittled a wooden peg leg from a stick of hickory David Martin was curing for double-trees. Gimpy Smith, at Martins Park, had one like that. But his leg was off below the knee and his scarrings tough as alligator hide. Just trying to fit himself made Milton's old wound raw to bleeding and brought the numbing pain back so he gave it up and didn't talk even to young Stevie for a week. Then one of the loafers hunkering an hour away in the little store told a long-winded story about a doctor who had lost both legs years ago and walked again at a spiritualist meeting.

"Hold up, now, Asa, you ain't goosing any foolish widow-woman, showing her transportation by ghosts in the dark."

"Tarnation, I ain't one to tack plumes on bullfrogs, like you. The magazine's right here," he said, hauling out a handful of tattered pages. "Picked it up on the dumps; wonderful place, the dumps of a great city, all the appurtenances of modern civilization."

Milton headed him around. "You was telling about the spiritualists," he reminded. "My ma's been going to some down near the levee since things been so unsettled, and when that letter come saying Spencer was killed in the mines. Likely the same kinda outfit."

"All the same, including Doc Mary Walker who cut Reb lead out of me, only in this here story it's the legs that come back instead of messages. Seems the doc in the story stepped around bright as a banty rooster on his own legs, and after they had been respectfully interred for years. Gives complete details here."

Toward morning, when the little store was empty, Milton looked the story over, lopped wearily over the counter, his hands flat over the pages as though they might escape. The wording and the paper too, seemed like the high-toned periodicals that Sarah used to have in what she called her library. The next day he asked Charley Powell. Yes, he had seen the story a while back. The magazine was dependable enough, dependable as a horse-faced old spinster.

After thinking about it Milton hunted up a spiritualist meeting, one where he wouldn't run into his mother. It was off on the bottoms, in a swaybacked old shack of a house, but folks were going in and so he followed to a room thick with a stink like soldiers long on the march, and dark as a crawdad hole. Near the back a little grease light sputtered and behind it sat a mammoth old woman, her eyes closed, her mouth fallen open, her breath loud in the stillness.

Somebody sang, thin, high from the roof of the mouth, and when the late comers were pushed down into the jam pack, a sheep bell tinkled, and another high voice came floating over the huddle of people, making them stir, hold their breaths, swallow in the darkness. The voice, somehow familiar, was bringing messages from the spirit world, outright hogwash, Milton told himself, stuff like: "An old lady comes calling for her Mary, saying, 'Take all the advice you can get here about the dark stranger, take all'" and "A young man in kepi comes asking for his mother," and "There's work for you come summer. In a month I can tell you where, in about a month."

Each time there was a sobbing or a shameful pleading for help to get somebody or something, always to get somebody or something. And so Milton began fumbling around for his crutch, but the high voice said there was a message for the young man who was running away with his lameness. Suddenly Milton wanted to laugh outright, for it was Billy Hugan's voice; Billy the Chicago boy who had made so much confusion in the army, particularly inspection time and reviews, by throwing his voice around, until he was sent home the first scratch.

"Shucks, I knowed you the minute you stuck that black mop-head of yourn inside the door. I was just wonderin' when you'd catch on," he told Milton afterward, admitting that this business was low-down as a bushwhacker's, but he and the old lady had to eat. She was deaf and generally managed to snore all through the seances. They made a good thing out of it here in Ohio, off and on. Some who claimed to be relations of the copperhead Vallandigham tried to get the old buzzard to tell where he'd stashed his traitor gold. Then some big bug come wondering if the plot by the dictator of Santo Domingo to sell his country to the United States for pocket money would work out, hoping to get his snouse in the trough first. Lately, there was the humbug of spirit pictures showing up on windows and looking glasses all through the country, even here in Cincinnati, and folks like that half-wit, Liz Matters, claiming they were transported through the air.

". . . But mostly it's some poor female who's man's been killed or skipped out and left her with her apron loaded, or maybe it's lawing or a job," he said. "Hard times is hell; makes even sharp folks suckers for any flim-flamming."

Yes, Milton thought, and made sucker-catchers of good steady workers like Billy Hugan. But them that can't fly like eagles had to crawl on their bellies like snakes. Afterward he remembered why he had gone to the meeting, and shamed himself for taking even that much stock in a fancy story about walking on legs. What he needed was enough sand in his craw to break away from the crutch that held him down like a pin stuck through a bug, and crawling around himself. So he tried the hickory peg once more, this time fitting the top with a cushion of sponges inside the deep socket of sole leather. He fell a dozen times and had to crawl to the door or the counter to pull himself up; bruised, swearing like a keelboater, sweating, humiliated, but determined not to use his crutch. God-amighty, what a lump of suet a man was without two legs!

But he learned to balance himself, his stump toughened, and he got around, first with a cane crooked ready over his arm, and then without. It took months and sometimes the old pain came back, but the day he walked the three blocks home without crutch or cane, the leather-tipped peg making a slow, even thumping on the cobbles, he felt as mighty and powerful as the day he and Johnny got on their twelve foot tom-walkers.

Lucinda met him at the door, turning pretty as a peach fruit at the sight. She kissed him, and then cried a little softly, as he pushed her against the wall like the wild man of Gillus Mountain, who jumped out in front of the maidens on the village path and took them on his feet. On two legs.

There was a lot of big talk about the Grand Army of the Republic, the GAR, organized, Charley Powell said, by another army arnica-shooter like himself, and then taken over by Stanton as a bodyguard to keep Johnson from throwing the Secretary of War out of his cabinet.

"Usin' the army against the Commander-in-Chief is revolution," some said bitterly. "Revolution, and we ain't firing a shot agin it."

"I don't know—lot of the Ohio Regulars think the GAR's worth joining," Milton reminded them.

The cobbler who turned the soles on Milton's odd shoes was in. He scratched his head. "Some of them joining is good boys. I guess they figger they better stretch the long way'n the blankets."

When Grant was elected to the presidency, even soldiers not in the GAR began picking up their feet. The General had won for them from Vicksburg to the end in spite of all the grafting at home, even with the Peace Democrats and the Radicals both pulling back. He could sure win the battle of the Potomac.

"Always talking war and politics! No wonder you have no good customers," Lucinda once complained when she brought Milton's supper. "Don't any of you have homes or families to interest you?"

But she never did that again. The loafers cleared out at her words, like turtles tumbling off a log, and Milton threw her basket through the window after them, splattering the little cake she had baked for his twentieth birthday and the broken glass all over the walk. The curious gathered to stand and look in, while Lucinda ran out the back, her handkerchief to her mouth.

Two days later Milton finally came home, silent behind his growing beard. Lucinda cooked up the little pig sausages she had ready, and apple fritters with plenty of syrup, for it was well known among the women that sweets would lay the taste for liquor in a man. Afterward she went to the organ and played a little until Milton pulled out the old fiddle sack and joined in. Young Stevie came from his crib to stand beside the peg leg for the first time, timidly touching it with a finger, then slapping it hard.

"Gun!" he said, for some secret, childhood reason. "Gun! Bang, bang!"

Charley Powell had been against Grant all along. "Gives me the fantods to see a political amateur in the White House; worse than in the operating room, where the mistakes are one at a time, and you can throw 'em in a hole."

Soon it was plain that Grant brought his own flock of buzzards, more and hungrier than those they drove away, and with no Johnson around to raise his voice against them. Even Milton had to admit that the war hero wasn't as sharp as he might be, or else sharper, and just pretending to think the presents given him worth thousands of dollars, hundreds of thousands, were nothing more.

"I wisht somebody'd try to bribe me with presents like them," one of the old Regulars said.

"Or me," Milton admitted. He had to dip into the pension last month to pay the store rent. Old Hiram was hired-handing it now, for the first time in his life,—clerking in a drug store, with Sarah back in a river bottom shack, smaller than the one where she was born, just two rooms and a little chicken coop out back. There she talked temperance and raised poults as though she had never had thirty rooms, and an iron deer on the lawn. Gradually Hiram got to be a regular at the Hound's Tooth, not saying much, taking his whisky barefoot when he had the money, or nursing a nickel beer through a meal at the free lunch. When Black Friday came, only a few months after the big hullabaloo of a great war hero inaugurated and the transcontinental, the world's longest railroad completed, it was like some great hop-toad puffing herself up to busting, or an old bull alligator story blowing up in your face. Hell's buzzards, Wall Street cleaned out by Gould, and Fisk trying to corner the nation's gold! and then getting off free as a cat on a doorstep, licking her sides.

When money got tighter than ever, and jobs too, even Hiram spoke up. "Why, the goddamn bastards had the entire nation by the yams," he complained. "Are there no laws left that such highway robbers got to respect?"

But many remembered that he was the brother-in-law of Senator Tolley, one of the rascals that made Gould and Fisk possible, and so they drew themselves and their steins away from him—not answering until finally Hiram had to look around into the silent, pooched-up faces. Slowly he set his half-empty glass down and went out through the swinging door with his hat in his hand, and nothing for Milton but to follow. The next evening the son was back and in a couple of weeks Hiram too, ready to eat boiled crow. But by then Steve Tolley had died with the snakes, the DT's, and nobody laid further blame on the old apothecary. "Seems that trash floated by a flood's the first to lodge . . ." some said. But they might have meant Stanton, who had fought Lincoln, refused to be fired by Johnson and got the impeachment against him going although it failed by a vote. Now there was a story going the rounds that he had slashed his throat.

"He's done it often enough to others. . . ."

The campaign of 1872 brought a little hope, this time from the rise of the Liberal Republicans, the Mugwumps, with solid backing in Cincinnati. They promised big things: to drive out graft and corruption, reduce the tariff, bring civil service reform, liberate the South from the army of occupation and the carpetbaggers, and get some of the fruits of industry for the common man—the fine, useful things so many couldn't buy because machines had taken their jobs, their living. The convention was in the Queen City, with a big delegation from burned-out Chicago. Even Charley Powell put a sign on his door and went down to the great Exposition Hall as a delegate. But the nomination went to the high tariff Greeley, and Milton saw the leaders of the Cincinnati movement go home with defeat in their faces, like from a great war lost—something he would see again, and almost a third time, but not for many, many years.

Nor did the faces brighten when the Democrats, called traitors for years by Greeley, swallowed his puke and nominated him too. But even with a protectionist candidate, the Mugwumps couldn't buck the millions poured out for campaign expenses and palm grease any more than the Democrats could overcome the old waving of the bloody shirt, the cry of traitor—and the GAR's order to "Vote as you shot!" So Grant was in again, and Congress had passed his currency act boiling down the nation's money still more, squeezing the little fellow tighter, and raising Grant's salary to $50,000. By then Hiram's poor job went to a younger, quicker man willing to work the clock around for the little sleep he would grab under the counter after midnight. Sarah talked more about votes for women like in the new territory of Wyoming and set more hens while Hiram peddled garden truck with a cart and a flea-bitten old mare that the Stangers, who hadn't been invited to the wedding on the hill, loaned him twice a week. On the side Hiram did a little swamp doctoring.

By then the country was hearing one scandal after another, stinks worse than a summer battlefield coming out of Congress, the Cabinet, the White House itself, the whole topped off like a bury wagon by the rotten corpse of the Credit Mobilier, the holding company of the Union Pacific railroad. Looked like the panic so long threatened was here, with the new banks going down like rootless trees in a Kansas twister—the starving and homeless swarming the city dumpings.

Maybe the monster guyascutus so long held up as a scare to the nation was really loose this time.

By the time Charley Powell was talking about the new Farmers' Alliance and planning to head out beyond the Missouri, Milton had lost his little drug store—"Too much on tick to people who got to buck God and the weather to onct," Scott said. When the bills piled up Milton began to smell more and more of the brown-topped jug of river corn under the counter, and finally there was another dawn when he came crawling home through the gutters.

So Lucinda joined Sarah in the temperance crusade that was spreading into Cincinnati, the women going right into the water-front saloons to sing hymns and kneel in prayer on the dirty sawdust, shaming their men so that when they came to the Hound's Tooth, Milton wanted to stomp up to them and order them around to the ladies' entrance—for such women as would come into a saloon.

But instead he slipped out the back himself, putting his peg down as softly as he could but mad as a polecat with his tail tied down.

One comfort, all those uncertain years, a tin roof against the rain, was the pension—twenty-four dollars a month now, so Lucinda could manage to keep Stevie decently covered, have something on

the table, and beds for them to sleep in, hers mostly a cot in the
corner now, the boy in her place beside Milton. From the day of
her return to the flat after she lost the twins she was what Charley
Powell called a reluctant wife. Even so he had to help her out once
and not graciously or easily and afterward she grunted around for
months, thin and yellow as jaundice. Sometimes when Milton had
been to his jug, her holding back made him mad as a tromped-on
bush rattler.

"Half a woman you call yourself? Why, Godamighty, you ain't
no woman at all!"

The first time he said this Lucinda held herself silent and still the
rest of the night, and in the morning she tucked her fair hair under
her bonnet and with what was left of the pension money hired a
cart to drive home, as she still thought of the place. Although there
was the newer road near the river she took the old overgrown one
through the timber of the breaks, the way the Martins came the
day of her wedding. She stopped several times, once to show little
Stevie a mother quail hurrying her covey of striped young away
under the gooseberry bushes bent by the rows of pale green fruit;
once to look up at a great trashy nest in a dead tree, probably a fish
hawk's, Lucinda said. They would ask father when they got home,
not clear if she meant Milton or if she was going back to him at all.

Farther on they saw George Shefton exercising one of his trotters
back and forth to an old racing sulky, the seat so close under the
breeching that his legs were spraddled along each side of the horse's
lean barrel, legs fine and straight on the shafts. And each time the
whirlwind of his passing blew Lucinda's skirts and lifted the mane
of the slow old livery horse, the spokes of the swift sulky making a
flurry like the fan of a stage coquette. But there was no sign of
recognition in the man's face.

At home it was good to stand between her sisters except that they
were quick to sense that Lucinda might be moving back, and so
they busied themselves making up a box of fresh eggs and butter
and preserves for her to take home while they chattered lightly of
their plans and prospects, Malinda still hoping to marry the young
minister who hesitated over a family connection that included the
notorious Senator Tolley in a drunkard's grave. Lucinda understood.
Plainly there must be nothing more for clacking tongues, and no

further expense—with barely enough money to dress the two daughters for suitable marriages.

So she kissed them all and started back to town in the middle of the drowsy afternoon, gay as any leisurely young matron from a call. In the woods she wept a little, silently, so the sleeping Stevie would not awaken. At the gooseberry patch she stopped to pick enough for a few pies. Leaving the boy asleep in the bottom of the cart she unhooked the horse and pulling up her skirt like an apron, started to strip the cool green berries into it, swiftly and expertly, getting few thorns in her soft fingers.

It was here that George Shefton found her. Tying his horse near the road he came climbing up the slope, fine and agile in his tight checked britches, lifting his cap, gallant as in a story book. What a pretty picture she made, in her rose gown against the fresh greenery, and her yellow petticoats! When he saw the blush he raised, he reassured her by asking about the sleeping boy. "You are a brave wife, a noble mother" he said, "and so young, so charming. . . ."

His handsome yellow-brown eyes were like sunlight over rippling sealskin, and his voice so gentle, his flattering words so disturbing that Lucinda couldn't turn them aside as she had been taught at Miss Farnsworth's. "Prettily," Delicia Farnsworth always said, "but firmly, permitting no familiarities!"

Instead Lucinda, who had been told last night that she was no woman at all, could only blush, suddenly as young and tremulous as that day so long ago when she came running through the lilacs behind the little station to meet her returning soldier boy.

It made her ashamed, and shaking afraid too, that she had to remind herself George Shefton was a rounder, a gambler who had been a member of the treasonable Knights of the Golden Circle and made a big business of smuggling arms to the South—Beecher's Bibles used against boys like Milton who stopped the bullets at sixteen dollars a month. By now she kew that Hiram and Sarah and her senator brother could have told where those arms came from. Indeed, they were a very pretty lot, Milton's folks, helping every way they could to get him crippled, and now here his own wife stood, listening all a-tremble to the sugared words of the gun runner.

Yet when the man laid his hand on her arm, she couldn't thrust it aside, or even hold herself firm and lady-proud, and so he drew her close to him, his lips moving hot over her cheek, her mouth, her throat. Once, in furious anger and contempt with herself, she tried to push him away, but under the man's insistent murmur of apologies, his gentle and diffident caresses, she softened, until his lips were on her mouth again, then on her breast suddenly bared, and she was like water, and let him lay her back upon the grass, the gooseberries from her skirt spilling every way.

Milton had tried several lines to make a living since he lost the drug store. First it was peddling a four-volume set of *The Great American War* through backwoods Ohio, dog-whipping the money out of women poor as poverty. But he wasn't much better off himself so he kept trying until one of them told him, "It ain't books on war-fightin' I needs, Mister Peddler. What I yearns to have is something to keep from gettin' in the fambly way every time I happens to roll over on my back."

Milton looked at the straggle-haired, gap-toothed woman, her milk-stripped dugs sagging to her apron, the young 'uns swarming around her scrawny and scabby, nigh as naked as jay birds. All he could do was hobble away to his cart, the woman and all the children looking after him so long as he was in sight. Hell's buzzards, if a man could only afford to give them a set of books, for there were pictures, even if they were of killing and war.

With the fall of '73 and the crash of Wall Street, winter shut down on the country like a December river over a mess of kittens in a sack. Times were never so hard, many admitted. Even the old bartender of the Hound's Tooth, who used to kowtow to the tall hats of George Shefton and Eph Dix was tootling another tune now that the town bloods never came there any more, not with river graft dead as a quick-limed catfish.

". . . We're next to dead, too, with our fat fried out from inflation to deflation, and demonetization," one of the free lunchers complained, looking sourly at the dry, moldy cheese. "Squeezed thin as hair snakes in a horse trough, and all to preserve the credit of the country."

"Yeh, an' judgin' by the interest them Wall Streeters is chargin', the government's credit wouldn't hold cornshucks. Inwhiles there's three million out a work, and all us little fellers swept away like hen coops in a cloudbust," Ash Scott said.

Those around him bent their loaded mouths toward the spittoons and then came up nodding. Ash, like Milton, had lost his little store because he couldn't say no to beans and flour and larrup on tick when the young 'uns were hungry.

". . . Some claim there's been too much speculation," Milton said, just back from his mother's. "Too many folks living beyond their means."

"Yeh, by God, payin' taxes for you pension farks," a newcomer put in, but he was shut up quick. The bartender laughed as he wiped his hairy arms. "Your ma say folks livin' too high, Milt? Then mebby what I see on the seat of your britches is a piece a that high livin'."

Charley Powell laughed too, but his gaunt face was bitter as hedge thorn. "Yes, Milt, we sure been living beyond our means, and there's no telling where the country would be if Congress hadn't cracked down on us. Probably folks'd be out of jobs everywhere, women and children hungry, strong men dying of starvation in flop houses, in alleys and on the turnpikes tonight."

The hum of the gas light was loud as a trapped dawbug in the still room, and Milton knew they were all thinking about the hundred men reported dead of starvation and exposure just the last week in New York alone, and stumbling over their own dead right here in the Queen City of the West. No telling who would be dumped in pauper holes by spring, and the Johnny Rebs coming North like army worms.

The men scattered into the freezing night, with no stomach left for stories or other brags; not looking Milton's way, holding his mother's foolish talk against him, and his pension too. So he drained his glass and had a couple more quick ones. Hell's buzzards, he was right onto twenty-five, with a big sprout of a boy calling him father; time he acted like a man, not a mangy hound-dog snuck away under the stoop. So he got up, tossed his cap over the end of his peg leg and throwing it up toward the ceiling, caught it on his head. He felt better than all the winter; his mind made up at last. He would take the offer Dunn had made him, go West with the spring.

Milton had tried a medicine show wagon down in Tennessee in November—Indian snake oil for the ills of man or beast. But he couldn't sing, his fiddle didn't draw enough these hard times, the loudmouth Mudheads broke up his spiel, and while he was turning cartwheels they stole him blind. So when the winter rains started he pulled back to Cincinnati, low-down.

Then Charley Powell told him about Aloysius J. Dunn, the drug manufacturer who got his start with a medicine wagon, an impressive belly, a tenor voice that slid up and down like a monkey on a greased string, and a magnificent, hypnotizing spiel that could coax the stitches out of a poorman's pocket. Dunn was picking agents to take his wagons into the new country west of the Missouri river—only responsible peddlers, for there was a future in it. Fisk peddled tin pans, and Astor and fifty others, even Rockefeller's father a medicine wagon man. Dunn wanted men knowing a little about boils and fever and maybe bonesetting, to build up regular circuits.

"No git-tar strummin', an' no goin' through a community like a shot of croton oil, suh," he said.

Out at Council Bluffs Milton was to have one of the orange wagons with DUNN'S WORLD FAMOUS FAMILY REMEDIES in black across each side. With a route established he would get a special kit: Dunn's Secret Liquor Cure, a tray of adjustable trusses, lancets for boils and felons, forceps for pulling teeth and to help an occasional piggy sow. Later there might be a side line for married ladies, . . . "to be prescribed only with great ca'e, suh! I may say with great and unusual tact and ca'e," Aloysius Dunn orated to his peddlers.

Before the Stones started West, Lucinda's father came to speak to this eldest daughter once more, walking up and down her poor little flat, his shoulders stooped, his face loose and sagging. "We have no affluence to offer you, my child, but with us you will be spared the humiliation of an intoxicated spouse crawling like a broken animal through the streets."

Lucinda didn't lift her eyes from the rag bag she was picking over. "Thank you, father," she said, so low he could scarcely hear, "but I have to go"—remembering an afternoon on the old hill road beside a gooseberry patch. That the man was the disreputable, the scoundrelly George Shefton was humiliating enough, but he never tried to come near her again, never gave her any opportunity to use her carefully planned dismissal. When they finally met it was by accident, and before she could escape she had to see the taunting in his sun-flecked eyes. Just another woman for a lay on the country grass.

So the Stones joined the thousands who didn't have the money to ship out on the cushions or even the hard benches of the emigrant cars, going without the boisterous singing of the Forty-niners or the Pikes Peakers, or the high hopes of the Oregon Trailers and the Mormons. But they went—urging their logey horses, their oxen over roads deep as battle mud, escaping the shadow of the landlord, the mortgage holder and the blank, locked doors of bank and mine and factory.

Many started from Cincinnati before the frost hove the ground, singly, like Charley Powell, or in groups and colonies, complete with minister, doctor and blacksmith, perhaps with a large block of land under contract and railroad cars chartered for the trip and for temporary living quarters. Hank Gibbs bummed it and Joe Deaver preached and exhorted his way. George Shefton went, too, getting himself shot by an angry husband out in Omaha the first week. Maybe men were more vigilant out there, with women scarcer, Lucinda thought, as she pushed her needle through the heavy wagon quilt she was piecing. But George lived, Doc Charley wrote, to move out to a wild place called Cheyenne with another woman.

The Stones had meachin' little to show for their eight years of married life: a few pieces of wedding linen still unsold, the old folding organ, the fiddle sack, and such farewell gifts as those left behind could manage, gifts with the extra warmth of sacrifice. There was the team and covered wagon bought on a note that David Martin signed, a crate of Dominiques for a few fresh eggs and a cheerful daylight crowing, a pair of little red pigs in a tub under the wagon reach, a handful of plants rooting in a box of wet sand; geraniums, a wax plant, wandering Jew and a sea onion that would bloom if they stayed seven years in one house, as old Mollie Stanger promised when she pinched the little set off for Lucinda. "Makes a mighty good salve for blood poison, draws like a williwaw in a tin chimbley," she said.

From Sarah there was nothing but an old flour sack full of silk and velvet scraps, for the giving had to go the other way now.

There were two surprise presents: a box with holes punched in it from Washington, a brindle pup inside, as soft-boned as a kitten when Milton put him into the fearful arms of young Stevie. Milton was uneasy that some outsider knew about the boy, and glad they were headed West. Then there was the muzzle-loading ten-bore from the bartender at the Hound's Tooth. "Used to shoot deer out on the breaks in sight of here with old Roarin' Ida," he said, patting the rusted lock. "A little oilin' and a pocketful of buckshot and she'll get you ducks and geese flyin' through."

The seven-year-old Stevie was up mornings at Milton's first toot-toot of reveille, whooping, bare feet flying; handy as a shoat under the table. He fetched stones or brush for the hub-deep mud holes, spied out any stick of firewood along the way, carried coffee water. Dark and spindly shouldered, with brows black as Milton's, campers said, "Ain't he the spit' image of his pa!" Back home there had been rumors about the woman who fell from Jimson Baker's window, and about a fine snowball bush on her grave, but apparently Lucinda knew nothing about these, nor did Sarah, although there was no telling about old Sarah, always one to sit on the hole in the carpet.

As the wagon moved westward, the earth warmed to the smell of spring, the timber greening as it thinned and settled down into the stream ways like April run-off water, the oak woods reddening on the hillsides, then the wild plum and dogwood and black haw making snowy patches. But it was the great lone oaks and elms that Milton pointed out to Stevie and the pup on the seat beside him, and to Lucinda too, working at the crazy quilt from Sarah's pieces, outlining each block with colored floss in rosebud stitch or perhaps in a graceful trailing vine that Milton and Stevie called turtle tracks.

So, with his peg leg on the dash, his pipe stuck in his thick, dark beard and the boy to wonder at each day's new sights, Milton bragged in his old doughfoot way about Sherman's marches, their evening fires, bean holes, coffee pounded in a rag, weevils toasted out of the hardtack, and the way birds fly up before a moving enemy. He even told about the punishments, men tied spread-eagle to spare wagon wheels, and the cat lashings they got, but nothing of killing. He told many great bull alligator stories too, showing them off like a willow withe of fresh-caught fish, and the stories from the bluecoats who had been out in the Indian country, about grizzlies, buffaloes and the gold fields, and about the man out in Texas who lassooed him one of those great serpent snakes seen floating around in the air the last year or so, dragged it right down, thrashing around like trapped lightning, and cut it up with a steam saw to feed his hound-dogs.

"I bet you could do that, pa," Stevie bragged, and when Milton laughed out loud, the boy's face got sullen. "You could," he insisted, "why, you marched your leg off."

"Igonnies, yes!" the man roared, punching the young one beside him. "I'm a swivel-jawed, double-jointed rattler and strike both ways. I went through the yellin' Rebs like a dose of croton oil and I fights gougin' somethin' gostratious!" At Lucinda's complaint he quieted. "Yeh, I'm a hell roarer fer talk, but honest now, we may run into a flock of wild pigeons, still scourging the Iowa fields like they used to around Cincinnati, clouds of them, so tame they could be killed with clubs or donnicks."

"We'll get us a lot of them, won't we, ma?—enough for a pie this big?" the boy bragged, making a great circle with his arms about himself and the pup between his knees.

Even with the crowded roads, Roarin' Ida usually got Milton something for the frying pan: ducks, plover from the hundreds running through the greening uplands; or bullheads, sunfish and bass with his willow rod. Sliding down the wheel from the wagon, Milton would vault away, Stevie having to run to keep up, and if the hunting was good he might even turn a cartwheel for the boy on the way back. So the days on the trail lengthened, the rains increased, and the wheels cut deeper, sometimes sticking desolate in some bottomless hole waiting out the downpours, farmers with dogs watching their woodlots in the evenings, and their pigs and chickens and haystacks, many with guns on their arms, while merchants all along raised their prices rocket high.

Every day there were fewer of the dashing young horsemen on a tear to get to the mines, and more child-bound women sitting the heavy wagons as uncomplaining as was in their nature, helping with the driving and the camping too, the wind redness of their faces showing how far they had come. There was even a woman among those who were walking it, driving a small flock of sheep, the ram with the wedding featherbed rolled in canvas on his back, the larger ewes carrying bundles too, a hoe and a spade, and one with a dishpan inverted over a sack of seeds. Milton and Stevie stopped beside her campfire, gave her a mallard for her supper. She rubbed a thumb over the glossy green head as she told them in her broken Bohemian that she was going to a homestead in Kansas—

this stocky, heavy-boned woman with her crook and her two dogs walking almost a thousand miles to her husband, and not going empty-handed. It was a mammoth fine thing to see.

Lucinda let his loud talking pass. At least he wasn't sitting batting his black eyes at some young girl around the camps, watching her climb into the wagon, as men did, particularly when not right from liquor, and the girls so bold nowadays, encouraging even a cripple if he was dark and handsome.

As the homeseekers leaned out and weathered, their tongues became more bitter on politics and the hard times, old soldiers among them talking pensions, bounty lands, and organization. Many asked about the Farmers' Alliance. Could the million and a half membership be jumped enough to break the grip of the railroads and bankers on Congress? In the meantime Lucinda, her netted hair still shining, her calico starched, visited among the women, stewed up onion syrup for the babies with the whooping cough, made rag nipples for their bottles of barley water when the mother-milk failed, or wrote letters back when someone had to be buried beside the road. She asked questions too. Did they make their own clothes, and had they heard about the new Women's Temperance Crusade?

Sometimes she went out into the night to someone sick or a baby borning, but cautiously since the night a man tolled her with a call and then grabbed her and clapped a handkerchief into her mouth. "You got me bucking the tailboard out a my wagon of nights—" he puffed, as he fought to carry her toward a rig in the darkness, push her into it, "no damn gully-jumper's gonna keep you from me."

But Lucinda had kicked out like Milton showed her for close fighting, a thumb in the eye, then balancing on his peg leg, bringing his knee up hard in the crotch. So she got away from the man in his surprise, jerking the handkerchief out of her mouth and retching from it as she gathered up her skirts and ran, her heart pounding from the scare, and the excitement. She slipped into the wagon without waking the others, happy that someone still wanted her, not easily, like George Shefton, but enough to run the risk of hanging, like the man left on a tree beside the road a piece back, where the emigrants strung him up for a woman-raping.

Milton was called out nights too, to fiddle for a quadrilling on some worn campground, drench a sick horse, blister a sweeny or to splint a broken arm. Sometimes it was the mending after a gouging, or a waller fight, or maybe to listen to the troubled talk of an uneasy man, like the one in a faded old blue overcoat who came to sit on his thin hams beside Milton's fire. At last he unrolled a brown-stained banner with BREAD OR BLOOD painted on it. His brother had carried the banner in the great jobless parade in Chicago. "The splotches are his blood—" the man said softly, touching his fingertips gently to the edge, "—but they got no jobs."

"No," Milton admitted, scratching the gnats out of his bearded chin. Nobody was getting jobs, not with the deflation, the graft and corruption and panic under Grant. It was the first time the son of Hiram Stone laid his tongue to such disloyalty.

After a while the man with the banner spoke again in his soft shy voice. "I was a craftsman," he said. "Fine boots and shoes. I quit my job to enlist, and now one man with a machine can make 300 pairs a day. Not like those we made, but cheaper, and for each machine there's 299 men who can't buy anything. So, at fifty, I got to go out West, learn this new trade of farming, to keep my wife. . . ."

"Well, by hokey, you're sure a-shootin' at decoys, you are," another man spoke out of the darkness. At the fire he turned out to be burnt and gaunt as a twisted, wind-bared root. "I give up farming," he said. "Quit my claim out in Nebraska an' headin' back east. Half the time I couldn't give 'way what I growed, then last year the grasshoppers come down on us like a cloudbust. This spring I see the ground's movin' with 'em hatchin', so, by God, I lets 'em have it."

Slowly the man with the stained banner folded it across his knees and, then buttoning it under his coat, went away into the darkness.

6 — The Easy-Walking Woman

Not until the day Milton Stone stomped out of the blacksmith shop with a piece of pipe for a leg did he become what he himself would have called a goddamn crip, one who used his mutilation against the world, either as an appeal to its pity and shame, or as a means of aggression.

It seemed to change the pleasant speaking, unassertive man entirely, made him stand taller, his beard and chest stuck out, his eyes sharper and far-looking, his voice roaring against the wind.

". . . It is like he find all at once the sunrise in the pocket," the Old Country blacksmith said to the loafers watching the peddler swing his pipe leg up to the seat of his medicine wagon.

"Or an old soldier who's just cut a new set of teeth on bar lead."

"Yeh, well, maybe a lot of other folks is goin' to do the same. Looks like the whole country's gettin' ready to rise up, come fall election time."

"An' ripe for it, by God!—this year bein' the Centennial. Hundred years since the Declaration of Independence. Time for a new shake."

But the Polish blacksmith shook his smoky head. "The crippling, it is bad for a man . . ." he said, the rest of his words lost in the roar of his foot bellows.

The next day an old farmer, a good customer for Dunn's horse liniment, tried to goose Milton a little. "What you say, Doc—— What'll you take to plant my sod corn with that there holler leg a yourn?" But he got such a loud bawling that he stepped back into his plowshare in his apologizing, "Hell, Doc, I didn't go to make you mad."

Maybe the change in Milton Stone really came ahead of the iron leg, for it was during a fight at a Polish wedding that he broke the wooden peg and found somebody had sawed it almost through while he was sleeping off the wine he got for fiddling. So, in spite of the blacksmith's warning that the metal pipe might draw lightning, come summer, Milton had it made. "Hell's buzzards, there'll be lightning in it all right, but it'll be me a making it."

Now he was known as old Iron Leg on the western routes. The nickname came easy because he had been so handy with the wooden peg, spinning himself around on it like a top on its point to make the children laugh, or, throwing himself back; use the stick like a bat to send balls whizzing out for young Stevie to catch. If necessary he could stand off attack in a frontier saloon, jumping into the air and swinging the leg up and around like a club, cracking heads or knocking out teeth neater than a plug dentist with spike and hammer.

"Oh, Milton!—a common barroom brawler!" Lucinda cried when he showed her a clipping from a Kansas newspaper: MEDICINE PED-DLER BREAKS UP POLITICAL FIGHT AT MEMORIAL REUNION. HELPS CLEAN OUT CLODE TAVERN GANG.

So Milton went over to Frenchy Brulley's, although he was just home and Lucinda looked almost like a girl in her rose-sprigged calico, her light hair new-washed and curling around her temples, for that morning she had seen George Shefton pass. But at Frenchy's he could sit in peace over a beer, pat the clipping in his pocket, play a hand or two of slobberhannes and talk about the little man's sudden feeling of power, even hamstrung as he was by no learning and no way of finding out what the Washington outfit was up to until the sack was over his head. Somehow this was his big year, with hailstones a foot around falling from the sky, cows shelling out twins, women with triplets, and talk of a set of six young 'uns born up on the reservation. The little fellow's year.

Milton was full of beans himself, and crick water and codding as he headed out into the Niobrara country. There would be prairie chicken, antelope, deer in the brush patches, and folks pleased to get his remedies, to see him come with the news from the railroad. Maybe there'd be a woman now and then, like the one over on the Republican, lonesome, with her man away, a fiery red wagon to be living alone.

He found new dugouts and claim shacks, some at least fifty miles farther out than last year, maybe deserted or with wind-burnt settlers pulling sunflowers from their strips of sod corn or the tree claims. There were many deep-cut new trails across the August prairie toward the Black Hills, where, two years ago, Custer of the Seventh Cavalry had reported gold at the grass roots and started a stampede into the Indian country that not even the army had stopped. Not that Custer was giving a foot-slogger's Godamighty for gold now, nor the hundreds of his men scattered dead along a ridge up in the Sioux country, but a raft of others did. Even old Clyde Winston, who thought he had been cured of the gold fever by California twenty-six years ago, was following the call of easy money again. With jobs and bounty prospects so bad, he was going like many others, shanks' mare, carrying his old canteen slung over his shoulder for any long dry stretches—chasing gold like a ball of swamp fire of a summer night.

". . . A ga'nt belly's as hard a driver as a determined woman," he told Milton as he worked through a few beers and the free lunch. Clyde was looking old even for a Mexican vet, the fringe of hair thin and white around his ears. He hadn't had a month's steady work since he shucked out of his blue britches eleven years ago; even tried marrying a widow woman who ran him off when there was no bounty. By now he'd got as worthless as folks always figured old soldiers were—worthless and hopeless.

"Johnny Stanger writes it's a genuine strike . . ." Milton comforted. "Placer pockets fat's a 'possum in a corn patch."

"Yeh, genuine . . ."

Milton gave old Clyde a lift out across the flatlands of the upper Blue, where the winding streams moved canal-slow and folks had the ager shakes. Lucinda watched the two go, sending Stevie to spy out if they tied up at Frenchy's. They did, and then hurried on, looking back as the orange medicine wagon crawled up the wooded breaks west of the Missouri. It was a fine stream, wider than the Ohio, but new, half-finished, without banks, the sandbars left in the bottom pushing up into the summer sun, shouldering the restless current aside. Clyde remembered when steamboats puffed their way from one wood landing to the next, against the gray flood currents of spring or, hitting snags, sank in the liquid mud. Before the wood burners, boats were cordelled slowly up the long, long water path to the Cheyenne, the White and even the Yellowstone River, with goods and whisky for the fur trade. He had been over it all, in the pushing out into the West, then down to Mexico, to Seward's Alaska, and lately into the leftover pockets, the Black Hills, the Little Big Horn—pushing out like Sherman's lanky bummers marching thousands of miles and more, or some unthinking young squirts on tomwalkers jumping the neighbor's ditches and maybe home too late for supper.

But now he was old, with a game knee and empty pockets and an empty heart. Four years ago he had been hopeful about the election when he saw the thousands of Mugwumps collect in Cincinnati for the convention, even a few frockcoats overrunning the Hound's Tooth, like Hiram's old banker broadcloth. Clyde was happy as a tomcat in the sun over a party sprouting for the little fellow . . . Carl Schurz's great speech greeted by a roaring like the doughfoots when Lee handed over his iron. Yeh, for a day or so that Washington gang was no more than last year's rabbit turds in a buffalo wallow.

But they picked Greeley, and so Clyde sold the last of his Mexican war souvenirs, got drunk as a flatboater, and then tramped out west to Kansas. Now, with Greeley as dead as the hope he killed, they were being tolled in again to vote for the old breed of rascals. Even a scalded hound could be coaxed back to the boiling kettle if his belly got lean enough.

It was the last night before Milton switched off northeastward and so he didn't try to turn Clyde's mind. The next morning the old soldier set on afoot, heading toward the gold fields, three, four hundred miles away. Gold seeking, when he had no stomach for it, no heart. A long time Milton watched him, an old man, small and alone on the empty, sunburnt prairie. Then suddenly he jerked his horses around and whipped off the other way.

Cutting across the trails reaching off toward the Black Hills, Milton watched for the wagon trains crawling along like ants on the move, catching as many as he could in camp, getting the campaign news and talking up Dunn's Anticholera. "Successfully counteracts the dire effects of strange foods and waters, and combats the bloody flux," the label said. One camp turned out to be Hoosiers overlanding from the railroad on the Platte, small-towners green as Wabash grass. Their horses were collar-sore and played out, the men galled until they could hardly walk or sit, one big, rope-haired young fellow so poisoned that his face was puffed up like a fresh blood stomach, his ears purple saucers.

"Hell's buzzards, but you're a stove-up bunch of tenderfeet!" Milton laughed as he pushed his gun aside with his foot and slid down the wagon wheel, his pipe leg gleaming in the evening sun. "Don't look like nothing worse than trail wolf and buffalo gnats," he comforted, handing out jars of salve for the chafing and sunburn, and a can of saleratus to bathe the sting from the boy's face. . . . "A red bandanna under your hat with the corners soaked in coal oil and flopping in the wind'll keep the little varmints away."

"You mean it's just them flitterin' dawbugs no bigger'n ground pepper's what's doin' all the damage?"

Yes, it was the buffalo gnats all right, millions of them, and dog poison for the lily-skinned, Milton said, always careful to laugh with newcomers who wouldn't know that it was polite words that were the bullet through the hat in these parts.

Around the smoking campfire of old buffalo chips Milton talked about other troubles besides soft horses and men—insects, rattlesnakes, mountain fever and the Sioux Indians who still owned the Black Hills and most of the country this side. No real danger from them, with the warriors all off, but they might run into some of the begging agency loafers any day. "Just hand out a little tobacco and coffee with sugar in it, and if the bucks get pushing, give them the broad side of the ax. The real scrappers are all north, fighting with Crazy Horse."

The circle of goldseekers about the fire grinned, their greased red faces shining as they moved their hands toward the brand new six-shooters, confident again, and hot to get a few scalps for souvenirs, and to avenge Custer if the Indians really weren't very wild. When Milton turned the talk to Tilden and Hayes and the presidential campaign, they got right back to Indian fighting and the gold laying around loose as hailstones at Deadwood.

"Yeh, there's gold—" Milton admitted grudgingly, a fresh run of anger in him that such soft, foolish men, one of them with the draft dodger's gap teeth, could go, but not he, "—gold and all the lawlessness that goes with easy money. Army telegraph reports Wild Bill Hickok was shot in a saloon up there last week."

"Wild Bill killed?" the blond boy looked as mournful as his

swollen face allowed. "I saw him 'while back with my pa in Chicago. But Buffalo Bill was the ringtail tooter. . . ."

"You got genuine ringtail tooters right around here, Jesse James's said to have a hideout up on the river a ways, and Doc Middleton's gang of horsethieves railroading their stolen stock up through here to the Niobrara and on west."

That put a stop to the big talk, made the men listen to the snuffing of the picketed horses and the coyote pups trying out their thin, uncertain voices far away—looking uneasily over their shoulders at the hoot of a prairie dog owl in the darkness, saying maybe the old peg legger was stringing them. But when he rose to stomp off in disgust to his wagon, the goldseekers coaxed the medicine peddler back with a jug from under a wagon seat. So he came, carrying the fiddle sack. It was noon the next day when he awoke, spraddle-legged and bruised on the prairie, the sun burning his painful eyes, his wagon upset, the bottles and jars smashed, with a hundred orange-backed Dunn's Family Almanacs blowing over the prairie. A little farther on his team and the broken double-trees were piled in a washout, the old mare underneath dead. Godamighty, he must have been hog-tight and horse-high last night, without even the sense to stay camped. And those Black Hillers had gone off and left him, a cripple stranded on the prairie, after he'd doctored 'em up!

Feeling mean as a skunk with his tail tied down for sure, Milton went over his misfortunes with the added martyrdom of self-blame and a bust-head. Maybe Lucinda and the whisker-chinned temperance women were right. Alcohol did make a fool of a man, and a double-hammered fool of a cripple. For a dirtied shinplaster he'd lay right down in the washout and wait for the coyotes and the buzzards. But he didn't, and with Roarin' Ida for a cane he started back the six miles over hot, sandy trail to the nearest house. He was galled too, when he got there, his pipe leg dragging like a mudhook, and he had to pay out more than the profits of the whole summer for another horse, a mare with foal. Too bad there were no high-toned customers for the Fairy Beauty Dew, water from a foaly mare, bottled with a little alcohol and sweet-smelling rose water— Fairy Dew for the Fair. But he would catch a couple of bottles, hoping for a sale somewhere when he got out of the dugout region.

Altogether it would be mighty small potatoes for Lucinda and the boy this winter but it'd all been wished on him, all of this wished on him that day they pushed him into marrying instead of letting him go to the mines. Then he saw an old woman stuck off in a little cave by herself to die of cancer. She had been to one of those acid cancer doctors down on the Missouri, the middle of her face eaten out so her nose was only a couple of holes above her naked jaw-bone, and suffering, making a noise like a gut-shot cavalry horse. So Milton had one of the boys come along to the wagon to get a little pain-killer. On the way the young 'un asked how he lost his leg.

"Snapped off by a coachwhip snake down in Georgia, son. Yes, sir-ee, bit clean off. But I gloms it away from him an' beats him to death with it, the onmannerly rep-tile!"

"Igonnies!" the boy said, his eyes sticking out.

Two years ago when the Stones came West they had rented a little place at the edge of Council Bluffs with a trellised porch, grass enough for the team and a cow, and a little garden that was mostly Stevie's responsibility, although the grasshoppers that cleaned out the Western farmers took most of it. With the velvet photograph album on the stand table, and her satin-stitch Farnsworth spray of wild roses framed and hanging over it for tone, Lucinda started to take in sewing, all she could get, to count against the note for the team her father had signed. Between times she worked with the Temperance Crusade against such places as Frenchy Brulley's little bar. The pension would be seeing them through the winters snug as the 'coons in the hollow stump Milton used to tell Stevie about, if it wasn't that most of the check went to Brulley's.

"Maybe like Grandmother Strathorn always says, you can't expect a bobtailed dog to walk a log without falling off," Lucinda complained.

"No, and you can't be looking for him to stay home if you keep kicking his rump," Milton replied. That stopped her like a scow running into a mudbank, and she bent her head over the sewing and held her tongue, but still with the righteous face of the Temperancers kneeling in the dirty sawdust of the old Hound's Tooth. So Milton stumped to the kitchen and made up a batch of sulphur liquor for the itch ointment, and finally went to bed half-frozen because Lucinda had thrown every window wide to the zero night.

The winter was a bad one politically too, the winter of the Presidential Steal. The news of Tilden's election had come through on the army telegraph while Milton was still up in north Nebraska. ". . . A new Declaration of Independence for the common man on this hundredth birthday of the nation!" a red-faced politician orated from the back of a buggy in a little Irish frontier town. Afterward he was hauled up and down the street in a spontaneous parade, Dunn's orange-colored medicine wagon with Tilden banners on both sides well up in front. They passed a racing sulky, the man familiar—George Shefton, Old Yeller Weskit George, probably up to the trotting circuit. But then Billy Field, with the hook for a hand, pushed out of the crowd calling, "Milty! You goddamn bluebelly, what in hell you doin' up here?"

So the two war cripples sat up all the night of the celebration, Milton playing a little on the old fiddle Billy gave to a boy in a hospital because a grabhook was no good for fingering a gut string. Then they told each other lies, bigger and bigger lies because there was nothing else to talk about, except old Clyde Winston and Morrie Rosen, both fighters against Mexicans and Rebs, one gold-seeking again, the other dead with Fetterman, killed by the Sioux. On the hard times Billy argufied like a GAR, against everything, looking on Tilden as a traitor. He ended up in a crying jag, cursing softly to himself until his mother found them and took him away, not even letting him look back to the old friend, the dirty old crip tolling a poor widow-woman's only son back into army profanity and rum.

Over in Springfield there was more election night excitement. Ghouls tried to steal Lincoln's body; actually got the casket to moving before the detectives shot. Turned out body snatching was no crime in Illinois.

Turned out, too, that the election kegs, tapped free as for a new railroad, had their bungs knocked in too soon. The carpetbaggers in Florida, Louisiana and South Carolina were enforcing their own electoral count, with Grant's troops to back them, making double returns from the three states, and bringing protest parades and riots all over the country. Looked like a buckshot war for a while but the show of naked bayonets scattered the civilians. Yet for all Grant and his army could do, Tilden had 184 electoral votes without the disputed states, only one less than the majority to elect him against Hayes' 165. There it stood when the cold drove Milton home late in December in spite of the buffalo saddle coat that he got from a soldier at Fort Hartsuff, for a dozen bottles of bitters and a box of clap salve. He had pumpkins, popcorn and a couple of smoked Canada geese in the wagon; a sack of sweetgrass for Bruno's doghouse on the snowy top; and a roll of soapweed roots to make shampoo as old Clyde had learned from the women of Texas. In his pocket was a handful of arrowheads picked up in a windy August blowout for Stevie and young Putty Gillard next door, and a present for Lucinda too—a pair of Indian moccasins. But he didn't tell her that he got them for practicing cartwheels at his campfire one evening, trying to turn fast enough to land standing up on the pipe alone, arms spread out, no help from the foot. When he sat down to catch a wind and smoke his pipe, he saw a man squatting on the wagon tongue, dark-faced with smooth black braids wrapped in fur hanging over his breast. In a few broken words he said he was Winnebago, out hunting, and wished to examine the leg, the thin one. Marveling at its metallic sound under his tapping, he waggled his head and laughed deep down in his chest. It was a leg of great power.

"Power?"

"Hou! Medicine power, not like in bottle, but power from the Great Ones—earth . . . sky . . ." the man said, spreading his brown hands.

Milton nodded, and passed his tobacco pouch. In the morning the Indian was back with the fine, blue-beaded, woman's moccasins. But he couldn't even tell the story to Stevie because Lucinda was so set against tricks with the leg. Sometimes it looked like she thought he got crippled on purpose, just to plague-devil her.

Without waiting for Lucinda to cut off his tangle of black hair hanging long as a Wild West showman's, or the supper to sober him, Milton swung into his buffalo coat and went over to Frenchy's spit and guzzle brigade, as the Temperance Crusaders called them. The Hayes men were ready for him as he stomped in out of the storm, even before he got the snow off his coat. "We sure got you sittin' on a buzz saw now, Doc!" they called out, laughing together.

"What you mean, buzz saw?" he demanded, peering around, light-blinded, for his friends. But the Grangers and the Farmers' Alliancers were all pushed back toward the frosted windows tonight, far from the fire. "Tilden only needs one vote and everybody knows the disputed nineteen are all from Demo states and so his."

"Think he'll get 'em?" the circle around the stove demanded, tilting their chairs down and spitting at the sand box. "Think so, Doc?"

"Godamighty, even if you was to get 'em all, it'd still be a tie," Milton argued but holding onto himself, as he broke the icicles from his beard. "The Constitution says the House of Representatives decides ties, and that's Demo, for Tilden——"

"Yeh, but try an' get it to the House!" they hooted, their eyes sly and sure as the buzzards' following a marching army. "Try—like hell!"

"I admit there ain't anything too shady for Grant and his highway robbers," Milton said uneasily.

"Who you namin' robbers, you old pension fark!"

There it was, the old name calling against a man who had been robbed by those war grafters, robbed so he wasn't half a man in their eyes, or his own, or any woman's. As Milton looked around the taunting faces a flood of battle anger surged up in his chest, ran so hot that his hands itched for the feel of a bayonet plunging into the bloat-guts tilted back on their chairs there, plopping them like rotten melons, jabbing fast as lightning.

But there was no bayonet, so the men could keep on. ". . . It's old soldiers like you's holdin' the country broke—" one threw up to Milton, but he stopped before the old soldier's face, the slow stomp of the iron leg toward him, ducking so his chair tipped over backward. At the thud Milton stopped, looking after the Hayes men scattering like a hatching of chicks before the shadow of a hawk. Then he swung around on his pipe leg, and kicking the outside door open, let in the storm.

Out on the street Milton Stone stopped, foolish and ashamed in the whipping snow, shivering, suddenly empty as a sack with the bottom out, only a salty taste of violence, of hunger for killing left in his mouth.

Next day the sun was out shimmering on the icy snow, and because he couldn't face Frenchy's, Milton hitched up to scout for a little local business. Dropping Stevie and Putty and Bruno the dog, for their Saturday skate at the gleaming, wind-swept river, Milton crossed to the Nebraska side and followed down the bottoms that he somehow always neglected—in too much of a hurry to get out to the territory or too anxious to get back home.

Mostly the people seemed to be river rats like the Tolleys used to be, fishing, trapping a little, with maybe a truck garden under the drifted snow, or a few goats to climb the breaks; not even a cow whose winter-cracked teats might need ointment. Finally he came to the big place called Riverside Pavilion standing out gray and bulky from the pinkening snow of evening, with a circuit track for horse and whippet racing, gambling tables and other amusements inside, and a chef who put out wild-game dinners—anything from buffalo to rattlesnake and beavertail for those with the money.

But today there was a winter-quiet over the whole place, the long galleries empty. Inside, a long room ran across the front of the building, the bar at one end, lobby in the center, parlor and ballroom around the side. Today the bar was closed until night but Milton leaned against the desk near the heater, warming his mittens, matching up acquaintances with the hunchback clerk, and selling him a few pills for his liver. Then the door opened and an easy-walking woman came in with a puff of frosty, evening air. She wore fur-edged gaiters under her blue walking skirt, a beaver sacque and a yellow velvet rose in her fur bonnet. When she saw Milton she stopped, looking down the bulk of the short buffalo coat to the shiny, iron leg. Throwing her head back, she laughed out loud, a fine, melodious laugh, her teeth shining, her black eyes bold as a cat-amount's.

" 'Sblood! a ragged, bearded Apollo! Apollo on a stick!" she cried. Then she swept her bustled skirts past the men and up the red-carpeted stairway, Milton gawking after her, helpless as a river bottom shirt-tail young 'un when he might at least have smart-alecked her back, or spun around like a Kansas cyclone on that leg she thought was so funny.

Finally Milton noticed the hunchback nudging him, stretching over toward him. "Calls herself Dolly Talbor," he whispered, lifting his hunch toward the stairs. "Used to be a famous actor woman, they tells me, lady friend of . . ." dropping his hoarse voice so low Milton didn't catch the name that sounded like Fisk.

Afterward Milton tried to remember what happened, but all he could recall was how the woman looked the moment he turned from the hunchback and saw her there in the late sun of the frosted windows, tall-standing, well-rounded and elegant, her hair blue-black against her white skin, her black eyes so fine and bold, her laugh even in its taunting, like music coming through an open summer evening window. But mostly it was her high-headed way of standing and her walking, like a black racehorse, held in, but lightning.

Godamighty, to be a man, a whole man tonight!

After that the Dunn medicine wagon made several more winter trips down past the Pavilion. There Milton, twenty-eight, strong-shouldered, the curls at his temples orderly and shining from the yucca shampoo, his beard clipped, stood cap in hand to watch Dolly Talbor walk past him to the cutter waiting in the frosty air or come in to climb the stairs to her sitting-room with Tom Colshire of the railroad beside her, or maybe a promoter from the gold fields; some Eastern investor or ranch owner on the way to look over his Western holdings, or an officer back from the Indian war. All Milton could do was hang around, pushed back to a bench in the corner farthest from the round oak heaters, alone, no big yarning, no talk at all—only watching for the woman, his brown eyes as soft and foolish as a newly housebroke pup afraid to bark his need.

By late February it was hell a-blazing and the river up all over the country, with inauguration day just ahead and the Grant crowd and the old Radicals threatening a filibuster—leave the country without a President unless their carpetbag count was accepted and Hayes given the White House. Once more the rioting started, but Tilden begged his party to let it go; the nation must not be torn by another civil war. So when the Republicans finally offered to withdraw the troops from the South if Hayes was given the election, the Tilden men agreed.

"Godamighty, it's an outright steal of the presidency!" Milton roared when he heard the news at Brulley's. Tying the strings of his earflaps under his beard he went out into the zero night to nurse his bitterness at home, away from the mockers. ". . . No wonder those crooks in Washington worked so hard against Tilden," he told Lucinda. "After the way he's been exposing the graft of the Tweed ring in New York City, there's no telling what stink his manure fork might dig up at the capital."

"It is discouraging," she said, but glad of anything that sent Milton home, as she poured him a cup of her night coffee that she made when there was late sewing, usually patching and mending for her menfolks. Tonight she climbed on a chair and fetched down a hidden jar with a fruitcake she was saving, and cut Milton a big piece.

"Yes, it goes to show what the Senate is, and we can't even vote the bastards out," Milton complained as he leaned back and brushed the crumbs from his expanding vest. "Anybody can get in with money enough to buy up a few legislators"—remembering his mother's last political dinner after that bank in Washington shut down on the Stone and Tolley money. "That's the way with Uncle Steve, so long's he could swing it, and mixing deep in all kinds of graft and bribery—selling guns that blowed up in a man's face to the army, stretching the war out, and now, Godamighty—the presidency's gone the same. . . ."

But Milton didn't finish. Dropping his face into his palms he hunched over, his strong back bowed like a water-worn boulder.

Quickly Lucinda took up her needle and pushed it through the worn jeans in her lap, anywhere, anyhow, to keep her hand from going out to him in pity. She thought his excitement about the president was foolish, but the other, that was appalling; the burden people would lay on those who came after them, one generation on the next. Shame, and the grief of young lives malahacked. . . .

Still, complaining patched no britches, and as Milton predicted, things were no better by summer, for all the fancy promises of Hayes. The newspapers howled for war with Mexico and with the Indians—probably contractors pushing it. Every day more people scoured the streets and the far roads, their bellies empty, followed by more layoffs and then more wage cuts. Some of the miners fought back, and while they had been eased along during the war, now with so many jobless around, it was the butt of the rifle in the snoot, the bastards, and hanging for ten, eleven of the Molly Maguires. Then the railroaders struck against a ten cent cut, the fourth in seven years, the walkout reaching as far west as Omaha. Milton went over with Ches Gillard and found a dozen men who had been with Sherman, but not picking their feet up now; whipped, with President Hayes crying revolution and anarchy and calling the army out against them.

"There it is, a precedent for all time—using the army to protect civilian property at the expense of civilian lives!" Charley Powell wrote from out in middle Nebraska. Milton read the letter to Lucinda and Stevie around the kitchen lamp, pounding the creased pages flat with his fist. "What else could be expected—a president who got his job by the bayonet!" he said bitterly.

With millions of people on wind-water soup, and foreign trade choked off by the tariff, the farmer's markets went like hen coops in a cloudburst. Milton heard the same story at dugouts, in dusty, worn yards, at country churches and post offices, in little towns with the pitch frying out of the store fronts from the Dismal to the fertile Nemaha. ". . . Hell, we can't afford us no medicine, not with ten cent corn and eggs three cents a dozen in trade. Cheaper to let the kids die an' dump 'em in a hole back of the house," a gaunt, scarecrow of a man down on the Nemaha said angrily when his wife looked at the vermifuge for her itchety-nosed young ones, fondling the dark bottle in her hands before she could give it up.

"Yeh, it's cheaper, but by damn, if we're gonna sit around on our asses and let 'em die like that forever!" a neighbor roared out. "If we don't get us free trade and cheap money to restore our markets soon, old Bayonet Hayes'll find hisself with a real revolution, a pitch-fork revolution on his hands!"

Lucinda was busy with the protracted meetings sprouting up these hard times, playing the organ, frying chickens, but she knew Milton would spend the rest of the summer arguing politics, railroads, pensions and prohibition, getting into rum-guzzling and no telling what trouble with his wild talk and that murderous pipe leg. So she sent Stevie along. The ten-year-old boy was slimming up too fast anyway, dauncy and blue as a pan of skim milk after a long siege of spring colds and the mumps that left him with a private swelling, so he couldn't go work on a farm with Putty, even if Lucinda consented. Awkwardly the boy let her kiss him good-by, looking back with concern toward the privy where Bruno, big as a brindle calf now, was locked up and howling as if he had been turpentined. But he'd be sure to pick up wolf poison somewhere on the road; besides Lucinda ought to have a protector, with her menfolks gone.

So they drove out into the street, Milton, low-down as a snake in a gully for months now suddenly laughing, loudly promising to bring great things home—a gunny sack full of golden eagles, double eagles, and maybe even a Kansas cyclone, hobbled and house-broke, to drive Lucinda's clumsy sewing machine. The next day looked like their chance. After a hot noontime, eight inches of rain fell in an hour and a half, flooding the Missouri bottoms high beyond the farthest spring break-ups, soaking cribs on the tablelands, so the corn sprouted and fired before the weather dried, along after the Fourth of July.

"We had one a them storms pa always tells about, sheds and barns floating by, and skunks and stuff on logs, and even muskrats drownded," Stevie wrote home.

Although there was little money around loose, the summer was working out well enough, except that Lucinda missed the boy and there wasn't much sewing. Then, early in August, Patience Ringer, daughter of Jack Ringer, the grain broker, came to have two Indian masquerade costumes made for the annual lawn fete—yellow satin instead of buckskin, with beaded bandings and silken fringe. Lucinda cut the costumes by garments the girl brought, and when they were basted together the two came for a fitting. The man was George Shefton.

Lucinda saw them draw up to the hitching post and she could hardly let them in, or fit the fringed trousers and shirt for the trembling of her foolish hands, the pins and even her thimble slipping to the floor as if she had the ager shakes. Finally she quieted enough to see that the man looked very gray, and remembered that a woman ages even faster. She was ten years older than the day on the wooded country road overlooking the Ohio, and twenty pounds heavier, her silver blonde hair grown mousy. He wouldn't recognize her at all.

When they were going Lucinda stood behind the fuchsias at her front windows, and saw George hand the laughing Patience gallantly into the seat. Steadying herself against the window casing, Lucinda dropped her face against her arm. Sobs for many things lost and gone shook her, long after the street both ways was empty.

The next day George Shefton was back, just passing, he said, and stopping for a little visit. He had known they were here, often saw Milton around Riverside Pavilion, and so on, he said, looking at Lucinda under a lifted eyebrow, and before she could make any defense he had dropped easily to the sofa, crossed his knees and was talking like an old acquaintance about the days around Cincinnati while Lucinda sat stiffly in her little rocker, wondering why she didn't send this man about his business, set Bruno's powerful jaws on him as on a common thief.

"Yes, Cincinnati was a pleasant town," he was saying as he lit a cigarette, the first ever smoked in Lucinda's house, "but there's nothing like a new country. . . ."

Finally the Indian costumes were done and they made a mighty fine couple, both dark, as was proper, the girl's handsome hair in two long braids, and there was pride too, in Lucinda's relief. But the day after the big storm that blew the roof off the Deaf and Dumb Asylum George Shefton came again, bringing cloth for half a dozen shirts. Lucinda was still nervous from the storm and so she couldn't say anything when he held the parcel out to her, although she stood with her arms folded against it, her eyes black with anger.

"My dear lady, don't be foolish," the man said, his lips red as a young woman's under the mustache. "I need the shirts and you, ah . . ." looking around the bare little room, at her shabby, wash-faded dress.

Telling herself that it was because of the mortgage on the team and wagon and her father pressed to pay it, that she accepted the work. Even knowing that old Sue Lasson would be out in her yard, watching—always hanging out clothes or something when there was anything to see—she took it.

"So you're tollin' in gents now," Sue called, laughing, and suddenly Lucinda remembered that Stevie was away too, that she was a lone woman. But there had to be a reply.

"Oh, no, not gents, Mrs. Lasson, and not tolling them in—just accommodating an old friend from Cincinnati," she said, making a sad, homesick face.

By the time the shirts were done and the velvet lounging robe too, dark raspberry with yellow silk frogs, Lucinda found herself lacing her corset snug and regretting that the silver blondeness of her hair was gone, although Milton's yucca shampoo kept it shining. Fortunately, her face was still oval, her color good, and her walk free enough so that her bustled skirts swished pleasantly as the passing George Shefton lifted his hat to her on the street. Hopefully she took a bottle of Dunn's Female Cordial and Tonic from Milton's supplies, even used a bottle of the Beauty Dew; although she knew what it was she barely hesitated, first patting it quickly over her cheeks and then splashing it over her whole face, desperate, without hope. She even figured her time carefully ahead from the checked dates of her Dunn's Almanac, and made a new nainsook gown, with sleeves daringly to the elbow, and medallions of ribbon-drawn insertion on the breast. But nothing came of it, although she went out everywhere, even to one of the lodge picnic dances where he was often seen, George wasn't there. A Black Hiller told Lucinda he had run into old Iron Leg on the road. By God, ma'am, there was a man. Stirred up a wind just settin' still talkin'. And when he picked up them coattails a his'n and took to turning on that leg it was a plain cyclone.

Then one chilly evening when the summer's bad spell of fever and ague was gone, the last cholera hog burned and the implement man, tired of his bundle of dead crop mortgages, had shot himself, Milton and the boy came home. The fall moon stood great over the farthest Iowa breaks and flying geese were honking somewhere overhead when Bruno suddenly struck off down the street, making almost no barking but tearing out and back, jumping the corner rosebush like a crazy pup, running in circles and off again. Then up the street jogged the medicine wagon, Stevie jumping off and loping ahead, wonderfully tall and brown and shy with his growing up, and Milton looking well too, the excitement and strangeness of far places around them both.

The wagon was full and piled on top with potatoes, pumpkins, sacks of apples, a tub of walnuts, half a bushel of frost-sweetened wild grapes, and under the seat a live wild turkey snared on the Missouri bottoms.

After they were cleaned up and had supper and felt comfortable and easy again, Milton took off his iron leg and from inside the top, pressed flat and warm, he laid out his little cache in a row on the red oilcloth before the lamp: silver and bills and gold, and so Lucinda put her contribution down too, making a hundred and ninety-seven dollars all together, enough to finish paying the note on the team and the twenty per cent interest—almost doubling the price in four years. That was the steal, the interest.

"But it's pretty good for an old soldier on a peg leg, eh?" Milton said, his arm around his wife, the ten-year-old Stevie counting the money out into piles again, spinning a silver dollar over the table like a shirt-tail young 'un, and then running off to see Putty Gillard, tell him about everything.

Later there was a little music on the folding organ and the old fiddle, singing the "Bone Picker's Song" they learned down in Kansas, and when Lucinda shuddered at "But a rattler was watchin'" that buffalo head . . ." they sang "The Dying Cowboy" and then talked about the summer, the great wonders they saw, particularly an artesian well that spouted high as Stevie's belly button, and the fire set to kill the grasshoppers moving like a carpet over the Platte Valley. The fire got away, racing into the dry upland, spreading a widening trail of smoking black prairie behind it, the sun red for a week, until a rain finally came. But they said nothing about the fine stories they picked up, or Milton's tricks with his leg. "It's good to keep some things between ourselves, like kids, like brothers. . . ."

Lucinda didn't say much, not telling that half of her money was from sewing for George Shefton. She didn't mention his name at all.

7—*Ants in the Butter Dish*

Late in the spring of '78, Charley Powell came through on the way east, looking windburnt and as tough and bony as an Ohio river red-horse, the flesh drawing back from his face the same way too, and his white mustaches hanging down into the air. He told Lucinda she looked fine and frisky as a grass widow, and talked new railroad surveys and politics and the war days with Milton until it was time for Stevie to come running in from school to draw water for the stock and get his shinny stick.

The doctor wooled the boy's black shock of hair a little and then went away with the sadness of an old wagon on a lonely road about him. A month later he wrote from New York. He had gone there because his wife was dying.

"Clear across the country!" Milton exclaimed as he tipped his spilling pipe away from his beard, "—and after a loose-twatted bitch who skipped off with a bounty jumper, a deserter, while Doc was off digging out minié balls and dosing trots and getting shot at!"

"Oh, Milton, such vulgar talk!" Lucinda complained, her mouth pursed up. "It was fine of Doctor to go to the poor woman, sick and probably all alone. . . ."

But even on this errand Charley Powell wrote much like his old self: ". . . Coming across the nation sure looks to me like it's ants in the butter dish," he wrote. "America's spreading like a Goliath since the war, talking over wires strung out, harnessing the lightning for our lamps, sending messages clear under the sea, and vaulting the continent on steam trains fast as the wind. And meantime we been building up trusts and financiers who vault individual rights and laws the same way, outfits like the railroads watering their stock out thin as orphanage gruel, and wildcatting, blue-skying and grafting everywhere. Looks like everybody's trying to be either a Jay Gould or a Jesse James, out for easy money, everybody wanting to be king of something: mines, railroads, cattle, outlaws—anything. The country's raising more to eat, piling up coal in mile-long ridges along the tracks, digging gold, building palaces at Newport and Virginia City, dragging home art stuff from all over the world, making more goods, and more machines to make more goods while millions get less to eat, maybe without so much as a sod roof over them this torrential night. No reaper or sewing machine saves their backs, no gold wears holes in their pockets, and no pearls adorn their rags. It's a little like a cloudburst over the bogs, the tableland left baking. Or like a bull of a man living high, eating and drinking powerful and well, but one of his members dying of gangrene and withering because no blood gets through. Maybe the coining of a little silver into dollars over Hayes' veto will help the circulation, but specie payment will take up that slack quick enough. It's no more a real cure for the disease than the acid poultice so many are using for cancer. The patient dies anyway, but much sooner and more pitifully. . . ."

"Oh! complaining like that, and his wife just buried!" Lucinda objected, remembering Miss Farnsworth's lecture on Correct Conduct for Mourning. "Soldiers seem to like Hayes, the GAR's——"

"Godamighty, ain't I a soldier?" Milton roared, "all just a bunch of sheep following the fat wether to the slaughter pens!" Pocketing his pipe he went out to Brulley's, to read the letter to somebody who wouldn't be knuckle-nosed, somebody knowing whose skunks were being skinned.

The twelve years since Milton Stone swung off the train on his crutch—four of them in the sun and weather that dulled the bright orange of his medicine wagon—had changed him too. Nearing thirty, his shoulders were thick and powerful, his dark skin ruddy from wind and Missouri corn. His beard was black, his hair thick, although a little dusty at the temples, and the years as peddler had brought a dance swing to his fiddle bow and a glibness to his tongue that could turn mean as a locust thorn or the flash of a Barlow knife. By now his name and the exploits of his leg had spread from Kansas to Dakota. It was told that he could bat a rock so high it fell in a shower of meteors 'way over Colorado and set the range afire; could jump the Missouri and back without touching the ground on the far side, and with a little oiling he would surely drive off the eclipse coming the twenty-ninth of July. Wherever there was a team-pulling, a rough and tumble fighter taking on all comers, or an epidemic of man or beast, Doc Stone would likely come swinging off his high seat, the polished pipe of his leg shining in the sun, his greeting hearty and loud.

So it was only natural that, when thousands began to die of yellow fever, some as far north as the Nishnabotna, he should bring Stevie home and make ready to go down South, although it meant missing the trial of the Olives, the cattle outfit north of the Platte who had killed and burned a couple of settlers. "It'll take martial law to keep the cow outfits from mobbin' the court!" settlers predicted, worried.

For two days Milton smelled up the little house below Council Bluffs with medicine-brewing so that Lucinda had to send the boy around to say his father was using the kitchen and would they come for their fittings Wednesday? Only Lola Peel, the Lucy Stoner and not given to humoring any man, came anyway, and regretted it.

"Pee-u!" she cried as she stepped on the porch, and so Lucinda quickly folded the blue mull into a box and followed the woman home with it.

When Milton was done he had fifty bottles of his yellow fever oil, a thick, stinking concoction that a southern soldier had told him about in the hospital—mostly coal oil stirred over a tub of hot water with a little sheep tallow, black wool-fat and water, and enough yellow soap to hold it together, give it body. Rubbed over the skin it was warranted to prevent fever at fifty cents a bottle.

On the way south Milton swung around by the Riverside Pavilion and so by the time he got down into the fever belt the death lists were climbing like Sue Lasson's tabby cat going up a tree ahead of Bruno. But as the old Reb had promised, no one who used the oil before he got sick caught the disease, and so word spread of a mighty powering medicine that a man in a yellow wagon peddled. Soon Milton had trouble hiding out long enough to make up new batches, using beef tallow and crude oil or even coon fat—anything, almost, so long as the coal oil and lye soap didn't fail him. As he got farther down the people looked poorer, sicker, and more scared, and below St. Louis they were running like rabbits before a Kansas prairie fire, dropping their sick and dead as they hurried on, some carrying bundles, or maybe a hen or even a pig, spreading rumors that in Memphis the dead were rolled into ditches like cholera hogs, or left to swell with maggots in the sun. Often the people ganged around Milton's wagon, sulky and feisty as starving hound-dogs, demanding all his stock, cursing him for a damnyankee when he refused their pay, even trying to pull him from the seat. But after the iron leg sent a leader or two rolling they gave him civil words for as much as he would hand out for money, if they had it, or a clutch of eggs, a mess of fish or nothing at all.

Nights Milton camped on high ground away from everybody, his skin greased, a good army grass smudge going. Although there was no fire they found him, perhaps a man on a work-stumbling mule hunted him out looking for Iron Leg, the Yankee swamp doctor.

"I aims to offer you anything I got to my name if you'll come cure my woman," he might say, standing dark beside the damped fire, stiff and awkward in his need. But Milton had no cure, only an evil-smelling preventative, and so the man would turn way, silent and gaunt and hopeless in the dim red glow of the smudge. On such nights Milton pulled long at the brown-topped jug and when he finally slept it was with his hand on the old gun loaded with buckshot, not depending too much on the reputation of his leg to protect him here.

Late in September Milton wrote Lucinda one of his rare letters and enclosed a money order for a hundred dollars to lay in winter goods—fruits and cellar vegetables, feed for the stock, a new pair of britches to cover Stevie's lengthening shanks, some warm winter clothes for herself and repairs for her teeth. "The papers say 20,000 died in Memphis, and almost as bad to the Gulf," he wrote. "I wish I could study out why some folks like those up on Stony Point didn't get sick and why my stinking oil seems to hold off the disease. A good doctor willing to experiment might find a real cure."

It was his first reference to his opportunity lost.

The fever ended as it came. A week of cold rain was followed by a frost that skimmed the ponds with ice. The next day the sun was out hot as summer, yellowing the steaming river bottoms. So Milton turned his weary team homeward, straight home, not around by the dark-eyed woman at the Pavilion. He was sober, his hair and beard trimmed by a grateful barber—not like other years, when Lucinda had to chop his face out of the dark thicket of hair hanging to his eyes and meeting in his beard. In the wagon were bags of yams and persimmons, and four new acorn hog-hams curing in a keg, ready for smoking. Under the seat slept a pet coon for Stevie from a man whose family of twelve, surrounded by dying, all escaped.

Milton had been away over four months but it was a happier return than other years, usually with so little in the pocket and nothing much to remember except wind-burnt men, and the desperation of drouth and grasshoppers and ten cent corn in the eyes of the women.

"I almost got to feeling good when folks come to give me stuff on the way home, almost like a—" but he couldn't say "a man." In his embarrassment he pounded his cob pipe against the iron leg and told a new Missouri puke story of the longest, out-daciousest coach-whip snake, that could rare up like a maypole, while Stevie rode the pet coon on his shoulder like an old friend. Milton had another John Wilkes Booth story, too. Seemed he was hiding out in the rough Missouri country, running with the James boys.

"Oh, such nonsense!" Lucinda scolded, but glad of something new to tell Lola Peel when she came for her fitting.

After Dump and Dolly were rested, Milton took Lucinda over to Omaha to pick out a good sewing machine, one with three drawers on each side and all the new attachments for the ruffled and pleated frills the fashionable wanted. While they were unloading it, Sue Lasson, hovering around like a hen hawk, came running over, her apron around her shoulders against the cold wind, her mouth full of talk. "My, my," she was saying, "won't this be fine for tuckin' them new shirts you'll be a-makin' now that George Shefton's back with us."

Milton stopped, rearing back on his peg leg. "She mean you been making shirts for that bastard?" he demanded, ignoring Lucinda's pleading face. "Godamighty!. . . ."

"Well, when the key is gone the lock hangs open, my ma always used to say—" Sue Lasson laughed, and off to tell her story at the MacMillans and the Gruenfalks.

"Oh, Milton," Lucinda tried to explain, "I told you about Patience Ringer bringing the work. I had it half done before I knew whose it was. Besides, we needed the money so bad——"

"I never need money bad as that!"

"It helped on the note, and he paid well. . . ."

"Paid well! Godamighty, my own wife talking like that about a gun runner to the Rebs, a feisty, lollygaggin' skirt lifter!" Milton brought his fist down on the top of the machine, splintering the wood. Then he got into the wagon and drove off across the Missouri toward Riverside Pavilion. It was a week before he came back, barking with a heavy chest cold, as though he had been camping out on the winter ground. All evening he sat with his one foot in a tub of mustard water beside the heater, Lucinda carrying hot camomile tea and the boiling kettle to him.

The winter was a cold one everywhere, for the Texas cattle driven up the trail to grass, and the Indians starved into revolt down south and now scattered through the freezing canyons of northwest Nebraska, the army hunting them down, firing into them, women and children and all, until nothing moved. On the Missouri the winter was a sleighing one, the frozen river a wide wood trail the two months that the bottoms lay smothered in drifts. Somehow Milton stayed close to his own heater, playing Crokinole or pitch with Stevie, ganging up to beat Lucinda when they could get her into a game, or joining her at the organ, Milton with his fiddle, Stevie blowing his mouth harp. Sometimes they walked Indian file to the school literaries, Milton ahead with the bobbing lantern to light the way through the drifts. Turned out Stevie could spell almost as well as the schoolmaster, although Milton was no slouch himself after an evening or two with the blue-backed speller. Sometimes they took the fiddle sack along, or even hauled the folding organ down for the singing and the play party games that were a little like dancing, but not really, because most of the people belonged to the Sunday school and had what Joe Deaver used to call Methodist feet.

Lucinda saw George Shefton several times that winter, but not with Patience. Seems he left last summer soon after the new shirts, and so Patience ran off with her father's bookkeeper, making talk, particularly when she came back a few months later, already plainly expecting. One stormy day George picked up Lucinda in his cutter, to sit uneasily as he tucked her knees in, remembering what old Charley Powell called the buffalo robe—the greatest single aid to the fathering of the first-born.

But at her door George Shefton lifted his whip to his beaver cap and let his horse out, the runner throwing frozen snow as he turned in the street and was gone. Inside, Lucinda dropped to the handiest chair, clasping her cold hands in her little round muff, glad Milton was not there to see, remembering the flutter the man's passing used to make among her girl friends in Cincinnati, remembering too, the afternoon beside the gooseberry patch on the hill road. After a while she began to cry, not for that day, but for now, when her only attraction seemed to be her skill with the needle.

It was evening, the house cold and dark, before she moved, but when Milton came home he smelled molasses cookies from far down the street and raced Stevie in a great thumping up the back steps. By the time the roads cleared Lucinda had other things on her mind: Stevie sneaking a smoke with Putty in the little shed out back, the bills piling up, and asking as tactfully as she could for her pay through a mouthful of pins to make it seem less hurting.

Farmers were complaining again, saying it cost them as much to ship a car of corn or hogs two hundred miles as the big outfits paid from coast to coast, Rockefeller alone getting ten million dollars in freight rebates. Although the Democrats controlled Congress, nothing was done about the tariff and so with the resumption of specie payment, money almost disappeared. Homes, farms and small businesses were swept away like Missouri sandbars before a flood. Even John Sherman of the Treasury was hooted and jeered when he came back to Ohio to make a speech.

"The old reprobate sure got his own dirt throwed back in his face. . . ." Sarah Stone wrote, forgetting the days in the big house on the hill and the crystal cake stand that a boy let slip through champagne-clumsy fingers at his wedding.

Milton tossed the letter over to where Lucinda was winding yarn from the hank on Stevie's arms. "Plain to see the Stones and old John ain't bugs under the same turd no more," he said angrily, and went out to Frenchy's to talk up General Weaver of Iowa, sure to be nominated for president by the Greenbackers.

There was complaining from Aloysius Dunn too, saying Milton had neglected his route last fall, kiting off south peddling quack remedies, hinting he might put in another, a more reliable man— one who realized his obligation to his work and his employer. So Milton tried to explain to Dunn that many people said he had helped them, and included the recipes for the yellow fever oil, the yucca shampoo and the Beauty Dew. Dunn denounced them all, and then in the next shipment sent the same remedies, packed and patented and under new names, with his orange and black labels. So Milton had to sell his own remedies at the small peddler's commission.

"I'll bet there ain't a drop a water from a foaly mare," he said holding a bottle of the whey-colored Dew to the light.

After a robin snow in May, George Shefton went to Denver and so Milton and Stevie set out on the road again, three shoes and a worn pipe-end on the dashboard while Dump and Dolly switched their lazy tails over the lines and the two on the seat talked free and easy as the brothers they were, exchanging the mouth harp between them, singing songs of the war and the Forty-niners or Stevie's favorites, "Down the river, down the O-hi-o!" "Jubilo," or "I had a gal, ugly as sin, her eyes bugged out, her nose bugged in." The boy's voice high and breaking a little, the man's a toneless booming, the pipe leg beating a tattoo on the dash.

It was fine to cook supper along some little stream and then bed down on the dry, warm earth, perhaps on a wind-swept knoll after thrashing out the rattlesnakes, or under some great cottonwood, the fireflies blinking, lightning flashing far off where some farmer was having rain for his crops, or maybe hail. Then suddenly it would be morning, blackbirds singing, orioles hovering around their swinging nests in the early sun and Milton already looking for a fish or two for breakfast, or quail, or young prairie chickens cackling on the hillside.

Once they were out far enough to see rifle pits dug by soldiers to stand off the Indians and once a great herd of Texas longhorns stringing north for the tall grass of the sandhills and beyond, to the Sioux reservations. They camped with the trail boss, the gaunt, leathery men with sagging guns around them, the singing of the night herders coming through the cool clear night. Several times they saw antelope, Milton getting one with the old muzzle-loader by crawling up a draw while Stevie drove slowly past, the curious pronghorns running in a wide circle around the bright colored wagon. That night the boy jumped up several times in his shirttail to see that nothing got the antelope hanging from the propped-up wagon tongue to cool for salting. If only it were the buffalo they saw galloping awkwardly over a knoll once; an old bull, Milton said, with hide thick enough to turn a ball, let alone the buckshot of old Roarin' Ida.

Often Milton talked about his days along the Ohio. Johnny was doing all right in Deadwood, had even been to the upper Yellowstone with a little prospecting outfit since the murdering Sioux were out of the country; up not far from what Jay Cooke once advertised as Banana Land to the suckers when he was promoting his railroad. They stopped on the ridge where the bones of Custer and his men lay bared by the rain. "By God, I know one young fellow mighty lucky he was doing his fighting under crazy old Sherman . . ." he wrote.

So Stevie had to have the story about how a Reb down on one knee had a bead on Milton when Johnny came up behind him and ran his bayonet through him like a toad-sticker. "I bet Johnny's off chasing outlaws all over the Black Hills this minute, and layin' in tons of gold——"

"Hey, back water there, young feller!" Milton said. "Ain't you forgettin' about the pick and shovel the miners uses? And nobody's heard from your Uncle Spencer in fifteen years, exceptin' that he disappeared from his claim."

But plainly Stevie didn't see himself as his uncle; he would be like Johnny Stanger, who was surely doing big things, probably almost as big as the stories told around the ranches and the country towns and post offices about a medicine peddler with an iron leg that was handy as a buggy plow. Seemed he could use it for everything from batting out balls for the kids to whacking back the bullets Wild Bill once fired at him. Whacked 'em back so hard he put a couple holes right through Bill's hat, he did. Then there were all those flowing wells that people talked about up north. Seemed Iron Leg bored them. Just grabbed up his coattails and whizzed around on that pipe until water came spouting out like a gusher, though mostly it settled later to just boiling up a couple feet out of the ground.

". . . Still a hell of a lot better's well-hoggin' or barrel haulin'. Why them folks off on that dry table north of the Platte, where it's four hundred foot to water, would pay him a dollar a foot for a dozen like 'em!"

"Whillikers!" the boy said softly to himself the first time he heard these stories. "Four hundred dollar a well!" Dragging old Dump and Dolly from the watering trough he looked for Milton back at the wagon. But when the boy found him he was sitting on an old box at the blacksmith shop, the pipe leg stuck straight out, the stump a pitiful thing in its leather that was like an old nose bag. So the boy slipped away to sit alone under the wagon. After dark, when there were only comforting night sounds around their camp bed, he managed to ask not about the well but about Wild Bill.

". . . It's true, Pa, ain't it—about battin' his bullets back?"

And when Milton awoke enough to understand he roared out laughing so hard the boy drew down under the blankets. But it was fine anyway, this being out with Iron Leg, even when he sneaked off nights, like he did down on the Republican river and other places, to some woman with a fat, jolly laughing.

Sometimes Milton and the boy got home for the Fourth of July or the GAR picnic. Taking Lucinda along, they loaded up with a grub basket under the seat, the old tent tied on top of the wagon, and plenty of bandages, arnica and limewater burn ointment. While Stevie ran after the fife and drum corps, it was the boxing and wrestling Milton liked, either catch-as-catch-can or what the breeds called Indian wrestling, both men flat on the ground, heads opposite, legs entwined, making a struggling, heaving two-headed monster until one was thrown into the air. He liked the races too, fat men's, sack, three-legged ones—any kind, whooping and laughing. At first the noisiness of the man who had been such a quiet boy offended Lucinda, particularly among the other old soldiers, many white-haired by now, old men; but gradually she came to think of it as an outlet for all his years of hampering. Even the time George Shefton stood off and watched them with what Miss Farnsworth called a superior smile, she joined Milton's laughing, although she cried a little that long night afterward. Charley Powell once said it was natural; the whole country came out of the Civil War so crippled it made up by noise and show, turning in blind adulation to the doer, the pusher; made gods of the railroad builders, the iron and copper kings—all the robber barons.

So, with a sunshade to protect her complexion, Lucinda went out to stand beside her husband at the team-pulling contests, the horse races, and the whippets running after the poor rabbit who could only flee blindly before the dogs that were so beautiful in their running. Even knowing that Milton might get to talking about soft money, or the railroads and the barbed wire trust, and have to be helped back to the tent by midnight she went to stand beside him for everything except the harness races, with their flying sulkies. She even showed Milton a clipping from the Custer County *Buckshot* that one of her customers brought in:

THE IRON-LEGGED MAN FROM THE MISSOURI

There was a great man abroad on the North Table last week, with thunder in his voice and an iron leg to ground the lightning, or flash out and rip the daylight from around your head. It is said he can hit a ball so it never comes to earth, and has catbirds slipping through his hair like through a plum thicket and bears roaring in his whiskers. We don't know, but we know he has the gift of Hippocrates in his heart and hand, for he saved three lives in one hour up there last week.

And when Lucinda asked Milton about it he didn't tell her much. "Oh, just some poor devil gone crazy; shot up his family. I happened to come along in time. . . ."

So the years passed, the sea onion grew great sweeping leaves and sent up a center stalk, the bloom Mollie Stanger had promised if they lived in one place seven years. Bruno, the pup sent to Stevie from Washington, died, still nobody knowing who sent it, unless perhaps Hiram did. Milton saw George Shefton now and then, whitened at the temples, with a bald spot showing behind when the wind lifted his toupee as he talked to some pretty girl outside a church or at a picnic—never with anyone from a place like Riverside.

"He don't pick up none a them overripe plums that's fell to the ground," Mose Randolph at Frenchy's once said. "He's the bastard what shakes the tree. . . ."

"Yeh, wonder nobody's barrowed him long ago."

The men around the sandbox spit and wiped their mouths, each enjoying the thought his own way.

Suddenly it was '83. The man who shot Garfield had been executed, Iowa gone dry and wet again, the Mississippi Valley endured one of its greatest floods, a million homeless from Ohio to the sea, and Stevie was sixteen, done with his short-term schooling, and ready to go West to dig gold.

"You want to leave your poor old mother all alone," Lucinda accused.

"Whillikers, of course not," the boy denied, shamed by the need for pretending. Women had no right to expect a man to hang around home all his life. Putty didn't have to, off being a cowboy. "Yes," Lucinda admitted, "and glad his mother was to get him away from that Cassie Sable. . . ."

The boy fussed his feet. "There's some who were through a war at my age. . . ."

Yes, the man he called father had lost a leg and become a husband when he was little older than this smooth-faced boy. But Lucinda cried so Stevie waited, reading Wild West stories, and about Buffalo Bill too, with everybody knowing he was a drinking man and a skirt chaser. Then Lucinda found the boy rolling in the hay in the little shed stable out back with that Cassie Sable. Horrified, she slipped away, watching the girl sneak out the back. And when she looked there was a bottle of cologne missing from Milton's stock. Miss Farnsworth was right, the nature of man was inherently animal and evil, and so she mended up the boy's clothes and folded them neatly into the box fitted with a strap for shoulder packing and side rope for Milton's shovel alongside. As she worked, Lucinda wondered how any mother ever let her own son go; how Sarah could have let Milton slip off to the war no more than a baby.

At the boy's begging Lucinda said good-by at the kitchen door. "All right, Stevie, if you don't want the men to see you have a mother—" she said, "—but I wouldn't be ashamed of you, son, for you are all I have—" making a sad, brave face before Milton.

But the man had already been to the jug under the wagon seat and felt good. "Oh, the kid'll be back; he'll come running home soon's his hanging parts freeze and begin to drop off. Gets sixty below zero up there."

"Aw, pa . . ." the boy protested, punching Milton playfully.

"And you be careful the road agents out of Sidney don't plug you before you get even a smell of the mines."

So they managed to cover up Milton's loss until he stood beside the track watching the boy climb into the mine excursion car full of rough men. Then suddenly it was like the day the train left a young returning soldier standing alone on his crutch at the little station of Martins Park. Quickly Milton stumped away, to sit at Brulley's all afternoon, alone, nobody daring to come near.

Before long Cassie Sable was having new dresses made up, pretty ones, elegant with satin and bullion braiding—getting more than a bottle of cologne now.

Five years after Stevie was gone the boy was still missed from his place at the kitchen table, from his side of Milton's wide bed, and from the closet-small sewing-room where he used to peek in when Lucinda was fitting a customer, to laugh at their screeching. She wouldn't even have another dog in Bruno's place; instead she welcomed a little blue kitten Milton brought back from a deserted homestead. "Came out crying and rubbing against the wheel when I drove by."

Lucinda had joined the new Oak street church, organized by a Campbellite preacher who had been with Grant, but she couldn't get Milton to go, and so she began to work harder for national prohibition, now that Iowa was dry again, and the Missouri river bootleggers were moving in thick as passenger pigeons in the old days. She wondered if perhaps even a Farnsworth girl might not join with the vulgar suffragettes to get temperance legislation. Her parents were dead now, died a few days apart, the mirrors not yet uncovered from the mother's funeral when the father followed her to the old private cemetery at Martins Park. Milton had offered to borrow Lucinda's fare on his pension but times were hard again, hard enough to bring in a Democratic president in spite of the old cry of traitor, and so she couldn't mortgage their future just to see the dead remains of those she loved in a life so long ago. Afterward Malinda wrote what had been done, and sent the family Bible to Lucinda, as the eldest, with the garnet earrings gone to Nittie, the opal ring to Malinda. Everything else went long ago to stave off the mortgage foreclosure on the home place, with things not going as planned for their husbands lately. Lucinda hadn't been told because there was nothing she could have done.

No, she thought, nothing at all, but it was hard to have it said by those who used to depend on her for even their nose wipings.

"Do not grieve yourself about this," Malinda, the minister's wife, comforted. "As my Richard said after the services, families come up and go down as the principles they stand for wax and wane. Grandfather Martin, like Grandfather Stone, stood for a public and personal integrity which has failed in these latter days. Once it seemed Hiram Stone was making the compromise with the new philosophy of arrogance and greed, and would ride the wave, but he never was ruthless enough, not even with old Sarah to push him. Father wasn't ruthless at all, so they both went down. But the folks missed you to the last."

This letter Lucinda put away into the old Bible that she placed on the stand beside the wedding picture, and if she grieved for her folks, Milton was not allowed to see it, and felt shut out and hurt. Lucinda, at thirty-eight, had a wing of gray hair at each temple and her eyes were failing from close sewing, but in her blue French serge with its neat-fitting basque and a little blue hat with green and magenta wings, she looked stylish enough to draw a few new customers from clear over in Omaha.

It was just as well, for Milton didn't work his territory much. Not sick, just slowing down, he called it, particularly after Stevie wrote that Johnny Stanger had a heart attack lifting mine machinery, and so was homesteading too. But the stories of Iron Leg kept growing until some even blamed him for the cyclone over on the Nemaha, since it was well known that by turning on that pipe he could make a wind that chilled everything around him so the ducks thought it was November and scooted off south, the grass died, and the cricks took to gurgling under ice. Some claimed he could whirl himself clean off the ground and sail through the air like a balloon, sparks from his pipe flying out behind him like a comet in the night.

After the Dunn medicine man in Dakota got caught in a blizzard and was found weeks later frozen in his wagon, even his ointment jars cracked, Milton never got far out from the time the first haze of Indian summer came creeping southward along the Missouri bluffs. He still went to Frenchy's, the shelves behind the bar wet or dry as Iowa law dictated but the results of the evenings were the same. Riverside Pavilion was open all the winter now, with the extra Iowa drinking business. Besides, there were the new western settlements and their railroads, and the flow of gold and commerce that the Black Hills brought through—the dark-eyed Dolly Talbor out with her matched team of white stockinged blacks, obtained, it was said, from the father of a son who drank too much and wrote her some foolish letters.

Milton Stone was a thick, stocky man now, round as a sorghum vat with arms and shoulders grown powerful to make up for the leg anchorage he lacked in swinging heavy cases in and out of the wagon, holding the horses in a hailstorm or lifting the hog out of the scalding barrel alone at butchering time these years since Stevie went away. Remembering Cleveland's obstructionism he had little hope his return would make things better for the boy, cured of the gold fever long ago and freighting out of Pierre to Rapid City now that he had a wife and baby to feed. Helga was the daughter of a Swedish emigrant homesteader, a good manager and blonde enough to make a towhead of the little girl, who was very sweet in the blue dresses Lucinda sent. Sometimes there were pressed prairie roses and once a mariposa lily, fragile as thinnest tissue paper, a splotch of yellow pollen rubbing off on the paper. And always the letters were signed, "Your aff'te son."

"He *has* made us a good son," Lucinda said, dabbling at her eyes, glad she never told Milton or even Lola Peel about Cassie Sable in the hay. Milton nodded, tilting his beard to keep the ashes of his pipe out of the ringworm ointment he was muddling in the mortar on his lap, fending the blue cat off his knee with an elbow. He wondered if Lucinda ever suspected the boy's parentage. Maybe after Sarah wrote about that Tilly Youngly, Hiram took up with for a while. "The man we have long honored as Husband and Father has proven unworthy . . ." still speaking like the lady of the big house instead of a moldy Ohio bottom shack that was so bad for her rheumatism and her heart. She still refused to admit that Spencer, the first-born, was dead, but holding that it was Milton who should be doing something for his mother now, and sometimes she hinted it was the high-toned lady notions of Lucinda that kept him from his duty.

Old Hiram seemed to be holding up in the usual Stone way, over seventy and still working on his feet, janitoring at one of the town schools. Better off than Milton, with old Dolly getting too stiff for travel, Lucinda's best customers making last year's gowns over, and the rains failing again, along with everything else. Maybe it was true that the South and the West were the economic stepchildren of the nation, their banks going down under the storms over Wall

Street like island seedlings before a Missouri flood. While corn was ten cents a bushel and a woman down in Kansas was crying to the farmers to raise more hell, Vanderbilt died and left two hundred million dollars that he made out of the West, while employers everywhere were using the blacklist against their striking workers, and in Chicago four men were hung. Harrison had defeated Cleveland, promising to make a hole big enough to drive a hay wagon through the Treasury for the old soldiers, he got a million more on pension but did nothing to help anybody make a living. In the meantime more settlers had to go West, and so the Indians were pushed back to make room, cheated and starved into the futile hope of ghost dancing, and then shot down.

". . . Your white brother is getting a kick in the belly too," Milton told his Winnebago friend. "Fewer jobs, less pay, and the new tariff upping the price of everything he has to buy."

A new party, the Populists, did start up, calling a great national convention, people coming to Omaha by train and ox team and afoot, their progress and their enthusiasm sending hope fresh as April green running over the plains. Milton, who had seen the Mugwumps of 1872 at Cincinnati, looked on with a sour mouth. A week after the convention, the steel companies began a summer of general wage cuts that set off enough labor explosions and bloodshed and bitterness to last a generation, enough to put Cleveland back into the White House by a landslide, in spite of all the scandalous stories revived against him.

So now the country was back on gold and safe, people were saying. All that ailed it now was too many shoes, too much wheat and cotton, and too many empty bellies. But the big bugs weren't making employment here; instead they hopped over into other countries, their money buying up plantations, factories, mines—anything where there were peons for starvation wages. At the first trouble they'd be yelling for the government to protect them. ". . . Where the U. S. dollar goes the uniform has to follow," old Charley Powell said angrily.

"Well, anyway we drove them tools a Wall Street out a Washington again, got 'em runnin' like a nest a skonks smoked out under the grainery," a Henry Georger from Kansas was bragging.

But even at Frenchy's many were more interested in the killing of the Dalton boys at Coffeyville, and just in time to give the poet

Tennyson an armed escort into Paradise. Before Cleveland was inaugurated Jay Gould died too, but he didn't have to kick himself out of this world in the dust of a Kansas town like a common outlaw.

"Ah, no, not the bas-tard who can corner the gold and leave the nation to hold the sack," Frenchy himself said as he poured from the bottle under the bar. "Steal the million and you die warm in the feathaires. . . ."

But hard times and drouth brought more personal saviors than Single Taxers and Pops and Free Silverites. Sky pilots walked the burning prairie, and the rainmakers came with their black boxes and their cannon to shoot the heavens. Aloysius J. Dunn was complaining again too. "He's right," Lucinda scolded when Milton brought the letter to where she was hanging out her wedding napkins for their annual bleaching, spreading them over the budding rose bushes to the sun. "Here it's almost June and you not out."

"Godamighty, I'd just be hearing that thin grub ain't binding."

"No need to be vulgar, Milton," Lucinda complained. "Many seem to have the money to go to the World's Fair, and from right around here—while all you do is sit around with a lot of old soldiers, like a bunch of crows cawing in a dead tree—saving the country."

Milton wadded Dunn's letter into a ball and stomped it into the ground with his pipe leg. "Godamighty!" he roared, "who's got a better right? Besides, that bastardly Dunn's slippery as a razorback hog in a wallow, selling my fever oil all through the South, every fisherman keeping the mosquitoes off with it, my yucca shampoo in every barber shop on my own route, and him buying into the railroads and getting a new steam yacht on my money!—mine and the other poor devils he's stole his patents from!"

All Lucinda could do was whip the moisture from another fringed square of linen and hold her tongue. Maybe Milton and that dreadful Free Silver paper, the *Broad Axe,* were right. Maybe Wall Street bankers really were withdrawing gold from the Treasury to keep Cleveland fighting for the life of the country instead of working to reduce the tariff and building up the foreign markets—increasing the revenue of the nation, making jobs.

". . . Breaking the country for profit when they know they'll go down like the worms eating, hollowing out a tree," Milton told those around his wagon at a foreclosure sale up in Holt county, saying it with a hopelessness that was bitter as ragweed on the tongue.

"Hell, yes," the sunburnt farmers agreed, "but we'll fight 'em—Wall Street, railroads an' all. We'll fight!"

Milton looked around the men. They were gaunt and gnarled as rock-rooted trees from hard work and starvation but, by God, they still had fight. For the first time since Stevie left he wanted to turn a few cartwheels.

One evening as Milton turned his team in at the house, a white-haired old man rose from beside Lucinda on the back step. By the time Milton had the tugs unhooked from his tired team he saw it was his father, still tall but thin now, and old, forgetting that he, the son, was gray too, and that this was the fall of '93.

They met halfway between the step and the wagon, Hiram holding his hand out formally. "It is in sorrow that we meet . . ." he said, and in the words Milton felt the influence of Sarah and knew that his mother was dead.

"Laid away Monday," the old man said, the wind blowing the thinning white hair a little.

To Milton this was like a surprise cavalry charge, a sneak guerilla attack from the worn darkness. His mother dead and buried and he could see her only as she came pushing into the carriage house on his wedding day. Holding her hoops sideways she had come through the silenced young people toward her son who had returned a cripple from the war.

Late that night Milton and his father were still talking. Hiram had lost his job; too many younger men dropping small turds these days, and so he was heading up to Stevie, out of a job now too, and taking up a homestead. He wanted Hiram to locate a place joining, giving him more grass for cattle.

Gradually, feeling his way as through some dark, long unused tunnel, the old man went back to his big days, talking of them to Milton for the first time in his life, to Milton who had even fathered his son.

"I get to feeling mean as a weasel in a hen coop when I think about the war days," he admitted, rubbing his knobby hands uneasily together. "There's no denying we were out for all we could get, and for as long as we could get it, and everybody else be damned. Now there's those who say that if the Radicals hadn't interfered with Lincoln's running the war, the fight would have ended long before it did, with many a life spared—yes—" he went on slowly, "—and many a. . . ."

But he couldn't finish, couldn't speak of the mutilations possibly prevented, not with his son there before him, the polished iron pipe of his leg shining where the lamplight fell across it.

But Milton nodded as though about someone else, some casual acquaintance, and made room for the cat on his good leg. He had gone over all this many, many times in his mind, got drunk on it and sobered up on it, and always the end was the same, done and not to be mended.

8 — Whole, Sound and Whole

The drouth of '93 and '4 lay like the dark path of a prairie fire over all the region between Ohio and the Western mountains. It wasn't enough that millions were out of work and following any rumor or hope across the country. Without snow enough for a gooseneck runner in the winters, any grass or crop that found the moisture to start at all shriveled and blew away in the hot winds of June. When the clouds did come they boiled up into thunderheads, sent a few bolts of lightning to shake the earth, and maybe a scattering of hailstones to bounce like door knobs in the dust. Then the storm dried up to a wind-streaking against the sky. Some remembered the old folk way of having a woman heavy with child walk over the seed fields to bring the sprouting through the hard earth, or a man with two ball potatoes in a tobacco sack hanging down in front. Nothing helped, but the newspapers carried stories of rain with the clouds opening in a gush of water. In Kansas a woman in her carriage was swept away in a dry gully, in Colorado a train rolled from its embankment. Elsewhere the earth grayed and broke, the starving grasshoppers creeping into the cracks to escape the sun.

"Buzzards're getting so hungry they've took to following their own shadows," Milton said in disgust, "And mighty thin pickin's, but the rockets are blazing up fancy from the World's Greatest Fair at Chicago."

With everything short but time and the wind, there were great stories going the rounds: the hell fire ones of the sky pilots, and some woman relating how she escaped from white slavery or a convent until a man shouted that last time she had claimed it was from Mormonism, and before that captivity by the Indians. Even the newspapers helped, carrying the story of a litter of eight boys born to a woman up in Keyapaha county, and of great lighted monsters flying through the night in the Platte River region, down around the Solomon and over in Indiana, and about a flying serpent that stampeded a night herd in west Texas. But many shook their heads, many who had never waited in soup lines, burned an ear of corn or saw a copy of Tom Watson's magazine. Maybe there was more than just bums' wrath and wind-pudding to the complaining; maybe the nation had been morally, even economically, unhealthy ever since the war. True, there were more millionaires, and even a short rally from common folks in the Eighties, but what followed now was like a relapse into black vomit, with the Wall Streeters up to their old tricks: collecting deaconed apples, big ones, for the knobby buckshot loaned; cleaning out the nation's treasury the same way, and Congress upholding them.

"Yeh," Milton admitted to his Populist friends, "maybe the drouth is God withholding the rains from sinners, like the sky pilots claim, but Uncle Sam's money troubles ain't nothing that a dose of vermifuge and a good shot of salts from the voters wouldn't cure."

"But for that they got to know what's goin' on, not just follow the rattle of one feed bag or another, only to find they got another frozen bit in the mouth and the exploiters solid in the saddle," Ike Ellers, a Weaver man, said.

"My gramp, at ninety-five, cast his last vote starting the Republican party, an' that's good enough for me," a man in baggy jeans spoke up.

"Yeh, your gramp at ninety-five was up an' coming enough to change to the latest improvements in politics back in the scythe and cradle days, where you're still standin'."

"Hell no, I ain't, I bought me the best, a McCormick reaper; had it foreclosed off a me!" the man protested, and got a loud drumming laugh from those around him, their mouths pouched up to hold back the tobacco juice and their words.

But talk still mended no britches, and Milton's profits for the summer barely paid for the horse to take old Dolly's place. Lucinda's customers too had vanished like pullets during a protracted meeting, and those left seldom brought new materials, mostly worn cloaks to be turned and skirts with frayed hems for new bandings which should make them look better than new.

As they became more demanding they got more familiar too, and freer with their gossip, even about Milton, hinting there were women along his route, finally asking right out if he wasn't being seen a lot around that Riverside place on the Omaha bottoms, making a show of himself, fiddling, telling stories and doing tricks with that pipe leg around a sporting house.

The first time Lucinda tried to laugh it off because she must, asking lightly how they could know so much about such a place, pretending to push away the blue cat rubbing against her skirts. Later she had an answer ready: "Oh, Mr. Stone has regular orders at the Pavilion for his shampoo and the Beauty Dew, you know, and for the—ah, female goods," dropping her voice, making a confidence of this for her customers. "Business is business, these days."

But to herself she admitted that even if this was only another of the stories that flew fast in windy country, she really knew nothing about Milton's friends beyond those around Frenchy's. There might be women, many in all those years since the twins died and Stevie took her side of the bed. She had always tried to put the idea aside while Milton was on the route, knowing how his bold dark eyes followed every switching skirt, even that sturdy Bohemian woman walking her sheep to Kansas. Oh, men really were animals, as Miss Farnsworth and even old Sarah herself had said, and Sarah knowing, with Hiram past sixty when he took up with that Tilly who scrubbed school floors.

But all that was lean comfort now, and so Lucinda tied a bandanna around her head and with the cat to smell out any mice, she cleaned the attic and then ripped down the window curtains and washed the rag rugs through the house, easing the disturbed mind by mortification of the flesh, as Grandmother Strathorn used to call it. Maybe they should have made friends here—have somebody to eat fried chicken with of a Sunday, as the Stones and the Stangers did when Milton was a boy, or go picnicking as they used to come to Lucinda's folks at cherry time. Her own friends were the Lucy Stoners and the church and prohibition people, with nothing but sour mouths for a drinking man, even an old soldier on one leg. And Milton's cronies, when they hunted him out at all, came to the back door as apologetic as a beery rag and bone man, never expecting to step into her clean kitchen.

So perhaps she should have known Milton would go to a place like Riverside for a friendly drink now and then, with its races and racing talk. Surely it was that and the little business he got there, not the women. But as she ironed the curtains she wondered, trying to lay it to the immoral times, with even good women reading about a harlot named Trilby. Perhaps places like Frenchy Brulley's ought to be encouraged—quiet, friendly places close to home, where a man could have a drink and a little talk and then go back to his family.

"You are backsliding in the work of the Lord!" the women of the church told her sternly, and Lucinda had no defense. Then, while she was still worrying her brow, a free-walking woman in a swirling shoulder cape of golden beaver, with a cloud of fragrance about her, came to have a dress made.

"You have been particularly recommended," she said, perhaps to explain how she happened to be in a rag-carpeted room.

From close up the woman's black eyes were sunken under their kohled lashes, her cheeks painted and her voice husky, but there was still beauty in her face and her bearing, and the material she brought was a lovely piece of imported wool, double-width, a soft, deep burgundy, with changeable green and gold corded silk for the shirred bodice and lapels of the basque—to be copied from a gown worn by a friend in a photograph. The photograph was from Paris, and the gown extreme, but turned out it looked fine on the woman, who had carriage and style; and when Lucinda stood off to admire, the blue cat jumping from the rocker and rubbing against her, she was given a check for the pay—a pension check like those she had seen for years. When she looked at it her hands began to tremble, the signature blurring before her eyes as ink runs in rain: Milton Stone.

Finally she had to look up. The woman was standing there in her new dress, the handsome beaver cape over her arm, showing she knew who this dressmaker was by the naked smile on her blasted face. So Lucinda compelled herself to go for her purse and make change, see the woman to the door as always. Then, from behind the fine spreading sea onion, she watched her get into the waiting carriage. Dolly Talbor, the cast-off, the morphine eater, one of the regular women of Riverside Pavilion.

When the carriage was gone Lucinda let herself slowly down into her little rocker, the check in her hand, the musky, foreign perfume heavy in the room about her.

Toward midnight Milton came in from the road, wet through by the sleeting river storm, with a bad chest and a chill. Lucinda was still up, numb and cold from long sitting with the stony knowledge of the woman at Riverside, although she had gone to an uplifting lecture with magic lantern slides of the Holy Land—and never heard a word of it. At Milton's stomping on the porch, she stirred herself, helped him undress and made a mustard plaster and hot camomile tea to sweat him. Then she carried the leg out to dry the leather behind the heater. A long time she stood with the pipe in her hands, finally she slammed it down so it fell with a clatter of iron through the silent house. It was not the loss of the leg she was resenting tonight but the independence, the arrogance the iron pipe brought to the man who had been a quiet, reticent boy, a homekeeping—even with his little drinking trouble—a homekeeping husband on a crutch.

The next time she went over to Omaha she cashed the check with the woman's signature on the back, but even there the man at the window looked at her a long time, until she wished she had dropped it into the privy hole where such things belonged. On the way back home she thought of all the things against Milton: the leg he never wrote her about, his family's foolish showoff ways, the drinking, the exaggerated stories, his political arguings, and now the woman—piling up like the stone wall that grew below the orchard at home as the rocky ground was cleared, until finally it toppled on the chicken coop below.

In her kitchen she washed her hair with a root from the yucca box in the cellar and pinched color into her cheeks, but still the aging reflection in her hand mirror was a grieving thing, and angered her that it should be so, for she was not in the wrong.

But Milton had other things beside the woman on his mind this winter. Since early fall he talked about a man named Coxey in Ohio with a scheme to relieve unemployment through good roads and other civic improvements to be paid for by paper currency—make work for the jobless, put money in circulation, give the country some badly needed roads. The newspapers called him a crackbrain.

"Godamighty, nobody who ever lived in Iowa can honestly call a man with a good road idea a crackbrain," Milton roared, remembering that soon the little frost in the ground would be lifting; then even one rain would turn the state into a mudhole, and surely the rains must come.

"Any man with a new idea's a crackbrain until he begins to threaten somebody's special privilege or profit, then he's a dangerous revolutionary," Ike Ellers said as he stuffed away a tin of Milton's clover blossom salve for his baby's eczema. "Coxey's got a hundred thousand men ready to start to Washington—coming from's far as Oregon, I hear."

After Easter, old Charley Powell stopped in at Council Bluffs on his way back to Nebraska. He looked in amazement at the thick-barreled man Milton had become, at the expansiveness, his arrogant carriage, his handsome head, his graying beard pushing out. ". . . Seeing you I sure can understand those tall tales I been hearing about the tom-walking medicine man. Maybe that comet a while back really was a rock you batted off that iron leg, or you spinning yourself clear off the ground, with your pipe scattering sparks behind. . . ."

"Oh, those horrid, vulgar stories," Lucinda scolded over her sewing, Milton grinning sheepishly at the doctor, tilting his chair back and easing his buttons, ready for a good evening.

Old Charley had been East to take a look at Coxey for himself. No telling from the papers. Turned out he was a quiet, self-made little business man with a big idea, but he picked up freaks like a sheep does burs in a brush patch. That Browne, for instance, with his whiskers cut like the Jesus pictures, and rigged out in a Wild West cowboy outfit, claiming he and Coxey together are the reincarnated Christ.

"Browne's a persuasive speaker," the doctor admitted. "He'd be a hotter'n a frying pan handle with a medicine wagon. Made such a stir at the labor meetings at Chicago the worried authorities ran him out of town."

"They probably worry easy," Milton said, pounding his pipe against his iron leg.

Well, they were only hired hands too. Anyway, he watched Coxey's petition in boots get off for Washington Easter morning, with flags and fanfare and flurries of snow. Around three hundred men marching, and as many more sightseers and reporters, only they had carriages, with storm robes over their knees.

Milton stroked the cat on his lap, the blue lights popping in the shadow. "You were planning to go along?" he asked slowly.

The old doctor hesitated a little. "Yes," he finally admitted, "If things looked all right. By God, Milt, a man can't just sit on his hunkers and let people starve. . . ."

Lucinda raised her eyes from the careful snip of her buttonhole scissors. "What you think will come of it all, Doctor—all this trouble-making?"

"Probably a few Pops get elected to Congress, to be out-jockeyed, or sell out for an invitation for their wives to some big bug's shindig. It's like giving the baby a bacon rind on a string," he said with a youthful bitterness that belied his lined old face, the hair standing up in a handsome cloud fine and white as linen lint. Still, Coxey might accomplish something if he could keep the lunatic fringe out, like those coming from the west coast seem to be doing, although the railroads had them stranded in a Texas desert just the same. Left them setting there on a dry siding with nothing but dust and rattlesnakes; no water, but a good view of the fancy private cars of the monopolists roaring past.

"What could the tramps—the men, expect—talking about the government taking the railroads over," Lucinda protested.

"Lots of others talk that way—all the Populists, millions of them, including that bright young lawyer, Bryan, over in Nebraska; and a lot of mighty smart women."

"Besides, the men didn't pay their fares," Lucinda finished stubbornly, drawing the knot of her thread hard between her fingertips. "Their place is at home with their families."

Milton scraped his leg on the floor, pushing the cat from his lap so violently she fled to the darkness of the kitchen, but he made no reply. The doctor looked up at the faded satin rose picture, one embroidered by every Farnsworth girl, and held his tongue too. No use throwing it up to her that women never saw any good in their husband's causes, whether it was Mary Todd's man or a one-legged medicine peddler on the Missouri, the cause the Secesh or the monopolies. Not unless they were only sixteen or so, and still certain of their loveliness. No use, either, telling Lucinda that men like Bob Mitchell were walking beside Coxey these days—Bobby, son of the old Mrs. Mitchell who claimed relationship to Grant and the Longworths, and owned a mansion on the Cincinnati hills all her life. Yes, hard times were biting high up on the leg nowadays.

It wasn't until Charley Powell asked Lucinda about the baby she carried out of his office twenty-seven years ago that the room was easy again. Milton reached for his tobacco, the cat came back, and Lucinda brought out a picture of the family: Helga, a round-faced, healthy-looking young woman, two children at her knee, a sleepy little one on her lap, and Stevie standing as unbending as a cannon tamper beside her.

"He could pass for yours anywhere," Charley Powell said. "That fine head of hair."

"Oh, it was never hard to pretend," Lucinda agreed, and so the old doctor knew that Milton had guarded the boy's parentage well, for all his loose, boozy tongue. . . . If man in the mass could learn to act with the dispatch, the generosity and courage he could muster individually there would be no hunger marchers stranded in deserts or sleeping on the cold ground tonight, no man with an iron pipe for a leg lost in a war.

Milton had barely reached the south territory when he came hurrying back, driving most of the night by lantern through the chilly rain. Kelly's California Army of Industrials, as they called themselves, had reached Council Bluffs on the way to Washington. There was great excitement in the region, the militia called out as though they were criminals, or a foreign invasion.

Lucinda took one look at Milton's purpled face and knew that he had been tipping the jug in the wagon, so with a thin mouth she set out his belated breakfast and laid his mail at his hand. There was an unaccustomed letter from Hiram. Dakota had burned out two years hand-running, so he trampoosed back to Cincinnati. It meant a squatter's shack on the river bottoms, but there was always fishing and he wouldn't be eating off Stevie's family. The marchers from the southwest desert had come through—a quiet, mannerly lot of laborers, small business men, with a sprinkling of farmers and old soldiers. A bald-headed old man, Andy Burke, said he knew Milton back in Company G at Atlanta, fought with the Americans helping the Russians in the Crimea before that, for the Czar who turned out a Lincoln man later and sent his navy over to keep England from joining the South. Andy was as ragged, footsore and hungry as the rest, and anxious about his family too. Then up to Mount Sterling the railroads got the militia out with Gatling guns —maybe practicing up for the labor troubles this summer, with miners and railroaders having more wage cuts coming.

". . . Getting ready to kill the sheep they been shearing. In Cincinnati, Labor and the Pops hustled grub for the marchers and if Sarah had been with us she'd been in it with both feet," old Hiram wrote, remembering only the young Sarah, back before the war, and the war contracts.

So Milton put the tired team back to the wagon and drove off to Chautauqua Park to see the Kellyites; Lucinda as always looking after him to see if he turned toward that woman across the river. He found camp broken, a long column of weary men moving out, wet and muddy from the nights in the sleet, their feet splashing through puddles that would be muck before the mile-long file passed. But they stepped briskly under the gray sky, their flags and banners flying, with Kelly riding in the lead on a fine black horse that Milton had often seen around the Bluffs. It beat any bull alligator story a man could think up—thousands coming together like this all over the country, so Milton turned his wagon over to a man with a swollen foot and fell in beside the marchers, swinging his pipe leg high.

But such a fine sight had to be shared, and so he got his team and whipped them back to the little house at the Bluffs, hurried Lucinda into a coat and boosted her into the seat before she could get her thimble off. And when they reached the top of the rise where the trees fell away before them, he pointed his whip and there below was the long line of men winding out across the spring lowlands toward the East.

"There it is, Lucie," he cried, using the old name for the first time since the day the twins died, "there's the greatest spontaneous movement of Americans since the Revolution!"

But Lucinda saw only a ragged line of men plodding through Iowa mud. "Oh, Milton, not those tramps! Why, they ought to have their britches taken down!" she said, before she could stop her tongue.

Slowly Milton Stone turned to this wife of twenty-eight years, his eyes squinted and red from the road and the wagon jug. Lifting his empty hand he swung it out and brought the back of it flat across her mouth. Lucinda gasped out a little cry, her palm to her lips as she shrank back to the corner of the seat, shaking in silent, broken sobs.

Milton, his face pale with Tolley anger under his bearding, turned

* 131 *

his team back and gave her no more notice than he would to a bundle of willow sticks that he was dumping off at home for the hogpen fence. So he left her standing in the yard, helpless, hopeless, her hand to her bruised face, the german silver thimble still on her finger.

That night Milton sat at his fire overlooking the camp of the Kellyites, orderly as a Sherman bivouac, the fires fine in the brightening moon of evening. It was a great camp, two thousand men at least, now that the Army from Reno had come today, and many local recruits. They had made nine miles and still had time for prayers and hymns as the setting sun broke through.

A few old soldiers gathered at Milton's fire, begging cough drops for the camp, looking through his newspapers, the Free Silver *Broad Axe* and the *Wealthmaker* of the Populists. But mostly they bragged about their trip from California, as though it were a battle march, except that Kelly was a stricter commander, tolerating no tramps among them, and no drinking atall, the men saying it uneasily before the red-faced medicine man stinking of Missouri corn, their eyes wandering hopefully to the wagon.

But Milton was too lost in enthusiasm to notice. "I hear you been having trouble here. . . ."

"Not with the people. They always come around fine soon's they find out we ain't the bums and rascals the papers make out, some driving in miles to shake Kelly's hand. But the railroads here, they rushed the Governor up from Des Moines by special to keep us out; only the good old U. P. had us across their bridge by then, and setting around fires from old ties they give us. So the militia's called out and we're marched off like jailbirds through the stormin' to Chautauqua Park and then moved on to the amphitheater that the owner and the sheriff, too, means for us to have because it's turned sleetin' and snow. But the militia gets there first and the CO promises us lead in the guts if we come close, so we builds us a few fires, best we can in the weather. There's talk that the railroad lawyer wanted us loaded on a train and a wild engine sent into us— kill an' cripple us, teach us a lesson."

"Why—the overbearing bastard!—and Doc Dunn, that I'm peddling for, owning a lot of stock in the outfit!"

"Yeh, well—" a gray-haired old soldier in the muddy blue uniform said wearily, "—at least he don't pretend to be a servant of the people, like some. But there's always good folks, and so they holds big protest rallies until the authorities offers to pay our fare to Chicago, only the railroad wouldn't even give us squattin' room on their rollin' stock. So this morning we has to hit the road—health menace, an' we stunk bad as a military camp, with the open thunder holes an' all."

He was interrupted by a commotion over at the camp, a messenger galloping in to say a great demonstration of Omahans at the Bluffs had ended in the capture of a railroad engine and some cars and were headed this way, even women helping to repair the tracks as fast as the company men tore them up. Milton hurried over as the headlight came burning out of the west, the whistle sharp and clear in the chill air as it used to sound between the Ohio river hills. The camp cheered; threw the night's wood on the fires and sang songs—religious and marching songs—even "After the Ball." But they wished they had a little of that heat before morning, for there weren't cars enough, and Kelly wouldn't take a stolen train. He sent those sick from the wet April nights back, and when the militia was called again next day, the Industrials were already moving into the morning sun, beginning what turned into a triumphal march through the greening Iowa countryside, with farmers coming for miles, some with brass bands and wagons loaded with butter and eggs and ham and baskets of new bread, while the women brought extra overalls, wash tubs and lye soap and spread the army's washing on the new grass to dry. The Kellyites made up a glee club and a baseball team to play local nines and the vaudeville troopers got up shows. Milton fiddled a little too, and did a peg-legged dance, and ended up by sticking a polished iron cap over the end of the pipe and whirling around on a piece of board until his coattails flew out wide, his gray beard making a blur in the firelight while the crowd whooped and the local recruits yelled, "Hey! We don't want us no flowing well here!"

With the Populists, the labor representatives and the mayor of the Bluffs making arrangements, the movement grew very fast and jealousy grew with it. Then one evening a troop of young people, mostly girls, came parading into the camps, filling the night with singing and high-voiced, inspirational speeches. A priest Milton knew got up and promised the army a hundred-fifty wagons, and the Woodmen some more, to cheering and more songs. It was a fine evening, but it ended in trouble between Kelly and one of the would-be leaders over a woman and liquor. Milton didn't see it; he had left early by request, jug and all, giving two of the singing girls a ride to their home. The sisters squeezed themselves into the seat beside him, pointing out the way in the fading moonlight, the shy one asking softly if he was the man with the sweet-smelling water in pretty bottles.

"Aiming to bait you a trap for a beau?" the medicine man laughed, the older sister scoffing, "She couldn't get her none; she's too all-foolish."

To the middle-aged cripple with the warmth of corn under his belt this seemed powerful funny and he laughed aloud and slapped his thigh. "No beau?—why, you're pretty as a new-feathered duckling."

"Ducklings is foolish *as* foolish," the sister said contemptuously.

So Milton admitted that he had a little sweet-smelling water, if she meant cologne, but mostly his wagon was full of bitter medicines and stinking stuff like itch ointment.

"I'll get pa to buy me some a that cologne in the morning," the older girl said confidently as she showed Milton the woodlot where he might camp, and maybe their ma would have a few flapjacks for him at breakfast time.

With the horses picketed, Milton built up a fire and lifted the gallon jug of corn several times more to help him forget the chill and the dissension in the movement that had looked so promising just a few days back. It seemed man could work together smooth as axle grease so long as there was nothing to grab; no money, no hurrahing.

As the fire burned down a warm comfort spread through Milton and then suddenly the foolish one of the girls was squatting beside the coals, saying nothing, her dark eyes not moving from Milton's loosened, watching face, her lips shining wet in the fire glow. And as the light dimmed she leaned toward the man, the red of the fire paling on her throat where her dress fell open. She was saying something softly, so softly she had to repeat it for him.

"The sweet-smelling water—you got it in the wagon?"

The next day it all seemed like one of those confused, terrifying dreams of morphine and pain, back when every morning meant a new facing of the empty sheet where a leg should be. But there in the Iowa mud were the barefoot tracks of a girl, and when Milton went to the wagon two bottles of the cologne were gone, the other things scattered to a williwaw as by a drunken, impatient man searching. So without making even a cup of coffee for his aching head, he drove homeward as far as the horses could go, and all the next day, too, trapped between the thought of what happened in the night woodlot and Lucinda with her mouth smashed against her teeth. But when he reached home she said nothing, a little quieter, maybe, the bruise almost gone. He made a short trip or two out west, but the rain hadn't reached that far, and so the bare earth smoked behind his wheels, the customers looking at him from wind-bittered faces. By God, they wished he could bring the cloud-busts the newspaper stories told about. Better to drown out like a gopher in a hole than starve to death.

He was jumpy himself, unable to get away from his thoughts, not even when Coxey's army was driven from the capitol grounds and Coxey himself arrested for walking on the grass. Or the strikes got violent. The Pullman troubles had spread to the railroads; 750,000 men out, some said, and Cleveland ordering the army out against them in Chicago, breaking the strike with the bayonet, while overhead hung the black smoke of the burning railroad yards, the fire set, it was said, by the company men themselves.

Then one hot, storm-darkened forenoon, a man swung his lumber wagon in before Milton's house and came stalking up the walk with a plow whip in his hand, the long lash caught up. He was tall and workstooped, a scowling on his gaunt, stubbled face, and anger in the set of his cowhides, while behind him, shrinking and frightened, stumbled a pale-cheeked girl not over fifteen, her blue calico dress faded, her brown hair in straggly braids. And when Milton came backing out of his wagon that he was packing for a trip north, pipe leg first, the girl began to sob.

The man stopped at the porch, pushed his sweaty old hat back and spit. "So you're the one-legged son of a bitch what's been fuglin' my girl!" he said, bawling it out like a hog caller for all the street to hear. Milton could only look in misery over toward the trellised porch where Lucinda had risen, letting the sewing slide from her lap into a heap.

"Now she's knocked up, and, by cripes, I'm here to pay you out," pushing his ragged sleeve up from the sunburnt arm, jerking himself free from the girl's vague, hopeless hands as he popped the whip.

"Oh, you wicked man!—talking so before a little girl!" Lucinda cried out in angry protest.

But the look on Milton's face settled it. A moment she stood, her eyes down, steadying herself; then she spoke again. "Come inside," she commanded, leading the way from the sight of the neighbors. In the doorway the man balked. "I come to get satisfaction, not to chaw the fat!" he roared out, standing stiff and angry before his barefoot daughter. Frightened, yet, she looked curiously around him into the room, and toward Milton over near the wall, his face pale above the bearding, awkward, hunched together, even the cat staying away.

". . . Satisfaction!" the man still roared.

Now suddenly, Lucinda was a Farnsworth girl in a domestic crisis. "Come in and lower your voice, sir!" she ordered. "Satisfaction, you say! What good would it do you to pound a cripple, even if you could! You would just get your teeth knocked down your throat with that iron leg," Lucinda said, seating herself in the rocker beside the stand with her wedding picture, rocking energetically. "The girl would still be in trouble, you know."

"Yeh, from a goddamn fark of a old soldier, a dirty old crip goin' 'round fuglin' little girls!" still at the top of his voice. "An' all he give her was some smellin'-water she dropped and busted."

That started the girl into a soft, desolate sobbing. "He said I was pretty—" she moaned, "—pretty as a new-feathered ducklin'."

All Milton could do was move his pipe leg awkwardly. What a fool's road a man could set himself upon; what a plagued, criminal, goddamn fool's road he had taken, trying to run away from a loss that was within him, within them all.

But Lucinda was pushing on: "So it's what he gave her that you resent?" she demanded, her voice as cold as to the loafers from Brulley's, "Well—what do you think the girl should have, besides the cologne?"

At first the man threw his head up like an angered animal, a scrub bull on a hillside, guarding his heifers, but in the silence that Lucinda put on him, his calloused hand fumbled with the plow whip. "Well, Jesus Christ. . . .! At bottom she ought to have—" looking around the shabby room without too much hope, "—five hundred dollars."

Milton laughed to hear him, an angry laugh, bitter as quinine dust. If he owned five hundred dollars he might have gone on to the mines, not been caught in his mother's marrying plans, or else got to be a doctor, helping smuggle away other men's bastards now, not standing here like a house-wetting pup, having his own nose rubbed in it.

But with the business down to money, the father began a horse-trader's dicker. Clarie's marrying chances were spoiled, but with times so all-fired hard, even a couple hundred dollars and that Jersey cow he saw out back would help. Well, two hundred dollars and the calf to boot.

When Lucinda refused him an answer to that too, he pushed at his sleeve again, curling the lash of the plow whip on the rag carpeting. "By cripes, a hundred then, and rock bottom!" he yelled.

Finally, when he had agreed to fifty, Lucinda ran out the back way to the bank, leaving the three alone in the silent room, the blue cat still not coming to relieve them until the woman was back.

"Here it is," Lucinda said, a scattering of more gold pieces on her other palm. "I'll add another fifty if you'll sign a paper saying he had nothing to do with it."

"He did so!" the girl wailed, her bare feet disturbed on the carpeting. "He said I was pret-ty!"

With the money shining on her palm, Lucinda moved to show them out, and so the man came to the signing. When they were really gone, Milton went too, not coming back until dark, then sitting just inside the kitchen door, his graying head in his hands. Finally he went to his waiting supper but he didn't eat until Lucinda sat down opposite him and poured the coffee, holding out his cup.

At last Milton looked up, his face shamed. "There don't seem to be a Godamighty thing a man can say. . . ."

Setting the cup down carefully to steady herself, Lucinda answered him, holding back her knowing about Dolly Talbor and many other things, "I'm not laying blame on you, Milton," she said, "I want you to understand that. You never got much from anybody except an empty pants leg. I failed you too, even that day on the hill watching the marchers. It was a fine sight but meanly I wouldn't give you that much satisfaction. . . . I haven't even been a friend to you, Milton—and no wife at all. Too afraid of dying, I guess, just yellow, yellow as . . ." but she couldn't get herself to speak the only name that came to mind and so she finished without it. "Yellow as bile, and now it's too late."

But it wasn't, for young Marty was born to her the next spring, soon after George Shefton went to Washington to lobby for extension of soldier pensions on the strength of his three weeks' enlistment under Lew Wallace, the time young Milton and Johnny helped dig entrenchments. They had seen Yeller Weskit run bawling to the General when he heard a galloping in the night, "The raiders! The raiders!" Turned out it was only a man come to join up, his wife after him.

Some said the soldier lobby was a blind of the railroads or maybe just an excuse to get Shefton out of town after that scandal with the preacher's young bride. Just before he left he passed Lucinda coming from the grocery, moving heavily, slow. He turned in his red-wheeled buggy to look back at her, and then drove on.

But he had looked back, and that night Lucinda settled herself with her side pillows and lay awake to remember. There was no accounting for the foolishness of a woman, she told herself, but there was such sweetness in it.

By now Milton and his Populist cronies were finding out that Cleveland had called J. P. Morgan in to save the credit of the nation. At inauguration time the country was diving deeper into depression, more payrolls closing, dutiable imports shrinking so the revenues were seventy million dollars below last year, ninety-seven million lower than before the McKinley Tariff. Cleveland sided with the big financiers, stopped the purchase of silver and then watched them raid the Treasury of its gold until he had to buy sixty-two millions of it back from Morgan to save the country's credit, with J. P. getting a straight profit of four millions, some said, or five.

"Hell, it's nearer nine millions he made on the deal. . . ."

Milton, still around Frenchy's, but weaning on beer, admitted it looked bad. "Playing rings around the rosies with us, and charging us big interest and commissions every time 'round."

"But you got to save the credit of the nation," a Clevelander argued.

"Dems or GOP—saving the credit of the nation's all I been hearing since the day I come home on a crutch," Milton said angrily. "And old Morgan's probably doing the same thing off across the sea, taking over everything with his money there, stepping across national boundaries, beyond all laws. Outfits like him're cooking up trouble and revolution from Cuba to China, and hollering for guns to protect their holdings. Look at the agitation we been working on in Cuba and Central America for's long back's I can remember, and now that Hawaiian sugar revolution going. Only Cleveland's being anti-imperialistic keeps us from taking over right now, although our sailors've landed there long ago to protect sugar property—a long jump over a broad puddle."

"Hell," Ike Ellers comforted, "Maybe it'll be a boy to your house, and he'll grow up like Rockyfeller, the oil king. They tell me his pa was a pain oil peddler."

Then one evening the voice of a neighbor came from the darkness of the swinging doors, calling, "You're wanted to home, Milt!"

"Home?" Milton asked, up on his leg immediately. Lucinda had never shamed him by sending for him like the other women did, not even the time Stevie cut an artery with the ax. It must be something pretty bad, for her time was still two months off. . . .

But the little house was lit up bright as a wake, and the neighborhood baby catcher met him at the door, showing her broken teeth in a grin, and from behind her came the wet, steamy smell he knew. And suddenly Milton Stone was thankful that at least his iron leg did not get ropy at the knee.

Yet inside everything seemed all right, Lucinda looked paler, a little grayer than when he left a few hours ago, and tired, but she smiled as she lifted the blanket beside her, showing the red and wrinkled face of a baby tiny as a new-born pup, the puffed and swollen eyes shut in the same tight frown.

"Not over four pounds, Milton, and we used your remedy—snuff-sneezed him into the world, bawling loud as old Sarah."

It was all cloudy as a hospital dream, this sudden thing, and he had to put out a hand to the bed post. Lucinda saw his concern and pulled the blanket clear back. In the yellow lamplight the little head was bare and red as a bull pup's, the wrinkled little legs sticking out of the baggy diaper no bigger than a man's little finger, and as bony. He touched them cautiously and together the graying parents laughed out loud, for the little booger had kicked his father.

Now, suddenly, Milton's thick chest filled tight, his heart balling up as it used to against the pressure of his crutch. A son; he had a son, small and scrawny as a new-hatched crow bird, but he was strong and full of fight and whole—sound and whole, with two good legs, and before God and man he would keep him so.

BOOK TWO

—rub your neck with lard; in this
way you will slip between the
fingers of calumny.

CHORUS

1 — *The Promise*

The standpipe on the edge of the tableland rose dark and lonesome in the morning sun. Below the bluffs a train whistled in from the empty prairie, slowing for the little town of Sidney, with its tall galvanized grain elevators just coming out of the shadow. At the station a dozen German-Russians, squat, sturdy men in broad overalls, got off, their wives in headcloths behind them. Stretching, yawning as the sunlight hit them, they made a few words among themselves and started away past the long, dew-topped ricks of coal paralleling the tracks. They walked heavily, in single file, the women behind their men and a little to the side.

One more passenger got off, a soldier in khaki, with the lonesome look of a uniform in peacetime. There was the untidiness of a night in the chair-car about him, his eyes red from loss of sleep, his thin face soot-streaked because the washroom had run out of water. Only his curly black hair, close-cropped under the cap, and his rolled puttees were soldier neat.

Carrying his grip into the empty depot he found a place to shave and dust off a little and when he went out into the morning sun he looked taller, and better too, his face less tense, in spite of the brows like the soot of black-powder on the pale face—much better, almost handsome. Setting his cap over one ear he looked around for a lunchroom with soldierly directness. Before him the main street sloped gently through the little town, past a few straggling creek-bottom willows and off toward the ridge beyond, where an eagle circled slowly, very high, like a Heinie over the western front. A firm little wind came up, chilly for May, but probably not unusual on these high plains. Martin Stone had often heard his father tell about this country, where the antelope used to run curiously along the rises to look at his orange-colored medicine wagon, but that was 'way back, when Sidney was full of cowboys and the miners from the Black Hills. The old man's last route had been out here too,

* 143 *

but young Marty's mother wouldn't let the boy go along as Stevie used to, although it was safe, with good roads and the Model T's, and the mail-order houses that were putting the medicine wagon out of business—back when poison gas was only for horror stories in the Chicago *Ledger* and the Denver *Post,* not something that spread like fog through the shell-torn, wire-tangled forest called Argonne. But Martin Stone had managed to stand off all the dead-wagons so far and was out of the hospital, with the red strip on his sleeve and looking for a plate of ham and eggs, and a cup of Java.

On a stool, with his grip safe and comforting between his heavy shoes, his breakfast coming, he spread Nancy's last letter out on the counter, its neat blue ink getting a little smudged but the words unchanged. She was awfully glad to hear her Marty was feeling better, putting the word "awfully" into quotations to show she knew it was too slangy for a schoolteacher. She was glad, too, that he might be released by the hospital after a while. She had been afraid all along that he was really much worse than he was letting on because he didn't want her to worry. As for herself, she guessed she would stay out here this summer again, helping Mrs. Leite a little and resting. ". . . Unless a better offer comes along, ha! ha! Lovingly, Ever yours, Nancy."

Slowly he folded the letter, remembering her more as the little girl in yellow braids who pushed doll buggies past his house than after she grew up. It seemed so long now since they walked on the spring bluffs overlooking the Missouri and planned his returning, almost five years ago, and somehow not even the picture in his watch had helped him keep hold of her face. But he did remember she had a mighty fine pair of legs, and it sure would be good to get his hands on her again.

The air was warming, the smell of morning dew gone by the time the old mail car started up Sidney hill toward Albers, the little tableland post office near Nancy's boarding place. The climb was steep, and after much sputtering and boiling the engine made it; Milton at the edge of the old seat all the way. On top the driver grunted, took his foot off the slipping clutch and let the car jump into high as he twisted and yanked at a plug of tobacco with his teeth. And when the gravel was hitting the running boards like shrapnel, the empty cream cans in the back banging, and the dust boiling up from the loose grade behind the car, he spit, wiped his mustache and was ready to start the visiting.

"I don't think I got your name, soldier," he said, as forty years ago a stage driver on this road would have asked a Black Hiller: "What name you travelin' under?"

"Martin Stone."

"Stone, eh? Got folks around Albers?" he asked, looking curiously over the young man's face, his service stripes. The short turndown he got didn't stop his civilian running off the mouth. ". . . Hain't no work if that's what you're after."

But it wasn't, and so the man held out a little white liquor in a flask. "Cheyenne Moon," he called it. "Made up the road a piece, and cheap, with that new outfit cuttin' in. I could put you next to a little game, too. . . ."

When Martin shook his head the man settled down to his driving, but soon he was trying again, telling stories, Martin taking the chance to plan once more what he would say to Nancy and how she would look when she saw him. Maybe she would be washing her soft brown hair as teachers did Saturdays, or be off at the schoolhouse correcting papers where he could see her alone right at the start, maybe show her that little trick he got from Helene in a cowbarn overlooking the Meuse.

But the mail carrier wasn't the man to put up with a silent audience, and so Marty had to listen to the long story of the slip of paper that made everybody who read it turn pale and jump over a cliff or dive off a ship.

"Hell, that story's damn stale gut-wash!" the soldier said. "I got a dad who never bothered talking about papers blowing overboard in a wind. He made cyclones."

"Made cyclones? . . . Yeh, an' by God, I s'pose it was you what cut out the Kaiser's balls and dried 'em to shoot craps with," the driver grunted, sourly, unloading his mouthful of tobacco juice as he pulled the hand brake to stop at a circle of mail boxes mounted on an old buggy wheel. Martin just nodded, holding his hands together, making himself wait quietly, looking off over the tableland that dished up into the hazy distance, like a saucer and as empty, except for the many clusters of farm buildings. There were twenty, thirty of these in sight, and except for a few gullies, some narrow as trenches, most of the land was broken up, great strips and patches in the bright, fresh green of winter wheat and rye, or in the brown of new-listed corn, tractors and four-horse teams creeping in dust along the edges of the dark corduroying.

"I thought this was wheat country," the Iowa soldier said.

"Yeh, and pretty good money in it, till the government got out from under the pegged price and pushed it down cellar so the bankers could foreclose everything."

"The houses look mighty prosperous," Marty said, contrarily.

"Yeh, mebby they do till you gets up close. Then you see they's mostly just shells, never been finished inside, like the Tedrow place over south, and the Mecheks and them four Millses. Art never even got the steps put up—used a box to get in the house to the day the sheriff come with the padlock. But they was all flying high during the war, mortgaging the land for fancy prices for fancy machinery and stuff—trucks and combines and tractors to run night and day— and needin' 'em, too, with the labor shortage and the government hollerin' for wheat. They was all hot shots, havin' to have silk shirts and big cars and Delco lights, and them square cement block houses you see stickin' up all around—ten, twelve rooms for folks what'd lived in a two-room soddy for mebby twenty years. Mostly they got 'em done enough so they could set up an old heater over the register that they couldn't use because the war boom was busted before they got the furnace in."

"Things that tough 'way out here?"

"Tough? Where you been since the war, panhandlin' the uniform?" the mail carrier snorted. "I had to get to rock bottom to keep my mail contract, half the county biddin' agin me. Ain't makin' my gas, scarcely. —Yeh, things been tough couple years now, for them as works for a livin'."

At Albers post office Marty got out and paid his dollar fare among a lot of farm boys hanging around for the mail, gawking at this unexpected passenger.

"Lookit—a soldier!" the older ones called to each other. "He's a corporal, infantry, see them crossed guns," while the younger boys stared without comprehension. The house across the road was pointed out as the Leite place, another square box of gray cement like stone blocks. Leaving his grip with the talkative postmistress, ". . . Might's well take the mail to Miz Leite, seein's you're going anyhow," he accepted the roll of papers and catalogues. The place looked empty, but when he got near the bare, weedy yard a dog tore around a corner, barking, and a young woman with a baby on her arm came out on the un-railed porch to look, another young one hanging to her short skirt. When Marty saw her his heart began to pound and he started to run foolishly, his feet awkward as over a soft, new-shelled field, calling out, "Nancy! Hello, Nancy, honey! Oh, Nancy, Nancy!" his eyes blurring.

But as he got closer he sensed something strange about her—fat, and her hair bobbed off high as her ears, like an army post chippie. Still it was Nancy, and so surprised to see him she couldn't say anything until he was clear up on the porch. Then her face got very red and when he went to grab her, she pushed the baby between them.

"Why, Marty Stone, what a surprise!" she said, standing there holding the baby before her, not even offering him her hand, and as he looked at her, puffed out like a Frog featherbed, it seemed like more of the gas dreams, all the dope they gave him. But no; that was Nancy, and he felt himself getting roaring mad, like when he first saw some of the things the Heinies had done to people in occupied territory.

"You—you're——By God! Show me the bastard got you knocked up an' I'll cut his goddamn heart out!"

"You don't need to be insulting, Mr. Stone. I'm a respectable married woman."

"Married woman!" he repeated after her, "Mar——" Then suddenly he caved in. "Married."

"Yes," she admitted, looking down at Martin's dusty puttees, his awkward issue shoes. "And you can't blame me. The war has been over three years—three and a half years, and it seemed you weren't. . . ."

"Wasn't what?" he demanded. "What?"

"Well, you didn't come back and didn't come back—" putting the blame off on him. "And I wasn't getting any younger."

"How long did you wait?" the man insisted angrily, seeing that the baby in her arms looked like her, and even the great chunk of a kid hanging to her skirt. "How long?"

"Well, I—I waited a year," she said, her face turning even redder, "almost a whole year. . . ."

"You managed to wait a year, almost a year! Why, goddamn you! you were married long before the night I got my gassing—and you never thought enough of me to write and tell me. Instead you keeps calling yourself my Nancy, not letting me know anything!"

"I couldn't," she whimpered, like a frightened child, trying to defend herself that way, just as she always had done, even their last evening together, Martin remembered.

But he wasn't the easygoing kid who grew up across the street from her in Council Bluffs any more. "The hell you couldn't! But you could bed down with the first hanyak you come across! Well, who is he, this slackin' bastard you was so pants-wettin' ranny for?" And when she said, "Don't you dare insult me, Martin Stone! We were married by a preacher and Harold was exempted for the battle of bread," he pushed his cap back and spit into the yard.

"I be goddamned! Battle of bread! That's a hot one! And I bet you got him tied up preacher-solid before you come across with anything, not unless he was willing to spend years warming you up, like I done! But what I want to know is, what're you gettin' out of it?"

"We own this place and I have a hired girl to help with the work and the laundry," she said, a little proud.

"A house and a hired girl to wash the kids' dirty pants. That's what outbid me!" He laughed, the taste of it bitter as the smut dust from a battle-shelled rye field. "Well, you got your price, and I hope that slacker bastard keeps you knocked up till your tongue hangs out."

So he left, the young woman standing at the door of the house built of cement blocks molded to look like gray stone. And when the ragged little dog came running after, to smell his heels in friendliness, Martin whirled and kicked him in the belly with the expertness of an infantryman taking out a Heinie. In sudden exultation he ran after the dog, kicking him again and again, until he lay a helpless and broken lump of hide and bone while Nancy screamed her anger from the porch.

Then shaking, and suddenly afraid, Martin Stone ran for the mail car. But it was gone, and so he set out toward town afoot, the bundle of papers and catalogues still under his arm, his grip forgotten, too. Seeing him go the postmistress came out and with cupped hand called to him and finally sent a boy with a car to get the Leite mail back. "What's eatin' you, soldier?" the boy complained when no honking stopped the man and he had to cut in ahead. "Pa figgers all you fellers from war's a little bugs."

But when he saw the man's face he dumped the grip to the ground and, reaching for the mail, turned on the highway and drove off in a volley of backfiring.

The road stretched across the tableland, whitish and empty except for a farmer's wife or two starting early to her Saturday afternoon trading, a horsebacker driving a cow and calf along a section line, or a tumbleweed turning over a few times, slowly. Here and there a bobolink soared up singing or the metallic sweetness of a wild plum thicket bloom rose from some gulley. But the soldier was alone on the treeless plain under the far wind-streaked sky, and feeling nothing except that his clumsy shoe seemed to be striking something, something soft and yielding, like the helpless side of a little dog.

He didn't notice when two cars roared, rocking, past him, boozehounds chasing a bootlegger, or a truckload of picnickers waved. Finally an old man in a brass-banded Model T came out of a side road, peered anxiously right and left over his beard, and then killed his engine in the middle of the highway right before the dusty, plodding soldier.

"Want a ride, son?—Hey, want a ride?—You kin do the drivin'," he called in a high, excited voice. When he got Marty under the wheel the old man relaxed into visiting. He supposed a boy who'd dig out a uniform nowadays must be going to a land opening—Wyoming, maybe, or Montana. "That's how my nephew what's been driving my Lizzie got the place up above Torrington— pretty good land, too. Soldiers with discharge papers gettin' preference."

Martin's hand was reaching out automatically, fiddling with the carburetor set-screw, getting the sputtering engine to pick up, smooth out. It pleased him that he could still do it, after five years, and so he finally spoke.

"Yeh, I guess a piece of free land wouldn't go bad. . . ."

"No, and with the service time off and all, it don't take long until you can prove up on it and get a little chunk of money from some cow outfit."

"That so? Is there land a man can take up any time?"

"Guess so. Ask Judge Miller, down in Sidney. He's got all the literature. Great for working with vets, the judge is. Lost his boy, you know. Sunk by a sub."

So the first westbound local out of Sidney carried Marty. He was sitting among a lot of the German-Russians and Mexicans getting off here and there for the beetfields, and as stiff and numb on the old green plush seat as though he were in a shell hole, tied down by days of crossfire. It wasn't until a train butcher came through with a tray of candy and gum that Marty remembered he had had no dinner, nothing since the ham and eggs right after sunup. He had been holding himself back on what happened today, as he used to hold back his breath when it tore him like a crosscut saw in a knot. But with the first bite of the chocolate bar, the stoniness in him broke, and with tears running down his sun-reddened face he stumbled away to hide himself in the washroom.

And when he finally came out he slipped into the first empty seat, not seeing the girl beside him. He hunched forward, his hands dropped to his knees, not noticing the heat of the afternoon car, the soot or the talk about the long ricks of coal along the tracks at the stations. "Getting ready to last out the mine strikes this summer," the men in the seat ahead told each other. "And the railroad shop men are going out too, got a twenty-six million dollar wage cut ordered against them."

Once the young soldier did glance out past the weed-grown Farmers' Union elevator. But beyond the right-of-way was a gray field turning back to grass, and in its center another of those cement block houses with empty window holes. Then he remembered Nancy's letter, and ripping it from his pocket he tore the sheet to bits, and then the picture from the back of his watch, a laughing, taunting face, too, and reaching over to the window he struggled against its stubbornness. Then he flung out the handful of scraps to swirl and flutter down the grade like disconsolate snowflakes on the wind.

Vaguely he noticed he had been leaning over a girl, even pushing her back against the worn plush seat, and he mumbled an excuse.

"Are things that bad. . . .?" she inquired softly, and he jerked his head in acknowledgment, looking at his wrists sticking out of the thick khaki blouse that had been sweating him all day. So he took it off and she folded it for him, neatly and handily, smoothing it over the seat, the wound stripe showing. "I had a soldier friend . . ." she said.

At first Martin held himself silent but the girl felt so friendly beside him, and a stranger, calling for no pretense, no more big talk than any bedpan rassler, that he started to tell her about the Nancy who didn't wait. ". . . After going together for years, letting me think all the while she was waiting, and today I find out she's throwed me over for one a them cement block houses and a hired girl to wash the kids' dirty pants."

The girl murmured, not saying that she was the oldest of the family and knew about diapers. Propping both elbows on his knees, his hands hiding his face, the soldier talked a little, as though to himself, and then still more.

After five years in the army coming home wasn't like he'd expected—more like walking into a land mine. First off his father had done a complete backdown from everything he used to preach. . . . The old man wasn't called Iron Leg for nothing, with as many stories told about him as about Mike Fink. Back in the Nineties he had tried to join Kelly's army of unemployed in their march to Coxey in Washington, and him with an iron pipe for a leg in place of the one he lost in the Civil War. "I'd lay in the hospital and think about him, a right guy, and now, night before last, he sets there talking about shooting the striking miners down for trying to hold onto a living wage, favors hiring thugs and gunmen against them, and he's the man who'd been voting with the Pops and talking about sloughing out the teeth of every Pinkerton man with his pipe leg."

"Old Artie—that's our dad—still believes like your father did," the girl said. "Mother calls it throwing his vote away."

"To hear my dad, you'd think he was an old moneybags throwing in with old J. P. Morgan himself, instead of a poor tom-walking old soldier living off his pension in that crumby dump of a room over in the Bluffs, with nothing left except his old fiddle sack hanging to a nail. He was making a little on the side as night watchman until a vet a third his age was glad to take the job for the five dollars a week, adding it to the hashing job his wife's trying to hang onto."

"M-m, that's too bad."

"Looks like we been running into rough terrain. I couldn't get even a chance at my old job braking a freight for the railroad; something I could swing because it wasn't heavy work like the section, and got me outdoors for my gassed lungs. But they wouldn't take my name, not even for trackwalking at greaser pay. My dad blames it on foreign agitators, the Reds and IWW's, while he pounds his cob pipe against that leg the way that used to tickle me to stitches, back in my crawling days, him telling great bull alligator stories. Now, after me in the war all this time, and him fighting for free trade most of his life, he's against the League of Nations, calls Wilson a crazy old schooldad who's pushed us into war. He's all for high tariff and getting back to normalcy, cutting down on taxes on excess profits and incomes. That means more hard times for us and more money for the big bugs to buy up Congress. And him without two nickels to rub together."

So they had gone at it, the strangers the two had become, until the son picked up his grip, slammed the door and caught the westbound train. Maybe he should have remembered his father was old and alone, took him out where there was a little home brew and women, but a man gets fed up on all that talk in the newspapers, shut away in a hospital, and keeps thinking that the home folks won't be sucked in.

"I guess they have been, though, a lot of them," the girl said slowly.

It sure looked that way. Well, he came straight out to surprise Nancy, making it a couple days earlier than even he had planned.

"Didn't you let her know you were coming?" the girl wanted to ask, but she could see he hadn't, from his stricken face. He had been so sure.

After a while he began talking again, low, desperate, as against his own thoughts, to keep them out. It wasn't that he couldn't have left the hospital long ago; he was really more on bedpan detail than patient the last year, with the help cut down, but he wouldn't marry Nancy until he was well. His mother spent her life looking after a man who came home to her a war cripple; working, trying to keep him sober and out of trouble while she took in sewing to put pants on her son's backside until he was able to swing a spike maul on the section and she could take time off to die.

"Oh, how sad!"

Yes. Well, her kind was gone. He had been a damn fool about one woman, wanted to have everything planned up to the fuse for her. When he couldn't get a job he arranged to go to his brother Steve, his wife and kids gone, and needing a young couple to run his little ranch up in the Black Hills country—even if the man had to be slow at first and didn't know much about stock or cropping. He could learn, and with his compensation and Nancy's Liberty Bonds, they'd have a place of their own someday; until then they'd have a hired girl if Nancy wanted to go on teaching. She liked the country —spending all her summer vacations out. Everything looked smooth as a Heinie camouflage; steam up and highballing west.

"God, what a fool a man can be!" he said, moving his shoes back so he wouldn't see them. A goddamn fool.

Because the girl couldn't make the soldier more miserable by sympathy, she looked away to the optimistic greening of spring along the hills of Wyoming. Yes, things were bad everywhere. Her own part-time job down in Lincoln had blown up—just ceased to be. "'A minor retrenchment is indicated, Miss Turner,' my boss told me. 'Nothing that isn't normal, you understand, just a temporary retrenchment.' That was last fall. The folks couldn't help me, not with prices down and the prairie fire burning their range in the best war boom days."

So she had dropped her university studies and hunted a job. But there were so many soldiers glad to take anything, and needing it too, with six thousand vets' families on Red Cross in Boston alone, she heard. So she was going home. She liked Wyoming, but every horsebacker on the trail would remind her of Dick, the man who wasn't coming back from France. She said it with her voice quiet, laying her palm over the little diamond on her finger, her face pale to whiteness. It wasn't that she would be sponging on the folks. With Joey missing off in Russia and young Artie dead of the flu, there was room for a little free help around the cattle and the haying. For fun there was always an old saddle she could repair, and an extra range horse loose. But Dick wouldn't be there, and besides her two sisters had the bedroom; a cot in it would spoil the effect of the bedroom suite Marilyn got from Sears Roebuck with her cream money.

"Maybe your sisters'll tear out and get married," Marty said, telling himself that was what women wanted—the house and the hired girl to wash the kids' pants and any damn man to foot the bill, first come, first handiest.

"Marilyn's been going steady for a couple of years but Ben's got no place either and they'll probably move in at home."

"Then what'll you and your sister do?"

"Probably build on a sod lean-to or something. Anyway, there'll be no more living on stale cinnamon rolls for weeks."

So Marty asked about sod lean-tos and houses and about crops and stock and what a man could hope to make in the way of a living on a homestead.

"You aren't planning to go dry-landing?" the girl looked at him curiously, and for the first time Marty noticed how large her brown-flecked gray eyes were in her thin, colorless face, her dress a soft blue not too much like a *poilu* uniform. "Yes," he admitted. "I thought I might try a shot at homesteading. Ain't much else left."

The girl considered the weary, dusty soldier. "You look a little delicate and soft for it. Homesteading's a hard life."

"Too hard for other people?" he demanded angrily.

"Oh, I didn't mean that, only that my folks knew the country, used to it. Mostly nowadays its jobless city folks that come blowing in on the hard-time winds. Been thick the last couple years, I guess, with all the vets, and things so bad in the East."

"I'll get stronger," Marty said, bringing himself back into the talk. "The docs say I got to be out in the open, best where it's sunny and dry."

"That's Wyoming, right out of the booster's mouth."

"Yes, but I got a mouth too—and it's long on chow."

"Oh, you learn to manage about eating," the girl said, without seeming to notice that she had shifted sides, jumped the fence like any breachy heifer. "You don't need to make much money for that out here."

But Martin Stone didn't seem to be listening, his eyes looking past the girl to the track workers waiting out the train at the edge of the cinders, with shovels, bars and spike mauls ready. Suddenly something ran through him—recognition, the recollection of strong young joy in the swing of the big hammer, steady and slow as the beat of a heart on the iron.

Gripping a hand on the arm of the seat he stared out to the running sagebrush swells. Not a house anywhere, only a wedge of gray sheep on a slope, and then a sheep wagon just off the right-of-way, and a woman behind it, looking after the train, waving, at home here. The girl beside him was like that; friendly, comfortable, too, with no bitching, Nancy ways—always working a man up, any man that came along.

So Martin Stone started to ask a question of a strange woman; one that should have been easy, with him a railroader, a soldier— but this was a little different from a lay. "We—" he said slowly, "—we neither one of us got much left out of the war, me a few dollars, you knowing how to run a place here. . . . Would you, could you think about us throwing in together?"

"Throwing in together?" the girl asked in astonishment, looking squarely at the man to see what he was meaning to say.

"I wouldn't ever step out on you," he said, making the one promise he could still imagine that a woman might like. "I done my share of stepping."

"I wasn't thinking about that," the girl said, considering him with the eyes of a stockman's daughter, the eldest daughter of a poor man's family. There was something she didn't like about the soldier's mouth—a spoiled, petulant droop, like her own brother Joe's. Probably the eldest son, pampered by an overfond mother too, with an inclination to self-pity, and no telling how aggravated by the war and the homecoming, and too old to have it spanked out of him now. He wasn't a tall man, not as they grew in Wyoming, but the sweep of his cheekbones, the high, straight nose, the dark hair curling a little, the clean wrists, the straight, strong bones were good. The damage of the gassing she couldn't gauge but she knew the high, dry air of Wyoming might do much for scarred lungs if the softness of the man's lips didn't deny him the serenity and patience. A lot of wives put up with mother-spoiled husbands. Old Grandma Corley used to say every woman ought to have at least eight children as fast as peas shelling out, and the first boy thrown in the crick so she wouldn't make a fool of herself over him and a whining fool of him. But it would be fine to have eight children, eight straight-legged boys and girls with maybe a little drake tail curling to their hair as Dick could have given them; Dick, with the dimple in his sunburnt chin, the eyes that had to come back from the far horizon when he kissed her—big, few-spoken, gentle-handed Dick, to be shot down.

Over four years ago—four dead years.

But the soldier beside her was getting up, gathering his blouse into his arms, his face sullen and angry. So she brought herself back, smiled contritely into his eyes and saw them soften quickly under her friendliness, her full attention, until he had to say something, apologizing sheepishly. But she stopped him.

"Shake," she said, holding out her long, lean hand. "That means it's a bargain, with a chance apiece to renege after you and the Turners size each other up."

So it happened that for the second time that day Martin Stone got off at a little western station with wedding plans in his head. This time it was Stover, Wyoming, and the girl, Penny Turner, was beside him, taking him up the dimly lighted street with a few cars parked along the center to hunt up old Artie. They found him still talking politics at the harness shop and forgetting he was supposed to meet the train. But when he saw them come down the aisle between the saddles and hames and fly nets, he drew up tall in his overalls and stepped forward to shake his daughter's hand warmly, complaining at her thinness. "Them flipper-flappers all got to look thin as fishpoles." Then he looked at the young soldier, bringing out his steel-rimmed glasses for it when he noticed the girl's trouble with the introduction.

"Well, son, we wasn't knowing about your coming; Penny here's a little closemouthed, but you're shore range welcome."

At this the girl looked to Martin easily. She had known how it would be with old Artie, and so they all went to the battered, cut-down car and rode, three in the seat, into the starry Wyoming night, the open wind in their hair, hunger empty in their stomachs. It was different from Martin's last night in the open, almost four years ago, with gaunt belly too, but from a seven-day push through mud and snow, with no time to notice what the stars were like, if there had been any in the battle-molten sky.

At the Turner house it was more difficult, a phonograph blaring "Dardanella" under the bright light of a sizzling gasoline lamp, two girls in their teens looking on, and Ma Liz's shrewd eyes sizing up the situation.

"Another poor house struck up, the neighbors'll be sayin'!" she complained as she wiped a strong hand on her apron and held it out to the soldier, while the two sisters giggled and old Artie shifted his tobacco and prepared to take the sting out of his wife's remark.

"Don't be letting Ma Liz throw you into a scare. You'll make out all right with Penny here to help you. She's like her ma at managing, and Ma Liz's kept our backsides covered come hell or Mormon crickets. Her tongue's sharp as bob wire, sometimes, but you get like my old Blue mare about my cussin'—used to it. If you was to settle down in this country, I'd give you a couple milk cows, not worth much, with cattle prices shot to hell, and I'd throw in one a them tough buckskin colts a mine for a saddlehorse. If you're still a ridin' the range when that buckskin dies of old age, you're a better man than I ever figured on for a son-in-law."

But Martin Stone remembered he could still renege.

2 — Welcoming Committee

It was June before the Martin Stones ate their first meal on their new homestead. They came driving in toward the evening sun, their open car piled high as an old-time freight wagon with farm tools and household goods, the loaded trailer behind pulling back like a reluctant milk cow on a rope. Across little Seep Creek from the hump they stopped and climbed out over the running boards. They were both in overalls, blue shirts and old Stetsons, as alike as two ranch hands, Penny a bit the shorter and slimmer, and almost as dark with wind-burn.

Like old ranch hands they went straight to camp making; Marty almost as good a forager as his father had been with Sherman. He grubbed dead sagebrush for fuel while Penny stomped the ground around the car for holes that might harbor rattlesnakes. Then unloading the grub box they cooked the supper together, the fragrant smoke rising thin and blue into the late sun that lay golden over the wide, gray-green plain while somewhere, far off, a sage hen cackled.

"Raising us a mess of shooting for the old double-barrel," Penny promised.

It was a good supper, home-cured ham fried with lumps of baking powder squaw bread, watercress salad, pieplant sauce with oatmeal cookies that Ma Liz made, and coffee with canned cream. And when the tin plates were empty they brushed the crumbs from their overalls and leaned their shoulders back against the bundles of the running board. Together they watched the two slim buttes darken against the sunset sky, Marty's uncertainties of the last three weeks apparently forgotten as he slipped his hand under Penny's arm.

Anyway, it was a new sector. . . .

Much had been done the last three weeks, with the Turners, particularly Penny, managing it all like HQ laying out a campaign, or the nurses at McHalvey chopping up a man's time. The day after they got off the train at Stover they borrowed Artie's old car, and with him on the down-wind side because of the juicing cud in his lean cheek, and Penny driving, they went homeseeking—dry-landing as Artie called it.

"Now don't you go planking them kids down somewheres more'n a thousand miles from home," Ma Liz called after her husband from the doorway. "It's bad 'nough to have my boy lost off around Laddyvostock or some other hell'n gone place without having Penny stuck so far away she can't come home to shell out her young 'uns."

Behind her the two younger girls were laughing and pretending blushes, but actually Martin was the only one embarrassed, feeling red as a Swede in a sleet storm, as he remembered Nancy standing big on her porch. He sneaked a look at Penny. Maybe he was getting one hung on him?

At the county seat Artie passed his plug of tobacco around, asking about land, getting boosts for everywhere from the badlands around Goshen to the highest reaches of the old Stinking Water. "The young feller plans to make a living off the place," Artie Turner reminded, as he good-naturedly reached for what was left of his plug to stow away in his baggy overalls.

"Hell! . . . Thought you said it had to be free land! . . . Ten thousand vets been in and gone. . . ."

At the land office the help came around from behind the cages to shake hands with Penny, who had worked there before Dick was lost, telling her how nifty she looked, a regular big-city vamp, sunburn and freckles all gone, and just in time for the barn dance at the Box Bar before they refilled the mow. Saturday. ". . . Be just like old times to have you there—you and your friend . . ." feeling out the situation.

"I bet you know all the new steps," a sta-combed young man said enviously.

"Well, just so it ain't that there Varsity Drag that Bud Keller fetched back from Chicago and was a-teachin' my Ellie," old Artie put in. "So help me gobs, I wanted to hokey-pokey his tail, like we used to on logy bronchs; get his feet to movin'. . . ."

So the talk went, Martin standing stiff and silent, wishing he had lit out at daylight from his bunk in the haymow as he started to;

not be a dud among hot-shots, a soldier among civilians—among home-front goldbrickers who never got their insides scorched like the firebox of the old C. B. & Q. But the night had been like the end of a week of artillery strafing, with him shaking between the blankets, staring into the empty dark, the everlasting twittering of the sparrows in the rafters loud in the silence. And when he finally slept it was all mixed up, war and the name of Nancy, and old Iron Leg, too—the pipe shining in the sun as he vaulted the iron fence around a grave that was marked Lucinda Stone, vaulted back and forth, while a machine gun chattered far off.

But when Martin got moving this morning, Artie and Penny were already among the cows in the lot below him, talking softly, milk spurting in the pails. Like the goddamn army, carrying a lantern. And when Martin rolled out, he saw sixteen-year-old Ellie switching her pretty little butt around as she fed the turkeys in the yard. A man might get a good piece there, he was thinking when the breakfast bell rang.

But it was land they were after today, Penny reminded them, and so the pale blue government maps were spread on the tables—plenty free land left but mostly ink-shaded, meaning rough country; breaks, badlands, buttes and foothills; or else blank stretches that were flat, streamless country where not even an Indian could hope to find grass or water. Artie had done some riding for a horse outfit over patches of range like that when he was a kid. "Great country for lizards and side-winders, it was, and so I lets 'em have it," he said, grinning. Seeing Martin's sullen face, Penny wished she had urged harder that he wait a while, get the feel of his stirrups before the chute was thrown open. He was welcome to the bunk in the haymow long as he wanted to stay, as was anybody coming through, and no obligation.

But he had to get settled. "I got to have something to hang onto," he had said, the white, hurt look back around his mouth. Yet here he was at the land office, pulled away from them all, sitting right beside Penny but a mile off, so Artie put it up to the young fellow straight out. What did he want to do, get farther away or give up the whole shebang? It was then Martin admitted that he had already picked a place.

"You have! Where?" Penny asked, surprise deepening the warm brown flecking in her eyes.

"Up on Black Earth River."

Old Artie pushed his glasses back on his balding head to examine this stray who sure wasn't acting like the kind of man he wanted his girl to marry—sitting there all this time, sulking like a jinny colt, when they were only trying to help him—and help he needed, as what tenderfoot didn't, coming to Wyoming?

But Penny wasn't looking at it that way, not noticeably. "Well, what do you know, Artie? Black Earth River! I remember some good land up there, but under irrigation, gone——"

"Not off northwest of Argonne post office," Martin said stubbornly, and stopped, thinking that he shouldn't have said the war name right out. People looked at you funny, like the man in the Bevo joint back in the Bluffs. "Get shut of that there uniform and stop running off the mouth about it! War's over!" when Martin complained about the railroad not giving a soldier his job back.

All the way home and afterward, too, Martin Stone was quiet, even to the teasing of the younger sisters, trying to find out how things stood between him and Penny. And when they cranked up their portable phonograph and put on "K-K-Katy" and "Valencia" and danced slow and close together on the old porch, their eyes on the soldier, he slipped out into the evening to lean against the wire fence of the yard and look over the weathered old Turner place. The house was like three, four lean-tos pushed together, the grainery and chicken coop just old claim shacks moved up, the swaybacked barn gray too, and behind the corrals and windmill a bald ridge with a few scrubby cedars. To the man from the cornlands, where cattle meant the stink of the feed lots along the tracks, the steers crowded too close to walk the fat off, this was a pauper run; the outlook ahead mighty tough terrain, and nobody of his outfit along, none of any outfit he could call his own left anywhere. But when Little Pretty Butt came running past to get in with a carful of Stover high school kids and tore off, honking, he looked after her until the dust hung thin and shining in the evening sun.

At the window of the summer kitchen, Ma Liz watched the young man uneasily as she stirred up the dumplings. "Blamed hard to make an empty sack stand up," she muttered to the beat of her spoon. "Oh, Penny!, I almost forgot to say that Bill Terrey stopped by to see you. Heard in town you was home. He's working up to Teapot Dome, driving a big car."

"He needn't bother," Penny said shortly as she pinched roots from an apronful of young, brush-bedded lettuce for wilting. "I walked home once; that's enough."

"You know he's tamed down since; a good boy, sending his mother to Florida, and all. Besides, I hear there's a lot of money loose up at Teapot, with oil boiling out everywhere."

When there was no reply, the old woman began dropping blobs of batter into the boiling chicken broth, her wide wedding ring shining in the late sun. "Pa been shootin' off his mouth about Wilson and the soldiers again?" she finally asked.

"No, why? If he's had anything unpleasant to say he's been cautious as old Nellie."

"Well, I'm relieved. Them as was in the war don't like to hear him. Jimmy Swanton left the supper table last Sunday, his plate full and it beans an' ham-hocks, when Artie tells him the soldiers is all pension bellyachers and that Wall Street put the war over on us."

"But he was all for world democracy and licking the Kaiser!"

"Yes, but come branding time, with young Artie buried and Joey not back to help he gets sore and turns again the war. 'Pull our boys out!' he says, 'Let them as wants to, fight the Huns!' Then there's this League of Nations talk in the papers and when he gets out a clean shirt that's all runny with that war dye, he gets madder, and agrees with all what that Hubert Mack and Lodge and Hi Johnson and old Flap-Mouth Borah got to say again it."

Penny sat up in amazement, the root scraps left in her apron sliding off to the floor. "Why, that's turning our backs on everything— on everything Dick. . . ."

But in a moment she was out for the broom. "It was that handful of spiteful senators, backed by enough big money to swing the newspapers, when the country really was behind Wilson. And poor Artie he's always argued you couldn't expect peace in one nation without it all over, anymore than you could have law and order in Miles County and not in the rest. It's heartbreaking."

Ma Liz sighed, whipped the cloth from her bread sponge and started to punch it down with her strong, brown arms. "Yes, but it won't do for me to open my mouth too wide—not with Hubert Mack's mortgage against us from back in the prairie fire year coming due by spring. All we been getting's hail and drouth, and cattle prices down to give-away, almost. Ain't a thing to see us through now, unless—" she choked, but the next sob escaped her, shaking her heavy bosom as she held her buttered hands out, trying to wipe her streaming eyes with her arms, "—unless it turns out true that Joey's been killed in that Laddyvostock place and I gets the insurance."

"Oh, Ma! Ma Liz! Things can't be that bad!" the girl cried, drawing the heavy shoulders of her mother to her breast, rocking her back and forth as she used to do her sisters and young Artie, thinking about Bill Terrey and his big oil job, sending his mother to Florida.

But almost at once the woman pushed the girl away, sniffing the tears back as she worked at the dough, punching it, spanking it hard. "What I can't stand to see is an old fool blubbering," she scolded.

The next day Marty was up early, helping the girls finish the bean planting and then dropping the late potato seed behind the plow. He even tried to hold the handles a couple of rounds himself, until his wind and his strength gave out.

"Maybe the altitude's gettin' you, but it'll be worse with a breaker bottom and a team that steps out," Artie warned. "Be slick and easy if you had you a tractor, but sod bustin' afoot's damned hard work."

"Yeh, but I think I can get the swing of it, if I take it gradual," Marty said, and remembering, kicked himself for a big mouth that night. What a laugh—a good railroad man planning to gyp the jackrabbits out of a living, and bed down with a woman he's never tried out, never had so much as a feel of.

But it had been a hard day, and so he dropped off, still whispering "Nancy, Nancy . . ." as he had for over five years.

By eight the next morning they were at Dunhill, on the Black Earth River. It was a pretty place, with high, black-stratified bluffs on both sides, the valley between a patchwork of greening alfalfa and the brown earth of beetfields, the irrigation ditches like creeks in Iowa, with grassy banks and clumps of leaning trees. In the little town, dusty cars were parked down the business street, with here and there a cowhand against a building or squatting on his run-over heels, while below the depot was a mat of shipping pens for

cattle and sheep, and a couple of tall galvanized grain elevators—
outlets for a productive region. Evidently the railroad was to keep
running through the mine strikes, for here, too, were the long ricks
of coal on the ground.

But the tableland beyond the bluffs was the color of a mangy
coyote, and as ragged, with Argonne only a hole in the side of a
bank along the mail trail, a padlock on the door of the dugout, the
key hanging on a string beside it.

"Yeh," old Artie said. "Law says post offices got to be locked up
so we does it out here too, and leaves the key handy."

There was no trail the way Marty wanted to go, so Penny cut
across, and from the top of a little rise it was plain why the region
was marked free on the land office plat—bare, graveled breaks, with
outcroppings of sandstone in the gullies, a few scattered squaw
currant bushes on the ridges, not even sagebrush. Like a long-dead
battlefield, torn by shell and mine.

Marty pushed his cap back and wiped his red forehead, feeling
foolish as the day he bayoneted an old sandbag, his first time up and
over. But Penny was already flattening out a map she had borrowed, her finger stopping at a faint line, like a fine, crinkly black
hair. "Do you suppose this actually means Seep Creek, up north
there, as it seems to?"

"Yeh, it's Seep all right," Artie decided after he got his iron specs
unfolded. "Something's probably seeping, water or oil."

"Oil?" Marty looked up. "Oil around here?"

"Possible. You run into it 'most anywheres over this part of the
state. Remember the dark seepings down to Dunhill, along the river
bluffs? Not in paying quantities like over to Teapot—mostly just
enough for promoters to drag money out of suckers for wildcatting.
Bear traps for the foot of the little feller."

"You notice Artie speaks with deep conviction," Penny laughed.
"He sunk a couple hundred in a dry hole."

"Hell, that's the way a man learns about a new thing. . . ."

Penny drove fast over the rough ground, Martin on the running
board to watch for sudden cuts and holes. That was how he saw the
antelope, standing a moment against a sage-covered knob, and then
gone in a flash of his white rump. "Deer, deer!" he cried. "No, it
must have been an antelope!" Like the antelope old Iron Leg used
to sneak up on, and not a bad piece of stalking either for a one-

legger, the son thought, his face excited. Old Artie looked at him. "By gobs! I would a missed seeing him! You got sharp eyes for a tenderfoot. Must be from watching for Krauts."

Turned out Seep Creek drained a wide tableland, with a lowish band of thicker sage and weed growth crossing it, the grass-edged little creek winding down through the middle—shallow, sun-dappled, a few red minnows flashing around the stones dropped in for bottom where the trail crossed—the whole stream not over a good man's jump in width. Here and there a tarpaper shack squatted in the sage, weed-grown, or perhaps with a couple of rusted barrels for gasoline and water, and a strip of plowing about thirty feet wide along both sides of the creek; string farming, Artie called it.

Penny stopped the car at one of the newer shacks and a woman with a purple scarf tied Theda Bara style around her coarse red hair came out to look.

"Yes," she said, in an easy-talking way, "there's land to be had around, and there'd be a lot more if we settlers could find work anywhere." With her husband's service time off they could get a patent to the place now so he was off to Dunhill that minute, wiring Pittsburgh about his old job; things maybe were picking up a little in the East. Marty tried not to look at Penny as the woman talked, both hoping to keep their knowledge of the hard times from their faces.

But perhaps the woman suspected. "Worse comes to worse, he may get in on some strike walkout."

Scab, strike-breaker, Martin thought. "Don't you like it here?" he asked.

"Goodness, no," the woman said. "Bad as camp following down through Deming. It's forty miles to a moving picture and only a rootin', tootin' Bill Hart at that. About as far to a tree, and hot as a bake-oven in the summers, the wind blowing incessantly, ruining your complexion, particularly with these topless cars the natives affect. . . . Everything's hard here, even the water in the creek, hard enough to bounce a rock."

"Probably some alkali," Artie said.

"Alkali! There's something makes the soap suds go like clabber cheese, to curdles. Wells are three hundred feet deep and don't bring enough water to pay for the gas to pump it, unless you turned it into bootleg by hauling in corn, like some do up the creek. We're getting out quick as we can, all of us. You could take your pick of the whole country for fifty dollars cash, Corporal, if you threw in a good meal."

"Everybody leaving?"

"Well, everybody except old Wheeler P. Scheeler. You couldn't get him and his hounds out any more than you could roll up Seep Creek and store it away against the dry weather."

"Old timer?" Artie laughed. "They got roots like a jack pine on a rock."

When they finally got away old Artie spit into the dust. "Did you get her slam about cars without tops? . . . Fresh-air fiends, the drylanders calls us, and I'll admit it don't come fresher than in Wyoming. But what makes my backside tired is that every slack-pants what fails at everything else thinks he can come squat on a chunk of land and get rich farming. All they do is ruin the country, like them that busted up so much loose ground during the war— soil that blowed out of the county in a week. You don't make a farmer by pushing a shoe clerk or schooldad into a pair of overhalls and a rush hat. Farming and stock growing's a profession, like doctoring or preachin', and you got it to learn."

"And find land that's not too barren to learn on," Penny added.

Old Artie grinned, winking at Martin. "Gettin' back at me for the hardpan in that valley a mine. Women's like that." Then he lengthened his lined old face into seriousness. "Yes, I'll admit that the ground oughtn't be too barren but it's pretty much like with a woman; if nothing sprouts it's mostly on account a poor seed or shallow plantin'," laughing out loud, making Marty feel ashamed. He had heard as much dirty talk as any section hand, any doughboy, but he didn't like a man talking free before his own daughters.

When they got out of sight of the last tarpaper shack, Marty suddenly called out, "Stop! Let's reconn." A low hump of land like a half a French bread cut straight across lay on the other side of the creek, the cut end almost up against the bank. "That'd be mighty fine at your back in those blizzards you tell about—and that little green slope at the foot looks good to a man from Iowa."

"Maybe, but in summer you better watch out for rattlers on them humps," Artie warned. Penny just laughed and pulling down her old Stetson, jumped the creek with the young man, her overalled legs flying beside his putteed ones, Martin thinking about his father vaulting creeks on his iron leg, his tom-walker—vaulting creeks wide enough to water a whole section of dry land.

And the pretty greenness turned out to be bog grass, with little threads of seepage water from the hump winding through it, the ground squeegy underfoot.

"No, no good," Marty said, rubbing his sunburning chin in disappointment. "It could be tiled like they do back home but that costs money, and the crops here'd never pay out."

But Penny got Artie's short-handled car spade and dug along the foot of the hump, baring a thin outcropping of sandstone, dark with years of water and mud. The seepage came from above this, running down over the stone like streams of tears over a sooted, grief-broken face. And when she diverted a patch with the spade edge, no water appeared under the blade. At another place it was the same, and at a third.

Marty was following close, his dark eyes shining. "Why, it'd be easy to catch and drain off if we only had some tile troughing or something that didn't rot right out. You could drain it off in a stream or two down to the creek."

"Yeh, Penny's studied a little geology and knows about ground water, and irrigating. She'd be wanting to spread that seepage over the slope for your garden truck. Be mighty good for cabbage and cauliflower and other stuff that wants rich ground," Artie said.

"Of course! Say, you are a smart kid," Marty told the girl, carried out of himself in his enthusiasm, "—and looks like that water supply would be steady."

"Steady and a little hard but no alkali," Penny said, testing the flow between her fingers and against her tongue. Nodding, Marty sized up the place. Probably twenty acres low enough for cropping along a mile of creek, say thirty at the most, if worked like the other string farmers, leaving six hundred odd acres in ragged sage. "Not much good for anything except sheep, wouldn't you say?"

"You ain't got a bad eye, son," old Artie said. "But sheep's been run out a here, herders killed and the flocks scattered. Not enough good water anyway. Yet with a windmill on the down edge of the hump you probably get enough extra water for the few cows you can grow feed for, and all the horses the rest of the place would run, range horses that don't need hay."

"At least it'd never turn to mud, like France," Marty said, smiling, his sun-reddened face handsome in its purpose as he squinted off across the shimmering, flattish plain, trying to see it as a stockman might. It was empty, without house or fence or tree; nothing in sight except the little hump and two buttes far in the west, like a pair of salt and pepper shakers his mother used to have, slim but spreading out at the base, and of the same pinkish color. They helped make him feel good, better than any time since he saw the baby in Nancy's arms. Why, on a piece of new land a man could build himself any kind of place he wanted, make it a little world of his own, in a way a kind of blow-hard story too, like old Iron Leg whirling himself around until he shot off into the sky, his pipe scattering sparks behind.

So Martin Stone grabbed the girl beside him around the waist. "Honey, how you think that buckskin Artie's plannin' to give us would look on the hump there, if this sector happens to be open to occupation?" and as he kissed the girl's wind-flushed face, old Artie looked away with the embarrassment of a father seeing a young man make love to his first-born daughter.

Now, barely three weeks later, they were bedded down on their own place, the moonlight a silvery haze over the sage, the rivulets from the hump gurgling softly on their way to the creek, and somewhere a coyote howling.

"Let's wish ourselves luck," Penny said as she settled her face into the pillow, "and remember what you dream. First-night dreams come true."

Skeptically Marty started to laugh, and then realized that she was joking, kidding, although she was twenty-five, only a few months younger than he, with hard luck in her life too, and sensible, a good manager. Yet she had these light ways that he had never seen in anyone near him before, not in his mother or father or anyone except the cowhand from western Nebraska who got killed beside him in the Argonne. But Slim wasn't over eighteen the day he fell running, his momentum so great that his head plowed his tin hat into the soft mud before him when the burst of gunfire came. And when Marty turned the boy up and wiped the mud from his face, there was a little round hole between the eyes.

It was a clean shot, like the one Slim used to talk about for beef-killing at home, and it kept coming up before Marty the first few months in the hospital, with his burned-out lungs tearing at every breath, keeping him reminded that even in battle the ways of dying were like those in peace, that the whole craziness of war was only an exaggeration, a speed-up, a kind of prostitution of the everyday things—working, eating, loving, dying; unless it could be that these things were always a craziness.

"Dreaming already?" Penny asked softly, her low voice penetrating the walls of his thoughts, bringing him back to the bed roll spread under the Wyoming stars. "Seeing Nancy?" making it as casual as she could and then holding herself still for what she had let herself say.

"No, I never saw her in a dream," Martin answered, making his voice quiet, "not even after all my years of practicing. Maybe I never really remembered her as a woman though I done as much waking up out of woman dreams as any saltpeter eater. It's more like she was the things all us poor bastards hoped to find when we got back—not the same as we left them, but better, prettier, through our long thinking about them. Then we comes back and there they are, hair cut up high around behind the ears like a army camp chippie and their bellies filled by some slacker's tail, and talking big about all the money and stuff they got out of our fighting."

"Oh, darling," Penny said softly, touching his hair, wanting to cry out, "Don't hurt yourself so. . . ." It was like having to watch an injured animal spring up from its quiet resting at every sound, or perhaps something more.

Burrowing closer to him as though for warmth, Penny did not let herself think further, and in return he put an arm over her shoulder and said no more nor inquired into her dreams. Not that he didn't know quite a lot about the rodeo rider called Dick whose embroidered white boots and purple silk neckerchief Penny kept stuck out of sight somewhere. Ellie, the one with the pretty little butt, told Marty all about them.

"You needn't think you're the only one who lost somebody by the war," she said angrily one evening when she found him out leaning against the wagon wheel. "Besides, there's half a dozen fellows right around here with their tongues hanging out for Penny."

"I know—I saw some of them in town," he answered, making marks in the dust of a wagon spoke with a spear of grass.

But today had been a hard pull for a man with so little wind, although Penny had driven most of the way, even opened that new barb wire gate this side of Dunhill after he strained and puffed until he had to lean against the post, played out. And Penny had loosened it easy by jumping on the wires in the middle, making a fool of him, a damn fool the way women liked, the way she did writing to his dad when Martin refused. As he thought about these things he pulled his arm away from her shoulder and was getting to sleep when he felt her lift up to listen, whisper: "Horsebacker coming. I hear a saddle creaking." The next instant something wet and cold was thrust into Marty's face and in the fading moonlight he could see a hound squat back, felt him put a paw on his arm, wanting to shake hands.

As Marty reached for his pants the horsebacker rode up and called out a friendly, "Hello, there! You the new couple's filed on this place?" And when Marty replied, the man said he was Wheeler P. Scheeler, and hoping they didn't mind this western informality.

Oh, no, Penny was from down near Stover. . . .

So? Then he wouldn't have to warn them about rattlers around the hump here, but if the coyotes got bad for their chickens, he'd run them with his hounds, and meanwhile he'd like to put in a bid to borrow any books they might be bringing in. He had a couple hundred himself they were welcome to. Started with a lot he bid in at a sale once, in a barrel, sight unseen, thinking it might be dishes, or stovepipe. Kept adding to them ever since. When folks left they generally gave him any they didn't want, so he passed them out to newcomers.

"Been here long?" Marty managed to put in.

Oh, yes, born in a covered-wagon coming back from Oregon in the Seventies, had whooping cough on the way to west Nebraska in the Eighties, smallpox down in the Indian strip in the Nineties and typhoid in a box car in Kansas while his mother was cooking for a section gang.

"I used to work on the section," Martin said.

"That so? Well, pa didn't stay at that long neither. Too hard work, he said, and took to moving again. When I turned twenty-one I come out here for a place where I'd not have to move till they hauled me out foot first. Ma was glad to settle down, too. She's been with me twenty-six years now."

"Twenty-six years around here?" Penny said in surprise.

"Yeh, at Seep Springs, about three miles up, where the crick starts. Got a couple neighbors up there. Been by to see you yet?"

"No, you're the first," Marty said.

"That's what I was figgering on. Well, call on me any time for a sack of books or anybody come bothering. I ain't no scrapper but I got the low-down on most everybody 'round, being here so long— enough to make 'em step a little easy."

Whistling his dogs together he loped off into the chilling moonset, the horse's hoofs loud on the dry earth.

"Well, there's your Wyoming welcome," Penny said, as Marty crept back under the blankets, shivering like a wet pup.

But he was awakened once more. The moon was gone, with only the strange, cold outdoor blackness around him and the sound of a high-powered car coming close. Then suddenly two brilliant head-lights swung around the hump where there was no trail at all, and stopped with their full glare against the loaded car.

"Hey, wake up!" a man's voice shouted. "Got any gas?"

So Martin pulled his pants on again and his shoes, and went out toward the car where four, five men were already standing around. At first they didn't speak, just stood, then one finally said they came from up the road a piece, looking for a man called Dunlap; had some kaffir seed. He wasn't Dunlap, was he?

"No, Stone. Martin Stone," he said as he came up through the beam of light, still stuffing his shirttail into his overalls.

"Well, you got gas an' we run out—need a little. 'Bout five gallons would be right."

Martin didn't like that, overbearing as a Kraut, but he let it slide. "I'd like to accommodate you but I only got just enough to take me back to Dunhill myself. I got to haul out lumber for a house, and get my team," he explained. And while he spoke one of the men fussing around the back of their car with a flashlight shot it out over the dead campfire and the bed until it hit Penny's woman-face, hesitated a little, and moved on.

"Hell, there, you be careful," Martin objected, but he got no answer and finally another spoke up. "You're new here, ain't you? Maybe you'd be wanting to come to the meeting Sunday to my place. Say, you ain't a mackerel-eater, are you? An' you sure your name ain't Stein?"

Martin was getting sore. "What the hell you aiming at? I said Stone and I mean Stone!"

"Well, you look mighty dark for a white man. Sure you ain't a son of a bitchin' curly-head Jew?"

"Why, you goddamn bastard!" Martin roared out, mad as in his old fighting days on the section, forgetting his lungs, everything. "What in hell's your game?" he demanded.

Another of the men in the dark, apparently the leader, stepped up now, as though taking over. "Better go easy, Mr. Stone," he said. "We don't know nothing about you and we aim to find out before we let you settle 'round here. For ten dollars we'll investigate you and if you're OK we'll give you a membership in good standing."

"The hell you will! Membership in what?"

"What you think?" the man laughed. "The Klan, of course."

"Why, you dirty, bulldozing bastards, get off my place!" Martin ordered, but instead of going they moved up through the dark from both sides, spread to get around him standing alone in the light, carrying car tools and no telling what else in their hands. So he jumped sideways into the darkness, his breath suddenly short and hard, tearing his lungs, and somebody already behind him.

But it was Penny, Penny pushing her old double-barrel shotgun cold into his hands. At the feel of it his fingers went around the grip gratefully—a fighting man with his gun.

"I said git off my place!" he roared out strong into the night. "Now I'll fire one shot in the air, then the next one to hit!" And as the men laughed easily at his bluffing, coming on again, step by step, in a semicircle, a hot, red flash exploded into the darkness over them. It was enough. Before the echo of the shot came back from the hump the engine was roaring, the gears crashing, the last man just making it to the running board as the car jumped ahead.

For a moment neither of the new settlers standing together in the dark spoke a word. But when the car was safely gone, Martin put his arm around his wife. "You sure know how to move up the artillery in the nick of time, kid," he said, his voice shaking a little. "I thought there for a minute I was back surrounded by Heinies, and not a grenade on me—and no iron leg like my dad. . . ."

"Well, we aren't far past the range wars out here, with sheep troubles still going. Now it's the Klan's moving in. I guess that's what W. P. Scheeler was warning us against. They sure seem to be in the money up here. That's an expensive car; gets under way fast."

"You think they really was the Klan?"

Penny guessed so. Lots of them, thousands, down at Lincoln, and her mother wrote about their nightshirt parades over around Stover, burning fiery crosses. About a month ago they whipped a poor Mexican who started a little garage and nothing was done about it. Maybe because the judge and the sheriff had joined up.

That was a hell of a note, Martin said. And why pick on the Mexican? Hadn't he seen a lot of Mexican beet workers and sheepherders around the last few weeks?

"Yes, but beet workers and sheepherders aren't competition."

"What'd they come here for?"

"Membership drive, probably, getting a good rake-off on each one, I hear. A plain shakedown for a can of gas and ten dollars on the way home from some other deviltry."

Once more Martin lay down on his new homestead, without pulling his overalls off this time, and with the familiar steel of a gun under his hand. Even so, it was white in the east before he went to sleep again and then he awoke almost at once, his face wet, and not certain if he had called out Nancy's name aloud in his crying.

3 — Trailing the Wether

As the June sun rose, the two pink buttes in the west reddened against the deepening sky. A little wind came wandering along the creek, making a rustling in Penny's strip of shoulder-high cotton-woods, the young leaves shivering like aspens long after it was past. As the sun climbed, bobolinks began to rise into the bright, clear air, spilling their song over the hump and the windmill and the little pine slab house at its foot, and over the whitening strips of wheat and the green of young alfalfa along Seep Creek. Somewhere a sage hen made a friendly morning chatter to her young, while far off on the road a blur of dust appeared and moved rapidly closer, a car coming fast.

At the pole corral Martin stopped to look, squinting his eyes into the sun. Then he dropped the empty milk bucket like a tin hat on a post, swinging over the gate and the little creek and ran foolishly down the road. And as the open car slowed beside him he hopped on the running board and hugged Penny close to him. He laughed boyishly, and when she got the car stopped, kissed her hard, his stubbles rough as a hoof rasp on her cheek.

"God, you're welcome as the sight of a letter from home."

Penny smiled and put a hand on his arm. Then she lifted the blanket from the box on the seat beside her, and said softly, "Here he is, young Milton. Here's your dad, his tail sticking in the air like an old dog wolf on a hill—your own dad."

Martin craned over to look. "Hell," he said, "he's a red-faced booger, redder'n some wild Indian! You don't expect to bleach him out and make a white man of him, do you—that scalded little wart?" in his mind comparing him to the solid white lump of young one he had found on Nancy's arm "—a runt!"

Penny laughed, with something of her old teasing. "Is that all you have to say to your nine-pound son?" she asked, folding her arms on the steering wheel and looking over their place beside the creek, over all that had been done in one year. Watching, Martin remembered Artie's comment when they were down there Christmas: "They're good breeders, the women on my wife's side—shell out their kids right on the dot and strong as mules again in a week. It's them high-waisted ones you want. Harder to seed but easier to harvest."

In the meantime Penny was noticing that the red creeper over the door stoop had leafed out thick as a blanket while she was away, the garden in the old bogs up in neat rows, the ground dark and wet from Martin's irrigating. He must have been up several times during the night to change the flow. Too bad the place wasn't better land, or had more water, a great. reservoir of water, for Martin Stone would make a fine farmer.

And the stock seemed to be doing well. The two, deep-bagged, brockle-faced cows at the corral were bawling for their calves, and in the lane the team of mares switched their tails at the early flies. Only the buckskin colt Artie had given them was standing off alone, up on the hump. Four years old now, and ridden at least every other day the last year, he was up there tossing his head, lifting his black tail as he ran a ways and then stopped to look back toward the car that he saw almost every day.

"Look at that goddamn bronch of yours—faunching around up there," Martin complained.

"Oh-h, you've been fighting Pete again."

"All I did was try to catch him yesterday to take old Floss to the stud. You see how he's acting. . . ."

"I've been telling you, you ought to wear an apron," Penny laughed, passing it off lightly. She could always catch Pete in the pasture anywhere by walking up to him casually and while she scratched his jaw, slipping her apron off and up over his neck. But Martin had struck the buckskin over the head with the bridle for snorting, back when he was still a greenhorn with horses. The bit caught Pete in the eye, a pulpy string of blood running down the black nose, the horse rearing back into the corner of the corral in pain and fright. Furious, Martin held him there, slashing at him again and again with the bridle, cursing himself breathless, until the horse finally stood still, but shaking, his bloody nostrils flaring, his uninjured eye wild.

Penny saw it, her mouth thinning in anger and contempt.

"There's never been a ranch worth the name from Calgary to Fort Worth that would tolerate a man who'll hit a horse over the head like that!" she had said, and quieting Pete as well as she could, led him away, still trembling but pushing close up against her, like a terrified little dog. It was a foolish thing to do, for behind her Martin beat the bridle against the corral poles until the bit flew off into the sagebrush. That night he never came in at all. Not until three days later, when Wheeler P. Scheeler stopped by with a coyote across the back of his saddle, his dogs panting and red-jawed, did Martin speak a word, even to his plodding team.

It was a dreadful thing to have standing between them, even after Penny discovered about the earlier things of that day. Martin had been talking to Benny Green, the vet who ran the post office he called Argonne for his dead brother. Benny had told about the highest tariff of all time just passed, and Harding strike-breaking again, with more soldiers and an injunction against the railroaders. Nineteen men were killed, the strikers driven back to take a sixty million dollar wage cut. All that money out of circulation, when there were already six million men jobless. Besides, there had been no rain for five weeks on Seep Creek.

Penny had doctored the horse the best she could, but the eye healed white as an agate and since then no reins would hold Pete if Martin happened to lift a hand quickly on his good side. And harder than ever for the man to catch.

But today's homecoming must not be spoiled by a buckskin. "The alfalfa's looking fine, isn't it," Penny said. "But maybe we better borrow Wheeler's mower for the wheat; it looks a little fired, probably because the back-setting, or rust."

"No, no rust, just heat and drouth," Martin defended, as if he were being blamed. Then Penny saw her turkeys far up the creek. "Oh, and old Turk's got out! Why, her young ones'll die from that wet bottom grass!" she said in alarm, not noticing Martin's soft lip flattening in the week-old bristles. "No use chasing her in nights; all but two of the little ones are A-WOL," he complained.

Penny turned to him in exasperation. Twelve young turkeys gone—and already feathering out when she went to Ma Liz's two weeks ago! They would have grown fat and fine on wild seeds and grasshoppers with no outlay, and made good eating in the fall, maybe even brought in a little ready cash. Besides, a coyote could sneak through the sage and carry off old Turk herself. Penny knew she shouldn't have said anything about getting the turkeys in nights when she left, with Martin himself touchy as a woman in the family way. For a moment she let herself slide down in the old car seat, discouraged, tired, but at her husband's darkening face she straightened up. "Oh, darling, the poults'll probably come trotting back. Let's go home."

Releasing the clutch she swung through the creek and around before the door, the old gobbler running up to spread his feathers and strut his finest at the car. And as Martin bent to take hold of the rope handles of young Milton's box he was suddenly afraid of the silence, afraid of the covered face. But when he pulled the blanket he saw that his son was only sleeping, his red little nose sticking into the air, one fist balled tight like a section hand ready for a scrap.

Martin Stone had put in a year getting used to many things besides the civvies that cost four prices. He had been in uniform once—Armistice Day. But then he had felt pretty good, with a healthy tan, a place well started, and a kid coming—probably his first, for he had always been one for women who knew their way around, like that Helene in the cowshed along the Meuse. Last winter, when people noticed Penny swelling, it puffed him up like new shoulder bars on a little man. But even when she had to run out behind the house with morning sickness as she cooked his breakfast he couldn't keep up with her cutting squaw corn.

In the parade at Dunhill he was surprised how many around had been in the war; only the silver stripers, the home ribboners always fighting the battle of Paris. Miserable, his blouse too tight, he sat among them waiting out the speechifying about the country's gratitude to her great heroes, and all that had been done for them: billions spent on compensation, services and hospitals—and business making every sacrifice to help the vets get on their feet. It would puke a dog.

The year past was like a recruit's cartridge belt, the shells all spent with little to show except that he had learned to find the target now and then, when he could keep himself steady inside, not blow up because maybe old Brockle put her foot in the milk bucket or Penny got another letter from his father with clippings of the stories running in the *Platte Vigilante* about old Iron Leg's exploits. Yet he couldn't resist sneaking in to look at them gathering in the drawer of Penny's what-not—the kind of stories his mother had kept from him until he got the job on the section, but with new twists, like the one about a cyclone that was a heap more powerful than the twister that killed people in Wisconsin this spring. Happened a while back, when Iron Leg was boring a well with that pipe of his and striking hard pan, he whirled a little too fast to get through it, his flying coattails making a cyclone that cleared a strip of country far away as Arkansas, driving straws through fence posts thick as caterpillar fur, and chickens running around plucked scald-clean by the wind. Even the flow from the molasses barrels was turned to go 'round the other way, and the whirlpools of the Missouri, and the earth too, so the sun came busting up in the west. But he had to unwind it all, for a delegation with sawed-off shotguns came tearing in from Kansas. All the state flowers were wringing their heads off trying to follow the sun.

"Isn't that wonderful, Marty?" Penny said, suddenly in the doorway and laughing. Martin turned with the clipping in his hand. "B. S." he roared— "All a potful of B. S."

"Oh, Marty, it's really wonderful that they tell stories like that about a man who's still alive."

"It's still B. S.!"

Early in the summer Martin had taken to squatting a while with Benny Green at the post office when he went for the mail. Benny was a pale, thin little man with bad lungs from the flu he took after ten months of fighting without even a shrapnel nick. His wife, Betty, was an easygoing slow-foot from Jersey, her weight mostly below her belt, like a small woman with one of those Frog featherticks around her for an apron—a slob about her cooking and with the children. But she thought Benny was a world-beater.

When the evenings got chilly the men moved into the little dugout, Betty and the children asleep early in the bunks along the wall while one or the other of the men pushed cow-chips into the little stove and talked about the war and Benny's brother who had been with the old 363rd; Martin even talking about the hospital a little, the months he lay with the burning in his breast, watching the quick turnover around him—walk-out or rolled away under a sheet. Only he stayed.

All the last year Martin got more and more uneasy about the peace, America out of the League but the uniform scattered to hell'n, gone—Joey lost around Vladivostok somewhere, Benny with a cousin on the Rhine, others from Nicaragua to China. And where the Springfield wasn't ready, capital was pushing in and no telling what day the soldiers would come shooting. No foreign entanglements! No, none that could be watched; none with responsibility. In the meantime Italy was accepting a dictator and Germany with inflation that made a loaf of bread cost a wheelbarrow full of paper money. Not that things weren't boiling here too, with bread lines, strike-breakers with gas and machine guns, and the story Artie told the last time they were down to Penny's folks, about the naval oil property over to Teapot Dome being leased illegally. Billions stolen from the public, and young Teddy Roosevelt, assistant to Secretary of the Navy Fall, sending the marines in to expel a little company whose claims against the naval reserve were still undecided.

". . . Them guns ain't savin' oil for the government but for them grafters what's got the leases," a driller hanging around up there was saying, until he got his teeth knocked in.

Seemed the Harry Sinclair that they once saw big-bugging it around Casper was getting the oil, and men all the way up to the president involved. "Yeh, there's a blow-up coming, with a stink that'd make a skunk welcome in the parlor," old Artie predicted, enjoying the prospect, but still for Harding.

". . . Sheep'll trail after a wether into any slaughter pen when they won't foller a ram or a ewe into a clover patch," Ma Liz said sourly.

There was talk, too, of corruption in the Veterans' Bureau, hundreds of millions being stolen, while hospitals were overcrowded and new ones stood unfurnished and empty. Martin remembered the overcrowding all right, and the gray, ragged sheets of the last months around McHalvey, the bacon rancid, the eggs that could only be scrambled, dispensaries empty and doctors laid off, but the money going just the same. Now Harding vetoed the Bonus Bill, saying the nation couldn't afford it.

". . . Can't afford to make up a little of the jog between thirty dollars a month for getting shot and killed, and the two, three hundred a month for staying home."

"... Profiteers made billions. ..."

"Yeh, but it wasn't all gravy; silk shirts was forty, fifty dollars ..." one of the post office loafers said.

The surprise of the year was Martin's son. He had been all for precautions and then gumshoed around for a pin artist to take care of everything for fifty dollars, cash in the palm, only Penny wouldn't listen; knowing children were a snare and an entanglement to a poor man, particularly a sick one, she wouldn't. So Martin went up over the hump with the hoe to take it out on the rattlesnakes. By God, there was no figgering a woman, the best of them trapping a man with kids these days, when it used to be their main fret and worry to get rid of them, even old Katy, with her five woods' colts on the Missouri bottoms, where the boys used to go to spy. She finally died, knocking one too many.

In the long evenings Martin often looked past the kerosene lamp to Penny's hands slender and strong on her sewing, with a quietness that filled him with a sudden softness, a tenderness he had never known for anyone; hadn't known existed. But gradually her face had taken on a remoteness, shut him out, and he realized how his father had been shut out by his wife and son all the years of Martin's childhood. And if he talked regretfully about the trips with young Stevie along, the mother would rise up unreasonably and take her son from the room. "It's not fit to be raising a boy around you old soldiers!"

Getting the place in shape for living had been hard work. Because it was late for breaking when Martin filed, they lived in Artie's old tent until the sod corn was in, the seepage water led away with cottonwood plank troughing and the dried-out ground plowed for the garden before they started the house. After that there was the pasture to fence, a little breaking for alfalfa in case there was another rain, and then the well and the windmill.

"Marty gets a lot of work done. I guess it's because he keeps at it," Wheeler P. Scheeler said as he leaned over his saddlehorn, his hounds trotting up in a string along the trail, their curved tails swaying.

"I get a lot of help," Martin laughed, pleased. "You old timers— loaning me tools and trading me on the heavy work."

"Yeh, well," old Wheeler agreed, his broad, leathered face crinkling, "It's always paid-out to be neighborly, but since the war, some that's blowed in take advantage . . ." and Martin knew he meant the Carters—the Kluxers up near him; one with an office at Dunhill now, Real Estate and Investments, people tramping up and down the outside stairs, mostly nights. They were always cutting through Marty's place with that big car, tearing the new fence down, but so far they never faced the shotgun again. Maybe his markmanship at the fall turkey shoots helped.

But beside the cream checks and a few sacks of beans, only half of them white enough to sell, the new place was all outgo. So when Jack Hall, who knew the Turners for years, wrote he could use a man and wife for his little place on the Turtle Shell, somebody not minding deep snow, old Artie mailed the letter on to Penny. The work wasn't heavy—sled-feeding and cake, with just themselves and old Hughie, the regular hand, to cook for—thirty dollars and found, including any rump-end of stock, say three, four cows and a team.

Penny handed the letter across the oilcloth to Marty, wishing old Jack had written to him direct. "Feeding cottonseed cake," she said, "probably wintering calves. Think the work would be too heavy?"

"Oh, I can swing it."

Martin had grown wonderfully strong through the summer, not up to pitching hay on and off a rack all day in the wind at thirty, forty below, but this was pushing hay to the platform of a sled and then dragging it off at the feed ground. Besides, Marty was thinking about the four months at thirty dollars—a hundred-twenty clear, except for his winter stuff that he had to have anyway, sheepskin coat and so on, and something ahead if Penny had trouble, had to have a doctor. Besides, Seep Creek was deserted; everybody except Wheeler P. Scheeler gone on six months homestead leave, even Argonne post office closed. A good time for a little skirmishing.

So they filled the woodbox and left flour and bacon and coffee handy in covered buckets for any stray, storm-trapped traveler. Then they started to the Turtle Shell, Penny ahead with the car full of chicken and Turkey crates, the shoats in the trailer, and Martin on Pete bringing up the mares and the cows behind—like boomers on the move.

The sky was fine, the sun warm for mid-November and Martin with a job for the first time in five years, so he sang that he was just a long, lean country gink, from away out west where the hoptoads wink. The Stetson sat on the back of his head, his face brown as a lean-cheeked, curly-headed Shoshoni breed, and at the gates where Penny helped let the stock through, he pretended to be a traveling salesman and she a farmer's daughter, laughing aloud at the OD twists he managed. But finally Penny sang him a little song about the wandering horse doctor and the farmer's daughter who had been out with a marine.

It made Martin furious, although he wanted to talk as free as he liked to his wife, and more, like the night he came home from Dunhill after wheat had dropped again, with corn and beef and cream following. He couldn't sleep and so he tried to get Penny into those tricks he learned from Helene, and from listening to the men at the hospital, men who might never have a woman again. At first she played sleepy and stupid, then let on that he was joking, and finally she told him off. By God, how she told him off: "When you get so far gone you need such practices, you just go to the experts and I'll find me a man who is still a man!"

So he grabbed the army blanket and went to sleep in the car seat, damning her and everything to hell, with only the cracked steering gear to take it out on. Around daylight a storm came sweeping down Seep Creek, the lightning like a night strafing, the thunder Big Berthas shaking the ground, so he crawled sheepishly back into bed beside Penny, wet and shivering. Another time he got to blowing about the girls that chased him when he was a kid on the section. Penny looked at him with almost no brown in her gray eyes. "Don't you think that a man whose wife is pushing her apron up to her chin might stop showing off like a staggy steer in a cowyard?"

Goddamn the woman!—talking rough as a roundhouse chippie. He jerked the buckskin, whipped him into a lather, spurred his sides to bleeding by the time they got to the Turtle Shell, Martin wondering if he hadn't ought to keep right on riding, ride off before something happened, with that woman getting him so damn mad.

The rambling old house was of log, with a rusty tin roof and alkali mud plastered around the windows, but there were bear and wolf skins on the floor, mountain goat rugs white as the snow on Cloud Peak before the beds, and a raft of wood and coal handy. The buttery was full too, a beef hanging in the grainery, and Penny's hens laying well, with plenty of rabbit meat and green cabbage. In a month Martin was putting fat along his ribs and sprouting a dimple in his dark chin—really getting handsome, Penny thought, maybe the sentimentality of pregnancy softening her eye.

Then old Hughie started his arguing, pounding the Denver *Post* with his fist to prove his side. At first he had told endless stories about the outlaws in the early Turtle Shell country, the German spy scares during the war, old Jack's hairy-eyed hellcat of a mother-in-law, and Windy Johnson, the talkingest man in the country fighting with Plew Tollins, who hadn't said two dozen words since he was a kid and his mother ran off with a corn salve man.

But the stories gave out and the men took to arguing politics even as they stomped the ice and snow off their boots on the porch. It was a heavy-snow winter and for the weeks the mail truck didn't get through, Hughie rode against the freezing wind to town for the papers and a new supply of hooch in his saddlebags. Then he would start again, maybe on the unions and the "I Won't Works." "All the same, wantin' millionaire wages and pink silk shirts for loafin'—damn dirty bolshies!" until Martin stood up, dark and trembling. "I was a union man when I was braking for the railroad and I know they ain't bolshies. I know, too, that wage cuts play hell with the markets clear out here, people hungry and no money to buy your beef."

But Hughie didn't back water an inch, just sat and grinned through his gray stubbles. "Just a lot of dirty bolshies, it says right here in the paper."

When Penny tried cards, pitch, five hundred, bridge, Martin complained. "Hell, I can't play for fun with a bastard like that. . . ."

So the arguments went on, maybe on the way the Reds were making a scandal of Teapot Dome, running down the Klan and trying to put across the soldier bonus, with Martin hotly denying that the vets were pension hounds, an army of loafers trying to live off the government. He wasn't even for the bonus—just a chance for everybody to make a living.

"By damn! a stinking idealist! Well, you seen what we done to the one what sat in the White House!"

There it was, Marty told Penny; the old coot talking like he owned a steel mill or a sugar company or was Harry Sinclair himself instead of a forty-buck summer ranch hand, twenty and time off for his piles in the winter.

Penny settled herself into a more comfortable position in bed, moving the extra pillow she used to support herself now, and yawning. "We only got a little over a month left," she comforted, "then you won't have to listen any more."

Martin turned his back, taking the covers with him. God, she talked like these times were only a stretch of latrine duty, done when you got the stink off your hands, instead of robbing a man of everything, his right to a decent living, to a peaceful world, even his right to a glass of beer. Finally he got up and with his sheepskin and spurs he went out into the sparkling cold, bright as a sniper's moon. Forcing the frozen bit into the buckskin's mouth Martin rode him through drifts and up and down breaks, until his flanks were smoked white with hoarfrost, his sides bloody and Marty's lungs burned, each frozen breath a stab of pain.

After the three day St. Patrick blizzard, Windy Johnson came pounding his shaggy broomtail along the barer ridges, scattering tobacco splotches from house to house, inviting everybody to a stork party on old Plew Tollins and his woman up Bottleneck Canyon that night.

Because it would get the men out, give them something new to talk about, Penny was pleased, asking what she could bring.

"Wall, from the look a things," Windy replied, tipping his mouth up to hold the tobacco juice, "I guess you better keep what stork stuff you can collect for yourself."

Penny laughed goodnaturedly. "I could make a box of sandwiches and bring coffee and the cream."

At first Martin wasn't enthusiastic. "Too damn cold for parlor skirmishes," he said as he stopped buttering a roll and felt tenderly along the edge of a frosted ear. Hughie laughed. "I'd a thought you'd be strainin' to go. Plew's one a your underdogs, one a them socially downtrodden."

So along toward evening they got into the bobsled, Penny in the hay of the bottom with a bearskin coat and hot rocks, the two men standing up in front, earmuffs under their hats, sheepskin collars up. The sun-reddened snow squeaked under the runners and Martin turned from the wind while Hughie drove and talked about Plew Tollins: Plew'd been just a kid when the W-Bar-W punchers claimed they caught his paw with a rope on a ranch yearling and dumped him off dead at the porch. So the woman and the kid buried him on the hillside, and next day several of the old free grass ranchers rode over to buy the little meadow and spring pond. But she wouldn't sell, so the range stock took to breaking into their hay and the kid quit school to watch the fences nights, getting peery-eyed and shooting up tall as a horseweed the whiles.

"But his ma didn't stick with him; she run off and the Plew kid got even more closemouth, special after Windy and the others took to dedeviling him, making up songs to send him on postcards:

> Mr. Plew Tollins aint worth a goldarn
> His shack is dirtier than a old barn
> His paw stole a calf and kicked the can
> And his maw run off with a corn salve man

"But Plew never let on. Couple times a year he'd go to the railroad for stock salt, pancake flour and a bucket of jelly beans, not answering when folks'd ask, 'What you hear from your ma?' or 'Never heard from the old woman since she lit out, hev you?'

"One time Plew picked up a hound pup in town where a car had run over it. After that folks'd see him with that pup in a syrup bucket hanging from the saddle horn and when the dog got too big, he'd limp along behind with Plew waiting on the ridges, yellin' out, 'He-ah, pup, he pup, he pup!' Finally the dog got some of Windy's wolf poison and the next day Plew come to the Johnson place and aimed an old revolver with both hands on their Buster dog, squinting down the barrel but afraid to shoot it. So Windy runs him off and tells it all around the country, hooting and laughing, still at it when old Plew goes down to register to fight the Kaiser. '. . . Something where there ain't no shootin'.—I sure don't like shootin'. . . . .' But the draft board runs him off for a bone pile.

"Couple years back he puts up a mail box on the Ganter route and Windy seen him meet a woman, a youngish one, getting off the westbound train, so Windy he stops at the newspaper office and come Saturday everybody in the county knows about it:

PROMINENT BACHELOR FROM THE BOTTLENECK HAULED OUT A LOAD OF COAL AND A HOUSEKEEPER THIS WEEK. ANTICIPATING A COLD WINTER, EH, PLEW?"

"Mail-order woman?" Marty laughed.

"Yeh, and some of the newer biddies in the country were for running her off, but the men just laughs down under their buttons and tries business over that way. Turns out Plew's woman, Florrie, is a scared little thing with hair the color of a muskrat sitting in the sun. He's begun to sell a little cream too, and buying stuff, even hauled out a new dresser, holding the crated glass between his bony knees all the way. Come spring, and she raises flowers you could see clear from the ridge, and Windy got to talking about sneaking over when Plew was away.

" '. . . Get your hide a full a holes,' somebody warned. That tickled him. 'By that he-jinny? Why, he couldn't even shoot my dog. Scairt of a gun.'

"Then it got around that Florrie was in trouble, mighty unreasonable, with nobody but old slack-pants Plew around, but that's how it is."

"You can't always tell by the pants," Martin said, and went to settle down beside Penny to get warm and to tell her the story of the pup that rode in a syrup bucket.

At the Biggles, who had brought this stork party idea into the country from off south somewhere, the teams were doubled up on the bobsleds, the bottles passed, and when they reached Plew's sod house, Windy put a shoulder against the door as though breaking in on a nest of Heinies when there was no reply to his knocking. The door gave and Martin and Penny followed the others reluctantly as they pushed past Plew just standing there, gaunt and stubbled in the frost the cold air made around him, a spattered white apron hung from his neck to his knees, his pale eyes red-rimmed and his short lip twitching. Even Mollie Biggle was a little embarrassed that no heavy-bodied Florrie was around to take the cake she brought in a dishpan. But Windy was undisturbed. "Surprise!" he whooped, hogcalling it out in the hot little room, "Surprise!"

That moved Plew, sent him stumbling back against the red calico curtain beside the bedroom door, his feet just missing a tub of water with some clothes floating. Uneasily the women looked at him and moved closer together, pulling at their mittens, their eyes sneaking curiously around the pleasant, whitewashed room, the stand of geraniums pushed aside from the frosted window, pans shining, everything put away, probably behind the red curtain that was like a deep, six-foot-long closet against the wall to the bedroom, with Plew beside it.

"Where's your party manners, Mr. Tollins?" Mollie complained. "You're supposed to say, 'Sit down, folks. Me and Florrie's tickled proud to have you.'"

There was an embarrassed laugh or two, somebody back near the wall snickering, saying Mollie sure ought to know about bachelor stork parties.

"Bachelor?" Penny whispered to Martin, sitting stiff as wood beside her. "Is this a bachelor stork party?"

"A course! What you think—they was married folks?" Windy boomed out. He was getting impatient. "Say, Plew, where's the woman? She ain't run out on you too, like your maw? . . . No, I bet not, not in her fix."

Still the man in the hanging apron stood silent beside the bedroom door, a hand on a fold of the red curtain, and so Mollie fussed around to start the pitch game, lengthening the table, eking out chairs with the wash bench and the ironing board when nobody offered to go past Plew for chairs in the bedroom. Windy dealt at his end, laying out a hand for Plew, with Florrie's in the set at the stove end. But the bidders got to rob both hands, and when Martin looked over his cards at Plew, the man was watching them, his face gray as moldy alfalfa, his lips moving to speak but without sound. From across the table Penny saw Martin's hand knotting on the cards, his aloneness among these strangers, on the side of the man at the curtain, as Windy loudly bossed the games, counting the scores, "High, low, jick, jack . . ." each time.

When Martin finally drew a hand with nine spot high he threw the cards down and went to sit in the cold window, scratching at the frost on the glass, thinking about these people come out this freezing night to dedevil a poor, defenseless man, and not a one among them with anything himself—no money, no security, not a sign of happiness to show on the face. All sitting there watching the bedroom door for a sight of the miserable hang-dog Florrie. By God, even the Heinies, out to get you, were better, making it quick destruction, no drawing it out, no pretending it was a goddamn party.

But Windy had been going set. Slapping his cards down he bawled out, "Damn it, Plew, fetch out your woman!" and when Penny shook her head pleadingly, he repeated the command, pounding the table. "Fetch that Florrie out here!"

Now at last Plew's weather-cracked lips moved in his gray, furrowed face. "I—I guess," he was saying softly, but clear enough in the silence, "I guess . . . if a man has a good reason it would be all right to ask folks to go . . . even if they was to come on a party, huh?"

"Go?" Windy threw his big head back, his open-mouth laugh roaring out.

Miserably, Penny motioned to Hughie, her head indicating the outside door, but he was laughing, too, watching Windy bait the man at the red curtain, measuring him like a ferret would a gopher for the strike. "You look mighty wild." Windy was saying. "You ain't pulled no gun on the little thing like you done on my dog, have you?"

But the man's face was so miserable and tormented that the women stirred uneasily, Mollie whispering to her Jake so he fetched in an apple basket lined with an old pink quilt for a bassinet. From it with a flourish she lifted a great battered doll that had been in the rain but still cried a little when she squeezed it against her bosom. The doll's bottom was folded into a huge bulky diaper made of an old piece of bedsheet sagging with knobby lumps. Holding it carefully, Mollie carried the doll to Plew, announcing "Stork shower!" even managing a giggle.

Automatically the man took the doll, holding it out before him like an apron full of cow-chips.

"Open it, open it!" everybody but the Stones cried, and when Plew just stood, Windy pulled the doll from him and dumped it on the table. So Mollie undid the big brass blanket pins herself and laid the knobby diaper open. One after another she lifted the articles from it high over the lamp for the rest to explain, with jokes and laughing, to the father-to-be. But somehow, with no Florrie heavy and embarrassed and blushing before them, there were no funny words, no noisy roarings for the bundle of hemmed flour sacks, good enough to diaper a gully colt until beef prices came back, or the chain of bent safety pins, the cake of dried-out toilet soap, a fly-specked can of talcum, a battered teething ring, and a bottle of skunk oil for chest colds. Jake chuckled a little at the skunk oil but otherwise there was only the sound of the wind rising in the chimney, the rattle of the stove lids as Martin built up the dying fire. Even Windy Johnson was busy digging at a cavity far back in his mouth, and Penny leaned forward over herself, very sick, not looking up for the faded outing flannel kimono, the bootees leathery from bad washing, several strips of flannel for bellybands, half an old gray blanket and a piece of oilcloth.

"Somebody sure aims to protect you from sudden showers," Hughie remarked, but without his usual mean laughing. Then there was nothing more except the dog-eared patent medicine book, *Motherhood Made Easy,* and the regular stork party tonic for the bachelor father—half a pound of plug tobacco, which Mollie held out to Plew. "Helps put you on your feet," she said, and Martin moved uneasily, remembering where he had heard those words last —from the Klan speechifier at Dunhill Armistice Day, talking to the vets—"Helps put you on your feet!"

In the meantime Windy had jerked the plug from Mollie, bit off a piece and threw the rest on the top of the other presents. "He ain't no father yet, and so far's we been showed tonight, he ain't never gonna be."

But Plew stood exactly as before, his hands clutched in the white apron, making none of the customary mock thanks. At the back Martin hurried Penny into her coat, to take her out for air, and so Mollie grabbed her coat too, and the dishpan with her cake, announcing: "Eats and coffee to my house!" and disappeared through the doorway into the cloud of frost that pushed in as the others silently followed, Jake calling back to hurry, the snow was blowing up into a blizzard.

But Windy Johnson was not done. Stopping directly before Plew he straightened his short, thick body and then deliberately bent to spit a big splotch of brown between the man's feet. "Old Jelly-bean

Tollins!" he laughed, as he wiped his mouth. "Well, tell Florrie I'll be seeing her come summer. My turn next, you know. But feed 'er up; I likes my ducks fat!"

For a moment Plew didn't seem to understand this either, but then he stirred and sliding sideways through the bedroom door, was back almost at once, an old revolver held straight out before him in both hands. Penny, who had hung back to say how sorry she was about coming, saw him, and saw Windy stop in the open doorway, the snow blowing in around his feet.

"Why, you gun-pulling bastard!" he bellowed, whipping an automatic from his pocket. Just as he fired Martin struck the man's shoulder, spinning him half around, so the shot rang out wild in the little room. It was followed by a second one, close as an echo, but cannon-loud. Before it Windy clapped his hands over his thick stomach, stumbled back as the thin, frightened squall of a baby came from behind the curtain.

At the child's cry, Plew looked up from the smoking gun in his hands and laying it cautiously on the table he pulled the curtain back and from the bunk against the wall he lifted the bundle of new-born baby, holding it gently against him. Beside the man Penny looked down upon a woman, a woman so motionless and white that she was afraid to touch even her hand. But Martin, who had seen much of this thing, put the name to it.

"Dead," he said. "Dead for hours behind the curtain here, and all the time we were sitting around, making fun, worse than a bunch of drunken Heinies."

Now suddenly Martin Stone could face the fear that had been with him the last two months, ever since the night he saw Plew Tollins, shy, gentle Plew Tollins, standing alone with his baby in his arms, his wife dead, the powder smoke of his revolver blue and stinking in the room, while outside were the neighbors who had come to torment his helplessness with dirty, shaming presents and with laughing until one among them had to be carried away with a bullet through his belly.

And as Martin looked down upon his own son, and Penny there beside him, safe and pretty and full of living as ever, he put out his arm and drew her tightly to him, shaken and silent in his sudden release.

4 — *Prayer in the Rain*

"You got to expect a lot of noise and little wool if you try to shear a hog," old Iron Leg used to say, and Martin remembered it as he looked from the hump over his place, the wheat rusted to dead straw, the squaw corn curled, the heat waves shimmering into a mirage lake around the pink buttes to the west.

But it wasn't the wheat, the drouth or the lizard panting under the sagebrush at Martin's feet so much as the big, dusty car beside his yard gate that made him mad. Bill Terrey, from over at Teapot, and promoting an oil company down near Dunhill, had made it past the Stones around mealtime twice in one week. He was down there this minute, smoking a cigarette with Penny over a second cup of coffee and blowing to her about her good dinner, her fine garden, her pretty baby—hers, everything hers, and Martin, the man of the place, having to sit there, helpless as a toad on a shovel, not even knowing until big-talking Bill stopped by that Penny smoked.

So he had pushed his chair back and walked out to change the water, out where he wouldn't have to see those fancy engineer pants or hear the man's smooth-talking way, paying fancy compliments to a woman as easy as if he wasn't ranny as a billy goat, saying them so you couldn't even throw him out, pretending everything was lacey-pretty, and high above the belly. Women were fools for such talk, even the mam'zelles over in France—always complaining that the American soldiers had no finesse, just grabbed a woman, saying, "Geev me the kees; geev me the piece; good-by. . . ." Rough like the pig.

But nowadays there were other things on a man's mind besides the compliments of a slacker who got exempted to support his mother, so Martin cranked up the old Chevvy and went to Benny's to sit in the shade of the dugout and talk army and how they had all looked forward to shucking out of the uniform—he, Benny, even guys like that Carter, the Kluxer, up the creek.

"Yeh, I could hardly wait to get Betty over on her back," Benny laughed, his wife giggling a little, down deep within herself, but motioning her head toward the children, the two eldest making foot-houses over their bare toes, and listening.

Well, Martin sure had been happy to see his father waiting at the depot and to walk on his good side to a restaurant for corned beef and a glass of home brew together. But right from the start there was something wide as no man's land between them, something more than the forty-six years in age and the five years away.

Maybe it was that Martin had come home from the war ten years older than his father, and with two good legs. Or because there was no house of thirty rooms, with plenty of money and an uncle who was a senator, even though that hadn't lasted. Martin found a peg-legged old man with one room, a gas ring on a washstand, and an empty pension envelope beside it.

"Yeh," Benny said, driving his pocket-knife blade thoughtfully into the hard earth, "no job, nothing but them dry-landing home-steads. Back in '65 if there wasn't thirty rooms, and no work, there was all the West open to the vets, with forests, railroads and mines enough to make a rash of billionaires—and millions of free homes for the taking. Rich land, with trees and grass and rain."

"But dad did lose a leg," Martin was compelled to say.

"Yeh, he did, and that was something that couldn't be hid, and the damage to the country neither, a whole section just battlefields, or stripped and overrun. My pa was in the middle of it and he pulled out north to get away from the sight, and from the carpet-baggers that come swarming like Mormon crickets. But the stinkin' grafters what made it tough for my dad and yours and all the rest's the same brand a skunks that's on top in Washington today."

Martin nodded. With his uncle among the grafters Iron Leg still had to spend his life peddling salves and colic cures, be left with only one thing to say to his returning son: "Well, we got you back in one piece. You won't be going to a wife half a man. . . ." It reminded Martin of his mother's complainings. "Never wrote me a word about the amputation and so what could I do, sixteen and all the guests and the preacher and the presents waiting?" shaming the boy for his father, and for her complaining, and even more when he saw Nancy stand there swelled up like a cow that'd been at the corn crib, and bragging about the cement block house and the maid.

As he poured sand from one closed palm into the other, he thought about Penny, pouring out coffee at home for Bill Terrey, with his big car and fancy pants, and no lump of scarred and twisted meat where a lung ought to be. The sand felt like sugar, like the sugar he threw into Pete's white eye once a month. "Helps clear 'em up," old Hughie had said when he recommended it.

But he said something else too: "A tenderfoot kin maybe learn to work a Powder river roan, or track a jackrabbit through sagebrush and bring down a buck at the first shot but it takes a gen-u-wine longhorn to handle a buckskin."

And when Martin got home that evening Penny asked if he might like a job with the new oil development coming near Dunhill. She did it while she was lifting him a piece of gooseberry pie, her eyes busy, but even so she broke it a little when Martin thrust his chair away. "Working for that goddamn outfit? I'll take to cooking mash at a still first."

It rained before the Fourth of July, hailed too, but rained, and so the Stones turned the wheat cut down for feed and leaving it to dry in the sun, went to Stover for the day, Martin even letting Penny take a snapshot of him and young Milton to send to Council Bluffs. They took it with the Kodak her brother Joey brought home from Russia. He just came walking into the yard before dinner, everybody running out, Ma Liz dropping the roasting pan and screeching. Nobody had heard more than the report that he got left behind around Vladivostok some place and finally given up as missing. Seemed he did get lost and sick and was picked up by some funny Russkies, trappers, who were heading off into the wilderness and couldn't understand a word he said, so he went along and walked all over hell 'n gone.

It was wonderful to see Ma Liz crying over him, but now there would be no insurance money to pay the mortgage and so old Artie had to look for a place, something on shares. No jobs for a man of sixty, with the young fellows such a drug on the market they could be shot down in the labor wars like over in Herrin. No telling when Joey would find something either, probably sit on his tail for months, years, before he could get himself out of OD's. Ran into a floating crap game on the way home. . . .

When people at Stover tried to get him to make a speech about the bolshies he wouldn't do it. "I don't know nothing about them; didn't see many that wasn't just like anybody, plain tired of being bled. Mostly trappers and herders, maybe two families to the township. God, a man with a good tractor and a string of gang plows could lay out a field a thousand miles long!"

"Oh, you soldiers are all alike. Marty won't even tell how he got gassed," Ellie complained. But when she asked about Joey's luck with the Russky girls, he grinned over his mouth harp. "You know me, kid!" he said, and played strange, whirling little tunes.

So Ma Liz took in washing for the ranchers around, her hands getting crippled with the rheumatism while Joey lost his grin and Martin wondered if perhaps his father hadn't been lucky to trade a leg for a little pension that no fast-talking demagogue, no Washington gyp game could take away.

Martin Stone was still not as tough or as handy as old timers like Mort Miller or Chuck Sherman—never would be, but he put on a little meat, and even where the hot winds didn't strike, his skin lost its blueness; the sun-squint of his eyes purposeful. He had to work slow, but by paying back double he got help with the heavy jobs. "A mighty steady young feller," Artie said to his daughter. She nodded, and did not say what always lived in the back of her mind.

Like in the army, things got easier. Last year even planting the blue corn with the spade had to be learned from Penny, along with the time of heat in mares, and stringing barbed wire around his crops and pasture for protection against the sheep drifting through. Mostly vets who lived off the country the best they could, getting a little flock somewhere and ranging it toward the railroad by shipping time, picking up anything handy on the way, stock, tools, or maybe a bullet in the ribs. The first Martin knew about them was when Penny pushed the old double-barrel into his hand and pointed out a moving blanket of sheep, grayer than the sage, far up Seep Creek. "They'll eat everything into the ground unless you stand them off. It's an old game . . ." she said. A couple of wires around the breaking established his claim. Then he could stand at the corner with his gun on his arm and the men would call their dogs to bunch the sheep down the road.

Later cattle took to wandering up from the G Bar, smelling green corn and eating up the little grass, so this summer Milton had to buy fencing for the whole section, the chattel mortgage secured by the stock and the old car. Without Penny to staple or hold the stretcher bar, it was slow, sometimes the wire slipped, ripping his awkward hand, and then he threw the hammer as far as he could. By God, a man shouldn't be expected to do everything alone!

So Penny put her son under the wagon seat and went along.

The millet, sowed on the wheat ground after the hail, was coming thick and green for feed. The garden was fine again, with enough water left over for the young cottonwoods that were to hold the northwest wind from sweeping around the hump. Besides the fencing and the line of wash flying every morning, Penny worked at the house, tacking pinkish building paper over the bare studding and making a long bookcase under the south window of the rosy barked slabs like the casings. Above, she hung blue-bordered flour sack curtains and brought out her books from the university courses she took after Dick was killed—including History of the West, for she always planned to come back when the pain softened.

In addition she had some books from Artie's Aunt Phoebe in Philadelphia, like Dickens, Melville, Austin and Howells. "Just whoring stories!" Martin roared out angrily one night, when he felt left out of the talk with Wheeler P. Scheeler. Martin preferred the bottom shelf: catalogues and government bulletins on bean growing, co-operative marketing, and irrigation. At the top were the books Wheeler brought over in a sack bouncing behind the saddle while he borrowed others, perhaps the stories and scrapbooks on the West. "Been neglectin' my stock and coyote hunting since my ma died last winter," he admitted. "Guess I never did have sense enough to pull my neck in when I shut a window without her tellin' me."

But even Martin was pleased when Wheeler found the old Indian trail that crossed just below his house, with a dozen tipi stones scattered around the large spring, and a cigar box full of arrowheads, some of shining black obsidian, probably from the ledge at Yellowstone, showing them everywhere. ". . . Get's worked up over them slivers a rock like some men does over them Frog smuts," Benny laughed.

One warm, drowsy, flying-ant day, Wheeler stopped at the garden, staying on his horse as always when Martin wasn't around. Leaning over the saddle, his round, red face darkened with embarrassment, he put a willow-framed mounting into Penny's hands. On cardboard, arranged in a fan pattern, were a couple of the obsidian arrowheads, several of flint, a great jasper spear point, two carved bone tally sticks and an awl, brown with age, underneath; and in the center two bird arrowpoints of pink quartz, delicate as baby fingernails.

"You folks been like a fambly . . ." he said awkwardly, and whistling for his dogs, loped away, a short chunk of a man sitting his saddle.

Penny put the frame above the bookcase, wondering about Martin. But he liked it, better than the what-not Dick had carved while he traveled with the rodeo. The next rainy spell Martin got out the tools and made cedar frames to hold Penny's watercolors of the Big Horns, Cloud Peak and Devil's Tower, painted the year Artie's car was new and beef prices, along with overalls and mowing machines and sugar, were sky high.

"We should have stayed home; the money might have put off the foreclosure on Artie's place."

"I doubt it," Martin said, admiring the cedar frame against the rose-touched blues and whites of Cloud Peak. "The banks managed to grab places from folks who had a lot more money ahead than Artie ever got his lunch hooks on. Even some of the big wheat farmers, like the Leites."

"You mean Nancy's Leites?" Penny asked quickly.

"Yeh," Martin said, sinking the nail for the picture clear to the head with one blow, and having to set another. "I hear the old man shot himself, the boys out hired-handing, so Fancy-Nancy'll have to wash for her own dirty kids after all." Not a word of how he knew, and as though it was not worth further talk, he took up the fourth frame and fitted it to the enlarged photograph of the Miles County agricultural exhibit last fall. To the upper-left-hand corner he fastened the two blue ribbons they had won with their summer squash and sweet corn grown on sod.

They stood together admiring the frames and the pictures, and Penny didn't say what she had planned for weeks, with old Milton's letters so lonesome since his grandson was born. They could just as well throw up a sod lean-to on the north for him. Maybe later, when there were more in the family, so Martin would feel less left out.

But the times were unsettling. One night Wheeler P. Scheeler stopped by to sit on the lighted doorstep refreshing his cud and telling the news he got at the railroad. President Harding had died, took sick suddenly coming back from Alaska, and, judging by the talk around Dunhill and Casper, wasn't beating the devil out very much, with suicides and maybe murders all around him, the indictments for bribery and fraud on that Teapot Dome business and the Vets' Bureau probably coming close to the White House.

"Wouldn't surprise me," Martin agreed, as he pared away the thickened nail where his thumb had been foolishly mashed, oiling the windmill on a blowy day.

"Yes, looks even worse than in Grant's time," Penny said from her mending, "when the president's wife almost got him entangled."

"Old soldiers like my dad say lots of high officers besides Grant's been henpecked. Maybe that's why they yell hell out of the underlings." Marty said.

The others laughed, Wheeler objecting that far as he knew, Pershing's wife was all right; a Wyoming girl, died in a fire out in San Francisco.

"She wasn't here to prod Black Jack into risking his reputation in politics like Grant." Maybe he wasn't as hard up, Martin thought. Anyway, even a labor-baiter like Coolidge couldn't be worse than Harding.

But Penny wasn't so sure. "In moving picture shots Cal looks like a bookkeeper at the stove works down in Lincoln, keeping track of the paper clips," she said with concern.

"Then maybe he can keep track of the clean sheets for the boys in the hospitals, get something besides a shot of salts for a sick man."

"Maybe," Penny said doubtfully.

A couple of days later, when Marty and Penny were going down for Joey's twenty-sixth birthday, they heard that Harding's funeral train was coming through. As they drove along the highway, a special did come past, running smooth and fast, everything taking to the sidings, track workers and a handcar crew looking curiously after it from the cinders, a Mexican among them taking off his dusty black hat as he crossed himself. For a minute Martin was a soldier before his dead commander-in-chief and he stiffened, eyes front, but the next he remembered the stinking eggs the poor devils in the hospitals had to eat, the junking of the League and all he had given his lungs for, and kids like Slim who fell running through the mud. Spitting over the car door he stepped on the gas, roaring past the Mexican still standing in respect.

With Martin away, paying back help, or down the creek grubbing sagebrush for next spring's breaking, Penny found time for her wandering over the place, pulling the sleeping baby in an old express wagon as she looked for the first salmon mallow set so close to the earth, its fragrance sweet on the wind, or the white poppy thistles, the flaming purple loco weed that would blanket the gravelly spots of the hump, lupines, the great yellow satin blooms of the bull-tongue cactus or perhaps the magenta of a late sheep sticker.

Sometimes Martin watched his wife walking in her free stride, her thick brown hair bobbed at the neck flying out in the wind when she took off her hat to watch a bobolink rising into the air, or to look after the antelope that showed up now and then, or perhaps stooped over a nest of blue eggs safe in a patch of cactus from the soft-padded coyote. Perhaps she stopped to pound the earth, killing a rattlesnake with the stick she always carried, and with her heel on the snake's head, cut off the rattlers for the glass bowl on the whatnot.

Walking free and easy anywhere, not afraid of anything for herself or her son, even among the rattlers.

At first she always showed Martin what she brought home: flowers for the yellow crock in the window, agates, or mica-flecked bits for the curio box on the stoop, or perhaps a larger piece for the rock garden—a gray-knuckled stone that was the petrified vertebra of some prehistoric animal; the bent, spongy core of a buffalo horn preserved by the dryness, a pinkish chunk of quartzite, a rusty nodule of hematitic sandstone. Then one day she brought in pieces of gray flint that were surely man-worked for knives and skin scrapers, cruder and heavier than usually, perhaps from some prehistoric man who camped here when the two pink buttes were still a ridge, or covered much of the plain—who could tell?

It was soon after Harding's funeral, with Coolidge already penny-pinching, and the weather so hot that a man's spit would sizzle against a plowshare in the sun, the squaw corn rattling, the ears only twisted cob; and so Martin blew up like a land mine, exploding with all he had learned on the section and among the fighting, the wounded and dying. He didn't give a good goddamn what any of the son of a bitching stuff Penny dragged in was, and he wouldn't have any whore-running, tail-teasing woman showing off what she knew around him!

Penny took it, silent and shut away behind her stony gray eyes. And when he was dry and helpless against her, Martin ran out into the sun and began to shovel at the new cellar they were digging, throwing dirt fast and hard while Penny watched from behind the window curtain, waiting with the army blanket and a cup of salted milk warmed over a twist of paper as for the baby. When there was no more earth flying she hurried out and found the man sprawled in the hole as he had fallen, his breath a low rasping, his face gray and cold; shaking all over like a horse worked down.

"Oh, you foolish child!" she wanted to cry out as she rolled him into the blanket to get his sweated body from the wet ground, and held the milk to his lips, hoping it would help. And when his breathing finally quieted and the shaking too, he pulled himself up, hunching forward, his arms tight around his chest.

"God, it's like a ripsaw tearing through me. I'm no good at all," he moaned, tears running down his drawn, stubbled face, "I used to be the best man on the section. . . ."

"You're all right now, if you just use judgment," Penny scolded, and seeing the anger rise into his pale face again, she told him the news she had been saving for the last, after he saw the flint pieces. "Reddy has her calf, and you won't need to trade it, for it's a heifer already, two of them—twins," she said. "We're going into the cattle business so fast we'll be accused of using a rope and a running iron in the night, like poor old Plew's dad."

But Marty wouldn't let himself seem pleased by the twins. Toward evening, a little steadier, he did go out to help get them in, Penny driving, Marty holding the two little whitefaces in the back of the car, old Reddy following in an awkward gallop, bawling, licking the little ears over the car door with a rumbling in her throat when they stopped in the yard. But as soon as she had the calves on the ground she threw up her head, mooed, and with them running in her flanks, bolted through the gate and out over the pasture.

"Look at that goddamn cow go!" Martin roared, jerking his hat off and slamming it to the ground.

"Well, you left the gate wide open. . . ."

Now, the second time today, Martin Stone turned on his wife, and used every word he could lay tongue to while she stood there, knowing she could knock him rolling with one good slap. Instead, she turned her back on him and went to round up the cow with the car. Safe in the lot, she milked her down until the calves could grasp the swollen teats, one on each side, bunting, the little tails busy.

It was late that night when Martin came in and stood beside the dark bed. "I guess I lost my temper a little this afternoon," he said, his voice sullen with self-pity, "I wasn't feeling so good."

Penny sat up and spoke into the darkness. "I know you're not feeling right, Martin," she said, "but what you did today wasn't the work of a sick man but a damn fool. The next time it happens you'll be homesteading alone."

Then she lay back, the straw tick rustling as she settled herself, not letting him know how long she held her breath against the thought of his hands on her throat, choking her down as he did the buckskin, only the horse could jerk loose, throw him backward into the fence. But in the morning light her fear seemed very foolish and so she was up early, changing the flow of water through the garden, cutting the flowers, marking blooms with calico strings for seed. She came in with her arms full, a hatching of Plymouth Rocks in her apron that a silly hen stole out, with winter due in a couple of months. There was already smoke from the chimney and Martin out at the pole corral, showing the white-faced twins to Mike Cannon. "Couple of chirky little devils, ain't they?" he called to Penny. "Pretty as a picture."

But there were other worries for the Stones. One of the milk cows dropped her calf from Bang's disease, next year's increase lost, and Penny insisting that her milk was dangerous, although even old Chuck Sherman thought it was foolish to ship a good milker at beef prices when she had to be replaced for the mortgage, taking all the cream savings. And at the county fair the Klan came out in full regalia, a parade so long it seemed everybody for a hundred miles around must be robed.

"Hell fire!" Chuck Sherman said, punching the peak into his old-fashioned Stetson, "I didn't know there was that many men in Wyoming what could get around on the hoof."

"A bodacious sight of good bed sheeting wasted," Mary Cannon complained, as they watched the robed lines march behind the big cars carrying the flag and the headmen, and Congressman Stilt, Nat Ridges of the bank, and the sheriff. Toward the end somebody stepped out toward Martin and growled, "We're a-layin' for you!" the voice familiar and the slovenly, stringless shoes under the flapping robe. Later Penny whispered that it was Windy Johnson all right; visiting with the Carters, Betty Green said.

Windy a Klansman! That explained the burning cross above the ranch on the Turtle Shell the night after the bachelor stork party, and why Jack Hall said it wouldn't be necessary for the Stones to stay out their three months; should, in fact, get the hell out, although the drifted roads were almost impassable for stock or car, and with Penny so heavy.

They knew Windy was out of the hospital long ago, Plew's bullet hitting only fat in that belly. Because the shooting was on his own place, after he had ordered Windy out, Plew wasn't arrested but there was the baby, the boy he named Stone Tollins. A petition was circulated saying Plew was not a fit father, the Bottleneck not a proper place for a child. Here Martin's five years in the service made him a good counselor. "It's like in the army," he told Penny. "They got all the power and the disposal, and you better keep sayin' 'Yes, sir, yes sir,' and sneak any ideas around back like you sneak up on Pete. Spread it around that Plew's keeping the kid'll save the county money."

"But it's so stupid!" the impatient Penny complained. "What child could have more affection than old Plew will give that baby? Look how he nursed the crippled pup! Everybody admits he's a whiz with young animals."

"That's another thing you can't say straight out—that kids are young animals."

So the county's money was saved. At the fair Penny took a couple of dollars from her cream money and went with Martin to pick a present for young Stoney, something the odd, reticent Plew would never think of. They selected a pink hood and jacket embroidered in blue forget-me-nots. A couple of weeks later Plew drove up to the garden in his old pickup, the baby in a willow basket beside him, wearing the new outfit and doing fine—except for the prickly heat because Plew was sure that babies needed more clothes than the government bulletins claimed. He stayed an hour or so, looking through the fall garden and admiring the twin calves, and when he was ready to go he stood with his old hat in both hands, his Adam's apple jigging above his faded blue collar.

"You folks been right neighborly to Stoney and me," he said, and started away, but turned slowly back. "You think maybe the boy could learn to run one a them machines when he's big—one a them flying machines that I seen going over my place? Seems like he notices them already, and his ma was a smart woman, Florrie was."

The Stones nodded and he left, even waving a little from across the creek.

"Poor man," Penny said, because there were no words for what she felt.

"It's a few decent folks like him, tending their own business and not always gypping, climbing with their foot in your face, that makes a man think maybe the human race ain't all shot to hell," Martin said, turning back to his onion tromping, stepping down the rows of tops to make the bottoms ripen and dry for winter.

Penny looked at him concerned. "Maybe you need a little fun, Marty, a little visiting with your own kin. Why not go down to see your dad when the potatoes are dug, or ask him to come here? We could build on a lean-to before the ground freezes over. . . ."

But Martin only brought his cowhide shoes down harder on the onions. ". . . When he turned against us all!"

"Then go see Stevie." And while he objected at first, he finally went. He suspected Penny was in the family way again, although she had been nursing young Milton right along and claimed that was fireproof. He remembered what she said about her brother Joey once: "Looks like God nor the devil can do much about a mother's eldest son, unless more brats come crowding him off the breast and the knees."

But he was afraid to ask, afraid he would blow up, and so be homesteading alone. So he got Mike Cannon to help with the chores in case of a fall blizzard, although Wheeler P. Scheeler offered; didn't want that old saddle warmer around while he was gone. Bad enough to have him tomcatting the place when he was home.

Martin looked fine with his Sunday coat over a new pair of overalls, his neck brown as leather puttees above the white shirt collar, bluish white where Penny clipped it out of the thick mat of drake tails.

"God, looks like you been working on a Galloway bull!" he said as she shook the apron from around his neck, the dark hair like a fur rug around the chair. He caught a look at the back in his old trench mirror. "Cut up high as Fancy-Nancy's," he blurted out, and reddened, Penny already suspecting he planned to drive around that way.

When Martin came back he was full of old stories about the Stone house on the Cincinnati hills, the war graft behind it, and the manipulations of the Radicals in Congress that old Hiram regretted later. ". . . Maybe because the money got away from him."

He was pleased too, but not admitting it, that Stevie loved the old man Milton and had a big scrapbook of the yarns about him. He had many real stories to tell too, mostly about the leg or the cures, like for yellow fever, and about the great flock of passenger pigeons they saw on the way west from Ohio in '74, the flock shadowing the ground like a cloud against the sun, and now, fifty years later, not one left in existence. It made a man think.

Stevie talked, too, about the long summer trips in the orange medicine wagon, the cartwheels Iron Leg turned, landing on the pipe; the hunting, the fights, the fiddling and singing for the dances, and maybe the old man sneaking off to some woman afterward. Martin wasn't surprised. He knew about Dolly Talbor at the Riverside Pavilion, remembered that she killed herself and that she had come to his mother once to have a handsome dress made and paid her with one of old Milton's pension checks.

"Your mother told you that?" Penny protested sharply, but seeing Martin's face set, she tried to smooth it over: "Talking about such things just keeps the grass from growing over."

But Martin was wondering about something else; how his wife would pay him back when she found out that Nancy got the money to renew her teacher's certificate out of him—the fifty dollars he had been holding back from his compensation, in case he ever reneged on the drylanding.

Turned out Coolidge was against raising the pension of old soldiers like Iron Leg as well as doing for the new vets. Martin had talked the bonus over at Argonne with Benny and Cannon and the others already in hock to loan sharks for all their prospects would stand. Besides, the bill was just a hoax to grab off votes by putting a few borrowed dollars in circulation, like sprinkling the leaves of a plant when the roots were baked in soil tight as the Vermonter's fist. Farmers were still losing their land, Steve's place going too, while the jobless from the town came renting where the experts had been foreclosed. Even the old M-Bar-M, set up with longhorns trailed from Texas in the Seventies, went under the hammer like a vet's drylanding. In the meantime forty thousand more coal miners struck, some close as Oklahoma and Kansas. But Attorney General Daugherty had to resign over the Teapot Dome scandal in spite of all the gravel Coolidge could scratch to cover him, and some people were saying Harding had really been killed, put out of the way before he was disgraced.

"Disgraced!" some snorted, the same ones who asked, "What's the catch?" when a few steel companies ordered a wage increase instead of a cut.

Martin had no way of earning a dollar this winter but he chopped posts a while over in the foothills for logs to anchor the earth dam they were putting in west of the hump—hold back the little snow water and the summer's cloudbursts. The hailstorm alone last summer would have supplied irrigation water for weeks. With work so scarce the settlers, even the Cannons, the Sauls and Carlsons, all stayed, and so the mail came out twice a week. It was there Martin got the news of Wilson's death. Twenty below zero, with the wind whipping the snow over the sagebrush, yet Martin didn't start home until long past midnight. Penny got up when she heard his stomping outside, swept the snow from him and made hot coffee that they drank with their feet together on the oven door. In her blue corduroy robe she was round as a barrel and Martin had to look away, holding himself from blowing apart, and after a while he pulled out a paper with Wilson's picture, one taken during the League fight—already like a dead man.

A long time Penny held the picture before her sleep-puffed, blurring eyes. She knew what her history professor would say. ". . . We knew that all chances of taking our stand for peace were gone; with the prejudice, the ignorance and misinformation even fooling men from the trenches. The Republicans are afraid to let the Demos get the credit for lasting peace; the great international financial interests afraid of supervision and responsibility. . . ." Yet Wilson's death made it so desperately final. She turned her head uneasily toward the baby sleeping in his box. "Somehow I can't see the World Court more than just tolling a hungry mare with an apron full of empty cobs."

"Yes, and by the time the public finds out, the frozen bit is in the mouth," Martin agreed, licking his wind-cracked lips, tasting their sting and salt. "It's a disease. Take my dad, yelling all his life because a lot of grafters got Lincoln killed, with the papers calling him crazy, acting like he was a traitor, the enemy. Now old Iron Leg falls for the same line about Wilson, saying he's crazy, maybe even with the syph, like some claim, telling me that while we was off fighting the Kaiser, the folks to home has a fight to save the country from a madman. So I says, 'You know what they done to Lincoln. Why, he was lucky to be shot quick compared to what you been doing to Wilson!' and the old man just about runs me off. But Lincoln *was* lucky, like that Slim kid was, with a bullet through the head. He don't have to sit here on his ass——"

"Oh, Marty!"

For a long time the man rubbed his cold-swollen hands and was silent, but finally he started to talk again, this time of what had been like a lump inside him all the way home through the storm, something from a letter Benny showed him. A buddy had been in Washington last Armistice Day and saw the people gather outside Wilson's house like they always did every year, some at daylight and staying right into the stormy night, some even praying. Finally Wilson came crippling out under the porch light, just hitching himself along, with his hair all white and hanging to his neck. But he had got into the old black coat and his silk hat, sick as he was, and managed to say a few poor broken words to those who came on Armistice Day to kneel before his door in the rain.

Martin Stone was no joiner, not even belonging to the Legion. He liked to talk to Benny but he seldom hung around with the post office loafers or at the sales or the turkey shoots, where his marksmanship had done so well for him with the Klansmen looking. He didn't like the arguing of the heel-sitters, yelling "bonus hounds!" to every complaint against graft or violence, or "slacker" and "profiteer." But mostly the blowhards talked about their horses, their dogs or their muscle, puffing themselves up like a Wyoming thunderhead—big show, big blow, no rain, no snow. Like that Mussolini starting up in Italy.

But the Stones did go to the Cannon dances and to the G Bar when the barn loft was emptied twice a year. Come hard luck, Martin was ready as a native to turn in to help, like the time the Millers were burnt out by the spring prairie fire sweeping down their long-grass slough, or little three-year-old Charley Carlson was found in the stock tank. Maybe because Martin had learned to make persistence do for strength and wind he could keep up artificial respiration for three hours, with a little spelling by the other men, until he got color to the boy, a little moving and a big throw-up of water and moss. Then Martin gave out, and when the doctor from Dunhill got there he scolded. But the little boy was alive.

Next Jack Landry got caught under the harrow. He was a city man, one of the vets who went to business college and then had to dryland anyway because there were no jobs—more hog shearing, with all the noise and so little wool. Like a greenhorn, he hitched four horses straight from the winter range to the drag-harrow; a rolling tumbleweed scared them, and whirling from it, they upended the harrow and threw it over on Jack before he could see what was happening. His wife Susie, who had never been on a horse in her life, came galloping to the Stones, bareback on the old mare she managed to catch, hanging to the hames with both hands, crying.

Penny, very heavy now, hurried out to see, holding herself together with both arms to relieve the strain of her running, calling to Martin over her shoulder. Then the three drove to the Landry field, the wheels throwing dirt in a fan at every curve of the road, Susie holding onto the seat as though she was still on galloping Dorrie, her eyes staring straight ahead, saying over and over—"He was trying so hard. . . ."

Jack was still alive, but every long bone in his body seemed to be broken, his ribs crushed, and no telling what else with the blood in his mouth. Together they got him into the back of the car, Marty and Susie holding him in their arms like a long baby against the jolts, and Penny in front so big with child now she was tight under the wheel. But she had driven Wyoming trails since she was fifteen and could take them better at high speed than anybody else; knowing every hump and chuckhole, driving for them with throttle and clutch and brake. Together they got Jack through to the Dunhill hospital alive, even with nine bones broken, as it turned out. And when the stretcher men had him inside, Marty found Penny scrooched down in the seat, sweating and gritting her teeth, and so he ran back for help and in half an hour her second son was born, just two days short of a year after the first, and the first one of her family to be born in a hospital.

But as Martin was going out the door into the spring sunshine, leaving Penny to rest and sleep, the nurse came running. "Mrs. Stone says where is her other baby?"

So he drove the road home even faster than they came down it, like a crazy man, thinking of the year-old boy alone in the house for almost three hours with perhaps fire still in the stove! maybe pushing the screen door open, toddling to the creek or the tank, finding a rattlesnake; or getting to the hog pen and the old red sow vicious, full of fight as a she-wolf with her new litter of pigs. He drove faster and faster, forgetting the bad axle, the old front tire and everything else except the toddling boy and the yellow-tushed old sow.

But as he cut through Seep Creek, the wheels throwing fans of water, he saw something blue beside the stoop. It was the boy. He had pushed through the screen door and was in the window flower bed playing alone in the busy way he had, digging earnestly with a sliver of wood. And when he saw the car coming he lifted both chubby arms in welcome and then, getting up, he started to run toward his father and fell just as Martin caught him in his arms.

A long time the father held the boy to him, his breast torn with his breath. Then he examined the little head, the cold, earthy little hands for hurts, the face for traces of tears that were not there.

"Oh, baby, baby," he said in wonder and in joy. "You wasn't even scared. . . ."

5 —Big Money

It was seven years after the Armistice when Martin Stone walked into the little slab house against the hump and pulled out a fistful of crumpled bills from his patched overalls, then another from the other side, silver clattering among the paper as he dropped it to the table. Penny stopped her work, the two boys came running to see, young Marty pulling himself up so his eyes reached above the edge of the table to watch his father smooth out the bills: several fives, a pile of ones and the silver. "Some money Nancy owed me. Made it out of the still they set up lately in the breaks of Black Earth," Martin said, busying himself spinning one silver dollar after another across the table for the boys. "Fifty with two and a half for interest at ten per cent."

Penny nodded, not saying anything, but seeming like always as she put the supper on the table. Martin couldn't even tell if she had noticed the sweetish smell of corn liquor on his breath lately, never much, but more than Lucinda would have liked, or the doctors at the hospitals. But when he got out the Montgomery Ward catalogue after supper Penny wouldn't let him add anything for her or the boys to the order for his new shirts and a pair of those engineer pants that Bill Terrey wore.

By now all except the jailed or the hospitalized were back from the war, even those who threw over the girls at home and hid out A-WOL as long as they could; and those from the Rhine, like Billy Sherman. Marty had seen Billy choring around for his dad when he went over to price a bull calf, talking a while at the corrals with old Chuck about Germany's reparations being paid for her.

"Seems funny, us jumping in there, when we been so set against all foreign entanglements," Martin said, making little circles in the dust. "Like a kid vaulting over a fence and landing in a briar patch when he wouldn't come in by the gate."

"Wall, to hear Bill, you'd think we been shootin' in the wrong direction. Sounds like he's married hisself to one a them there *frauleins.*"

"Him and Coolidge! Old Cal's all for feedin' the murdering Krauts, ten million dollars for their relief, but he don't give a hoot about our kids with their backsides out. And okaying them a loan for a couple hundred billions to pay debts, and easy to guess what outfits Banker Dawes'll be building up with it. But watch old Cal snap that turtlemouth shut against any poor bastard what dares ask how the American farmer's going to pay out."

"Yeh, it's a hard row, but the farmer and the little cowman'll jest have to pull theirselves out best they can," Chuck, an old McKinley man, argued. He was in up to his tits but he'd make it, with Coolidge for economy and Sears Roebuck selling implements on installments. Besides, what was Martin bellyaching for? He got his bonus certificate payable 1945.

Yes, after Coolidge vetoed it to please the economy outfits, and the party passing it over his head to catch the soldier vote, and the loan sharks getting the benefit. But what made Martin maddest was him trying to sell Muscle Shoals into private hands, and cutting the income tax on the rich. Who's to pay the taxes?

"Wall, business got to be encouraged. . . ." Chuck said. "The reward for initiative's got to be maintained if the American way of life's to survive"—saying it slow and careful, as from a school primer.

"By God, Chuck, you sound like you got a hunk of the millions in war profit taxes that old Andy Mellon's give back to his aluminum trust outa the Treasury."

Thoughtfully Chuck spit out his tobacco and wiped his wind-scarred lips. "Son, I ain't even able to meet my interest this fall," he admitted. "My steers ain't bringing a third what they oughta, and ma's got to go to Mayos. . . ."

Some of Chuck's neighbors didn't try to keep cool with Coolidge. When beef prices didn't come back they went into moonshining, maybe with a little pine board dance hall at first, then price wars and hi-jacking, protection and politics. Their daughters shortened their skirts above their knees and learned a new lingo from the eastern hot-shots, their mothers disturbed or stirred to competition; the sons slicking their hair down and wrecking their fathers' new cars. Klan memberships jumped, with picnics and maybe a squad in sheets marching up some church aisle of a Sunday and laying a purse on the pulpit. Abe Abrams of the Dunhill Bargain Store, Father O'Shinn and Judge Lerrig no longer fished together in the Big Horns. People drove hundreds of miles to hear the Six Brown Brothers, see a shimmy dancer or maybe Queen Marie, and ran out of gas on the way home, or missed a bridge like Coldin Tinner. These were Coolidge times.

The Stones had voted for LaFollette, although Mike Cannon, whose brother worked up in Butte, said he'd be damned if he'd back an Anaconda Copper man like Wheeler, old Bob's running mate. "I claim you can tell a man by the company he keeps. In a prairie dog town you watch out for rattlers."

With the election news came word of Senator Lodge's death. "Well, that's something to feel good about. Lodge done more than any other man to lose the peace," Benny said as he emptied the mail sack on the floor.

"Shootin' off your mouth again!" Fred Carter, from up the creek, roared. "I was in the war too, remember, and not no damn buck private, and I say Lodge was a great man!"

"Great man? May he burn in hell," little Benny replied, quiet as always, sorting out Carter's *Klansman* and the Dearborn *Independent*.

"Say, bud, you better step easy if you want to keep your post office," Carter said, his little eyes like a ferret's on Benny. Martin shook his head cautiously to his friend. No use making trouble. Besides, what Lodge had done was beyond any man's cursing.

Martin had been down to see Nancy Leite several times lately. A while back he had a letter from her, saying she could get ten dollars a month more teaching up around Black Earth, where Harold was going into a little business. When Martin drove down he found the little business all right, off in the brakes, and Nancy fetching him a sample in a tin cup. Martin sniffed it, burned his mouth with it, and felt better for the refilling, or maybe it was because this time there were no children hanging at her skirt and she was light again, light as a filly twitching her butt around.

So he went back. And as he drove home the old days on the railroad seemed very near, the carefree summers of work and noise and roughhouse, the winter lay-offs that gave section hands such a big-bug feeling while they ate up their summer's wages. In those days Martin had a leopard plush robe for under the buggy seat when he took Nancy riding, but he always kept an eye out for any likely looking piece come to town. Even with the brakie job he wasn't married when the war came, and so he went in the first draft, not complaining much—not like those who died before they even got into uniform, going around with the look he saw later in the eyes of a stuck hog with its blood gushing over the ground.

Turned out Martin didn't mind the army. He was a good shot, tough as rail iron, and used to a foreman whose cussing carried above a dozen spike mauls in a cyclone. Besides, he liked the attention the first soldiers got: community send-off dinners, the band escort to the depot and a lot of girls besides Nancy crying around him, the troop train tooting like a presidential special through the country, with flowers and fancy eats and kissings from girls you ordinarily couldn't get close enough for a knock-down—Marty always out in front, like a good railroader, one with a mop of dark, curly hair.

Nor he wasn't scared by the first battle like old Iron Leg warned, but then he and Johnny Stanger had been just kids, thirteen, fourteen. Hearing artillery made Martin a little deaf for a while, and then gave him a feeling of privacy, a tent of sound in the middle of a battle. Not even the blood and the dying bothered him too much after the brawling section gang and the railroad wrecks they had cleaned up, women and children scalded, burned, crushed, scattered in pieces. It did hit him when that happy ranch kid from Nebraska caught his, but still not to worrying. Maybe you ended hanging by your guts to the barbed wire out there some night, with star shells breaking overhead; maybe you didn't. In the meantime a man gave as good as he got; better, for many a Kraut jerked himself together when Martin's old Springfield jumped.

But the gassing brought him home like a wind-broke old crowbait, to find nothing the way he expected, not his father, or Nancy, or the country. It was like a stomp in the crotch with heavy Heinie boots and an endless march under full pack with no falling out at the roadside, no falling out and no end.

He had tried to say something of this to Benny soon after he found his son playing in the dirt after three hours alone on the place, the time they took Jack Landry to the hospital.

"Here I am, galled every minute, while that kid knows there's things all around to hurt him—horses, cows, the tank, the snakes he calls 'wums,' the fire, the creek, but it don't weigh him down."

"He's a bright young 'un," Benny said cheerfully, "and a toughy. You got some pretty bad breaks in your time but things is running your way now, looks like. Chuck Sherman was just saying the other day what a damn fine stockman Penny was making out a you."

Yeh, *making* out of him, and making him feel like a goddamn rookie.

"I wisht to Christ my wife had some of her get-up," Benny was saying, laughing a little at the idea; Betty, who ran to sagging breasts and stomach, and stringy blonde hair. "She put in three years in the sixth grade. I caught her there, on high center like, her wheels still a spinnin' maybe, but not much, so I pulls her off and runs away with her—" bragging on her shortcomings as a man would his own.

Coming home from Black Earth, Martin thought about these things as he saw Betty Green sitting in the evening sun nursing her dirty baby. He couldn't put up with slobbiness like that; all the women he liked were quick and smart: his mother, Nancy, Penny, even that little Frog, Helene, who used to sneak him eggs and knew every trick in the straw. But when he got near home and heard the hum of the cream separator, the cows milked, everything except the calf feeding probably done, he hit the gas and banged out the back boards of the garage again. Then, as the boys sneaked up timidly, drawn to look in, but ready to run, he sat there thinking about Nancy, her wide mouth rouged blood-red, her breasts heavy and warm as honeydew melons in the sun.

Although the Stones were good managers, there just wasn't more than what Chuck Sherman called a thin gut livin' in a string farm on Seep Creek, and so winters Martin took to going to the irrigation meetings, hoping for a dam on upper Black Earth River, with a reservoir and ditches along Seep, fields a mile wide, green as the garden watered by the hump, fields rich as Iowa.

"Soil's OK; what we need is water."

"Yeh, water's what this world's been needing for a long, long time; water in the right places."

But there was almost no foreign market except from the foreign loans—and no telling to what purposes they were being turned, or

what might be uprooted, like some powerful Missouri turned recklessly from its bed, perhaps to wash away unknowing towns and
cities. And already a surplus of farm produce was piling up, with a
hundred million hungry. Once Martin got on his feet to talk. How
could they hope that the trap-mouthed Coolidge would understand
the thirst of land where no rain fell or the hunger of people who had
no money?

"We'll shove the legislation past him," the others argued. "With
the raise in salary Congress voted theirselves, they'd ought to be
getting some good men; not so many bums to be bribed, and millionaires who're their own sell-outs."

The summers were still dry, and when Artie got a late haying
contract down the river Martin was glad to run a bull-rake for him;
rough riding on an iron seat and right through Sundays and all because the old man had shaved so close to get the bid. They finished
up in a dry spell, the hay fine, the air smoky from a forest fire, thick
but not as bad as a couple of years ago when great black tracts were
burned from Oklahoma to Canada, the sky blood-red for weeks, the
nights ablaze, the smoke stinging the eyes and bringing Martin's
cough back. That's what came of rainless springs and summers,
with tin-can tourists loose everywhere—grass and timber destroyed
for a generation, and more.

Other things of hope were going too. Bryan was dead at the
monkey trial, and old Fighting Bob. But Artie had no regrets for
the things they once represented to him.

"Perhaps it's natural for even my father to get cautious and
afraid too, as he grows older and gets less able to adjust to new
situations," Penny replied to Martin's complaint, giving him the
strange, stiff words because he had corn on his breath. But she still
asked no questions.

By now Artie was loudly behind Coolidge on the war debts, repeating, "They hired the money . . ." sticking his weathered old
lip out stubbornly, Ma Liz laughing. "When Artie goes to buttin'
that lip out he knows he's run himself up a box canyon. Penny's like
him, only she manages to get around you, make you think she's all
noble and givin' in. . . ."

"By God, she does do that," Martin agreed, surprised that he
hadn't nailed down what ground on him so.

When the hay contract was done, Martin came home lean as a

sweep tooth himself, but all right, for the work had left him no time for brooding. Penny saw the old car coming and ran out to catch up a couple of young roosters crowing around too bold lately. While they fried, the boys watched their father from beyond their mother, approaching cautiously, and then finally whooping around his chair, young Marty, still weak from cholera morbus, soon snuggling against his father's faded blue shirt. Penny stirred the gravy and told about the Cannons anxious to sell out. Mike wanted to go back East, now that the stock market was on a steady climb. He made enough to buy a little place out of copper stock or something; started with a couple hundred dollars inherited from Mary's mother and ran it up on margin. So they were going nearer to the market, and where there was shade without a sun eclipse.

"What's he wanting for the place?" Martin finally asked, jiggling Milton on his foot as his own father used to, on his only foot.

"Oh, I don't know, probably not over six, seven hundred dollars, with those improvements, the shack good enough for a school house, but that single wire horse fence wouldn't hold old Flossie Boss with both legs broken and a crimp in her tail."

"Crimp—in her tail! Crimp—in her tail!" Milton sang as he was jogged up and down. "Crimp. . . ."

"I hate to see them go, and they had such a nice start in colored horses for the dude ranch trade," Penny said regretfully. "A pretty sight when they came flying in to water over the sagebrush."

After supper Martin figured a little on the back of an envelope and when they were in bed he finally spoke out. "What you say we mortgage the place and buy the Cannons out—you'd like that?"

Penny took a long time to answer. It would be a fine thing to have another section if they could get it stocked and he took an interest. "Maybe you could borrow enough extra on the two places for a colored stallion. . . ."

But Martin didn't, for he drove down to the breaks of the Black Earth several times, and the money borrowed for the stallion went to get Nancy's Harold out of jail. Booze running. Harold turned out to be a little runt, no taller than Nancy, but accommodating; making errands after supper, leaving the place to Martin, and for a short while it seemed he was back with Nancy before there was a war, and no war even imaginable. Once Martin stayed almost a week, with the early spring farm work on Seep Creek to be done, five cows to milk, new calves to break to the bucket. Two weeks later Frances Carter stopped on the way from Dunhill to beg a start of the white peonies. But as Penny was spading up the roots, with their red fingers pushing through the winter covering of straw, Frances didn't seem so interested, talking mostly about a big new car she saw Martin drive around Dunhill lately. "Must have an important job down there," she said, her face with the same ferrety look as her husband Fred.

Penny watched the woman out of sight, a puff of dust toward the two pink buttes to the west, telling herself it was just the Carters getting even for that first night when she gave Martin the old shotgun against them. But still she looked anxiously down the Dunhill road, past the boys playing at the crossing with Bruno, the brindle pup old Iron Leg sent. There was no sign of Martin and she wondered how long it would be before that Carter outfit and old Windy Johnson made an excuse to take him out for a flogging, like they did Wash Gilshire last summer, claiming he hung around a waitress at the Acme. Poor Wash left the country; no telling what it would do to Martin. . . .

Then one morning late in May, Benny came hurrying up in his old Ford. Penny ran out to see if Betty's time had come, but it was about Martin. "Oh, they've hurt him," she cried, going white as a summer squash.

No, he was being held in Dunhill, witness on a murder. That Harold Leite running a still down the river the last couple of years was found dead, head bashed in with an ax, the place deserted. Sheriff's men watching, picking up everybody who came near.

"Harold Leite dead. . . ." Penny said, her hands going to her denim jumper, hiding in the pockets—and Martin a witness. Then a face came up before her, wild and terrible, Martin Stone lashing the buckskin, knocking his eye out, trying to kill him. Slowly she drew her hands out and held them steady at her side. Benny was shielding her, telling her gradually that Martin had blown up, with an ax handy. And she was to blame; she had known, and should have done something about him long ago, protected him from this.

Penny left her boys with the Greens, the two standing white-faced together, afraid because their mother had never gone away without them before. At Dunhill the town was full to the sideboards, so Penny had to park clear out beyond the elevators and walk through the crowds around the bare old brick courthouse, a stir like wind on drouthed corn going over them when she was recognized. Inside she found Martin but not behind bars, and a relief that was pain swept over her. But he looked bad, ten years older than yesterday, and suddenly grayed at the temples. He had been crying as he had that first time she saw him on the train, and so she sat down beside him, silent as a stranger. Once he turned his bowed head to look at her faded house dress, the blue denim jacket, her hair blown about—an aging woman from a girl in six years. So he could only drop his head again, a hand on his black stubbles, and when he was called out one of the others whispered to Penny that he was just going in for instructions as a witness. Nancy Leite and one of the protection men from the East had been picked up near North Platte, in Nebraska, her maroon car ditched on a slippery turn in a shower, the man dead, Nancy with a broken leg, claiming the man had kidnaped her, that Harold had been killed in fighting for her three days ago.

Three days! Why, Martin was home then, so——

But the man interrupted her thoughts. "Fighting for her!" he laughed, "with old Harold himself solicitin' her business?"

When Martin came out he picked up his hat and still without a word between them, the Stones went out to the old car and drove around the back of Dunhill, along the irrigation ditch road to avoid the crowds gathered not only for news of the Leite murder but for a sensational trial already on. Nora Boyles, from below town somewhere, had taken Nat Ridges of the First National Bank into court, claiming he was the father of her gully brat and not paying for his keep any more since his engagement to that mine heiress from Denver.

"Like his old pal Harding," some said when it first got out. "Like that Nan Britton. . . ." Anyway, few able to sit up and take nourishment would miss the trial.

There was still more news today. A lone flier had crossed the Atlantic, a tall, silent young man that a friend of Penny's knew around the flying school at Lincoln. "And what a pill!" Penny saw Chuck Lindbergh a time or two herself, long-coupled as a pitchfork handle, with a little-boy head twenty years behind in growing stuck on top of that lanky body. Nothing like the sad, thoughtful face of his father in her scrapbook of midwestern liberals that fitted beside men like LaFollette and Norris.

But it was something to break the silence that still held the two when Artie came up that afternoon to see about his daughter. Sneaking a look at her under his faded eyebrows, he talked loudly about the news. Hell, the Atlantic had been flown eight, nine years ago, he recalled, spitting into the dust at the stoop. Used to know the boy's father too, ran into him at Socialist meetings, along with Bill Terrey's dad, and Bill now almost a milliona——He stopped, spit, and went back to Congressman Lindbergh. He was an earnest man, denounced during the war, but the loudest holler came from the trusts and the profiteers he had been fighting. Worked for the little man all his life, and in the end got abuse and a rotten egging from them; even his wife walking out and taking the kid along. Women were funny that way; no telling what they'd quit a man for, or what'd make 'em stick close as a sheep bur.

But Penny had slipped away and came back with two aspirins for Martin, and so Artie shifted his cud uneasily and went on talking. No denying these were showoff times, he said. Bootlegging and other shameless stuff, the papers full of gangsters, Aimee Semple McPherson, human flies, channel swimmers, Atlantic hoppers; and dried-up old farks with nothing but money bags hanging any more, marrying up with sixteen-year-old flappers while a hundred thousand people got drownded out by the Mississippi because nobody would spend a cent for flood control. No money to dam up that water, fetch it to land that needed it to raise grub for all the hungry folks. Old Lindbergh had fought for them all his life and never saw as much altogether as the $25,000 his son picked up for a newspaper stunt.

"I ain't so sure of Coolidge like I was neither," Artie admitted, whipping the dust out of his old hat against his ragged knees. "Over a million people drove to leave farms and ranches the last ten years and him encouraging this here speculatin' instead of getting money paid out for work and produce from the little fellow—widenin' out the base and butment. 'Stead, seems to me he's building his haystack mighty top-heavy. First little wind comes along 'll start it to slipping. . . ."

Martin sat beside his father-in-law on the stoop, the aspirins beginning to work, and the good meal Penny set out, quietly, her face pale under its tan, her eyes without light, her woman pridefulness gone. Even the boys, who had crawled silently into the back of the car at Benny's, sidled up to the table timid as the bunnies in the garden, and afterward Milton tolling his little brother off to bed as soon as he had eaten, whispering him a story in the little lean-to.

In his misery Martin felt warm toward the old man who had come up with his last bit of gas to ease this bad day with his impersonal ramblings. But he couldn't say so—beyond agreeing that if the Coolidge slide was to come now, not many of them were in shape to take it.

Somehow things moved on through the next year on Seep Creek. Penny missed Mary Cannon since they bought the place, and got so she depended more and more on Wheeler P. Scheeler for a friendly word, and on old Iron Leg. She wrote him almost every week now, and he replied; once sending out a second-hand headset radio he got for curing a woman's leg ulcers like Katie Shea back in Cincinnati, with a poultice of moldy bread. An old car battery would run the radio, and it did, Milton getting to stay up the first night to listen, and every day Martin caught the market reports and the weather. It was a handy little hootenanny, but he wouldn't write his father that.

Once old Iron Leg sent a sad little letter about Sacco and Vanzetti being executed. Why, he had advocated as much as they, seemed to him, and this was a country of free speech. He included a new set of clippings about the great deeds of Iron Leg; for fun, not for publicity, like the preachin' woman who got herself kidnaped, or like flying the Atlantic for the money.

Old Wheeler borrowed the collection of tall stories out of the what-not and brought them back pasted up in a scrapbook with polished, silvery cottonwood covers, the words IRON LEG burned on the top. Although it got Martin's back up, he saw the pleasure in Penny's tired face and the excitement of the boys, and so he smiled too, but the buckskin got wilder these days. Once when Wheeler saw him whip the horse with a twist of barbed wire he stopped off at the garden, his face pooched up, red and angry. He saw Penny knew about it, hearing the horse rear and kick and squeal in the corral, and was swinging her hoe the harder.

"If you was ever to find things gettin' too thick, ma'am," he said stiffly, his old hat in his hand, "I would be mighty proud to do for you and the boys. . . ."

The woman bent to pull a weed among the cosmos, a tear slipping down her lean, brown cheek, but she didn't look up until the man and his hounds were gone across the sagebrush to scare out the coyote getting into her ducks. The boys, sent beyond the grove when Martin began his whipping in the corral, watched old Wheeler go too, hanging to their Bruno dog, barking and whining to follow the hounds.

Before Labor Day it was plain that the election was sewed up, the brown derby stomped into the dirt by the Klan and other bigots, even with some help for Smith from outfits big as those talking Republican prosperity. But lower down and across the water there was still hunger and violence too, although war was outlawed, and a man named Briand was hoping to make the outlawing stick, through a kind of United States of Europe. Here, too, Penny had to hold her silence, for Martin and Benny had been across and were certain the hanyaks over there could never get along.

"There wasn't much friendliness among our thirteen colonies either at the start, but it was unite or die," Penny wanted to say.

Nancy Leite was never mentioned through the long months of preparation and trial, although the paper carried her picture, with the three children she had put in a home four, five years ago—when she had to start washing their pants herself, Penny thought bitterly. But that hadn't mattered to Martin, not even that she was the chippie she looked to him when he came home from the war. Now as an accomplice to the murder of her husband she was at least out of circulation for a while.

By then Argonne had a visitor. Betty's young sister Maidie came through with some cousins and stayed behind to see Dunhill Days, what Chuck Sherman called a popstand rodeo—a little roping, riding and bulldogging, with a county fair and a traveling carnival attached. Benny drove over to borrow the old tent. Couldn't put his wife's relations in that hole in the ground with him and Betty and the seven kids ricked up in bunks like stove wood and smelling high. But he didn't seem in a hurry to get back. With a foot on the running board he rolled a cigarette and when it was going he wiped his bald head thoughtfully.

"You know, them girls make me feel foolish as a old barrow hog around a boarin' sow, with them loud ways and skirts that may protect the property but don't shut off much a the view. Seems they been gettin' wild ideas the last couple years, movies and such. Maidie showed Betty a pocket flask, carries her gin right along with her lipstick and what she calls her protection."

"Protection?"

"Yeh, henskins, rubbers, safeties—and explains 'em to the wife, who blows up like a land mine; and so Maidie tells her flat there's some others might be usin' a little protection, not hatchin' a rabble a snot-nosed kids like gophers in the ground. She says she ain't gettin' herself caught and havin' to settle for the first man handy. Talkin' like that before she's been with us half a day!"

"How you takin' it?" Martin laughed.

Benny shrugged his stooped shoulders. "Hell, she ain't no more than a kid, just seventeen, but a looker, one a them flipper-flappers you hear about, and them cousins a hers is about as bad."

At Dunhill, Penny and Martin saw the girl, in a sleeveless yellow dress, the skirt showing rolled stockings and her knee bend in the back, the belt down around her snake hips, and a row of spit curls pasted across her forehead. She had a pair of dangling earrings and a string of red beads long enough to choke a cow in a brush patch. She was hanging around with Larp Miller who had been jailed a couple of times for bootlegging. Both were a little high, maybe advertising his stock of Mariposa Moon. Anyway she was teaching him the Charleston on the pavilion at Main Street, her feet flying out sideways, her beads jumping, singing, "Yes, sir, that's my baby . . ." the old timers gathered around slapping their knees and yahooing.

"By golly, she's better'n one a them Sioux braves when he hops on a red hot coal!" old Birdsell shouted out to all too far back to see.

Betty Green suddenly had a raft of women friends, especially among those with daughters. Many who had never spoken to her came nosing around, "Your sister is mighty popular," they might say; or maybe, "You should ought to put that young sister a your'n wise about Larp Miller's wife."

A couple of months later Maidie was still around Dunhill. "She's goin' plain hog wild out here," Benny told Martin. "She ain't never been where there's a man for every woman, let alone where there's four, five. . . ."

"Looks to me like she's got a taste for paunches and stringy meat."

"Yeh, says older men appreciate a girl. Well, Larp Miller shure must be appreciatin' her, and Chuck Sherman's sunk himself for a new sports roadster he's lettin' her drive around, with his wife's doctor bills not paid. Even old Wheeler P. Scheeler's been down looking at cars."

"You don't say!" Martin laughed, slapping his patched knee. "That old poddy pants!"

Next people were saying that maybe some folks closer to home were getting interested in Maidie too. Wasn't Benny sporting a new purple rodeo shirt and how about Martin Stone, suddenly running to all the dances and wearing a full suit, vest and all, like a city dude?

"He always takes his wife along since that Leite woman——"

"Yeh, but it ain't his wife he's hangin' around at Barteks, or sneaking out with for a drink in the dark. Some say he's even doing a little sellin' for old Larp."

Maybe there was something to it because the Dunhill *Lariat* carried an item:

> Martin Stone, prosperous young rancher from
> Seep Creek was in town Wednesday ordering a
> new Chevrolet for his growing family.

But by the time there were two cars in the Stone garage Maidie was gone, left rather suddenly, right after she won the popularity contest the paper was running, a new Chevvy too, for the most votes on subscriptions. Seems she got a black eye the same afternoon, out in front of the Golden Rule store, from Larp Miller's wife. Then it got around that it wasn't Maidie's eye that took the punishment. Seems Big Maggie turned the girl's bare bottom up and spanked it before the Saturday trading crowd, a hundred yapping yahoosers running up to see.

So Maidie left but Martin Stone still stayed away nights, and days too, ever since the beans were pulled and the potatoes in; never reading Iron Leg's letter about the election, Hoover yelling the guyascutus'd be loose if Smith was elected, and grass growing in the streets—but it wouldn't keep the customers from wanting their money's worth. Martin wasn't even around when Coolidge signed the bill for Boulder Dam, bringing water to millions of desert acres. But circus week he had come home to take the boys to Dunhill. It was an exciting time, from the long colored poster he brought to hang against the door, to the days of talk after it was over. Then finally Milton finished it all up. ". . . But nobody spun 'round to make a cyclone like grandpa. . . ." old Wheeler and everybody laughing.

Often now there was lemon pie for Sunday, rich and tart, with the meringue two inches high.

Sometimes Martin was gone as long as two weeks, with no letter and no explanation except what the dust on the new car told, or the strange mud under the fenders, the stranger money in his pocket. Once he pulled up grandly before the house in fancy dude rancher clothes, with a new radio, an express wagon, skates, base-balls, bats and mitts for the boys, and a fur coat for Penny, a Denver label inside and as surely mink as the pair Penny trapped last winter in the banks of the reservoir, or the twelve dollars they had brought.

Martin had the interest all paid up, he said, and was putting something into stocks lately—multiplied faster than any amount of cows, would pay off the mortgage and buy them a new house, maybe in town some place. Soon they'd be stepping high as a rooster in a puddle, like a couple of regular tom-walkers. He watched Penny's uneasy face as he said it, flipping young Marty around between his arms, like skinning a cat, while Milton hung to his neck. If they had grandpa here they bet he could swing around on the iron leg until they zoomed far out like a comet. He could *so*.

But Martin only laughed, happy and proud doing for his family, and after supper while they picked over beans he taught the boys a steamboat song he learned from Iron Leg long ago: "The old Miss'sip', she got so low, in the bottom of the river the dust would blow. . . ." and laughing at Milton's protest, "Why even Seep's bigger'n that."

Because there was so little time to read to him, the boy had begun dragging his book or paper to his mother, or even to his father almost as soon as he could talk. Pointing a smudgy thumb at a word before he could be sent to look after his baby brother, he would demand, "Wad it say?" By the time he was four and Penny even busier, he could read The Three Bears and The Little Lakota to young Marty, and was starting on the tool and implement pages of the catalogues. Next he wanted all the experiments in Penny's science texts done for him. In his better times Martin made button buzzers, tin windmills from old tomato cans, and even let the boy burn himself with a paper spiral over the tea kettle to learn how steam worked the trains Martin used to run. Winter evenings Wheeler P. Scheeler showed the boy how to drive a needle through a penny, if the cork didn't split, make knives and forks hang to the edge of the table, bring fire from the air above the kerosene lamp, and draw water into an inverted tumbler by burning a tuft of paper inside. Finally Penny had to warn that there would be a good tanning for a certain young man if he set the house afire, comforting herself that at least young Marty would be safe, out around the cowshed, the stable or the hog pen, for if no old sow ate him and he didn't get his head kicked in by a colt, Marty would surely grow up to be a stockman.

"Those kids are sharp as hound pups," old Wheeler told Martin. The father was expansive, if sometimes a little drunk, and Penny couldn't show her resentment or concern, for this fall and winter there was almost nothing of the sudden bitterness left in Martin, so much like the dark dregs of a water glass, ready to roil up at a touch. He even took Pete over to Saul's to be shod for winter ice, the first time he admitted the buckskin was worth the trouble, and on the way home he shot at an antelope with the automatic he always carried now. "Jumped high as the cottonwoods when the bullet hit," he bragged.

But Penny was uneasy. She knew Martin was working with Larp Miller who had spread himself far beyond peddling his Mariposa Moon—a bad and lawless business for any man, particularly one with no security in himself. Martin needed a chance to do for himself and his family like a man, and not in something that was shaming to him. Besides, anything could happen, with hi-jackers everywhere, and booze hounds, and the long, wild drives over side roads in the storm of night, with sleet and sudden blizzards of forty below zero, and Martin never sober.

Then once more Benny came hurrying up in his old Model T, this time with a telegram from Martin, glad enough to hunt up his old friends when troubles came along.

"Oh, I'm afraid he's killed somebody," Penny cried. "Carrying that automatic. . . ."

But it was only booze hounds shooting the tires out from under him last night down on the Cache le Poudre. The car went over a bank and smashed, with Martin all right; probably too drunk to get hurt. "I can't raise the money to go down for him," Benny said apologetically.

Penny got Wheeler P. Scheeler to stay with the boys and headed south in the old car. This time she found Martin behind bars, with his head bandaged and a knee wrenched.

"Oh, Marty! You might have been killed!"

"Yeh, Penny, I sure been acting the fool!" he said, hunching down on the bunk, his fingers in his tousled gray hair. "Last night when I was a little high, somebody reminds me that Wilson's dead, and I got roaring drunk and run off the road in the chase, just a little chase, like I got away in a dozen times, with that extra high gear in the car. He was a great man, Wilson was. . . ."

Feeling stiff and ashamed, Penny went from office to office to get Martin out. It took money here and there, every cent she could raise. Martin was silent most of the way home—past the empty short-grass tableland, with the gray strips of breaking where some drylander had given up the fight, past the badlands of the Chug country and the blue of Laramie Peak, with a thunderhead rising white into the sky like the smoke of a great bombardment. When he finally started to talk, to dog-whip himself for a fool, Penny moved from under the wheel. "Drive, Marty," she said gently. "Think about the road. It looks like rain up over Seep Creek and the reservoir's full. It'll be a good year."

The next week Hull Jacobs came to Seep Creek. He had a dozen regular runners from the border, and he offered Martin one of his best routes, a bulletproof car and protection. Martin shook his head and took to carrying the old shotgun everywhere for a while, since crossing Hull wasn't too healthy, not with his walking tommy guns.

The story about Martin's night in jail was lost in the excitement over Ike Brown, the hermit of Rock Canyon, swearing in court that he was the father of Nora Boyles' son. Afterward he got roaring drunk on the money Ridges gave him before he went honeymooning to Europe with his Denver bride. So Martin decided to put in a bid for the Argonne mail contract. It was only three trips a week, leaving enough time for the farm work if he hustled; besides, he could watch the stock market, get a little start to working for him again. Maybe he could put enough away to subcontract the route in a few months, put in a telephone line, or move to town. And if there was a letter now and then from Nancy it would be his business.

When the contract was signed he told Penny. With Milton, six now, looking after himself and his brother, she was freer, and he would be home over half the time. Besides, he might be able to hire help soon, and better later.

Penny was fetching her mending basket to the lamp when Martin told her, and so she sat down with it in her lap, looked at the man and began to laugh. Rocking, she laughed until tears ran down her strong brown face and dropped to the torn overalls.

"You made me pay the interest instead of putting the money in the market," Martin said angrily. "Now you want me to sweat my ass fighting sagebrush for another start."

But Penny wouldn't let herself notice his anger. "You never get one calf into a chute but they all want to crowd in! I've been thinking a sister would be good for those two young wild men of ours; besides, when Marty was so sick with the cholera, I thought we ought to have another boy. So I'm surprising you with one or the other along in April."

Martin held himself until she was done. Then he broke loose. "Another kid! By God," he roared, "a man can't win! Try to get ahead and your woman'll block every turn like an armored tank! I suppose you're thinking I ought to give up my mail contract?"

"Of course not," she said. "A contract is a nice thing to have on hand. But I could use a Maytag washer, just a second-hand, or maybe a windcharger. You're handy; you could make one."

The man softened. "Well, maybe. A windcharger wouldn't be so hard."

He was interrupted by a whooping in the lean-to, Milton standing in the dark doorway, bony as a chicken above his wrinkled pajama pants, his brown hair tousled, his dark eyes blinking in the lamplight. "Gosh, dad, a windcharger!"

Penny started to scold, but the boy had no time for woman stuff. "Are you gonna make it out of a magneto, dad, like the Cattlets, huh—ah," caving in as he remembered how his father got when he was sore, white and hurting anything handy. He wanted to run, but as the eldest child the boy sensed he mustn't let on. "I—I forgot," he stammered, meaning about the ranch hands of the G Bar driving off the Stone milk cows when they trailed cattle through; when Martin went for his stock they called him a belly-aching vet working for that co-operative agricultural marketing with those Reds from Alberta, Canada. Martin got the cows home but the buckskin's head was bleeding, his sides roweled raw, and so played out he dropped before the saddle was off. For two days Penny had sneaked water and corn to him nights. And just because the Cattlet ranch hands let the cows mix with their stock.

But early this week there had been a rallying on the uneasy stock market; Albert Fall was finally sent to the pen for his Teapot Dome dealings, and there was the mail contract, and so Martin forgot the Cattlets. "OK, son, we'll build us a windcharger, put the old Wyoming blows to work," he said as he pushed the boy through the dark doorway toward his bed.

On the way to get the mail-order catalogues for chargers, he stopped to kiss Penny's sunburnt neck. "Martha Saul's planning a little steak fry in the grove here Sunday," he said. "Move the tables into the cedars if it's chilly. She wants to kick her feet in the leaves once more before they blow away. Says the cottonwoods, couple weeks ago, made her homesick; golden as the old Missouri Valley."

Penny nodded. Bending over her needle she planned for the steak fry, knowing it would be all right for the new baby, forgetting about the folksy news reporter on the seed corn station that afternoon:

> Well, neighbors, this is October 16, the
> seventieth anniversary of John Brown's raid.
> Had a little raid today, too, on Wall Street.
> I dropped twelve bucks, twelve sim-o-le-ons, but
> tomorrow I'll be making them back and double.
> Only a little chuckhole on the high road, folks,
> only a little chuckhole.

6 — For Cottonwoods and Children

By the time little Rita was two years old she was pretty as a yellow-maned colt on a hillside smelling the first snow. She was shy too, and uneasy under the hand until she could be certain. Then she would snuggle down, hiding her face up under Martin's arm and trembling a little at first, and her father trembling too, but as she quieted, the warmness of her was like a glow against the man's body, and a happiness all over him as he cradled the little bare feet in his palm.

But sometimes she ran from his heavy step, hiding in the darkness under the bed of the lean-to. If young Milton was there he could coax her out, and sitting on the floor with her in the circle of his squatted legs, tell her the story of the little red hen or the peanut-shell boat. If he was away, she would cry softly to herself under the bed, until she slept.

The times were hard. As old Artie had predicted, the top-heavy Coolidge haystack had slipped, bringing down everything with it except Mr. Coolidge. He got out from under with his sour, regretful "I do not choose to run," while over in the Black Hills. Now he was writing for the newspapers and magazines, words so dull they made old starch-collar Herbie look gaudy as Buffalo Bill, and as intemperate. But Canny Cal wasn't banking on the authoring business too heavy, Artie reported. Had took to selling a little insurance on the side.

Yes, a paper-clip saver trading on his luck, Martin said. By God, it would have been great to see him in the White House now, scraping up the droppings of all the chickens come home to roost. "Wall Street's yelling that the guyascutus is loose," Old Iron Leg wrote, "clearing the tent of fools who want something for their money, but their stampede seems to be bringing the tent down."

Right after that the Dunhill bank had closed on the money Penny insisted on putting aside the last year toward the interest and taxes, and a little against the mortgage. Early in November they went to draw it out for margin to hold Martin's stock for the rally sure to come, Penny reluctant and uneasy. But it was already gone, the bank door locked, people coming up to look or just standing across the street like cattle drawn to a butchering. "Closed to protect the assets," the notice on the door said. So Martin's stock went, even after a hurried mortgage on their start on colored colts. Then Ma Liz's hospital bills took the rest, along with everything Martin and Joey could borrow on their soldier certificates. Penny cried a little, almost the first time since Dick was killed, so long ago. Now, with the soldier certificates gone, there was nothing.

But Martin was optimistic. His mother had three hundred dollars of her sewing money in a bank that closed along in 1906 and she got every cent, with interest. They just had to wait.

"Well, we'll hope," Penny said, rubbing her rough, calloused hands together. "But I'd feel a lot better if Nat Ridges had our money recorded on his mortgage instead of on the books of one of his banks."

"Same thing. Anyway, he wouldn't take the money when I offered. . . ."

Thousands of other banks went down that first winter, with news of suicides and arrests in all the papers, factories darkening, and mines, businesses and homes too. "The winter of '73 all over again," old Milton wrote bitterly. "But that year there was space to stretch your legs. You could head west when spring come."

There were a few who managed to look beyond mere survival, and talked about another greatest World's Fair in Chicago, the government loaning millions to Charley Dawes' brother to make it go. "I hope the investment turns out better than old Hell 'n Maria's plan in Germany."

But there had been celebrating closer to home that first hard summer. A hundred years ago the fur brigade left their initials on Independence Rock on the old Overland Trail, the Mormons passing that way too, and the Forty-niners, and a million others. the *Lariat* said.

"Golly, the old rock's one of the wonder spots of Wyoming!" young Milton exclaimed from the newspaper spread on the floor. "Probably almost as good as seeing Devil's Tower, don't you think, dad? Wish we could go."

"Let's! Let's go!" young Marty cried, busy with his scrapbook of square-bottomed bulls and bucking bronchos, but always ready for a trip. So the seven-year-old Milton had to shut the eagerness from his face and take on the pretense of a grownup. "Gas costs money," he said seriously.

"And so do tires," Martin added over the pipe he was filling. He had begun to smoke a little the last few months, when he couldn't sleep. Penny didn't look up from her work, not able to face her husband and the eyes of her sons. They hadn't been anywhere in so long, and there would be the big mound of rock and all kinds of oldtimers camped around—overlanders, trappers, miners, bullwhackers, pioneers, cowboys, Indians and just plain fakers —mostly fakers, and perhaps the most fun. Camp out with the old tent a couple of nights, have something to talk over the rest of the summer.

But every nickel counted on the interest, and gas was still eighteen cents a gallon at Dunhill, four more than for the same product hauled clear down to the Missouri river towns. A combine of oil companies, Artie said. There seemed to be a lot of combines lately, as that Fred Strong from around old Fort Laramie, the one called the farm relief crank, was saying.

But young Milton got to go to Independence Rock. Old Plew Tollins was taking his boy down and decided it would be more fun if they had another young sprout along. "Me and the boy would feel right proud if you was to let him go, Missus Stone," he said, apologetically, the tow-headed son watching from behind his father, the blue eyes round with shyness and a daring hope.

So Milton went, but only after he took a last run out around the turkeys, the garden and the gopher traps in the alfalfa, instructing his brother to look after Baby Rita, not let her fall or get flies on her, or go crying and spoil her pretty mouth. Even when they were off down the road he turned to look back from the pickup.

"He's a good brother," Penny let herself say of her first-born as she carried the baby back to the house, the dark eyes staring soberly up into her face.

Yes, Milt was a great kid, the father agreed. Already figuring the leveling they would have to do when irrigation finally came through. "I ain't had the heart to tell him Nat Ridges won't wait when the mortgage comes due, if the bank's still closed on our money; not even on the interest this fall," he said, rattling the worn, wire-wrapped spade handle in the metal shank, wondering if wedges would help. "Still, I guess the kid knows."

Yes, Milton had known. Although he was only seven then, he was in the fourth grade and had proved that the world was round to old Tres Pilters, coming to complain to Penny, the school director, that his kids were being taught lies. The boy did it with one of the gray puffballs off the prairie and a nail stuck in the side. "Now just think this is Devil's Tower—when you travel toward it, does it just get bigger all over or does it climb up out of the ground like this nail comes up when I turn the puffball?"

For a moment Tres' hairy face looked blank with surprise and then he began to laugh, slapping his greasy thigh. "By God, the kid's right! I seen it do just that a hundred times when I was riding for Sallmers outfit up around there." But Milton was still unsteady and apprehensive when he went to his mother afterward. "Golly, I was scared! The geography says use an orange for the earth, and I'd never seen the Tower."

The household seemed pretty empty the evening after the boy went with Stoney to the celebration, and Penny realized once more how the Greens were missing twelve-year-old Ben since he hit the road with a bunch of boy tramps; missed him even though they could use his space in the dugout.

Young Marty was lonesome without his brother to bicker with, and the baby cried herself to sleep without his hand to hold her bottle. Even the radio was bad, and in the gloom of the evening it seemed the hard times had moved in permanently, like a lean and starving cat that had slipped in under the table.

Somehow the depression made Martin Stone feel as sold out as he did the day he ran shouting at the sight of Nancy, and found her with her apron full. Hoover had moved into the White House with an optimism warm as the March sun against a barn door, predicting a prosperity more extensive and a peace more permanent, and so Martin bought his wife the mink coat. Now, two years later, not even Chuck Sherman was repeating the poor joke about prosperity just around the corner when he came by to sell a few blooded bull calves for fall delivery. Dirt cheap, not a cent down— just the promise so he could hold the bank off a little longer.

"Money shore kin scurry out a sight like them sheepherder bugs when the sun comes up," he said slowly as he shaved a paper-thin sliver from his plug. "You can't give the calves away. . . ."

Maybe Hoover never was too sure about that more extensive prosperity, for he had called a special session immediately to consider farm relief and the tariff. Martin had been too busy with his fat run from the Canadian border to Denver just then to notice, although he had voted Hoover along with the big shots. He knew Penny favored Smith and his anti-prohibition stand,—a square slap at her husband's whole living. But he just laughed and raised a little more money to put on the market. Now, back to string farming and visiting at Argonne. Martin claimed it was Al Smith's Wall Street tie-up he couldn't stomach.

"Hell, Hoover had a dozen financial tie-ups, and besides he was in Harding's cabinet," Benny said impatiently.

"That's calling the critters as they run the chute," Wheeler P. Scheeler agreed, for once taking part in an argument. "You don't look for an honest man riding amongst horsethieves—not unless he's too loony upstairs to tell one brand from another."

But looking back now, Martin argued that he was hoping a man who had been a poor orphan in Iowa would sympathize with the needy, although plenty could have reminded him that sometimes those not too secure themselves are handiest at kicking the ribs of the underdog.

So Hoover's special session turned out a joke. ". . . Like a breech blowin' back in your face is a joke," Artie said ruefully when he was up at Seep Creek for a few days. Instead of farm relief they got a federal farm board of big operators who never had to sell a crop at the field but could hold out for the speculator's market, and weren't above a little gambling in wheat themselves.

"Well, they got half a billion dollars to buy up surpluses," Martin argued. "That ought to help."

"At what price they buyin' and what are they aimin' to do with it?" Artie demanded, completely back on his own side of the fence by now.

Ma Liz snorted to hear him. "My old man ain't the first what's had to lose his underpants before he knowed which way the north wind was blowin'."

Grass-fat cattle followed wheat downward, Martin's steers barely paying out on the shipping and the commission, with no market for his spotted young horses, but the farm board dumped its holdings just the same, pushing the domestic market still lower. The tariff revision was even a worse sell—up instead of down, up high as the skyscraper Al Smith was building back in New York, and followed by reprisal tariff walls against American goods. Exports fell billions of dollars a year; produce, farm and factory, piled up in spite of Hoover's sour pouring out money—but not into the hands of the consumer—to the financiers and corporations. In Washington a couple of women—the sister of the Vice President and the daughter of old T. R., married to a Longworth of the great vineyards on the Cincinnati hills—were squabbling over who should come first at the White House table, while outside the grounds over ten million jobless roamed the streets and roadways, or threw Hoovervilles together, their children hungry.

Looked like Martin Stone wasn't the only one who bought a mink coat he couldn't afford that inauguration day in 1929.

Billy Sherman was home again, this time from back East; the school where he had been teaching social studies doubling up its classes to save money, although there was still enough around loose for ten-thousand-dollar debutante parties.

"Hell, there's always plenty of money for show and for vote-catching!" Martin growled, pounding a postcard addressed to Penny, a picture of rows and rows of crosses with an X marked far back, where the white blurred. "Spent millions to send the Gold Star mothers to see the graves of their sons in France last year."

"Still, it must have been a great comfort to some of them," Billy said. "And with so many older folks losing their poor, cautious savings, it was probably the first decent meal some had seen in a while."

"Worthless outfit!" Martin exploded, taking it out on Dick's mother. When he got home he threw the postcard on the table where it landed face up on the old oilcloth. Young Marty grabbed at it as the boys did pictures in the mail, only this time his father roared out "Put it down, goddamn you, put it down!" as he struck out with his fist, knocking the boy sprawling to the floor. Slowly Marty straightened himself, crawling away out of reach like a dog, pulling himself up at the protection of the wall. From there he backed to the door, his mouth bloody, his eyes on his father's wild face, his bare feet soft as uncertain mice on the floor. Then suddenly he bolted outside and ran, looking back once, in terror.

When the boy was gone Penny stood looking after him, tense and angry. Finally she picked up the postcard and, laying it on the table, went out. Martin had seen young Milton's frightened face at the window, and down in the corral was old Pete, head hanging almost to the ground, thin buckskin sides whitened with dried lather, and heaving. Penny would be thinking that it had come to this—a grown man not satisfied with taking out his spite and helplessness on a horse but on a boy too, with his fists on his young son. Judging him, measuring him every minute, maybe even thinking he was jealous of a dead man.

Goddamn the woman, and her goddamn sons!

Letting himself down into the old chair Martin Stone pushed his palms against his temples, trying to hold himself from the shaking that was inside him. When he calmed a little and looked out he saw that Penny was with the children at the edge of the hump where Marty had a cave and a sod barn with corrals and dipping vats of sticks. She would be talking and laughing, making the boy forget his father's blowup, and at this his anger against the woman rose until he could have twisted her neck, or the neck of anything else that stood in his way, even the little Rita in her blue dress, with Bruno beside her, playful and watching. Everything—he could break and destroy everything, but mostly the woman.

A long time Martin Stone hunched in his chair, until he heard Penny calling loudly to the children, "Watch out for snakes," knowing it was as much to warn him down in the house that she was coming, chasing him out. So he slipped away up beyond the grove and the drying string patches as she came, promising himself it was the last time. Let the world go to hell; Nancy was being turned loose next week.

But that night when a prairie dog owl hooted for more dry weather and the young coyotes up north started to yap, Martin was still there, shivering in the chill darkness of the hump. Hidden in the sagebrush he had watched the evening work done without him, young Marty leading the buckskin to water and rubbing him down as far as his arms reached with a sagebrush curry, even on the blind side, the horse quietly nozzling the water. He saw Milton bring up the milk cows and Penny take the shotgun out to where a sage cock was strutting and bring him in for soup, the blue dress of little Rita a bright spot in the evening sun as she ran to meet her mother.

Now it was night, the light from the window laying bright on the flower bed, blotted as Penny or the children passed. Martin was still unable to rid himself of the afternoon's foolishness because a boy had grabbed at a postcard of white crosses in France. Before Martin Stone had always thought of his spells as just not feeling right, but today he saw his own son run from his fist, run like a rabbit from the jaws of a gray wolf.

And yet it wasn't the postcard that made Martin blow up but Billy Sherman's news that the police were using gas against the unemployed who demonstrated before the White House, gas against hungry Americans, vets and all, at their own president's door. All the way home Martin's lungs had burned as though his scarring were new and raw, every stir of air a searing. It was like trying to hold his breath in the hospital, until his eyes popped and lights exploded in the shrapnel of night, the gasp ripping his breast. Now, somehow, this other thing in him had grown like that, until it, too, broke in him, broke in a blind fury that made him strike out, hurt anything in reach until it quivered and shook in squealing terror, or was destroyed.

First it had been Nancy's dog that he sent rolling with the OD shoes in the ribs so the cur lay like dead, and kept kicking him, to a lump of ragged fur. Then he knocked the buckskin's eye out— spurring and whipping the bull-headed bronch until the blood ran and he shook and cowered, paralyzed, helpless. And yet Martin had always liked animals, his father's horses, his own old Shep dog, the squirrels he tamed until his mother made him take them to the woods.

But it wasn't only animals any more. He had cursed Penny out twice in one day like a crazy man, probably would have whipped her like the buckskin if he could, and if she had been afraid. And when he came in she hadn't even been crying; just quietly warned him the next time he would be homesteading alone.

Yet things had gone along all right when he was making a little money with the Leites in the breaks—hanging around for Nancy, too, but mostly for the money and the feeling that he could make it, especially the big money with Larp Miller. He broke only one hoe handle those days, even had the buckskin so he could catch him, and Milton following at his heels, young Marty talking to him about white-faced cows and horses so big they shook the ground walking, little Rita snuggling down into his lap. And at night there was the warmth and sweetness of Penny in bed beside him, her daytime independence forgotten.

But mostly there was so much to bedevil a man—drouth, hard times, corruption and stupidity; everything sold out, war and all, before they got home, everybody grabbing—the little man be damned. Yet what could people do, with no way of knowing what was going on, the trap hidden like on the trail to the alfalfa, until the steel jaws snapped on the rabbit's foot. By God, no wonder a man went wild.

But it was cold on the hump in shirtsleeves, and a long time since noon, and so Martin got up, stretched the stiffness from his legs, and went down the slope.

As Iron Leg's letter reminded Penny, calamities gather to a panic like wolves to a kill. The depression was followed by a drouth that moved northward from the Red River through to the Saskatchewan, the hot winds bleaching the cornfields of Kansas and Nebraska to dead fodder by midsummer, the sage plains of Seep Creek gray as January. Then came the grasshoppers, driven from the baking prairies to cluster thick on every spear of green left in lowland or watered garden. Over vast stretches the sky took on a silvery look, vibrating with a high, rustling sound that grew until the 'hoppers began to fall, pattering on the leaves of the cabbages and the zinnias like rain on a dusty yard. They crawled stupidly over everything, clinging to the screens, floating on the water tanks, clogging Seep Creek and the grills of the car radiators, and making the curves of the highways greasy and dangerous. They cleaned up everything green, following roots and potatoes into the ground, until oldtimers like Iron Leg talked about '74, when the clouds of 'hoppers darkened the sun and dropped so thick on the rails they stopped the trains.

When they first appeared on Seep, little Rita went around making her happy little singing sound, her fists clutched full, as she clutched any small thing she could catch: june bugs, dung beetles, even wasps until she learned better, and worms, laughing as at a great joke when they tried to scare her about big worms that would bite, be little rattlesnakes. "Wums!" she cried, grabbing at her father's pants leg for attention. "Wanna see big wums!"

In the alfalfa the 'hoppers jumped in waves before Martin's dusty cowhides. Plainly this was no problem for his old go-devil with the trough of water filmed with kerosene like other years; this called for poison bran spread at dawn to catch the 'hoppers stirring to feed. So every day he hauled out a load of sacks from Dunhill and at dawn Penny helped scatter, Milton too, the boy shooting up like a horseweed under the hard times and the knowledge of bills gathering. Every morning the grasshoppers ate, sickened and crawled away to shade, until they were thick as scoop shovels of brown manure under every Russian thistle, and the moisture of a shower or a dew made the place smell like a battlefield thawing in the sun of spring. Magpies came to scream hopefully as they flew along the hump, a buzzard or two circled lazily overhead. A preacher came sky piloting in an old tin lizzie, but when he saw how scattered the settlers were, and poor, he moved on.

"Ain't no pretty girls around to be saved," he complained to Wheeler. "Can't have us no revival without no pretty girls."

Even the Mormon crickets were bad, and Penny stretched old gunny sacks and rags sewed together in a two-foot wall around her flower patch to save it. If that went, then really everything would seem lost. Perhaps Martin felt that way too, for sometimes she saw him stand at the fence a long time, looking into the plot bright with poppies, calendulas, cosmos and mourning bride, with hollyhocks along the back. Once he spoke of smelling the mignonette far out on the road. It reminded him of home on the Missouri.

Penny was worried about him now. He was so leathery and gaunt in his patched and wash-faded old overalls, his dark eyes sinking back under the thick, black brows, his hair graying to the back, his teeth going, and his cheeks sunken under their bristles— more a man of fifty than thirty-six. The children felt the change too, young Milton no longer slipping away from his work to follow his father, not even out to where he had planned a dam across Seep, or with the old shotgun for a young sage hen or a cottontail for the frying pan.

Finally August brought a cool, rainy spell; the 'hoppers vanished and new grass pushed up green as spring along the creek banks, the starving cattle breaking in for a mouthful. Martin disked in what rye and millet seed he could scare up for feed, and a few turnips, but at best it would be wind-corn and post-hay for the cows this winter, so after the frost he pulled out of the yard with the old mower behind the hayrack, once more trying to get a little something outside of the law. Three days he searched the deserted country, mowing every stray hatful of grass to get even a jagging load. He came home hungry and silent. The cattle couldn't even be given away, with their ribs already like bed slats, and so little feed west of the Missouri; he would have to watch them starve. Better he had taken up Hull Jacobs on his booze running than depending on the stock market. No jumping out of the window for old Hull. He was running guns down in South America, helping build revolutions. Tom-walking, as old Milton would call it—pushing in on people.

Not that Martin wouldn't do it too if he could. "By God," he kept saying, "it looks like there ought to be some way for a man to make a living, crooked or anyhow. . . ."

And there was nothing Penny could say to him, or Benny, or Billy Sherman.

Winter came cold and dry, lonesome too, with everybody except Wheeler P. Scheeler gone who could get away. The Stones stayed, and the Greens, cut off from news except the mail carrier's gossip and Wheeler's county paper since the radio went to howling. What they got was mostly local news, like Governor Emerson dying— things that didn't matter, with state government going the way of the counties since the old lumber wagon days. It was Washington that shut off the foreign markets and helped bring on the crash by encouraging easy money and speculation, misusing even the Federal Reserve that Wilson set up to control just such times—to tighten speculative capital, not to ease it. More and more money had gone into gambling instead of industry; or was sent abroad— Morgan making a huge loan to the King of Spain to hold off the Republic a little longer.

This year there wasn't even the fun of a pretty new teacher to draw the school-ma'armers around, now that there was nobody with room for her. So Billy Sherman took the job at fifty dollars a month, baching in the schoolhouse and keeping old Chuck in grub and plug tobacco. He was at the Stones an evening or two a week; talking history and the world to Penny and maybe old Wheeler; reading the Iron Leg stories to the boys; or going hunting week ends with Martin, for antelope or packing into the snowy foothills after deer, getting a couple apiece along the trail from one feed ground to another, and once a bear wandering foolishly out of his winter nest. They always came home chilled and weary but feeling fine, standing Chuck's old snowshoes against the house to dry and sitting up late to talk and to clean Wheeler's 45-70 that hadn't been used since the sheep war. But Billy was already reported as a Red, probably by some of the old KKK's, the ones who had blocked Martin's mail-carrying contract the second year, although the man who got it needed it too.

Fortunately the boys liked their teacher, with so little cheer this winter. Not that the Stones had worse luck than other people. Young Marty broke his arm falling off one of the colts summer before last, and there was Penny's operation after Rita was born—trouble left over from having the boys so close together, and paid for by the diamond from Dick's ring. She took it from the little velvet box with no feeling at all. Everything was lost; even the sorrow. But the biggest setback to the family was Ma Liz in the hospital so long with her spine and still taking treatments, the girls and Joey married—more poorhouses struck up. It wasn't bad luck so much as that everybody's working margin was too narrow, too pitifully narrow, and in a country with its elevators and warehouses bursting, and billions of dollars loose for big outfits like Standard Oil to scatter from Mexico to China, exploiting, raising revolution and misery.

Penny thought about this when two of Benny Green's children died of diphtheria the same day. Put off calling the doctor too long, hoping it was only sore throats and flu. So Martin pitched the old tent off from the dugout for Benny and his post office, and carried over fresh bread, syrup buckets of chicken broth and jars of jelly. Betty needed a night nurse but Penny was afraid, with Rita still small; so Wheeler P. Scheeler went. Turned out he had had diphtheria too, the summer his mother cooked in a tie camp in Colorado. He sat up nights for almost a month, until everybody was around again and little Clara was crying to go home with him, making his round face turn red clear to the fringe of hair around behind his ears. So he made a doll baby from a nubbin of blue corn and his bandanna for a shawl and, with tears standing in her big eyes, she finally consented to kiss the doll and stay behind.

The old bachelor took a lot of kidding about this around the sales, and the Saturday afternoons in town. "Hev ye heard about old Wheeler robbin' the cradle?" "Yeh, catchin' 'em younger'n that there Peaches Browning—" until he would bang the door of his pickup, whistle his dogs into the back and hit for home. But he only grinned sheepishly when Martin told him that a mighty fine father was lost in him.

"I ain't never been able to see my way clear financially," he mumbled apologetically.

Perhaps others should have waited for a clearer financial way, Penny thought. The day of the funeral for the Green children kept coming up in her mind. It was chill and stormy, the sky gray as a dirty blanket. One of the out-of-jobbers walking the roads had stopped to help Billy swing a pick on the hard ground. Martin had made a double coffin of the pine bark slabs and so Wheeler, Billy Sherman, Penny and young Milton stood beside Benny at the frozen grave, the dark-faced stranger off to one side, shivering, not horning in. Betty couldn't come, with all the other children sick. Just Benny with four of his neighbors, and a stranger.

Bareheaded, Billy Sherman led them in a song, "Safe in the Arms of Jesus," as a little snow, like gray chaff, began to fall on the rough bark of the coffin. Then Billy spoke a little, with the quietness and the sorrow of a man who had seen too many die.

"In our Father's house are many mansions, the Good Book tells us, and on this earth, Your footstool, there are many fine mansions too, glittering and warm, full of music and abundance and happy cheer. But the best we could do for these who were also Your children, was a cold dark burrow in the earth—no better than for the least of Your lowly creatures. A burrow no better than that of the mole and the gopher and the prairie dog—for these two of the children of God. . . ."

In the stillness of Billy's speaking, Milton moved closer to his mother, sniffling in the cold wind, Penny angry and bitter as any man there, her mittens tight on the newspaper twist of wandering jew, something green to drop on the coffin, to soften the fall of the frozen earth.

As they neared home, Milton beside the stranger, Billy driving, they saw a horsebacker hurrying back and forth along the hump, young Marty on one of the plow mares, looking for something. Then old Martin showed up on the buckskin, galloping down the road to meet them, a blanket flopping across the saddle before him, his face wild and desolate. "Rita's lost!" he cried, "A storm on the way and Baby lost!"

Lost!

Yes, yes, they had looked everywhere, under the bed, behind the stove, out in Bruno's house, the privy, the barn, around the wood and cow-chip piles, everywhere; young Marty crying as he rode up too, "I let her get lost, ma, ma. . . ."

A two-year-old lost out in the sagebrush in winter. "Why, it can't be; she never runs away," Penny argued, talking for herself, "and where's Bruno?—Here, Bruno, here."

But the dog was gone too, Rita and Bruno had been watching the Martins open the turnip hole to feed the starving cows a little, and when they finished slicing, the two were gone.

So now they all scattered, Milton trying to call the dog, Penny running to the house to get into her overalls and take a look around. Young Martin slipped in fearfully behind her. "She was crying, ma, Rita was—scairt because dad kicked Bruno when the turnips was about all gone, and he wanted to smell around for a mouse— wanted to dig. He kicked Bruno real hard," the boy whispered, looking back over his shoulder.

"Oh!"

Outside Billy and the stranger had run to the tank that Martin had already drained, and through the grove to the reservoir, the ice unbroken, the light chaff of snow running over it in the wind. Then they started separate ways from the house in a circle, coming together and then swinging back, wider and wider, until the father gave up his wild riding and took up part of the circling, and Milton and Marty too, while the hungry cows came running home, bawling, hoping the commotion meant feed.

It was young Marty who found the bloodspot, maybe because he knew better what to look for. From that the stranger moved carefully back and forth through the sagebrush, stooping his dark eyes close to examine every bit of earth while the others kept to the enlarging circle, and Penny ran along the creek, calling "Rita! Rita!" looking through any bit of rushes, grown up since the grasshoppers, for the faded little corduroy coveralls in the little skifts of snow.

As the early evening darkened, Martin brought out the lantern, his stubbled face pale and narrow over its light, his sunken eyes watering in the wind, his call, "Ree-ta!" echoing from the hump. Then Billy got his car, moving his spotlight over the whitening sagebrush as the stranger's arms motioned. And at last they found her, almost half a mile away, flattened into a little depression between big sage clumps, close up beside Bruno, her crying chilled to a broken whimpering. The dog was stiff, his eyes glazed, a pool of blackened blood at his mouth, the snow whitening his brindle hair.

With the girl inside his coat, still making the soft, broken little sounds, Billy started back, the stranger bucking the car over the sagebrush, honking the horn. Martin reached them first. Jumping to the running board he threw the blanket around the little girl and held her close.

At the house the boys stood blinking in wonder and concern, so Penny put them to warming a blanket and milk while she stripped off the corduroy coveralls and rubbed the frosted little hands and feet that would be swollen with chilblains, perhaps the little chest filled with pneumonia. When she finally laid the child down to get supper for them all, Martin took her up, but Rita awoke and seeing who it was, started to cry, pulling away. With his face stricken the father crooned to her in a choked, wordless little singing, stroking her tangled hair with a gentleness in his rough hands that promised never another fright or unhappiness.

Finally she trusted her eyes from his face and creeping up against his warmth, buried her head under his arm and slept, while outside the chaff turned to thick snow, piling around the door and the windows and over the new mound of Benny's children.

Long after the boys were in bed the others sat up around the fire, the rising wind loud in their ears. Finally Billy spoke. "You know, you're smart as an Indian about tracking," he said to the stranger.

The man nodded, rubbing his smoky, roached hair. "Yeh, I am Indian, on my mother's side. Went East for steel construction work; good in high places. Now there ain't nothin' to build, won't be until we get us a Hitler here to rid us a them Jews——"

"Jews?" Martin demanded, looking up from the child he still held.

"Yeh, yeh—all a them big bugs East is Jews; got their fists in everything, banks an' all. You don't get wise to stuff like that out here in the sticks, but I got proof," he said, patting his breast pocket. "Taking it home. It's the Indians was the real Israelites, and not the Jews. Them old Bible stories is all Jew frauds. That's why our land was took away from us, here and all over. Jews gettin' Indians killed off, shuttin' us up. . . ."

Billy Sherman pushed his tawny cowlick back with his elbow as he fed the stove more fuel. "Too bad to spoil a good Indian like you—working on his racial injustices with racial flattery. But it's an old game and a big one. In Russia when times got bad the Czar's henchmen whipped up pogroms to give the people a little bloodletting and lootery, and in America when the pressure got heavy the bloodletting and thievery was against the Indians, their land stolen because that was all they had. Now that mush-mouth Hoover stands up there in Washington talking his more permanent peace while the boys he's talking for whip up nationalism and racism all over the world—Seep Creek, New York, Germany, where that Hitler's Nazis are howling it through the streets on our money while the French soldiers are being withdrawn from the Rhine."

"You don't know nothing about conditions—not here on the range."

"On the range? Let me tell you, Big Chief Lost Israelite, I lived with the Germans along the Rhine four years, ate with them, slept with them, and they had me fooled too. But they looked mighty different in the shadow of the Koelner Dom with a *fraulein* in the feathers beside you from what they do when you look back from Wyoming." He pulled out a squashed package of cigarettes, passed it to the Indian, who struck a light for both, breathing his first puff of smoke toward the sky like his forefathers did. "There's

Japan, moving in on Manchuria, old Musso talking blood, the Heinies drilling and marching, and us building up their war industries. Stopping the bolshies, the Hoover boys call it, but one fine morning it'll be another one of those tom-walker tricks you find in the old tall stories. Then all the seed us Jews left over there under the feathers along the Rhine'll be bombing your boys, Indian and Aryan, to chicken mash."

The stranger moved uneasily from the roaring stove. "You don't look to be no Jew."

"No? Well, maybe you been getting nearsighted, fenced in by those tall buildings off in New York, so you couldn't tell a Becky Goldstein from Jean Harlow."

Martin laughed a little, and Penny too, the stranger silent, and so Billy turned to talk of hunting in the old buffalo days, when his grandfather was freighting for the Laramie traders. And here the Indian spoke up again, but quietly, as one who walks on ground securely his own.

Late in February Martin went down to the G Bar sale, riding a little sorrel mare because he must not let the buckskin get him worked up again, not after he scared Rita into running away.

Although it was in a cold snap, nobody who had put up with Robin Cattlet's swelled head the last thirty years was missing the sheriff's sell-out. In the boom days of oil promoters, speculators, tourists and hot racketeers throwing money around, the old cowmen going broke in cattle set up dude ranches and took to chambermaiding.

Robin Cattlet had gone into the business too, pretending it was friends he was entertaining, rolling the names of movie stars and New York playboys in his mouth with the cigar stub; telling the guests they were eating sugar bought up clear back in the war, at thirty-seven dollars a hundred. None of Wilson's damn bureaucrats was going to tell him what he couldn't buy—not reminding even himself that it was his friend Hoover, or how much the food administrator was said to have made out of the rise in sugar. What Cattlet expected was a tip or two on the stock market from any guests who laughed—Cities Service, maybe, or American Can, with even Mariposa Moon coming tinned now. He got the tip, and it broke him, except that he had actually been broke long ago, driving big cars he didn't own, full of gas he never paid for, talking about the pink-coat Cattlet Hunt Club he was organizing while he worked against everything that might have saved the cattle business. He was still at it today, laughing sourly when Artie reminded him that farm and ranch prices had dropped forty per cent since 1919, while the things he had to buy went up thirty; that one-fourth of the nation's population got only one-tenth of its income, the average farm paying less than eight hundred a year net for pa, ma, and all the boys together. ". . . And that includes them big outfits—cat farmers, citrus and cotton growers and the millionaire wheat boys up north," Artie reminded him, blowing on his thin old mittens in the cold.

But with no loose money around for the Cattlet outfit, what could the Stones on Seep Creek expect? So Martin welcomed the news that the man from Fort Laramie was getting the farmers organized to hold their produce for a better market, delay forced land sales, and push for favorable legislation. If the farmer and the working man would ever pull even on the double-trees. . . .

It was Bill Terrey who bought up the G Bar, Bill in a hard hat and a gray-green overcoat with the shoulders out wide as a ridge roof.

Toward sunset the next day Sniffer, the little yellow dog Wheeler brought Rita, began to bark. Penny scratched a hole in the frosted window and lifted the little girl up for a look. It was her brothers from school, flying up the creek on their old skates, the late sun glinting from their dinner buckets as they took the frozen curves, Milton's bulky, homemade coat unbuttoned and sticking out behind.

But when the boys saw their father coming along the Argonne road they pretended to look toward the sundogs and the range horses running and kicking before the storm that was coming. Although Martin had been gone three days, the boys dawdled in the cold so they wouldn't have to face him first with the knowledge of another cow dead last night, the second this week, both so starved their backs showed every warble lump, their hip bones worn through.

Perhaps Martin guessed they were avoiding him, or remembered Bill Terrey, for suddenly he put the young mare into a hard run and wouldn't let her take a smell of the sanded ice of the crossing, whipping her until she took it in a frightened leap, and slipped to her knees. But she righted herself under the lash of the reins and came tearing up toward the corral, the man's face red from cold and anger as he whipped her head.

Slowly Penny turned from the window, wondering what the year now breaking toward spring could hold for Martin, for them all, knowing that it would probably be their last on Seep Creek. At the stove she fed the firebox with cottonwood, pushing it full. The trees had struck their roots deep to soil water and had done well here; the cottonwoods and the children, and what in God's name more could one ask of a piece of ground? A sob came up in her throat, but she choked it back and reached for the coffee pot.

7 — Death of a Buckskin

Penny and little Rita leaned against the pole corral watching their colored horses line out down Seep Creek into the morning sun, a golden cream in the lead, long, pale mane and tail blowing in the wind. Behind came the pintos, bays, a stockinged black, two sorrels and a wall-eyed blue, with several colts running close to their young mothers' sides. Behind them rode Martin on a white-shouldered roan, and the boys too, bareback, sitting their horses close and having a hard time to contain themselves, not to drum their bare heels against the ribs, tear along whooping and hollering as they saw in the movies once.

When they were gone Penny got ready to follow, packing a picnic lunch for out along Black Earth River somewhere, with a baked ham and watermelon pickles—have the car ready for the men folks if everything was sold, everything, and they were left afoot.

When she got to Dunhill Penny found the horses at the sale barn and young Marty railbirding it on the fence, his father and Milton off to the closed bank, trying once more to get enough money out for the mortgage. In the corral an old Indian was beside Sunspot, Penny's favorite, a three-year-old with great golden patches on white, the wild young animal somehow standing for the strange hand on his neck. "That's Eagle Grass," Marty whispered as Penny lifted Rita up beside him.

"A chief's horse," the old man said, half to Penny, half to himself, a smile wandering over his withered face, but sadly, for he didn't have the five dollars for the mortgage Martin told him about. But his hand lingered on the strong young neck and so Penny let the boy ask him to eat with them, Marty shy and excited before this old man with the thin, dusty braids. Eagle Grass came, bringing an old blanket-woman at his moccasin heels. They sat off a little from the others, silent, but in a silence that was easy and friendly as they cleaned up everything, gnawing at the ham bone, sucking out the marrow. When they were all back in the old car, half a dozen ragged and dirty boys burst from the brush along the road and headed for the washout where the paper sack of scraps had been thrown, kicking and gouging for it, one of them scarcely older than Marty—boy tramps, thousands and thousands of them on the road, like young Benny Green.

Later, when the sleeping sickness struck, Martin wished they could have given Eagle Grass the horse, for Sunspot was the first to go. But to the poor, the luxury of giving joy comes high and seldom; instead, Martin had to watch the horses sicken, and then drag eight of them off to a gully. It had been hard enough to take that nice start in colored horses to Dunhill to the sale—all that was left, beside the mink coat, of the few months of big money. To the last he had hoped to get a little over the mortgage amount so he could hold onto a couple of mares.

Many had come to look that sale day, but they were like the old Indian, without money, and so the bank took the horses over and Martin had to drive them back, pasture them until winter for the unpaid interest on the chattel mortgage. The horses hit for home the moment the sale barn gates flew back, Martin following, the boys galled so they were mighty glad to ride with the womenfolks.

But even belonging to Nat Ridges, it was hard to see the horses die.

June was dry this year, dust coming up like a wall in the south, or rising right out of the sage plain, unlike anything Martin had seen. "Looks to be a year of ground winds," old Wheeler said. "Every eight, ten years they come along, bitin' down into the dirt like you was blowing into a bucket of ashes."

But Martin wasn't listening much. Since the evening Walt Henry at Dunhill refused him poison bran for the grasshoppers on credit he was like a man with a sentence on him, like a sick man who wouldn't live to see grass.

"We won't give up yet," Penny had said when he came in from town to stand numbly inside the door in his patched old overalls, his black, desperate eyes blinking in the light, like a stranger lost. "We'll manage the grasshoppers somehow," and for the moment he believed her as trustingly as her sons would. Carefully he washed his hands in the basin, wet down his springy gray hair, and went to sit beside his supper as though the ground weren't moving with the 'hoppers hatching. Once more the children were hushed and silent, and Penny wishing Martin were back running booze—a good car, money in his pocket, bringing home foolish presents, risking death—anything, so he could feel like a man.

But the 'hoppers were growing fast and when Penny finally decided to try trading the mink coat for a little poison, she found Martin alone in the house, the coat out across his lap, stroking the lustrous brown fur gently. She slipped away, and finally one night he told her the rest.

"Sorry, Stone," Walt Henry had said, standing among those seed bags of his, their tops rolled down, running his hands through the gold of the alfalfa, "no credit for 'hopper poison for you this year," and when he saw Martin getting sore, he dusted his hands hard. "You damn fool, I'm doing you a favor! You'll lose any crop you make to Nat Ridges, and you know you won't be running the place next year."

"The hell I won't! I got almost enough money to pay out right in Ridges' own bank."

"The Dunhill Stockmen's? Ain't you heard?—It's closed."

"Yes, of course, to conserve the assets."

Old Walt laughed, mean as a cowkick. "That was over two years ago! Assets vanish, and your mortgage is to Ridges personally. Besides, your land's in line for irrigation some day. It's an old game, my friend. Steal your money with one hand and your land with the other."

"Yes," Penny admitted reluctantly, as though she hadn't known it all along, "and if there's any kickback, some minor official takes the stretch in the pen or puts a bullet through his head." She stopped, for there was movement in the dark slit of the lean-to door, young Milton's frightened face in the crack of light.

"Git to bed!" the father roared, starting up, but before Penny had to interfere the door banged and the strawtick was rustling like a frightened little animal in dead leaves.

Martin sighed, rubbed his dark stubble. "They got to know it sometime. We'll all be on the road soon, Rita and all, like ten million others, fighting over garbage dumps, sleeping in hollers and brush piles like the coyotes. A man's a criminal to bring kids into the world."

But toward morning there was a soft tapping outside, like grass-hoppers falling, and when Martin went to look into the dark sky, something wet hit his face. Rain. It rained slowly for three days and ended up with a light frost—even the 'hoppers left alive crawling slow and stupid as dung beetles. By the end of the week the stalks of beans and alfalfa were greening again, and spears of new grass sprouting among the sage, the flax patch coming out of it too. When the fish truck came along, the men dropped a few trout off into the creek-bottom addition to the reservoir. "We've had some good meals here," they shouted to Milton, and drove off. The boys went to tell their father, hoeing the lower bean patch, but slowing as they neared. Turned out he was all right, said a start in trout would be fine, and if they would fetch him the shotgun, he might get that old hawk flying around. Leaning on his hoe he watched them, running like happy colts.

After three years of stalling, the World Court bill was finally defeated, denounced by Democrat and Republican and by telegrams that ran into the tens of thousands, the attack led by Hi Johnson, Borah and a Father Coughlin.

"Defeat I expected, but who's financing all those telegrams?" Billy Sherman asked thoughtfully.

"Who's this here Coughlin?" some of the post-office loafers from over southwest wanted to know.

"A priest Fred Carter was telling about around Detroit," Wheeler recalled. "Works with one of that Hitler's big guns that Ford imported from Germany, fellow called Fritz Kuhn. Fred says they were getting up something like the Klan together, maybe including Coughlin's followers."

"Anything low-down for a living suits that Carter outfit," Martin said, angry as though their coming to his place that first night on the homestead had been yesterday instead of ten years ago.

Benny was away, off with the Bonus Army. Early in the spring a lot of jobless vets talked about hitch-hiking to the capital to push immediate payment of their adjusted compensation certificates. When their bill was shelved they began to move like mountain jays gathering for the south. "You know I'd like to see something did to give every poor devil a chance, vets an' all, and it ain't like we was asking for something we don't have comin'—but we want it before all our kids is under the ground," Benny said when he came to borrow Marty's grip and the army blanket; catching a ride on a truck rolling through from the coast.

As old Iron Leg predicted, they had no more luck than Coxey's army. They settled in some old deserted buildings in Washington and threw up a great sprawling Hooverville out on the Potomac bottoms where the mosquitoes were big as turkey buzzards in Wyoming but not so mannerly about waiting for you to die, Benny wrote.

When the bonus bill was defeated the vets didn't have the money to start home so they hung around like a bunch of army mules around the smell of an old feed wagon. Benny had been sick a couple of times, malaria, maybe, Betty thought, all feverish and beat-out. She didn't like him away from home, sick like that, with another young one coming in the fall.

She didn't get over to the grove the Fourth, but five of the children came, smelling of mustiness and bedwetting. It was a shame, such well-spoken, bleach-headed young ones, little Clara a really pretty child, even with her dress not ironed, and busy as a bumble-bee around the swing in the cottonwoods, the first she had ever seen. The boys, with the young Stones and Hughie Saul, chased each other through the big trees, scrambling up them with their bare feet, swinging out across the creek on the old rope tied high, dropping off into the alfalfa, the dog Sniffer crazy with excitement, trying to be with them all.

Wheeler, who had brought the Sauls and the Green children, handed out a little stick candy and some firecrackers, a few giants among them, but not loud enough to bring Martin from his bean hoeing until the boys went down for him. Wheeler seemed low-down too, his broad face sober. But there was fun after all, with a strange woman showing up right after the eating was done. Seemed she had broken down in her tin lizzie at Wheeler's day before yesterday, the engine just choking and quit. She was mad enough when he twiddled the carburetor set-screw and started it, saying, "There you are, ma'am. . . ."

But she didn't leave, and now she came following him to the Stone's grove, introducing herself as Wheeler's lady friend. Martin looked at his neighbor and then over at the woman, her coarse face rough with windburn under the powder, her hair rope-bleached, her darkish little eyes mean and cunning as a trapped coyote's.

"Lady friend? Why, you old rounder!" he laughed. "Just wait till your wife and kids hear about this!" making Wheeler's face even redder. The woman misunderstood his embarrassment. "Married! Why, that goddamn dirty greaseball to Dunhill charged me five dollars for his name!" But she'd get hers. The rancher had taken advantage of a poor unprotected woman; kept her there, not letting her go for two nights!

"I wasn't even on the place after sunset," Wheeler protested, "and just long enough to do up the chores daytimes."

"You got no witnesses. . . ."

"Oh, yes, he has," Martha Saul put in, laughing contentedly over her folded arms. "He was to our place all the two nights, wasn't he, Elmo?—sleeping on the floor, poor man."

The woman looked from one to another of these weathered Westerners around the cluttered picnic table, the Saul twins between Penny and their mother, staring round-eyed, all the older children drawn up around the outside by the unusualness of a stranger.

"Hustling getting pretty tough for you, toots?" Martin asked as he swung a leg over the picnic bench, his eyes bold as in his old railroading days.

That beat the woman. "Well, you can't blame a dame for tryin'. . . ." When the noise of her car was gone there was a loud laughing and kidding, Wheeler turning from sheepish gratitude to enjoyment and concern.

"Yes, she probably's one of the seven hundred thousand people supposed to be returning to the farm this year," Penny said. "She and that poor couple up north of the buttes, living in a pile of sagebrush they collected. Not a spade or a frying pan, and trying to snare rabbits and gophers to roast over the coals, enough to live on. Probably be setting the prairie afire, some windy day."

"It makes one think," Martha said, wiping her sentimental eyes. "Millions of people like us, having to live like animals."

But Martin was thinking about Nancy, probably working the country like Wheeler's woman. She'd written several times since he didn't meet her when she was paroled out around Sheridan, away from her old associates. A job in a laundry, washing dirty pants for other women's kids. Finally she hooked a ride with a traveling man headed south to warmer country. Then there was a postcard from Arizona and nothing more when he couldn't send her even five dollars.

Maybe she was gone, like everything else.

The screen door banged over at the house, the boys whooping in a string around the garden to the grove, Marty carrying the Iron Leg scrapbook, crying, "My gran'pa is so taller than the windcharger, tall as anything," Penny trying to shush him. But Martin heard. His face went flat with anger, and kicking his picnic bench so it tipped and fell into the grass, he stalked away, leaving the others silent behind him, young Marty clutching the open book against him, his mouth quivering.

As soon as the Independence programs were done the radio went back to the old line, scattering crumbs of hope: a factory in Saginaw was putting on nine more men this fall, a store in Kansas City two new clerks, and Hell 'n Maria Dawes saw improvement ahead, although thirty-nine more banks closed in Chicago in June—perhaps a Communist plot. Hoover saw a plot too, a Democratic one, in the bonus march, while down in Nebraska 4000 farmers attended a Holiday Association picnic with an old soldier called Iron Leg one of the speakers. The hard times of the Nineties were bad but nothing like this, with the sluggings, blackjacks, guns and tear gas forcing the farm sales. One in every twenty-five farms that had survived the eleven years of foreclosure since the war was doomed to go under the sheriff's hammer in 1932. "One in twenty-five? More like eight in ten, and farm prices still dropping," Martin said, with no hope of getting anything out of the fifteen nice steers he had managed to winter. The last time in Dunhill, Penny got only five cents in trade for her eggs, limited to five dozen from any customer, so she gave the four crates to the county Red Cross for the hungry, and scratched sugar, a little powder and shot for the gun, and Martin's new socks from her trading list. Luckily she had enough money for gasoline at the old price, to get home, and so she tried to remember how fine Martin's flax field looked in the morning sun. But Bill Terrey had passed her on the street that day without recognition, and no wonder—lean, the brown of her hair graying, her face lined and weary, the fun Dick had loved, and that had surprised Martin so much those first years, all gone. Then, at Argonne, there was a letter in Nancy's handwriting, the postmark Rawlins—back in for parole-breaking or worse.

At the house Martin took the letter and came in to supper as usual, hunching over the radio he had managed to repair, tuning out the presidential campaign talk—a devil's choice between Hoover again and a wheelchair crip who'd been governor of New York and a corporation lawyer. Apple selling or nothing.

Then suddenly Benny raised the money for the railroad fare and was home, being helped from the mail truck, so weak and pale that the loafers looked the other way, even Martin, after all his years at the hospitals, as he steadied the shrunken little man with his arm around a shoulder. Inside the dugout Benny dropped off to sleep in a minute, Betty beside him, holding her arms around her swollen apron.

It was dusk when the buckskin finally moved out of the yard, rolled the dried sweat from him and began to eat a little, but Martin never came in for his supper, or to tell Rita good night as he did even when he knew he would wander the dark hours away through the dried-out crops, finally driven to bed by weariness, the strawtick rustling, the smell of dry dust from the fields about him.

But sometimes he would come upon Penny in a frantic urgency, needing to conquer, and in violence. Tonight it was around midnight when he stomped in and flung his clothes off, but because it was the wrong time with Penny, he grabbed her in fury and, grunting at the exertion, dumped her feet first out of the side window before she could stop him, crushing the clump of sweet mary, the velvety leaves fragrant, the woody stalks tearing her old nightgown and cutting her skin. Then he banged the window.

Outside Penny gathered up her gown, pushed the playful Sniffer away, and stumbled through the dark to the stack of new rye hay behind the barn, stopping to pick sandburs from her bare feet, sobs of anger and concern shaking her, for Martin and for the children, with Milton already noticing as an adult. Once she stopped to listen but surely the father wouldn't harm them. His anger was against her as one of those who sold him out, those who stayed home and sold them all out. That she could understand, grieve over, break her heart over with him, but times like tonight any cowman who ever saw a staggy steer in a cowlot should understand—the drive of frustration and defeat. Martin's lungs were better; he had built up a place where, with fair prices, he could make a decent living, even a very good one if the water was ever brought down from upper Black Earth. But for all his work his backside was always out, his children's too, because a few unknown people somewhere, people unknown and unknowing, had the power of life and death over him—unlimited power and no responsibility. Yet no man could escape responsibility for the whole, and it was a sickness to pretend less, and brought sickness upon all the helpless, the sickness of frustration and defeat.

But Penny had worked with the water and the garden all day and then followed a covey of young grouse a mile to get a couple so she pulled out armsful of the loose, fresh hay and burrowed into it with Sniffer crawling close, trying to lick her face on the sly.

At cold dawn Penny awoke to a sound of bare feet in the dry scattering of hay around. It was Martin, grumbling to himself, "Goddamn the woman! Catching cold; nothing on—Penny!" And suddenly he was at the corner of the stack holding his pants up with his hands, his hair standing tousled in the pale light. "Goddamn it, where you been? Why you got to devil a man so? All I wanted was for you to ask me to let you in . . ." he said, aggrieved.

So Penny let it pass, going to the house with him behind her, his suspenders making sad little noises as they flapped at his heels.

When Plew Tollins came by about eight, Martin wasn't around, although the sound of a car used to bring him fast enough. Penny was watering the flowers, the late poppies reaching almost to her shoulders in great balls of pink and white and red, fluffy as shredded tissue paper. Plew looked bad, old and almost as frightened as the night of the bachelor stork party nine years ago, when he stood against a red curtain shielding the dead Florrie, his lip twitching the same way as he began to talk hesitantly. Yesterday the bank closed on the seven hundred dollars he had scraped together for his mortgage and it due next month. They wouldn't take it ahead of time and he had been afraid to keep it to home, with old Charley Grunner tortured and murdered like he was for the few dollars he had hid out in a pickle jar. Now it was all gone.

Wearily Penny nodded. There really seemed no end to this taking from those who had nothing. She remembered the young Marxist at college who saw capitalism driven to self-destruction by increasing economic injustice, and he seemed less fantastic now than Pat Hurley, the Secretary of War, telling the bonus marchers there was a job for every man who wanted to work. Probably a farm and a home too, and all those camped on the road preferred to be tramps.

But here was poor Plew in his battered old pickup, his thin, weedy boy silent beside him. "Hold off the bank a while if you can. Maybe we'll manage a little help from the Farm Holidayers," she said, without too much hope.

"I know you'd do anythin' you can, Missus Stone, but I'd be agin any trouble like some places. I wouldn't want any shootin' trouble. . . ."

So he left the son for a visit while he went to the Holiday get-together in Iowa to see. The boys stood soberly beside Penny and little Rita, watching the car out of sight. "You don't think maybe we got to lose our place?" young Stoney finally dared ask, his pale eyes turning fearfully up to the woman's face. She shook her head and offered to race them all to the house and got beat too, although she let go of Rita's hand, while her pounding heart was sorrowful that even children needed to be afraid. Yes, they were getting too big for her, she admitted, and now if they would try those long legs against a couple of young roosters. . . .

While Marty and Stone carried the squawking chickens to the chopping block, Milton slipped in to whisper they had found their father sitting out behind the haystacks. "Not doing anything, just sitting," he said uneasily, "and he chased us—looking—looking. . . ." But the mother could not let him give this the reality of words. "He feels bad because Benny's sick," she interrupted, wondering what was to become of them all. If only Artie and Ma Liz weren't living in a Hooverville themselves, and old Iron Leg in a poor bachelor room. But Martin's need was for his own, secure.

The boys got the mail on the old plow mares, Milton, as host, taking it bareback, Stone and Marty with the saddle, carrying a sage hen or a fat chicken for broth or a couple jars of jelly to the sick man, although Penny knew the hungry watching eyes would keep him from tasting anything himself. But Benny was soon out, sorting the mail again, so Martin hooked a ride over and squatted beside him in the sun that was hot after the frost the night before, the children noisy and excited as fall wasps buzzing against the dugout window; Betty, heavy-footed and silent with the imminence of another time.

Benny did look better, even had a little color above his two weeks of mousy whiskers and brightened when he got to talking about Washington, like old Iron Leg recalling the Kellyites, marching across the Missouri bottoms beside them, his iron leg swinging high. But Lucinda had seen nothing except dirty tramps who had been sleeping out in the rain.

"There were over twenty thousand bonuseers at Washington," Benny said, "some chronic bellyachers and radicals too, and night-shirters like Fred Carter, and that Father Coughlin sending money. But they were orderly enough until the bill was voted down, although the slumgullion was mostly water, and eight, nine hundred women and children were in the rain and mud at Anacostia, including the twins of Bert Andrews from Martin's old outfit, Bert with an arm off at the shoulder. He had Jud Hudson along, his back in a brace, hurt scabbing at the packing plant in Omaha when he couldn't get anything else. The turn-down on the bill came hard, with all the talk about the government's ninety million loan to Dawes bank in Chicago, twenty-two millions to the steamship lines, and millions more to a railroad so Morgan could collect on his mortgage. Hoover had money for everybody but the poor man."

"Boober Hoover, Hellin' Mellon!" one of Benny's boys began to chant, the older children shouting him down:

> Mellon pulled the whistle,
> Hoover rang the bell,
> Wall Street gave the signal,
> And the country went to hell, Whooo! Whoo!

"Hush your noise," Betty commanded from the blanket she had spread for herself in the sun. "Hush now!"

"That is what you all was a singin', wasn't it, pa?" the boys demanded.

Benny had been in the packed gallery the day the bonus bill was defeated, grafting senators sticking out their gut-bucket bellies and yelling "You aim to bankrupt the Treasury!" up at the vets and the eight thousand more spread over the lawns and steps outside. Then they all got the bum's rush, everybody broke, so a hundred thousand dollars was voted for transportation, deductible from the vet's bonus money. Benny accepted the coffee and doughnuts handed out free and then sold his ticket for fifteen dollars to send to Betty, knowing the kids would be hungry.

"We was down to the last smidgin a flour," the woman said as she shooed the fall flies from her youngest, catching a nap against her stomach.

So their fair-weather friends, like Hearst, who'd been using the vets to club Hoover, turned against them. The bridges to Washington were closed, the marines out like they were over to Teapot Dome during the steal, breaking up the death watch of vets around the Capitol, turning the sprinklers on too. Hoover wouldn't see the delegation with their petition or come out to adjourn Congress that sneaked off home like suck-egg pups. Maybe they thought the old timers' guyascutus was loose sure enough. Anyway, the bonuseers were ordered out of the old buildings in town, a bugle sounding one morning, with ten minutes to get moving. Two vets were killed there by the police and then the soldiers came. ". . . Long's I live, I'll never forget MacArthur at the head of them tanks and trucks and machine guns rumbling along Pennsy Avenue, all dyked out in that flashy uniform. We heard he said it made him sick to his stomach to do it, but he was chief of staff, scattering his own men like a nest a Heinies with tanks and gas bombs."

Soon as they could slip away Benny and some others got over to the Anacostia camp, where most of the families were, feeling safe, on land nobody wanted. But around eleven that night there was the rumbling again; tanks and trucks full of soldiers and machine guns coming over the bridge in the glare of searchlights and the squawk of sirens.

Benny stopped, rubbing his palm over his thin, tattered knees, his eyesockets pinkening as he recalled it. ". . . Women grabbin' kids and hittin' for the dark; men tryin' to help 'em, or tearin' out with clubs to face the soldiers. It was like them night attacks on a camp a wild Indians, folks runnin' every way, screechin', cussin', dogs barkin', the shacks and tents blazin' up in the night as the soldiers come throwing gas bombs ahead, one a them explodin' in the face of a man tryin' to get his little baby away. It choked and strangled and died. The Red Cross sent the baby home."

"Godamighty!" Martin wanted to roar out, but his throat was

closed, his lungs stiff. After a while he found that his hands were fists, tight but empty of weapon. Even if he were strong as before the war for democracy, his hands were empty against a bunch of bastards who would gas a helpless man's kid to death in his own arms.

It was evening before he could strike a blow to relieve himself, lifting the manure fork against Milton when the boy came running around the corner of the barn chasing Sniffer. In a sudden fury the father cracked the fork down on the boy's shoulder, exhilaration roaring in him like a match in a thistle pile, and as Milton cried out and went down, the man sprang on him, the fork lifted, as the boy's face turned up white and twisting in terror, his hands digging into the manure, his feet pushing foolishly.

Then, suddenly, the man dropped the fork and began to run, his shaking hands to his head, and when he was played out he slumped down in a little gully and held himself together, scared as he never was in battle, for this time he had almost come to the end; almost killed his own son.

The Big Dipper was swinging around toward midnight when the boy came tip-toeing from the privy path to the haystacks, calling softly, "Dad, dad!" Martin rose up, and the boy stepped back, hesitating, but managing to stay. "I—I didn't get hurt much, dad," he whispered. "Slipped and fell out of the hay loft into the manger's all; hardly hurt enough to tell about."

A moment the father stood in the vague darkness, and then understanding, he went slowly toward the house, the boy slipping back the way he came.

All the week there had been stories about the Farm Holiday meeting at Sioux City—Communist agitators trying to embarrass the state governors gathered in convention there. Then a letter came from Plew, cramped and painful in indelible pencil, with many tongue-wetted spots. The town was running over with farmers, twenty, thirty thousand, and on the prod like a cow with her calf took away, parading right through town when they were denied a permit, and the jail too little, so they were loose to sleep out on the ground and looking like bums. "I an Fred Strong been tellin everybody farmers in Wyoming cant pay no interest an taxes and we aint the folks to stand in no bread line or fight over no garbag dumps like folks in Chi or Newyork or Souix City is doing. I seen em, even old ladys and kids. Makes a man sick to his stummik and plenty pork and milk and stuff rottin on the farms in yellin distance. They got the milisha out to help push through the sherif sales but there wasnt enuf. I been feelin some better."

For the boys he sent a book about cowboys written by a man named Will James, with drawings of bucking bronchos and big steers busted. Marty was so excited he jumped around like a calf on a rope himself while Stoney just looked with his hands held tight to his sides, afraid he would be reaching out to grab.

Even Milton came closer. "Books like that cost a lot of money, don't they?" he asked anxiously, but Martin was hunched before the radio again, his fingers in the peppery mat of hair and not listening.

"Yes, Milton, a terrible lot of money," his mother answered, wishing the windcharger would blow down if there was never to be anything but violence at home and abroad, fighting and civil wars going on in Chile, Brazil, Mexico, Siam, and a dozen other places, with the Japs pushing into Manchuria, Germany building up an army, with those murderous gangs on the side.

But there was another letter today, one from old Iron Leg. He had heard that the big boys had sent a billion gold dollars out to Switzerland and other places, expecting the USA to cave in, and so doing what they could to dig out the financial foundation, like back in '95. "The five dollars enclosed is for the kids' school stuff. I had a big slate when I was old as Marty and I broke it over Johnny Stanger's head. . . ." There were some clippings too, one that made even Martin look up when Milton started to read it aloud:

HELP WANTED: Good position for reliable, respectable man with iron leg to unwind revolutions, hurricanes, sunspots, reverse psychological tailspins and blow open closed doors of nations' most substantial edifices, confine the guyascutus, and deliver job lots of twin cars for garages and chickens dressed for pots, positively before Nov. 8. Comm. to Investigate References and Equitable Salary app'td. Apply No. 1 Just-Around-Corner, White House, Washington, D. C.

The day Plew Tollins was expected home started chilly, with gray lumps of fog flying out of the northwest until the sky was like a matted old sheepskin—a proper day for the sheriff sale of an honest oldtimer like Chuck Sherman. Some of the Holidayers were coming up and wanted local help but Martin didn't go. The spread of foreclosures was like a Missouri flood eating away the fields of the bottoms, except that the forced sales couldn't be stopped by throwing in bundles of willow loaded down with rock. Even in the push of the Argonne a man had a gun, and grenades hanging ripe for the picking at his belt.

When Wheeler P. Scheeler stopped on his way home, Penny was piling the tomato vines against the freeze coming if the sky cleared. She straightened to ease her back when she heard the car, wondering about the Sherman place, and looking over their own, with its mortgage almost due—a fine little strip of irrigated ground, with wagonloads of cabbage and cauliflower broad as her dough pan, neat rows of bean shocks, and the second cutting of alfalfa since grasshopper time in thick, green windrows, the cottonwoods in a great golden bank behind the cedars.

"Yeh, old Chuck's place's gone. Sheriff had the crowd planted with armed deputies and gas bombs. Brought three hundred dollars, leaving twenty-two hundred against Chuck if he ever gets a cent to his name—three hundred dollars for thirty-five years of work, when he turned down thirty-two thousand not four years ago. Made me kinda mad, so I decides not to chill my rheumatism." He spoke mildly, wiping the wind-water from his cheeks and eyes with his bandanna. "Maybe I couldn't face old Chuck. . . ."

Toward evening Plew Tollins came by, the boys and their school buckets in the back. Penny sent Milton out to pull an armful of late carrots and turnips, young and sweet. In the meantime Plew stood with his hand on his son's shoulder, speaking uneasily about their failure to stop the sale today. "Looks like they always got the guns agin us, and the law. . . ."

Martin didn't ask about the sale when he came in, just sat silent before his supper and went to bed without listening to the radio news. Late that night one of the Green boys came riding hard for Martin. Benny was pretty sick, he said, his young face white and frightened in the lantern light. Took sick to the sale today, trying to get a few together to buy in Chuck's old team for him, or get Nat Ridges to let him keep them. It didn't work so he climbed up on the corral fence in the wind and talked to the crowd, trying to make them hold up the sale. Took to coughing, and just sort a caved in, blood busting down his front and since he's been bleeding several times. Just spouts out. . . .

"Oh, how dreadful!" Penny cried, trying to think what must be done, with no gasoline. While Martin dressed she caught up old Pete, the only saddlehorse approachable in the pasture at night, and only by her, hoping that Martin wouldn't think about that now. But he was in a rage by the time she got back, striking the horse over the head because he moved as the saddle hit him, then spurring out of the yard ahead of the boy. Penny looking into the darkness a long time after their hoofbeats were gone, until Rita cried out in her sleep, as she did so often now.

Inside the dugout at Argonne the sick man lay so pale in the blankets he seemed already dead, the flesh sunken from the bones, his eyesockets deep shadows in the lamplight, his mouth a gray puckering. They were taking him to the hospital as soon as he rallied, the doctor said, speaking calmly enough, Betty crying softly on her arms stretched across the table, the children looking with frightened faces from their bunks along the dusky earth walls.

There was nothing Martin could say; all such words dried up in him long ago.

It was afternoon when he started home, leaving little Benny with his hands folded over his poor shrunken breast, his face set and white. Martin rode slowly at first, slumped over the saddlehorn, as though something more than a friend's life were ended, as though time had died in the ebb of blood from a soldier's breast.

Then Pete went lame in the left forefoot and finally Martin felt the jolting even through his numbness. He kicked the horse, jerked his bony head up, and whipped him with the reins, but the limping was even worse, and so it took a long time to get home. The boys, pulling the last of the beans in the lower patch, stopped to look, holding bunches of vines in their hands.

In the corral Martin unsaddled and tried to lift the buckskin's hoof to look at it, but the excited old horse jerked back from the approach on his blind side, and when Martin yanked the reins, he reared into the air, snorting and pawing, breaking away.

Now a cold fury broke loose in the man. With the lariat he got the horse choked down, jumped on his neck and looked at the hoof.

It was too long, cracking with old age and dry weather, and no wonder—staying away from the tank because it was near the house and near him. Well, by God, this time the bastard would get something to make him limp! Something to stay away for. . . .

With the horse stretched out, blind side up, awkwardly roped across the corner of the corral, hind feet tied to one side-post, neck to the opposite, the nose snubbed close to the bottom rung of poles, Martin went to work with the rasp on one hoof after another. He wasn't reaming down the bad one but cutting into the tip of the hoofs, cutting wedges to crack deep and laming.

As the rasp bit the horse began to jerk, throwing his snubbed head, his whole rope-trapped body, breathing hard, his blind eye rolling. An excitement like of battle rose in Martin. Astride a fore-knee he bore down, driving the rasp into the black hoof time and time again with the fury he used to put behind his bayonet. His hat fell off, his dusty hair slid down over his whitish forehead, his whisker-rimmed mouth working, but he knew nothing beyond the exultation running through him.

At a sudden gasping sound he looked up and saw Penny standing outside the corral with a sage hen in her hand and the old double-barreled gun. "Oh, Martin!" she cried, letting the game slip from her fingers.

But the man paid no attention. Instead he bore down heavier, bloody hoof meal rolling along the rasp, the horse struggling harder, his body lifting between the restraining ropes and hitting the ground with a great thumping as he let out a low, wounded cry, the man increasing his furious rasping, slaver running down his chin.

Slowly the white-faced woman lifted the gun barrel, pointing it between the poles, stooping her shoulder against it. The man looked up again, saw the eyes cold and firm behind the sights. The rasp fell and his arm jerked up to his eyes, his mouth soundlessly open as a shot rang out and he fell back from the blast.

But it was the horse that kicked, and then let his head sag against the rope, a big shot hole below the ear streaming blood over the side of Martin's overalls.

Setting the gun down against the post, Penny turned and started away. Behind her the man rose stiffly, reached through the fence for the fouled weapon and, breaking the breech, saw there was still a load in the other barrel. At this his hand tightened on the gun, his whole body taut as he slammed it shut, his finger slipping to the trigger, his black eyes going beyond to the woman who had seen all his humiliation and his failure since the day he came west to Nancy. There she was, walking free and easy as always along the path to the house, the turkeys running up around her, the gobbler strutting his feathers for her coming.

Slowly Martin Stone rubbed a wrist over his eyes, feeling his hand begin to tremble, his whole gaunt body shake as a new exultation and wildness ran through him. He lifted the gun and looked along its sights. But even now the woman was calm, free-walking, not looking back at all, as though he had no gun, wasn't even anywhere in the world, and suddenly he was drained, empty, his arms limp. Slowly he set the gun down and climbing through the pole corral fence, went to the road and down it toward Argonne. Along the creek his three children stopped their bean pulling, little Rita starting toward him, the older brother reaching out a hand to hold her back.

So they stood, the three together with their dog, seeing their father go, afoot, alone, without even his hat, and not looking back. And at the house Penny clung to the door jamb to steady herself as she watched him go.

BOOK THREE

*Come, read them out to me and
especially that one I like so much,
which says that I shall become an
eagle and soar among the clouds.*

DEMOS

1 — *The Portable, Extradimensional Hole*

Young Milton Stone looked out as the plane climbed fast from LaGuardia field, up through the clear air, with no cabled balloons straining, or showers of aluminum foil like swarms of shimmering grasshoppers; the scattered white tufts not shell-bursts but the last rags of morning fog rolling up round as floating bolls of cotton. The earth dropped away, and Manhattan grew smaller, until it looked like the little finger of a lady with a teacup—a smudged little finger extended over the corner of a mirrored table that stretched away into the sun, off to where the young soldier had been almost four years, to other landfalls and other seas.

But now he had sweated out his last x-rays and caliperings for a while and was heading home, with no flak to climb over, no bringing down in enemy country; never any more mortar shells, booby traps or Tellers, and no skulking patriots trigger-happy with American guns. So he stretched his long legs, eased the bind of his suntans, and settled back to hold himself quiet as sleeping. But he stopped, for the island of Manhattan was suddenly gone, a great, gray, gold-burnt cloud rising over it, rolling, billowing upward, mushrooming into the sun. Automatically the soldier clapped a hand to his eyes, the lump under his patch of ribbons turning in his breast, sharp, cutting his breath. It had come, the sudden, monstrous thing; flown in by drone plane or rocket as many had feared, among them a halo-haired gentle man of science, a line-faced old fighter under a marble slab up the Hudson, and perhaps even some of the eleven men sitting so futilely around a crescent table at a girls' college in the Bronx.

Yet there had been no blinding flash of light, no terror through the hollow body of the plane, no great air push tossing it like a corn leaf, and so Milton made himself take another look. New York was there in the old way, the piled blocks smoky blue in the haze, the cloud only a foolish boll of sun-limned fog drifting away over Long

Island now that the plane swung west. The young soldier wanted to laugh, sheepish as a pants-filling repple, but the other passengers were busy shaking down, flusteringly or quiet, even the two men looking back toward the city. They had never seen a bare, debris-strewn spot under the Japanese sun where a city disappeared in just such a second of time; probably talked about the A-bomb and the coming Bikini tests like the Joes did their Buck Rogers comic books, or old Iron Leg his tom-walker stories—the old hoaxing cry that the guyascutus was loose.

By now the seacoast retreated and the silver arm of the Hudson too. One of the men pointed up the river, talking soberly, shaking his head while the other slapped his folded paper. ". . . Trying to use his infernal UNO to oust Franco, let the Reds move in there too!" he roared out above the engines. "It's war with Russia by September sure!"

Wearily Milton leaned back and closed his eyes, trying not to hear this again, clearing his mind of it as he used to mow hay back in the barn loft, or strip a new field for the water. Pushing everything away, like old Iron Leg building one of his stories. So they had shut out the mortars and the 88's falling mathematically nearer to some blasted mountain curve under repair, or to the swaying pontoons pushed across a swollen river softening the focus, drawing the senses inward as in sleep—as in the long nightmare of Milton's litter carry to a mud-walled hospital.

So here he was, a smart apple with a skyhook, taken in by a chunk of fog like any recruit diving on his face into a thunder-gully because a truck popped off somewhere. By God, he was the one who needed that slick piece of equipment he had dreamed up for modern escapists—Sergeant Stone's Portable, Extradimensional Hole. Transport you into the sixth dimension, unknown to atom or wily guyascutus.

So Milton turned his mind ahead to Wyoming, where he would be when the sun stood straight over the western mountains. His brown eyes softened, and the battle stiffness of his mouth, but he laid his arms flat along the chair to relax against his happiness too, as he learned back when he was a boy on Seep Creek, and handy now that he had to be quiet as a fledgling in the old cottonwoods, until the day when, for all the deadpan, his heart would jump and stop from the dark spot on the x-ray, a bullet skulking like a coyote within the corral of his ribs.

But, hell's buzzards, as old Iron Leg would say, there're more ways of getting mud in your belly button than crawling under a fence, and a cautious man walks sideways. So Milton settled himself to sweat out this last flight, looking down upon the Pennsylvania mountains sticking out of their innocent blanket of creek-bottom trees like the knobby backbone of an old gray mare, one of those Indian crowbaits he used to see around Dunhill. And at Independence Rock that time with old Plew and his Stoney, who made it to a medal at Anzio, with one of Nancy Leite's boys beside him. But that, too, Milton mustn't think about, or Nancy's daughter Agnes, whom he ran across in the UK when Hazel hadn't written and his britches were getting mighty full of fleas.

"The mountains are beautiful, coming home, aren't they, Sergeant?" the stewardess asked at his elbow.

Milton nodded. "Looks like the bulldozers pushed up a lot of rubble and the timber's just taking over," he teased. But it was pretty hill country, like some of Italy, only greener, and no battery nests or the old stink of battle hanging to the gullies. But she'd ought to go eye-balling in the Himalayas sometime, or their own Big Horns, where he used to hunt deer with his grandfather, the old man letting the boys call him Iron Leg, if they didn't tell their mother.

The girl laughed. She was pretty and well-stacked, fit whistlebait for any Joe, and suddenly it was like a jungle fever coming up, his ears drumming with far mortars starting as he thought of the wife he hadn't seen in four years, not since he was nineteen. But there was the x-print of the bullet in his pocket.

Yet he was ahead of Iron Leg or old Martin returning. He had a profession so long as he managed, and in his wallet was another picture, the pretty daughter he had never seen, and his wife beside her, handsome and a stranger, but writing him no Dear John letter as so many did, no: "Dear John—I don't know how to tell you this. . . ."

Slowly, carefully, Milton let himself look at his wristwatch but, for all he'd had, the face blurred out like the first time he checked off the seconds to attack.

Young Milton stood ears over any Stone since Hiram, leaner and lighter skinned too; more like Lucinda and Penny, although his hair was dark, even the narrow mustache over his war-burnt lips that had thinned to seriousness back when he was seven, the time his father quit running booze. Milton couldn't be sure it was joy he remembered in old Martin those days, or only Larp Miller's Mariposa Moon. There had been laughing then, and the swagger of money in the pocket, until Penny fetched him home from jail. But perhaps it had been like the rest of those boom days, an exhilaration like a spree of grappa or jungle juice, to vanish in a night in jail or a day of crash in the place called Wall Street—a sort of thunder slit between old stone buildings, narrow enough for a Big Horn sheep to jump across, or a man to lob a grenade from the cluster at his belly.

Mostly Milton's recollections of his childhood were as a sort of second-string parent, a lance jack, from splinting Marty's broken arm to telling sleepy stories to Rita, so that he got emotional appeals from her at the remotest mailcall:

". . . The goopy old government says I'm too young for the WAC's, and Sadie Saul's just too *darling* in her uniform! Look, Milt, the air base is *moving out.* You just gotta make the WAC's take me. . . ."

His little sister a Jane, turned loose with the mud and the wolves and the buzzbombs! Yet he had seen Partisan girls even younger, with tough service behind them, grim, selfless, heroic service, like the one they found, stripped and mutilated of her woman parts, her gray face twisted like the granite of Thompson Canyon. But she had told no name or place of her fellow Partisans. An Antigone, like the sister in one of Penny's books, and barely fifteen.

But all that was past now, the Ohio farm lands below the plane smooth and greening, with not a familiar shell pit or rusted, broken tank, not a gutted house or wall—nothing except a thunderhead mushrooming up over the Lakes. So Milton eased the persistent bind of his pants and shook his head to the magazines of the stewardess, one opened to a story, "Is Hitler Alive?" with the picture Milton had seen blowing all over much of Europe, cheap colored tatters ground into the mud. He didn't want a newspaper either. He had seen them the last two days, dealing out the old bushwa of latrine rumors, time reversers and williwaws stirred up in bottles. He had a better line in his Portable Hole. The Old Man, his colonel, and all the Chinese kids had liked the routine, and Iron Leg would too, maybe even old Martin.

Now, there was something he had to think about today—meeting the father he hadn't seen in fourteen years, not since Martin walked away from the dead buckskin in the corral, past his watching children.

After the telegram came from the vets' hospital up in Sheridan, Penny had told the boys their father was sick from his war gassing and the hard times, while they looked down guiltily, knowing about the wedges filed in the buckskin's hoofs, nodding soberly when she explained it was like old Bruno getting coyote poison and having those spells in hot weather, or if a rabbit got away.

Then old Wheeler P. Scheeler came along, and Penny walked out through the bare cottonwoods with him, Milton watching from the shed, throat balled up, afraid. But Saturday the mail carrier brought a heavy old man with a faded red calico fiddle sack to the yard gate, and drove off into his own dust. From their cow-chip piling out in the pasture the boys watched Penny go down to look, Rita beside her. A wave of the apron released the boys from the silence of their father's going, and whooping, they cut straight through the garden, jumping the tall, frost-yellowed asparagus rows like colts, and stopping beside their mother in silence, for the old man had a pipe leg, a shiny iron leg.

They all stood off from their grandfather in the GAR suit, his hair short and white as a weasel's in winter, his beard a peppery nest, but Sniffer went up to smell at the man's foot and then sat down beside it, his tongue lolling, his long-browed eyes blinking. Sheepishly the old man rubbed at the ashes on his bulging vest and explained that Martin had wired. "Made out you been wanting me, so I come right off. Scairt as a gun-shy pup to write ahead," trying to reach past Penny's politeness to the children. He'd make a good farmhand when he got his belly cut down. Agile too, if he wasn't much at jumping sparegrass rows on the run. Could dig a well with that leg, he bragged, jamming the pipe down hard, picking up his coattails and giving his heavy body a spin so Marty's eyes stuck out like brown doorknobs. Then suddenly they were up around the old man tight as a fodder shock, Penny's face against his coat, crying hard as Rita of nights because her father wasn't in his chair outside the crack in the lean-to door.

And the old man turned out a pie biter all right, driving disc and mower, pivoting on that iron leg to lay into pitchfork or hoe, and as good with a knife around pigs and colts as he was on the fiddle. His bragging he took out on Seep Creek, talking their place up fancy as the G Bar, and surely the Stones' for permanent.

In the meantime he scraped his pension together like a muskrat laying up roots for winter, making his tobacco and the school overshoes for the boys by fiddling as he used to at Iowa hard-time parties, only now it was all hard times. On the side he muddled up a little salve from silver sage decocted on the back of the stove. A good, clean smell, not like that old wool-fat and kerosene for yellow fever. But it had worked, maybe because it kept the mosquitoes away; saved so many it busted the previous-minded coffin-makers.

"Le's get us a medicine wagon," the eight-year-old Marty coaxed.

"No—that's gormed out; all the catalogue houses, and cars. . . ."

Young Milton remembered something else this uneasy day of his return to a family and a wife who were strangers to his maturity: his mother sitting opposite Iron Leg with Martin's telegram spread between them, going over the situation together like engineers reconning a long-time site. "Fellow on the train tells me the Sheridan hospital's got a lot of psychopathics, vets snapped over . . ." the old man spoke up, his heavy face concerned. "Maybe too much of the killin' smell hangin' over 'em. . . ."

Milton watched his mother make an answer, trying not to blame her husband and yet blaming. "I see now it was my fault too," she said, tracing the worn pansies on the oilcloth. "But at the start I had to go ahead. I knew how, and could do the hard work."

Iron Leg wiped a hand over his white, furred head. "Takes a fit man to be around a handy, go-head woman, an' me comin' home on a crutch stick that way. . . ."

Penny Stone looked away from the old face, with the hurt still naked on it after sixty-five years. "I—well, little Benny's wife over at Argonne managed it. He was puny as a bucket calf, and she a shiftless piece, but to the day he died he could feel like a man around her; even with his children smelling like the outhole down the slope and his overalls in rags."

"Seems Martin felt we'd sold him out, all of them . . ." speaking slowly, haltering his feisty tongue.

"You were sold out the same way."

"Yeh, we was, but nobody claiming the obstructionists, like my dad and Uncle Steven, was out for anything exceptin' graft an' profit. With Marty, the outfits jumpin' in's far off's China, had the Lodges and the Borahs to pretend noble motives an' such asswipe, 'stead a profits and plain spite again the man'd been threatenin' the profits. Now Marty's in a hospital an' you an' the kids losin' the roof over your heads because folks get worked up on war like on Missouri rotgut an' don't care, with Marty feelin' helpless as a broke-back snake. A gassed lung don't show but it's like fever, the whole godamighty world in a fever nightmare."

A nightmare. Uncomfortably Milton shifted in the plane seat, trying to read his watch again, but he kept remembering Jim Becker, one of the best in the old outfit, back in New York all in good shape and peddling gripes, giving the vets a bad name. Claimed he went to sit in the USES now and then, all dry runs, with the jobs going to women or paying less in the pocket than his GI twenty a week, and taking it all sour as a run of KP, wearing his folks down, and Milton too.

"Too bad, chum, about the bullet," he had said. "You'd have a chicken on your shoulder in two weeks when they get the war rolling again, be bossing the bulldozers through Red Square on the tail of the Geiger counters. . . ."

But old Iron Leg had managed to keep joking that bad winter, right up to the starred telegram about Stevie in South Dakota, hurt in the fight at a sheriff sale. When the old man came back to Seep Creek his face was slack and gray. The Stevie boy who used to ride the medicine wagon beside him hadn't even a pair of pants to be buried in. His daughter had to wash the blood out of his old overalls and patch the blast of bullet holes across the front. Poor little dawbug, born of a war grafter and a window-jumping woman, and ending up with a belly full of forecloser's lead.

So Penny had locked her sheriff notice in the trunk and baked up some little bread men with dried chokecherries for eyes and buttons on the front, one for old Wheeler too; to please Rita, she said. Evenings the grandfather recalled riddles and sells while they picked over beans; told stories too, maybe about the great earthquake that shook the Mississippi River like Sniffer would bullsnake, rumpling up the ground to a bed blanket, like the hump there behind the house—until little Rita couldn't keep her eyes from the window, and she had to move closer to Milton's shoulder.

Sometimes they sang, songs like:

> He took me where my pants hung loose,
> An' fired me over the fence . . .

for Marty, and the "Johnstown Flood" or "Ole Big Muddy" for Milton:

> Eatin' land an' droppin' it flat,
> Drownin' steamboats an' river cat . . .

Secretly Milton had already figured how much water would be needed for their 800 irrigable acres. He had measured the land with a rope for surveyor's chain and old Wheeler's level, looking over it, seeing the ground in his mind from the first ditching to the finished crop in spite of all possible cloudbursts, winter interruptions, even scraper breakdowns. In the end there would the 800 acres green, except for the sheriff sale. . . .

Sometimes, pinned down by shellfire out there, Milton had thought about those winter mornings in Wyoming, Penny up early, calling that it was thirty-five below, the grouse like silver on the sun-tipped, glistening cottonwoods. Perhaps the antelope was snuffling over the feed ground or sunning himself on the slope of the hump, to be off at the first careless sound of the door in the crackling air. Sometimes, if it was Sunday, they got to jump back into the warm bed and a little half-awake dreaming, as much fun as an Iron Leg story, and if it turned bad, Milton could wake himself.

But there had been men and boys plodding the snowy roads all that winter, warming their frosted hands around a bowl of the hot soup Penny always had for them, and then shaking behind the roaring stove for hours, as though their bones could never be warmed. Often something swappable left with them, the hammer or a saw blade, Penny scolding, glad that Martin was at least warm, although he didn't write. Or to Nancy either, a letter finally coming from her to Argonne: ". . . I'm doing all right, I guess, cooking for the mission here in Denver. It's room and board, not bad these days. . . ." For a week the envelope stood in the calendar pocket over the table.

Now and then old Milt sneaked a look into the scrapbook of tom-walker stories, and once Milton found him with his old fiddle sack open, holding a picture of a handsome, proud-headed, black-eyed woman, the play actress he heard his mother tell old Artie about when their money was going to Nancy. Women chasers, all the Stones. But Penny did nothing about it, and after his father left, Milton understood about breaking up a family, and remembered it when the "Your Woman" letters started to come to them in the UK, saying his wife was running around in a big car, a banker's car. He better throw his gun down; all the GI's better throw them down, demand a negotiated peace and come home to look after their women. Thousands of others gathering for the invasion got the "Your Woman" letters—like back in old Iron Leg's war, the copperheads and Peace Democrats jumping the desertion lists 20,000 in one week with them.

So that's what it was again, but the faces were long as windsocks for a few weeks in the English winter, and nothing but wait.

There had been waiting that other winter on Seep Creek, too, with the sheriff sale due before the geese came north. Finally the round-topped trunk had to be dragged down from under the ridgepole, a couple of big boxes hammered together from boards out of the horse stalls for the bedding and dishes. At last Penny tried to write one more letter to Nat Ridges, but the paralysis that had struck even the banks in all but foreclosing reached her too, and she dropped her graying head and slept. Young Milton shivered at the slit of the lean-to door and then crept back under the covers, to shut out the realization that old Wheeler was going to get his mother after all. Or Bill Terrey, if his wife didn't come back. Better they go up to Seep Springs, with the coyote hounds and the old Indian camp.

But the mortgage moratorium came through, the face of their new president looking up from the county paper with such confidence and determination that they had sugar on their corn mush that night for the first time since Christmas, and nobody noticed the picture of another man with a foolish cowlick like Oakie Judd down at Dunhill.

The next two years were clod-corn and post-hay, with the drouth and the ground winds that stirred up black blizzards. But they got paid for killing a few of the starving cows, enough to help with the interest and taxes to hold off foreclosure. Then a man came from Ridges, offering to take the place over at full mortgage value, a substantial loss, but Martin Stone had fought for his country. They might even throw in a little house at Dunhill, where Penny could get washing and cleaning. Always a job in America for anybody willing to work.

But Penny shook her head looking off toward the west. "Martin liked those two pink buttes," she said. Next week the government announced the plans for the Turtle Shell irrigation project. Martin's water was coming at last.

"That thieving bastard from Ridges!" Iron Leg roared out. "If I'd a been sixty again I'd a wanged his front teeth out, scattered 'em like corn for the hens."

But really the old man was feisty as a land agent in a rainstorm. "You'll be seein' sugar beets all over the place, hump 'n all, with Milt there makin' the water run up hill, an' Marty growin' prize cows off a the four cuttings of alfalfa," he bragged.

Milton remembered sitting quiet, with Rita leaning against him, letting the warmth of the news spread slowly through his lankiness as he watched his mother's face pinken while Wheeler big-talked the future too. Turned out as soon as the dam was started there was a market for all the truck they could raise, Grandpa Milt making three trips a week in the old car he learned to drive when Milton got his right hand mashed trying to load the hayrack to the wagon in a wind. But he had shifted to the left hand, so it grew even faster than he did that fine growing year. Then there was a new Iron Leg story for the scrapbook: Brought water to Wyoming, boring a mess of wells over in the foothills and just letting the water run out over the sagebrush, with Iowa as his home state taking her claim on the water rights to court. And up around the dam they offered to pass the hat and send him over to clip old Musso in the mush, maybe turn around fast and blow him and Hitler and their kit and kaboodle scattering like a whirlwind in a fodder pile.

Sometimes the old man roared out songs all the way home through the beer on his whiskers. None of them told Penny that

Nancy Leite, camp cook up there, always had a bottle or two for Iron Leg and cookies for the boys. Good cookies.

Before Milton was sixteen he was on an engineering fellowship down at Nebraska, working for his board. After summer school he hurried home to lay out the new fields, slosh in boots, change hands on shovel and hoe, or help Marty build the tarpaper shacks for the Mexicans east of the hump, with their chicken yards and flower gardens. Evenings Milton talked to his mother about his courses, the importance of climate and water to man, and about world history and the coming war. The last year, two hundred dollars came in a bare envelope from Martin and Iron Leg slipped Milton twenty-five, from Nancy, he knew. So he cut down on his little job and changed to the four-year course. In December the Japs struck and by the end of January Milton took his degree, married Hazel, and enlisted.

Now the soldier was coming home, his heart stuttering at the thought, like a walky-talky running over broken ground. And below the plane the patches of green and brown were overlaid by roads regular as crossbar gingham, even the streams robbed of their curves, following man-made cuts straight as a compass line through ridges and the darker patches of old forests and lakes and swamps—through everything that held back the waters, slowed their torrential wash toward the lowlands of Ohio, where old, old Milton had goaded his cows west to the settlement of Cincinnati before the vanished woodlands even became stump.

Yet a stump can put out new shoots, and the seedling sprouts; cuts fill in like shelled hillsides, grow over, gather humus to darken and rot; but the atomized streets build no new pavements, no new houses, and a bullet in the heart is no boulder rolled into a stream, to shelter fish and grow green.

At the Chicago airport, Milton stretched his legs in the sun that was hot and yellow under the storm mushrooming high over the lake, flashing red, the thunder rolling in like a barrage. Even around the crowded port some looked after the tall, handsome young soldier, his shirt paved with tin and fruit that suddenly made him feel very rear echelon on parade.

As a radio somewhere roared out news of Truman's bill to draft striking railroaders into uniform, the flight was called and they headed west again, toward the Missouri and the country beyond.

Now he couldn't hold himself any longer, but Hazel's face was still only a blur, the remembrance of her like a Chinook blowing in at some frozen midnight—a far, thin singing sound, high up, over a hush of air, then a soft warmth against the cheek and a roar of water rising under ice.

She had shown up at Brace Lab for a course in engineer's physics, willow-slim and scared, but she clung to the knob of the door like a Nip to a bluff, saying she wanted to know about electricity and the quantum theory. When the class laughed, Milton saw the yellow light blaze up in her eyes, her cheeks the sudden color of a wild plum ripening in the sun.

Turned out she was good in the stuff, deadpanning any sabotaged experiment, or any skyhooking. He wished he'd had the Portable Hole routine worked out then, the day he found her with an article on Grand Coulee over a coke. After that they studied together, went to a few student tea dances, even a ballet; only once though, with her working too, secretarial, to stretch the insurance from her parents who were killed at a grade crossing up on the North Platte. Soon there was more between them—a kiss or two, and then, with their diplomas, their caps and gowns rolled under Milton's arm, they went to the courthouse and started the round of the new army camps, Milton mostly detailed to some troubleshooter. He wouldn't go out for OCS. "There's been a Private Stone in every one of our major wars and I'd like to round it out," he said, feeling red-necked and stubborn.

Looking back on it now from over the Iowa cornlands, Milton's American service seemed a sort of wind tunnel with nothing to remember except the habitations of the campfollowers. Even when Hazel was working and could afford better, it was some hole more cramped than the old lean-to, a smoky kerosene stove or an electric plate on a box, the community bathroom stinking with other people's lysol. And always held up, like the army of occupation they were, and taking the women like an enemy too.

Somehow Hazel was always at the camp gate or the bus stop, a breathless joy about her, as though she had never expected to see him again. Perhaps because her parents were killed so suddenly, or from the contagious exhibitionism spread by the fatalistic wives of the fliers, until every camp Jane kissed her man good-by forever if he so much as went to dig a sanitary ditch—weepy children playing a desperate kind of house. Even those like Hazel, who knew the soldier needed an easy mind for his training, did it, knowing, too, that all these able-bodied young women should be at work making equipment instead of drifting across the country like wind-driven tumbleweeds or frantic sheepherder bugs caught out by the sun. Instead, they fought with a million other bedraggled, suitcase-packing women for a spot to love their men; made a melodramatic virtue of their irresponsibility, as many did of their "Dear John" letters later. No wonder the Joes would pay anything they could scare up to a fortune teller to send their women home.

Milton himself had shook down with the take of a crap game. It was after Hazel followed him 800 miles by bus, kid-pukey as old Betty Green of a morning, and not a room or flop or even a booth in a beanery empty. So he broke into a parked car for her and made it to the last bus for camp. The next day he had to bail her out—soliciting, a young woman waiting in a strange man's car. She had been given a Wassermann and was sick before the judge. That was when Milton cleaned out a visiting bomber crew with some passes Iron Leg showed him from the old Ohio River days. But the fortune teller didn't work; three weeks later Hazel was making another bus jump to another crowded, miserable little army dump.

But finally Milton's time came, Hazel lovely in one of those deliberately pathetic upsweeps, a bunch of white feathers in it and a bit of veiling to catch in his iron work. They laughed very hard, clinging together to hide their faces. Then suddenly she left, before she needed to, but making it slow and steady. Outside the gate she turned to look back, her eyes dry again, smiling, standing straight and no more than chubby from the baby coming. She threw him a kiss and walked casually to the corner, but she started to run too soon—when he could still see, only the line of GI shoes was moving by then, shuffling him along.

That was the summer of '42, and since then his head had been landing-shaved from the UK through Africa, Italy and the Balkans, Normandy to Austria, and then on to the Philippines and Japan and finally China. Always on the new fronts, a time or two ahead, using any weapon that came to hand when it was fight instead of work, from MI and BAR to Jap toad-sticker, and that old brass cannon in Yugoslavia. Twice he got nicked and left behind, once with his right hand out, but his left grown hard as a maul. Usually he was pulled away ahead, perhaps over grounded brass—the eyes and rule-of-thumb for the Old Man, who was co-ordinating plans for munitions and supply, emergency airstrips, safe water, and looking into slack and lag. And when there was a moment Milton slipped out to look at the country.

"That Joe's sure'n hell crazy to walk over ground—hills er flat. Gets him worked up like a woman on 'er back," he once heard a mine detector say wearily, fanning the awkward finder before him.

Milton knew it was his gall that made him useful, his easy Western know-how, and his goddamn Wyoming way of getting along with any man on earth, as he was told by an angry two-bar when he overheard Milton and the Old Man shoot the bull about hunting in the Jackson Hole country like a couple of GI's chewing the fat over their Saturday night prowls. The colonel liked to watch the Chinese children around Milton when he got ready with a sock and some sticks, to do his Portable Hole routine: ". . . So, when the big Japanese bird of fire comes flying, bang, bang—quick, all of you inside, into the hole like these sticks, and then it is all gone —safe," making the sock disappear, but not before the Old Man recognized it as from his own line.

That had been after Hiroshima, when the isolationists at home were already whooping for a strong Germany against Russia, the colonel roaring, "Hell and goddamn! Handing everything back to the boche again! I'm glad I'm heading into reclamation; get my mind off the politicians!"

Hazel's last letters, five months catching up, brought news of a nice raise in pay with Ridges' bank, and snapshots of Kathie at the bomber plant nursery. It made Milton itch to get home, but instead he went to China for a reclamation study of the upper Yellow River. A fine opportunity for a boy from the high plains, he cabled Hazel. Then a couple of weeks before starting to the coast and home, Milton and two other observers were sent on a special winter reconn into upper Shensi. The Chinese interpreter found their equipment wrapped in an old Chicago newspaper that denounced the war as Roosevelt Imperialism, and here they were, those imperialistic American soldiers. So he killed two of them over the breakfast fire and put a bullet into Milton, and then helped carry him a hundred miles because no one could drive the jeep.

His clever hand dressed and packed the wound with the skill from long warring, pulled the plasma string, administered emergency tablets. At night he kept the fire burning beside the wounded American and all day he trotted with the shaking litter until they reached a mud-walled little hospital with one nurse left for the new troubles coming. Before he slipped away he admitted that the newspapers must have lied, for were not the gun, even the cartridges from the Americans—from one of those who died flying the Hump? But it takes only a little to kindle the ember that wills to flame.

It was like one of those half-dream nightmares, but not to be broken by the will to waken—a long stretch of troubled fog filled with a regular clockwork of pain that sharpened and died and came again. Then, when the wound was almost healed, he sat up to write his report. Moving his cramped left arm a little, a sudden pain crumpled him upon himself, fingers grabbing at his shoulder. After a while he could see the window still before him, the odd gray tree outside, and the little nurse running in, on silent feet. She had been with the retreating people and so she had Milton taken to the nearest x-ray. The bullet had neither dropped out nor been removed by the contrite man who shot him, but still lay, like the tip of a dark finger pointing deep into his heart. And from this, too, there was no awakening.

Since then Milton had been 'rayed and probed and measured and told that the bullet was too deep for removal. Probably it would move, then it would be swift as a bolt in the desert, or it might be walled off, or even work outward, and perhaps be removable. A period of observation was indicated, but the trend seemed predictable.

"Bad?"

The doctor pooched his mouth out in consideration. "Take it steady, like walking against the surf for a landing. In other words, live quietly, moderately, without unusual physical exertion or emotional excess."

"But my wife. . . ."

"That's your gamble," the doctor said slowly. "But don't think about the slug too much. Every man carries his death within him from conception; you may have seen yours in my peepshow."

It was a mean knowledge to be carrying around, to write home about, sweat out an answer. Hazel's letter came, calm and with a little woman-blaming. It was too bad, when he might have been home, with the war all over. She was to be loaned to district head-quarters for the election campaign at a substantial increase, and with good contacts. Who could tell what might come of it for him?

Come of anything connected with Nat Ridges, tied in with the Klan and all the old isolationist gang; the old Nat who closed his bank on Martin's savings, almost grabbed the home place?

But when a man is knocked out, and no repple. . . . Besides, there was a color shot with the letter: a poised and lovely young woman in the sun, with the little Kathie that Milton had never seen, a serious, pale-haired child in a blue dress, her hand trustingly in her mother's.

And there was still waiting ahead, with nothing to kill time, no plans to draw up, no skyhooking, not even a gun to clean, so Milton buried himself in everything he could get on nuclear fission and the infinite possibilities it offered for attack on the ills of man—disease, hunger, calamity—until his heart was pounding and the nurse took his reading permit.

So Milton's color came back and the gloss to his thick, dark hair; his mustache grew; his weight rose until he looked so well in his reds that when a photographer caught him giving his Portable Hole spiel to the paraplegics, the newspaper caption said:

Visiting GI comic dons hospital garb and makes 'em laugh.
Uses Colonel's sock like magic carpet to transport imagination.
Comes by it naturally. GAR grandfather made Kansas cyclones.

But it was all right, for it caught the same happy, puzzled look on some of the men that he had seen on the faces of the hungry Chinese children. Happy and forgetting.

Yet he still found himself looking inward, intent on some inner ticking of time, doubling up suddenly with pain. He tried to realize that everyone was, in fact, brooding the egg that would hatch his death. But not from a newspaper like the one in the hand of the man just ahead of him, a newspaper built from the rich earth and the labor of the American midlands into the arrogance to destroy those fighting to preserve it; so powerful that one crumpled old copy could bring death to two men—not in the rumble and blast of war, but on a far errand to bring water to desert lands, food to the hungry.

Even now Milton's anger climbed like steam under a stuck valve, and so he turned to look at his watch. But it was all sand in the transmission and a long back soon broke, so he deadpanned himself and put a hand into his pocket, on the sock that made people laugh, trying to imagine Kathie's face. When he looked out again they were over the green-gray prairie of Wyoming, over the West with so many great engineering developments planned. Perhaps they would end up on the Missouri, in a MVA boom town, but settled in a place of their own. It was true both he and Hazel had been children, caught in the surge of war emotion, the marriage not what it might have been with, say, Nora, the little Yorkshire schoolteacher, or even Agnes Leite, if he could have affronted his mother like that, or his father. But perhaps the time with Nora had been war too, the dented pillow beside him empty that last morning as much war as the six hundred GI's entering divorce action in New York in one day.

Uneasily Milton set his collar. Hell's buzzards, he was worse than any repple fresh into combat—a shaking, scared-pants, redeployment depot civilian. But tomorrow he would be shucking out of suntans, with no more need for deadpanning and skyhooks, or the escape of a Portable, Extradimensional Hole.

Suddenly he began to dig in his bag, bringing up a little Chinese doll, for the deep, dark canyon of Black Earth River was just ahead, and not a cloud in the whole wide sky, not one white boll of cloud anywhere, while down there a young woman and a small girl were surely waiting.

As the plane coasted and stopped he saw a waving in the crowd at the fence, the bright head of a child suddenly lifted up, an arm pointing, the wind bringing a gay cry: "There, Kathie, there!" and Milton began to run; holding up the little Chinese doll, he ran.

But only a few steps. Remembering, he slowed himself, and so he came up to the handsome young woman Hazel really had grown to be, and the little girl in her arms who looked in concern to her mother and then turned her dark, serious eyes upon the stranger. Lifting the light curls, he kissed the fine delicate forehead, and then the lips of his wife.

Another Stone was home from the wars.

2 — *Lemon Pie for Sunday*

Fall came early to Seep Creek. Mornings the sun sparkled on the frost of the bottoms while at noon the heat still shimmered in a mirage lake around the two pink buttes in the west, the air heavy with the smell of dying sweet clover and alfalfa, and the frosted muskmelons swarming with drowsy wasps. It was October, almost five months since Milton was roused from that first sleep after his homecoming. With the immediate and complete awakeness of long danger, he had stopped his breath and listened. But there was no artillery or bombing, no stealthy step of an enemy, no rubber-wheeled dead-wagon passing, or the scream of sudden pain and torment in the night. Then the sound he had heard came again, and Milton let his breath go. It was only a coyote echoing along the breaks of Black Earth, his pointed nose stuck into the sky. A warmth came over the returned soldier, and a sweet, boyish happiness. He was home, home in Wyoming.

That was last June, and now young Milton was in the faded overalls of a choreboy, thin and sunburnt, his mustache gone as not fitting to his new life that was somehow as unmanning as the old instinctive mutilations of combat: the ironed bootheel in the crotch of the fallen enemy, the stallion whirling to kick, the bull with his lifting gore. So Milton squatted on his heels beside a dry ditch looking off to the black ribbon of oiled highway while strings of beet trucks rolled toward Argonne Dump, sometimes several heavy haulers snaked along by a tractor. Like the engineers on the move, the eagle circling high against a windy cloud over them a Focke-Wulf, prowling.

As Penny complained, Milton was thinking more and more in terms of war instead of demobing himself. She pretended it was because he got old Iron Leg excited, with so much new war talk around anyway. They did shoot the bull lately, outmarching and outlying each other, although the old man smelled that Penny disapproved.

". . . She'd oughta know penned pigs is gonna whistle, even if they ain't got the mouth for it," he complained, after several beers in the Stockmen's Cafe at Dunhill, where Nancy Leite was putting out good meals, best this side of Cheyenne. "Like the women around here, cluckin' about Nancy, usin' any club to whip a handy dog." He glowered over his shoulder toward the merchants' table. "Wore-out old farks! Their women ought to know a rim shakes loose on a dried-out hub, an' 'most any old pumphandle can use a little primin'."

Yes, old Iron Leg had tried to make the summer pleasant, Milton thought gloomily as he looked out over the place that the plans and management of his teen years had turned from ragged sage-brush to this fruitful ground. Now, a man grown, an engineer, he had to spend a whole summer odd-jobbing. Nothing to strain or press a leaded heart. Just puttering, feeling mean and low-down as a yard bird, with less for pride as his own than a six-year-old. Not even his suit of civvies could be bought without his wife's pull, and then at $150 for a forty dollar job. So his joy at being home had gone crumbling like a solid old house on a bombarded Italian slope, bit by bit, the shelling steady to the last firm stone.

Part of it was his concern over the off-year election campaign, the problems, from inflation to A-bomb control and world co-operation, lost in labor-baiting, racism, the American Action's isolationism, and the old cry of the 1920's that the Communist guyas-cutus was loose. It was like setting a jungle fighter up for the knife by the old, old trick of chunking something into the leaves ahead of him.

In other ways, too, the summer seemed a time for which there was no measure in a world that was unknowable. First there was Hazel, changed from a bright, pretty girl, in love with the romance of a soldier husband off to the war, into a handsome young woman, cool and aloof in her shining hair, and calmly looking out for herself and her daughter, as she had these four years.

By herself, as she said, and as Milton would believe.

At the airport the day of his return she took him to a new convertible, yellow as a meadowlark's breast, with black upholstery, standing a little away from the other cars, battered, dusty, prewar. Easily she drove her soldier and her pretty daughter standing between them through Dunhill, waving here and there to acquaintances who called out, "How are you, Hazel!" grinning in their friendly western way, their teeth white in their brown, curious faces, eyes a little envious for the car.

"Say, you sure take over," Milton said, pleased that she was so well liked in his country. "Folks act like you were the pie wagon moving into occupied territory."

"A smile and a personal word for everybody, we always say," she agreed, half serious. "Gets votes. I'm on loan from district headquarters to Senator Potter for his stump of the mountain states, you know."

Milton snapped to attention. No, he hadn't known; she would be away. . . .

"And includes the loan of this car," bringing up something that he hadn't meant to think about at all.

But he had grinned, as four years at GI'ing taught him, holding little Kathie and her doll close, the child's body so delicate and slender in her tiny pink dress. Then he remembered that she must not be frightened by sudden, aggressive affection from a stranger, so he set her down into the seat, smiling into the dark, disturbed eyes. By now people in the street had discovered who he was, calling out, "Hi ya, Milt! Ya lookin' good." Even Nancy Leite, calling it out gaily and loud as she would have to the boys up at the Turtle Shell dam. Milton relaxed. Here people still shouted in the every-day street, not in anger or abuse or fear, as over so much of the world, even New York, but neighborly. It was fine, and with his wife beside him, and a lovely daughter, both within the reach of a man's arms. . . .

Toward the upper edge of the town, Hazel stopped before a modern little house set back on a grassy terrace, the entire southern wall of glass, no, some war plastic, perhaps, from the bomber plant. Uneasily Milton got out, looking around. Inside, the living room was cool and pretty, the slip covers pale gray, with more meadowlark yellow, and a touch of the blue Milton saw in some old vases in China, matching the wall hanging he had managed to pick up.

They sat on the couch together and made talk that was stiff as a Joe corraled by a duchess for tea, the green-flowered dress Hazel wore bringing out the light in her eyes, like sun on goldstone. Yes, oh yes, the trip was good—a fine day, barely a cloud on their route except a few round fog puffs over New York, one a big one. Then there were the ribbons and the ironware to be explained, Kathie stretching the tallest of her going-on-four and putting her small finger on one after another: American, European . . . making him name them all a second time. After that Hazel said, "You might show Kathie the tricks that got your picture in all the papers," but he shook his head, and so she could only repeat, "You do look well, after all the trouble, and handsome."

So Milton's heart began its uneven drumming and he had to remind himself: steady like walking against the surf—and bring up the first diversion, more dull, impersonal talk about the house, built for a bomber plant superintendent, Hazel said, and loaned to her by the bank since the plant shut down last year.

"But, with the housing shortage, the rent must be high."

"Oh, they loan it to me, no charge," Hazel said easily.

Slowly Milton laid his arms to his side, close against him, and finally the maid came with a pretty tray. When he hesitated, Hazel said, "Lemonade made with lemons, and gold cake!"

"I'm remembering the time you had getting butter for that last one, just before I was shipped."

"Oh, yes," she laughed, permitting herself something of her old rueful exasperation, "and it turned out to be whipped butter, mostly gelatin and milk, so the cake got runny and fell. For your last supper home!"

"Home?—that stinking, ready-made foxhole, with the bed jack-knifing every time you sat on it, and the granite washbowl rooting out for spring with the rags in the holes of the bottom. . . . Yet, I guess it was home at that," he said, his voice suddenly soft. "You cried about the cake," and because there was such a shaking in him he reached his big left hand out along the couch to steady himself, almost to a fold of Hazel's dress. He wanted to touch it; shut his eyes against the house and everything and touch the dress like a patrol man who had lost contact wanted to run, a rocketing bronch twister grabbed at the air.

"I doubt it was the cake that upset me, under the circumstances," Hazel started to say, calmly, but she stopped when she saw the whiteness of Milton's face and then, before she had to say anything at all, several cars were outside. So Kathie was sent to the nursery, crying a little, softly, and people filled the house, carrying cocktails around, shaking hands with Milton, congratulating his trimmings until he managed to ditch them in the bathroom. Then it was time for early dinner at the hotel and on to Casper, where Senator Potter would introduce one of the speakers of the rally—General Daunce, who, off the record, looked like presidential timber for '48.

"Old Fauncy-Dauncy?" Milton complained, cross at the interruption this first day home. "So the old windbag's still kicking around, even after the pictures of his Adolf's been wiping paper all over Europe? Anyway, what'd an exhortin' preacher know about running a country in the atomic age?"

"Sh-h," Hazel laughed. "He'll make a good compromise candidate in a tie, get backing East and West, and pull the solid, the right-thinking vote of both parties. Besides, military men make good chief executives. Remember a certain general named Washington?"

"Yes, and another one named Grant, of considerable political ambiguity too, and a couple of molting capons called Hindenburg and Petain."

It was long past midnight when they got home, with a little blowout after the Daunce talk, and later, after too many drinks, Milton had done part of his Portable Hole routine, angrily, to show them what he thought of the outfit. But it went over big, everybody laughing like hell, slapping him on the back, so the sock that had vanished slid halfway out of his sleeve, making them laugh even more.

"A natural-born comic!"—while a pink-skinned, dude-shirted publicity man from New York was saying he knew somebody. All he had to do was say the word and Milton would be in. Always glad to help a fellow vet. "All you gotta do is build your stuff up over a little song and dance business, needle the Commies and the pinkos, and cut out the GI slant. That's corn strictly from the cob, Mack, positively."

So Milton had hit him, just once, with a left, but Pinkie went down like a sack of potatoes. It bent Milton too, in a clutch of pain, but straightening himself against it, he stumbled out through the watching crowd, the sweat suddenly heavy and cold on his face. Outside he slumped to the running board of the first car, Hazel finding him there in the pale moonlight. "Oh, Milton!" she cried, down beside him, her arm around his shoulder.

But he seemed all right, so she scolded a little, gently, "Our best publicity man—and over an old sock!"

Slowly Milton lifted his head. "That gum-beatin', short-arm kibitzer!"

Toward morning they slept, Milton to be awakened by the coyote. The next time it was bright sunshine and he was alone. Holding his head he tried to wake himself out of a late morning dream, half-sleep and half-awakened recollection. But he was not asleep, for there was a dent in the pillow beside him, a faint fragrance, like yellow wallflowers wet with spring dew, and suddenly it came to him—Hazel, his wife.

But it seemed the pillow was to be empty in the morning just the same.

Toward noon Hazel came back from the office, bringing Kathie and her black-eyed doll from Sabbath school, and the Sunday papers, and a box of flowers for Penny's dinner table. "Now take it easy today, darling. You really have been out of touch," Hazel said.

Milton looked off over the oiled highway, smooth and water-miraged, the sky blue as over the plains of Shensi, a thunderhead far in the northwest rising like the billowing smoke from the London blitz, but flattening at the top, mushrooming.

"A genuine Wyoming cumulo-nimbus," he told Kathie, trying to lay it with a name, and with it his annoyance that Hazel blamed him for last night.

But then there was Seep Creek ahead. Even before Milton left for the army it had become the mid-rib of a great leaf-shaped region turned lush and green by the water from upper Black Earth, the little creek no longer clean and sun-dappled, with minnows flashing. On each side lay wide fields of grain and alfalfa, soy patches like chenille rugs, and dark, wet soil striped with young sugar beets. On the lower Stone place the first cutting of alfalfa was still on the ground, the windrows thick as the close-running waves of a rising sea. Although it was Sunday the bucks and stacker were going, the two Martins out with a couple of hired hands to get up some hay without rain. Hazel stopped, and old Martin swung off his tractor-driven buckrake that rolled up alfalfa like a bulldozer rooting out brush. Wiping his palm on his overalls he came to hold it out to this son he had not seen since the nine-year-old stood between the youngers, watching their father go.

"You have done well for yourself, boy," he said, motioning toward all the plunder pinned back on Milton's chest for Penny and old Iron Leg. The son smiled into the face of a stranger, a stubbled, sunburnt and healthy face, with a pleasant twist at the wind-dried lips, leaning them from the softness that had made Penny hesitate that day on the train, after another war. Milton wondered about her now, and about Nancy Leite, with Nancy running the cafe in town, as Hazel said, and before that the cafeteria at the bomber plant, where Martin Stone had worked three years.

But they went over to the stackyard together, the father and the son, the stubble crackling under their feet—much alike, except that Milton was a hand and a half taller, hospital pale, uneasy. Once he stooped for a lost slobber of alfalfa and sniffed the sickly sweetness he had always hated. But today it was something familiar, and good.

When he saw them come young Marty slid off the stack, stopped at the thermos jug and went to meet them, his teeth gleaming, his face battle-grimed in dust, his hand horny. Together there was sizing up, measuring back to back, Martin still the shorter, but stocky, with bottom and draft. Admiringly they punched each other, and when Kathie was up beside them, Marty kissed the new doll and led her over to the broken body of a rattlesnake. "The stacker tossed him up to me. Pretty scared, he was. Came slithering off and beat it so fast he about ran the legs off a Charley there, getting him."

Soberly the little girl looked from between the brothers. "Oh, it moves, it moves!" she cried, drawing back.

"Yes, some say his tail won't die until the sun sets, and cools," Milton agreed, looking away from the mottled gray body with its slow meaningless twisting, like a grenaded entrail, twisting that same slow way as the body beside it stretched and lay still.

"Oh-h?" Kathie asked, looking to Martin to see if the strange soldier man was joking like her Gran'pa Milt did, but with no laughing in his eyes.

Leaving the hands to top out the new stack, the Martins rode the car doors in to dinner, proud to show off their postwar improvements already done: new sheds, graineries, bunkhouse, two big barns. Even the house Milton had built in 1940 was only a wing of the new place now, and all accomplished under the foolish shortages and restrictions. Damned expensive too, old Martin complained. Not that they couldn't afford it, but every stick would have been paid for if the A-bomb had held off another six months.

"Held off!" Milton started to roar out against the sour joke but his father's face was without laughing too. "People always get to feeling too rich for their stomachs," he finally said, carefully. "So inflation balloons, like back in old Milt's Cincinnati, and Cattlet's thirty-seven dollars a hundred for sugar in 1919. Makes hoarding and black markets."

"Oh, Hazel got us the lumber through Ridges. But we had to pay the hold-up prices, labor's hold-up. Maybe old Harry's draft'll get 'em back to work. Anyway, come election time we're putting in a congress that'll get the bureaucrats off production's neck," the father promised, talking big as the old booze-running days, with Nancy, a mink coat for Penny, the stock market, and a vote for Hoover. Now he was taking credit here, when he was only back on the place a year—one year for all the changes since the old string farm.

But Milton remembered his father those months before Benny Green died, and so he looked away toward the house, two-storied, gleaming white, with lower, wide-porched wings on each side— set against the shelter strip of cedar, olive, Chinese elm and cottonwood that he had planted, with the yellow-gray of the hump behind. The green marsh that attracted Martin that first time was a smooth sloping lawn before the house now, with shrubs at the sides, pink and white with bloom, and cascades of yellow roses.

Penny was down to meet them, pretty in a flowered dress, a little heavier, her short gray hair well-set, her face glowing at the return of her first-born son. And from the barrel chair under the trees old Milton came too, much thinner, tough and bony as an old carp, his hair a silky white halo, his beard sprangly. He walked with a cane but his iron leg still shone. "Godamighty!" he shouted over his growing deafness, "he's dyked out with ribbons like a goddamn studhorse to the state fair! Looks like he's been every place, a reg'ler tom-walkin' trampooser!"

And in the old way Marty was making shaming fingers for a showoff at his brother, so Milton held his cap over his chest and got away to the house to ditch the stuff while the hayers washed up, to shut his eyes a minute and give himself to the feeling of home.

In a striped chair on the terrace, with a grape cooler, Milton leaned back and put his hand over Hazel's. Slowly he looked all around the family, and then out over the irrigated fields that reached from the gully where the buckskin was buried, off across the creek to where the Indian had found little Rita and her dog in the sagebrush with the snow already running. Enough land to keep two dozen men busy all season, and house room here for half as many families—at least a dozen families, the way people were living.

"I know," Penny said slowly, perhaps thinking back to the slab shack. "There's been a lot in the papers about a housing shortage, but one never knows how much's propaganda."

"That's all it is—government fighting the real estaters along with the farmers. If the East's that crowded, why don't people come out here?" old Martin laughed, stroking his freshly razored chin with his pipe. "Plenty room in Wyoming!"

Yes, plenty of room, Milton wanted to say, as there was for Sally Gault, living with her Bill in their sagebrush hole up northwest back in '32, poor as any DP. She had plodded the five miles to the Stone cottonwoods for a tree big enough to hang herself. Sniffer found her one frosty morning, the boys right behind, drawing close together—the way the skinny woman's hands hung down, her eyes popping. And in New York two days ago Jim Becker showed him eight, ten people, vets and their babies and all, jammed into one two rooms the size of the Gault's sagebrush hogan, or a good-sized foxhole.

Always plenty of room, and hell for breakfast in the morning.

Somewhere in the house telephones rang, Penny and Hazel and perhaps Martin too, waiting. When the maid came to say that Senator Potter was calling, the others looked after Hazel, smiling a little, proud. But not old Iron Leg. "Potter, you say? Deadbeat—catwater under the bed!" he shouted into the silence, like a surprise flanking. There was a shushing, and a turning to other things as

* 292 *

Hazel didn't come back. Milton really must have seen a lot of strange sights, the years away in far places. . . .

But he just sat and stared down into his glass, even Kathie beside him forgotten in the knowledge that he could tell them nothing they would hear. So Iron Leg, who had come home like this eighty years ago, sounded off. "That old copperhead Potter's sure been skyuglin' around the last couple years! One a them Eastern imports, his vote's handy in the Senate from one a our shrinkin' states as from New York, and cheaper bribin'. Cheaper electin', too. Power companies' five thousand dollars goes a long ways to buy up them little newspapers out this way—ranny as a chambermaid to get stood up in a dark corner an' make a extry quarter."

"Hush, Dad——little ears!" Penny warned. "The Senator's really been a good fighter for the West, getting us war plants and bases, working to raise prices on meat and sugar, and he's been wonderful to Hazel. Selected her out of the whole country west of the Missouri. Really depends on her."

But old Milt was on one of his tears. Pounding his iron leg on the ground he demanded if it wasn't true that Potter made a million out of army sites, picking up options ahead, holding up the government, with his cahootsers in the Military Affairs Committee and the War Department. "Even got the air base and the bomber plant switched to them dog towns him an' Ridges had tied up at twenty cents a acre. Made a haul right there, an' all over the country. Investigatin' committees kickin' the underbrush fer Reds, while Potter's——"

"Now, Dad, that's giving Milton the wrong impression."

"Don't make much difference either way, with the government taking it all," old Martin complained.

"Don't I remember you griping about the seventy-five million war profit taxes Andy Mellon paid back to himself out of the Treasury," Milton laughed but listening to the far voice of Hazel on the telephone, soft and gentle, very soft.

"Now hush," Penny whispered, "You'll get Dad excited." But old Iron Leg was still roaring: "Them big bugs got their tails over the dash an' the brush afire!" with Martin talking on too, ". . . I was like you fellows then. Coming back from the wars, you won't face things as they are, reality, as the docs call it. You probably won't for ten, twenty years."

Milton could only look down at his GI shoes. So his father had had to accept it after all, the point of view old Milt offered him on his return, and Hiram and old Sarah to Milt before that. It was almost like the day he had to watch his father walk down the Argonne road.

But Penny was protesting that they weren't making it a home-coming. "Why, Milton hasn't even seen the new dairy barn. And hurry back, for there's lemon pie for dessert"—his favorite lemon pie for Sunday.

Leaving Kathie to look after him uneasily, Milton went out of reach of Hazel's voice, briefing himself to admire his brother's stock with the interest of the old days, when he used to come home from high school week ends to help. It had been settled even before then: home things and laying out the fields for Milton, the stock Marty's.

And the new barn was fine—white and clean as a base hospital inside, with more floor clear, the clean smell of good hay, the gleam of the milking machines.

"Remember the knee-deep manure of the cowlot, and the cracked teats in winter? The cows sure used to kick us rolling," Marty laughed. "Even with lard on our hands."

"Yes, the Turtle Shell has certainly changed this country," Milton agreed, looking along the rows of Holsteins, down, chewing quietly, their heads in the stanchions, feed and water in reach. Nothing like the cows on shell-torn fields, their legs lifted in bloat. ". . . And with the new discoveries, this is just a beginning. . . ."

But Marty cut his brother short. "I guess we had about enough of that kind of stuff, like tunneling under the Divide down in Colorado, and that talk about damming the Missouri. But with the power companies buying up big space in all the papers, we'll get it stopped. Time we got to doing for ourselves, individual initiative. . . ."

Only long GI'ing helped Milton hold his hand from his brother, kept him from reminding Marty that under individual initiative this was a string farm—as life still was over so much of the earth, with the gamble of drouth and flood and handtilling on remote, impoverished lands.

Then before he had to say anything a car drove up to the barn. The brothers went into the sunlight to see, Marty predicting:

"Harvest tramps," as one of the men, lean, unshaven, got out and came over. No, there was no work, Marty told him. Never hired drifters.

"Drifters? We was tore loose from our jobs by Uncle Sam," the man replied, with the quietness, the straight eye, the buttoned-up face that Milton recognized—long, solid soldiering, a good man to take on patrol. "I'm thinkin' maybe you was glad enough to have us workin' for you when we was standin' off the Japs."

"Yeh? Well, Japs are damn steady workers, and you better learn it too," Marty replied, and before his shavetail boss-way, the man turned and climbed soberly back into the old car and nursed it out of the yard, hating his guts, Milton knew, hating Marty's bossy guts.

"They looked hungry—— Probably have kids," Milton said uneasily.

"They ought to be hungry, if they won't settle down! Too many bumming vets; two-three million loafing off the government, and millions more drawing pay around schools and shops, pretending to be learning. Learning, hell! Nobody's paying me to learn!"

As the family settled in the cool north dining room, young Milton hoped the awkwardness, the strangeness of a soldier home among them might wear off; that they would quit fighting the air as though holding off an attack. He looked around the pleasant table, with its centerpiece of red brown and yellow and white, unfamiliar hothouse flowers smelling of musty wetness instead of the old-time spikes of bluebeard's tongue in bloom on the hump, or the wild roses sweet through the gullies. His mother looked younger than the day he left, and Martin well too, like a determined, white-haired sportsman in his loafer slacks of biscuit brown, in everything except his work-knotted hands.

Beside him, in her old place, was Rita, the red slacks and bushy permanent unkind to her stockiness. But she would slim out to whistlebait again, now the baby was here, and look like the girl of the exaggerated letters who had cried "Hubba, hubba!" when she saw her brother, kissing him with affected lingering, "Mm-mm, Van Johnson, you send me!" showing off, making a fuss before Hazel's reserve.

Yes, Milton saw how she came to run away with a tongue-tied

young ranchhand at fifteen, with the bomber plant closed, the air base shutting down and millions of men out of circulation, dead or hurt, or married elsewhere. ". . . I'm afraid the war has spoiled our young girls," Penny had written, apologetically, as though reporting on a guardianship. "Rita was crazy over a sergeant from the Bronx, out all hours, barely fifteen, and wanting a car because Hazel has one, and a mink jacket. We just about had to tie her up when he left. The next week she ran off with Al, who can't jitterbug or even one-step, but at least she's married. So many who should be aren't, even in good families. Something like that would have broken her father's heart. But she and her dad are getting foolishly pally since he's home, and she may be regretting Al."

Now there was the ten-pound boy they called Vannie. "Enough Miltons and Martins greebing up the joint," Rita said.

"Yeh, thick as sheepherder bugs under a rock," her father laughed. The girl screwed up her face at him. "A square!" she announced to Milton.

"A square, a square," Kathie chanted out suddenly, and then, shamed by her daring, turned her face against her mother's arm, quickly remembering to wipe her mouth on her napkin.

Yet there was discontent under the chatter of the sixteen-year-old, Milton decided, probably over trading the fun of high school and the GI's for baby pants and a cowhand who had never been beyond Dunhill—a big house, pretty clothes and spending money for a ranch shack, with the reminder of Hazel always before her. But Rita was good stock; a couple of toddlers reaching for her skirts would take the goose fuzz out of her britches.

The resentment in Marty was more disturbing. He had the style of a cowman, his gray-brown eyes sun-narrowed, his mouth at twenty-two a wind-scarred line. They teased him about a girl called Nollie, who jitterbugged him most of Saturday night and then off to church the next morning, Marty turning red as the old gobbler's wattles, but pleased that his brother wasn't getting all the attention, after he had been the whole show here for three, four years himself.

"Hm-mm," Milton pooched up his face as though considering a serious piece of snafu. "What you think of taking on a new daughter, Penny?"

But Marty shook his head. Not with taxes taking everything, just to be shoveled out for boondoggling all over the globe. ". . . Like

Milton, off there plotting reclamation for a mess of Chinks and then getting a bullet, and his mug in all the papers."

There were the OPA restrictions on Marty's yard-fat steers too, with the extra feed it was taking to hold them off the market all these months. Everything a man had to buy was out of sight, and now the sugar company might close down, let the beets rot, unless the growers' association got the ceiling off.

Milton let his fork clatter against his plate. "Why, that's the old technique they used in the early '30's! Old Man Jarnes from the North Platte valley used to tell how they finally sold below contract price and later the sugar company bragged that they put nine millions profit into a holding company that year. You remember, Penny—Roosevelt cracked down on holding companies afterward."

"Yeh, well, Roosevelt's done crackin' down, and old Harry Truman won't," Martin said, as he helped himself to more chicken and split biscuit. "Not with old Harry trussed up like a shoat going to market under the seat of a drylander's wagon. . . ."

A murmur of agreement went around the table, a little laugh, Penny too, comforting Milton. "You've been out of touch," she said, and tried passing the chicken again, Hazel sighing her regret. It was a fine dinner. "Those biscuits!"

But Penny shook her head. "I don't think Milton cared for them, and after all we heard about GI's hungry for home cooking," Hazel smiling into Milton's eyes. "Maybe just a little too much liquid celebrating last night," she comforted, the Martins glad of a chance to roar out laughing. With him just out of the hospital!

So Milton had to act sheepish for them. "You got me with the crossfire, just a Joe tied down in a wallow," he admitted, watching the maid carry away the plates, old Iron Leg clinging to his, giving her an angry look under his jagged white lashes. The other plates weren't half empty either—enough on platter and bowl to feed a dozen more, most of it headed for the hog trough while millions starved, millions more with their skin sticking to their bones like the hide of a bleaching carcass.

"We did cut down on the baking," Penny was saying, "but when Hoover came back you could tell he didn't find it so bad, with the crops coming." Martin nodded, while Milton looked down, remembering all the children like his little Kathie, starved into bellied old dwarfs, or fierce and fighting as wolves. Slowly he rubbed his finger-tips along the table cloth, wrinkling it under his pressure as he tried to hold himself. "Old Herbie once saw prosperity just around the corner too," he said quietly. "Talks like he's been hiding out in my Portable, Extradimensional Hole. . . ."

"Oh, now, don't start that, darling; not after last night," Hazel objected. "He got rowdy about it, knocked our new publicity man down!"

"Oh, not Milton!" his mother laughed, the others skeptical too, except old Iron Leg. "Shudda had my Little Jim Dandy Noggin Knocker," he said, thumping the pipe against the floor as he chewed.

So the talk swung to the primaries and politics, little Kathie shushed several times from a limerick she wanted to tell. "I try to keep her away from such things," Hazel said to Penny, "but she gets them from the men around headquarters, and even at the summer camp. Almost as bad as before Roosevelt died."

"Yes, there was never a more hated man," Penny said soberly over her salad, and Milton having to remember the first day that the water came creeping along the new ditch on Seep Creek, slowly, the dust so dry it floated in a thin, gray layer on the water, all of them running like wild beside it, and nobody noticing until afterward that they were all crying. Like the liberated people when the star-marked armor broke into their villages. He remembered too, the faces when that other news spread over Europe, worn, tired old women crossing themselves, or folding their hands a moment, and then stumbling away, their eyes blinded, men standing numb and vacant and silent as the wound-shocked.

Now, here at home there was only Iron Leg left for Milton, the old man not saying anything, once lifting a bushy eyebrow to him and dropping it down as he mashed his food with his fork, chewing slowly, as though his jaws were bare and barefoot. He had been through this before as a returning crutch-cripple, and then on the stay-at-home side, like these others around the table here, seeming not to care about anything except some strange spite and venge-fulness against the ones who managed to win a war for them—spite for the highest, and for the poorest now come begging a little work at the barnyard.

Godamighty, Milton thought, his father ought to remember; he saw it in '22, saw it close in around him until there was nothing else, only little Benny dead.

Or was Milton like the Jim Beckers, carrying a gripe.

As he thought about this the talk washed around the table, breaking against him like a flood against a sudden boulder, or a man alone in a rubber boat, bullets spitting. ". . . 'Minds me of that half-wit Oakie, blowing up the house trying to make a steam engine out of an old gas can," Martin was saying, the others laughing too, old Iron Leg still chewing. ". . . Only a sick mind could cook up that hellish atom bomb."

Now Milton had to look up, starting to rise, and then sitting down in confusion before the faces turned in surprise toward him. It was no use trying to tell them what he, an engineer, knew. They knew it too, at least enough, and not caring, talked faster and faster, even Hazel, forgetting that she had studied about nuclear fission all of six years ago, that there were atomists, 400 BC. Instead she was nodding there to Rita's Sunday supplement stories of monstrosities deliberately created by the A-bomb—two-headed babies, or born with their brains outside, embryos growing in the testes of the men, old Iron Leg grunting angrily at such talk from a young girl. "Shame your tongue!"

And as Penny murmured her concern about the stories, Milton wanted to shout against them that such monstrosities were old, old as the causative rays, known and labeled many years.

It was then that young Marty spoke up, loud, angry. "I claim we got to use the A-bomb quick. Bomb the Russian cities off the map, the English and Canadian too—anybody who won't give up to us, let us run their industries, mines, everything. We got to bomb everybody down and keep 'em down!"

And in the silence there was no surprise around that table, no objection from Penny, not even from Hazel. "Yes. The Senator says . . ." talking like the Germans who knew of the Buchenwalds and saw no horror, felt no guilt—all struck by the same horrible disease, a swift and dreadful paresis that spread even to remote Seep Creek.

And as he sat there, his first day home, Milton Stone tried to grip his hands together under the table against the rising anger, the hatred against his own family here, against all those he had left in the world to love, hating them as he hated the bombers of St. Lo, as they ripped their own attack concentrations to shreds, annihilating them, while responsible men turned their crying faces to the sky, cursing it and the wind that had moved the guide lines of colored smoke so carefully laid down.

But the bomber crews had wept as bitterly when they found out, while around this table there was joy in perversity—in these people and in all the others who were determining the future of the world around their dinner tables; joy in their destructiveness, deliberately willing to know nothing, to feel nothing except hatred for the responsibilities they would neither face nor recognize.

Now, finally Milton had to get out, and pushing his chair back, he stumbled away into the sunlight, leaving them all behind, even little Kathie, the child looking after her father, silent and disturbed, a wishbone in her hand ready to pull. Uncertainly Hazel started up, suddenly remembering Milton's attack of pain last night, but old Iron Leg stopped her. "An oak wedge'll split the seedling tree to the ground," he shouted angrily, "but you ain't no call to woman-shame him on top of it!"

So she sat back down and almost at once the dessert came. Penny poured the coffee. "He had to find out sometime how things are," she said soberly, and then everybody began to talk about other things, only Kathie's eyes returning to the empty chair. The maid passed the lemon pie with meringue two inches deep, and a silver server, while out beyond the windows the beet rows were growing green in the dark, wet soil where once water was so alien that the earth resisted its coming, floating on it in dust, gray and dry.

3 — *Tame Cat on the Doorstep*

So Milton scraped his mustache off in the back of the Stockmen's Cafe, Nancy Leite looking on while she rested her feet on a chair. His hand was unsteady, dropping the shaver, yanking the cord from the socket, but finally he rubbed his thumb over the bare lip, examined it closely in the blurring mirror and returned to his new song:

> So I'm off to war again,
> I'm off to war again,
> The bravest fightin' man abroad,
> A bare-assed monkey home.

But, as he explained carefully to Nancy's good-natured listening, he was a fraud, off to no wars anywhere because he was a disab, disabled by a bullet tucked inside him like a pebble clutched in a fist. So she went to dish out the pair of thick pork chops she was frying for him and rounded up her Agnes, back from her clerical job in Europe, to drive Milton home. Not to Hazel's, or to the big white house on Seep, but to the bunkhouse. "Nobody looking down her nose at you tomorrow morning before you find your feet," she said.

When he awoke himself out of a half dream of the fighting, it was noon and he had to go explain to Penny about the re-enlisted Mexican vets that came along yesterday after he left the table. They were from Okinawa, had a guitar and offered him a lift to Dunhill. First he bought them a drink, and they bought him one because he was low-down, and sang him their new song. Finally they all got hungry and then it came out that these Joes couldn't go eat with him because they were greasers. After that things weren't too clear, except that he skinned his left hand somehow and was hit by the pain again. Then—well, she'd hear about it anyway—Nancy Leite got him away before he was run in. Fed him, sent him home. Now he felt like hell, his head exploding, his chest and arm sore, his knuckles busted. "Your menfolks don't do well by you, Penny," he admitted.

"It's all right, son. Eat your breakfast," she said, exactly as Milton had heard her speak to his father in his worst days. Then in the afternoon she took him down to a doctor at Cheyenne, a heart man. "But he can't tell me anything I don't know," Milton objected, "and I have regular checkup dates at the vets' hospital, free."

"Government doctors . . . !" Penny replied. And because he couldn't start hitting women, not his mother, he went, old Iron Leg taunting him: "Hay waddie who was down to Dunhill yesterday tells me you had them yeller-bellies headin' fer the breaks every direction. Looked like you was a real hell-roarer, thunder in your fists and your whiskers blowin'. But it's gonna be tame cat on the doorstep, lickin' your sides."

And it turned out that way, both Penny and Hazel watching that he followed orders: quiet, no strain, nothing. Like a child or an old, old man; not Iron Leg—old! So Milton wrote and wired everywhere, trying to corral a job, get off on his own with his family. But it was slow as moving a scraper pan in mud, and so Hazel had Kathie sent home from camp for a week end now and then to cheer him up. Milton even got the girl to himself for an hour once, and took her up through the old cottonwood grove that Penny planted before he was born. Together they watched the orioles flash through the trees and slip into the nests swinging against the whitish summer sky. Carefully, with his right arm, he carried the little girl through the marsh that was the old storage reservoir, breast-high in rushes now, and gay with the call of the blackbirds—red-wing, red-head, or with yellow, and all singing. Together they looked down into the nests in the rushes, with blue-green eggs or naked, big-mouth younglings, while brownish birds fluttered in alarm and cunning about them.

"See—the mothers are afraid we will hurt their babies."

Slowly the child turned her dark eyes down to her father's face, considering him soberly, and a little uneasily, as with some remote and frightening monition behind her reserve.

So he lifted her a little higher and plowed energetically through the rushes to set her feet on dry land. The wind along the hump fluttered the plaid ribbons at her braids and the water in Milton's shoes squashed to make them laugh, and gathered dust. They picked an armful of flowers for a thick lei of blue and yellow around Kathie's neck and looked at it together in the father's pocket mirror, the girl putting her hand shyly to it, her wondering eyes upon her reflection. Afterward they went to see some calves, white-face cow-calvies. There were a dozen right together, some standing, those sleeping flat on the ground curled up lifting their heads lazily as the two approached. One even let the fearing little girl touch his wet nose, stroke his curly white back while he reached around for a nip or two at the flower chain, until the big steer with them stopped his cud and got up to look, shaking his head threateningly, as though it still had its intended weight of horn. Milton smiled to his small daughter and she went on patting the calf, but her eyes were on the watching steer, until, at a warning rumble in his throat, the calves all jumped up and ran off down the hill in a little bunch to the other cattle, the steer staying behind, still looking.

Then there had been old Plew Tollins to face. Quiet, taffy-haired young Stoney had gone into uniform from his second year in Animal Husbandry at Laramie. He looked fine when he stopped by Seep Creek to say good-by his last time home, and now his father was coming.

Penny watched him plod up the walk. "The old man's been getting strange," she said, seeming to forget the wintry night of the bachelor stork party, and all the years since.

Milton went out to meet the old man, his work-stooped shoulders almost a hunchback under the blue shirt, his hands work-gnarled as a Polish slave laborer's, helpless tears running down his gullied stubbles.

"Don't feel too bad, Mr. Tollins," Milton tried to comfort. "He did all right; he went down with his gun in his hand, shooting. . . ."

Surprised, Penny looked at her son, and hurried to get the old man inside, talking away his embarrassment while the maid brought iced tea and cookies—asking neighborly about things in the Bottleneck. "Raised turkeys, thousands of them; grazed them across the country like sheep," she told Milton. "Thanksgiving for everybody in uniform."

And after a while Plew got his stumbling tongue to speak,

to ask how it had been in Italy. So Milton told about Anzio, full of dead to be buried, shells dropping accurate as though magnetized from the high ground when Stoney's outfit came in to help consolidate the beachhead, extend it, keep it supplied. They made their way up toward the first artillery emplacements where the land began to climb. The boy led a squad of volunteers to clean out a gun nest in a pile of rocks. The jerries got most of them but the guns were knocked out.

"You s-s-saw the place?" the old man persisted, needing this much.

"Yes, the exact spot, with the stuff still scattered around. It commanded a slope about three hundred yards but Sergeant Tollins cleaned it out, Stoney and—the others," almost naming Harold Leite, Nancy's boy, although Penny must know he went down beside Stoney.

Old Plew rubbed a hand over his leathery, bald head, his eyes far off, proud. "He was a great boy, my Stoney," he said slowly. "They gimme some kind a medal for him." Not a word of wishing that it could have been otherwise, only needing to have something of how it was, and as Milton looked at this father he wondered, as the other Stones had before him, if there was any way to return from the wars but dead.

Then Iron Leg came stomping in, his old eyes sharp. "Godamighty!" he roared, "world's sure goin' t' hell standin' on a box when Plew Tollins wastes time gallivantin'!"

Marty finally sold his steers. He had held them over in the Argonne feedlots for three months on the advice sent out through Ridges to all the stock growers, with the promise, backed by the packers, finance cattlemen, NAM lobbyists and five of their senators that the OPA would be broken. With millions for publicity and easy tide-over loans, the scheme worked, and now the steers brought twenty-eight cents, $25,000—steers that wouldn't have paid out on the shipping and marketing back in '32, old Martin said bitterly. The next day Penny asked Milton not to call his brother "Marty" any more. She preferred his right name, Martin. He was to be county committeeman, had ordered an airplane, and with his father bought a good block of utilities stock through Ridges. ". . . He's one of the important men around here now, and only twenty-two."

Milton held himself together until he got away and caught a ride to Dunhill, to take it out on anybody making a crack about him or the other vets, or perhaps even less, like the time he knocked down that yahooser from over south for spitting on the Senator's car, Hazel driving, although he knew it was only a man trying to show his contempt for a woman out of his reach. The vets had started an AVC but somebody got to Bill Deevers through his father's job with the oil company, and to Chuck and Mary Wilder through their business loan. With the Mexican vets and Solly Hoff, the one Jew, the method was more direct—twisted barb wire whips left against the door at night. So the committee had fallen apart.

For those without jobs and maybe without a house, there was just the sitting around waiting, like in the army, but with no guns or equipment to clean, no beating their gums about home. Sometimes they talked a little about their soldier ancestors coming West for free land because there was no welcome at home; grandfather to Kansas, maybe, father drylanding here or up in Montana. Now there was only Alaska, and that took big money.

Perhaps somebody asked for Milton's spiel with the Portable Hole and his latest variation, maybe: ". . . And this stick is the bird that's building the roadhouse and those tourist camps and shutting them up over winter. Fold him in so—and so, and presto, the hole's gone with him, and you can move into the camps next week."

Usually they squatted along the shady side of Main Street, eight or a dozen of them, just waiting, like Ash Wilbur, still hoping his wife who had run off with a cake salesman might return bringing back his car. "Service man marryin' just wears down the doorstep," he said sourly, but still he waited, maybe beside Cal Johnson, who had a couple of cornea operations coming up, telling him when to wolf-whistle, with all those thirteen, fourteen-year-olds switching their pretty butts past, looking back with tolling eyes, like the girl children of Europe, but without the need of hunger.

Others coming home joined the loafers, some war workers too, but not old Artie's children. They were stranded as far as California since the plants closed, the old folks themselves buried at Argonne beside the Green children and Benny and the Scheelers, Wheeler's mother and Wheeler too, dead from a horse kick, after sixty years in the saddle.

Sometimes Bert Cattlet, the son from the old G Bar, came down to chew the fat. His back was twisted from a Jap knife, and hot, dry mornings he liked to stretch out with the others under the cottonwoods along the big ditch to watch the cattle come in off the range; steers in steady mottled red streams sweeping down the bluff roads and converging on the gray mat of shipping pens. Dust rose, punchers whooped out their "Yip-pee!" and "Ya-hoo hoo!" swinging the knot-ended ropes against the lean, dusty white backs that should have had the meat of three more months of grass on them, the fat meat of seed-filled, curing grass. Now they were being gunned to Omaha to the highest market of all time.

Sometimes, when Marty needed an extra freighter, he phoned for Milton, even before the market crash made him ornery and sour and so penny-pinching that he canceled the plane order. Milton usually got the word through the Stockmen's Cafe, Nancy bringing it to him at the counter or bar. "Your folks want you," she would say, offhand, never mentioning the name of either Martin. Often it was the old truck of the Mexicans that Milton drove, maybe Iron Leg coming along to sit at a table at the Stockmen's, his bony hands nursing a beer and perhaps talking about the rockets reported over Sweden.

"There's always a lot of fireworks shootin' the sky, August 'round to New Year's, an' with that vitty water I seen Swedes drink . . ." he laughed, "but I bet what them Swedes been seein' don't compare to the flyin' serpents we had back in the Nineties— quarter mile long, an' smokin' flame. Feller in Texas drug one down with his lassoo an' chopped it up for his hound-dogs."

They talked about their wars too, Milton matching old Iron Leg's bull alligator stories with Mat Gray Goose, possessor of the longest pair of legs in the army, regular double-jointed tom-walkers. Folded up behind the wheel of a jeep he looked like an Indian's head spying out between khaki scantlings. But he rode his army truck like his forefathers their wild horses; could take that old strip-hauler up Devil's Tower and down the other side if he had to, without unfolding. Once, when the outfit was cut down by a dose of the GI's, the African trots, with even Milton unable to keep his AS books read up ahead of his need for paper, Mat got to trailing pretty far. At one of his squats, five jerries hid out since the retreat came sneaking in around him, each way. Handicapped by his position and his pants, Mat grabbed a handhold on the truck door, swung up and planted his big GI heels in one German's mouth and then back into the stomach of another one, while he let out a Sioux war-whoop that lifted the dust from the rocks two miles away. Kicking his pants off into the wind he grabbed the Nazi guns and rounded up the other three, weaseling it for the hills, and brought them in on top of his load, dallied with his towrope. When the outfit ribbed him about his bare shanks he gave them a slow grin. "My grandfather put up a pretty good fight against Custer without no pants."

Milton wondered where Mat was now—probably listening to the organizers of the Klan or the Christian Vets, who promised to push a bulldozer through the Treasury for him, give him what labor and the Jews had, maybe the Catholics too. "Keep your tail down and the sand outa your gun!" and the stiff arm salute—all smooth as a wind-swept stretch of African road before the first mine went off.

But Mat, drylanding on the family quarter-section on Pine Ridge, might be taken in along with his white brothers by the sell-outs who voted against irrigation, against anything for those who work the earth like Mat ran his truck, loving it as they might a woman, like the bald little Russian, Mat found in Iran. It was spring, and the broad, Slavic face spread in pleasure at the words "Ukraine" and "Dnepropetrovsk." He jumped up and down, making scraping motions while his mouth burred like a child's imitation motor, and then plowing motions with his hands, and sowing and reaping. But with fallen face, his fingers became the enemy marching eastward, the explosion of his hands the destruction of it all, and the retreat. Then his motions changed: his fists, rolling tanks; the index fingers, cannon pointing westward, making "bang-bangs" and "pfoofs" until with one forearm raised like a hill, his fingers marching up, he looked over, and then spread both arms out in joy, his strong face shining in tears, his arms a sweeping encompassment—miles and miles of his home earth free.

"Good as the goddamn signtalk of the old ones," Mat had bragged.

"Yeh," Iron Leg agreed. " 'Minds me of them Russkies, Andy Burke used to tell about at Crimea, pockets full a sunflower seeds and spittin' hulls," he said, craning to watch Nancy come by with her beer before the supper rush. Milton grinned into the old man's eyes. "Still ranny as a GI!"

"Hell's buzzards, you wouldn't stop a wore-out studhorse from r'arin' his neck an' poundin' his belly a little."

No, no, Milton admitted. But thinking about Mat and the Russkies, he talked of his uneasiness ever since he looked in on the UN Security Council last spring, watched the gray-heads around the bent table wrangling like a high school student council—the principal's stooges railroading through the edicts from above. Nobody except maybe Dr. Lange seemed to know the purpose of diplomacy. Fighting over oil and ports and spheres of influence as though nuclear power, finance cartels and A-headed missiles were no more than mooley cows against a barbed wire fence.

Iron Leg waggled his thin old beard and pushed his glass back. "Yeh," he shouted, "act like diplomacy meant burnin' a man off his range if you don't like his breed a stock, or how he's runnin' 'em."

"Or want his range. Instead of sharing waterholes, keeping the fences up, rustlers and range-burners out. The business of diplomacy is to compromise conflicting interests and points of view; not defeat. That's the business of war, of fist and six-gun and A-bomb."

"Hell's buzzards, no use denying we're up to our tits in a dozen Johnson county wars, our troops tearin' in every place to hold off the settlers from cleaning out on the blood-suckin' outfits. Our planes like chicken hawks over the ground, with A-bombs to back the bayonets."

Still 'n all, what young Milton needed was being freed in his own bed, something to do for the bullet like Charley Powell's buffalo robe done for a crutch-cripple. So they had more beer and when they started home somehow the lights went bad, and the steering gear. Anyway, at sunrise they woke up in a ditch near Argonne, the truck on its side and the old man so chilled he couldn't get around much for a week.

Then Hazel came home unexpectedly. Milton and half a dozen others were squatting against the wall of an empty war-time pool hall that the bank wouldn't turn over to be partitioned for room for vets. They were talking about the transmutation of elements; gold or anything made in a factory like plastic or buta, Chick Hanks scoffing, "Hell, that's just more a your Portable Hole stuff!" So

Milton didn't see Hazel stop the car across the street. But Ash, still watching for his Dallie, nudged him. "Wife looking for you." The way he said it made Milton sore but he got up, dusted his hams and went reluctantly over to stand beside the door of the yellow car, unshaven, his hands dirty from drawing in the dust.

"Get in, Milton," was all Hazel said, and so he went to the house with her, feeling foolish as a runaway six-year-old. After cleaning up, and supper that Hazel had sent over from the Cafe, she did complain a little. ". . . With those bums, dear, looking worse than any of them, and the whole country talking about you and Grandfather hanging around the Stockmen's. Have you no consideration for anyone, not even your mother? I hear the Leite woman has her Agnes there too now. What kind of a daughter is she, coming in with the mother who was an accomplice to. . . ."

Her father's murder, Milton finished to himself. And he, too, hanging around his father's woman. So he had to strike out, as with a fist. "That Agnes comes mighty well stacked up."

Quietly Hazel went to pour them a little brandy with their coffee and asked about his job-hunting. "I've got to go back," she said, "help get the primaries in Montana lined up, and then on to the coast. If you haven't any work in prospect, you are to come along."

For a moment Milton looked at Hazel, anger drumming hard, but there was the bullet, and this was his wife, so he laughed, threw his head back. "Me? You expect me to turn into a goddamn camp follower?"

"We'll skip the implication of that remark," Hazel said easily and began to clear away the dishes. But afterward Milton got her to say she would go on a fishing trip to the Big Horns with him the rest of the week, although it would take her a month to get her skin bleached out again. With tent and tackle in Hughie Saul's jeep they could get around in the mountains up where old Iron Leg took the boys in the cut-down Chevvie long ago.

They started into a clear Wyoming morning, clouds like a bright row of shell puffs rising over the pink buttes to the west, the sun already warm. In shirts and levis, with old ranch hats, they drove up miles of Seep Creek, the old sage plain fertile as the Nile now, big houses set back in shimmering groves, good roads, with the smell of the yellow sweet clover along the shoulders. A couple of times they stopped for moving stock, the flash of white teeth in greeting, and then they turned off on a trail toward the mountains and were suddenly out in the ragged sage, clumps of bull-tongue cactus with the blossoms like satin cups of lemon-green, here and there a purple thistle swaying in the wind, and an eagle off very high.

It was then that the coyote jumped up, and Milton pulled out of the rutted tracks and cut across the plain after him, whooping, bouncing over sagebrush, across hollows and out along a clear stretch cut suddenly by a washout, Milton yelling, "Hang on!" as they plunged into it and scrabbled out the other side like a Big-Horn sheep going up a crag. Honking, they started to make up the time lost and the coyote, scared now, struck off down a slope of a couple miles toward some breaks, stretching himself lower as the jeep roared up, then beginning to duck and dodge, Hazel hanging to her hat and the seat, whooping now too, as the jeep teetered in Milton's short turns. A couple of times he ran clear over the coyote without hitting him, and had to switch back and pick up speed, but going it hell-for-leather, like on the blacked-out roads of the Italian mountains. Finally the coyote lit into a straight desperate run like a Nip afire and his ammo belt popping—heading for the rough country, Milton, afraid of going over some bluff, cut in around him along a crest, the wheels kicking gravel, Hazel crying out as the wheels hit the coyote, bumping softly. But they were too close to the loose edge and before Milton could stop or turn, the jeep went over, spilling the two down the side of a graveled slope into a patch of purple loco blossoms. Milton pulled himself up, afraid, but Hazel was right beside him, lifting her head, shaking gravel from her hair, laughing as a sheep cactus that she jerked off her arm stuck to her fingers, no matter how she shook them. So Milton helped her get rid of it and together they looked for more cactus and for skinned places, laughing until they were weak, for it was like the old days around the university—like the time they worked late on lab experiments and got locked into the building and had to climb out of the second-story window between the suspicious rounds of the watchman with his flashlight. Hazel's hand-hold on the window sill had slipped and she missed Milton's arms held up for her, hitting him so they went down in a pile. But when the watchman came running at the noise they had shushed each other and were safely on the walk, with no necessity for a girl to go explain to the dean.

It was wonderful to remember this now, with a clear, rocky creek below the breaks, and the mountains beyond blue as night sky while Milton picked sticks out of Hazel's hair and out of the back of her shirt. Her shoulder was moist and soft under his hand, and suddenly more dear than ever. Gently he turned her face to him, wiping away the dirt from her forehead, her sun-flushed cheek, and suddenly he was kissing her as though all this summer had never been, with a new urgency that grew to her sweetness, her soft response.

But only for a moment. "Oh, Milton, you—you must quiet yourself," pushing him away, making it his need.

So he closed his eyes, drew himself together and went up to see about the coyote, still alive, snarling and snapping at his broken back as he dragged himself toward a clump of squaw currant. Milton took him out with the jeep shovel, one good lick behind the ears, and lifted his scalp for bounty, Hazel close behind, crying, "Oh —you delight in killing!" in sudden woman waspishness, turning away as Milton looked up in astonishment, the eared bit of tawny skin fresh and limp in his hand. "Why, he's a varmint, as old Iron Leg calls them, and his back was broken. . . ."

But it was no explanation for what stood between them, and so Milton worked with jack and rope to make the jeep pull itself onto its wheels and up to the level. After a while they were back on the road and talking a little, deciding to stop for hamburgers at Yellowhorse although they weren't hungry, with no emptiness to fill.

It was there, in the crowded lunchroom of the little foothill town that the trouble started, with a commotion around the door and a loud voice calling in: "Where's the goddamn Jew with that jeep out there? Git it the hell outa my sight!"

Milton and Hazel looked around the side of the booth, rising a little to see over the seated crowd. The old counterman was trying to get a stubby, hawk-nosed man in a big white hat out the door. But he kept up his roaring, his eyes searching for strangers, turning in the direction some of the crowd looked, towards the Stones' booth. "Ha! There's the goddamn kike!—hidin' out!" he yelled, and pulling out an automatic, started toward the booth, and when several tried to stop him, a foot reaching out to trip him, he jerked the gun up and fired—a little slow, Milton taking Hazel down behind the booth wall with him as the bullet hit the plaster behind them. Chairs fell back, women screeched, and somebody upset a table as the crowd rushed the man.

But he held them off until he got out the door, shooting back into them twice as he ran for a parked car, leaving the old counter-man face down on the porch. Several stooped around him, a woman slipping her hand under his shirt. She looked up, shaking her head.

"Got old Johnny! The bastard finally killed a man!" somebody shouted over the roar of cars lining out into the road, rifle and shot-gun barrels pointing into the air, the dust kicking up, horns blaring.

"Your tail-breaker'll easy catch my car he took," a man called out, running toward Milton, motioning several others along, all with guns. Milton looked back to Hazel in the doorway. She nodded, so they bucked the jeep out into the street, Milton and two others in the back where the tent roll had been, a man in greasy coveralls under the wheel, one who knew the country, the short-cuts.

"Mack drove brass all over hell'n gone with Patton's outfit," the man beside Milton shouted into his ear as they tore up the road toward the mountains. "I guess that Carl Weigert's always been a little on the prod, with his ma always makin' the fool over him. He's been peddling stuff from the Silver Shirts, America First and the Nassis, even smuggling some into the Jap relocation center, and hiding out in the hills from the draft. When the army finally caught up with him he was out a dog tags fast enough, with a medic dis-charge, PN. Been peddlin' the hate stuff from Butte to Denver since, and tryin' to get a jeep for it, bellyachin' about that."

Suddenly the driver turned the jeep from the dusty road, crashed it through a plum thicket, a sloughy pasture and a creek, and then climbed back to the road beyond, into the middle of the speeding cars, the man still shouting to Milton. Weigert claimed his wife lit out whilst he was off to war, but it wasn't so. She'd worked here slinging hash until a couple months ago, feeding him, covering up for him in fights and thieving, carrying a black eye around. But when he busted her nose she up and left with the TB who had a hemorrhage at her table on the way to the lung hospital at Denver. She drove him down and didn't come back. "Weigert claims the Jews got her. I—say, you don't look much like one a them. . . ."

"I'm not, but the jeep's in Hughie Saul's name. His father dry-landed after the first war, down on Seep Creek."

"You mean Hugh Saul what's got the Congress medal?"

Milton tried to nod, grabbing a new hold as they struck down into a deep wash and back to the road again. Now the thickest dust was behind them, only Weigert ahead, and not over half a mile, the man beside the driver pulling his rifle up, ready to fire fast at the curves. Finally, on a long upswing, he got a tire. The car swerved, jumped the trail and as the white hat sailed off, the car went over a sidehill, turning, rolling, until it stopped in a thicket near the bottom, dust rising like smoke around it.

From the trail the men in the jeep looked down, watching Weigert crawl out and duck behind the wreck, yelling a warning.

"Let me try to fetch him in," Milton asked, but the others refused. "He'd shoot you down. Better to surround him," as the other cars queued in behind, the men out and running with their guns, spreading out beyond pistol range to work down over the broken ground while Milton kept shouting: "You better come in, Carl. The jeep does belong to a Jew, but he's had it like the rest of us, from Pearl to Formosa. Left a leg there. That's how he got the jeep."

But it was like whistling into the wind. Weigert only roared out more talk, and when a hat was pushed up above the brush patch on the lower slope in the old trick of hunting and war, he whirled and shot, so they knew they had to waste him out of ammo before he hit somebody, or killed himself. Milton wasn't afraid of suicide. He'd seen too many men like that, Nazis of whatever nationality, mean as rattlers until their guns snapped, then coming out begging, only to spill their old hate in the questioning. Weigert would make it a lurid trial for the papers: WAR PSYCHO PERSECUTED! While the counterman lay up in the little cemetery, Carl would get a few months in the asylum and then be loose again.

But the man was already coming out. A bullet sent in from below glanced off the metal beside his head and brought him up, hands high, his stringy black hair over his eyes, bawling like a cut calf.

"Psycho, hell!" Milton roared. "Maybe he is—but it's a mighty familiar pattern to a lot of us."

And when they got back to Yellowhorse, Hazel had taken the bus to the railroad; the fishing trip was done, and it wasn't until weeks afterward that he found out why she consented to go at all. By then the trip was already like a morning-time dream, with the hopeful happiness of the drive out, and the swift turn into senseless violence; like a hospital dream, like this summer everywhere.

So now it was Milton's first election night home, and cold, with the unprecedented snow Saturday, and blowing again, another storm warning to cattlemen on the radio: a night like those Milton saw two years back, when they were bridging the streams into Germany, the flood waters boiling as they worked under a roof of artillery, but stationary, ranged by sniper and 88. Here, on Seep Creek, the living room was pleasant, fragrant with old Iron Leg's chokecherry wood on the open fire, and comfortable in soft red-brown leather against the pinkish buff of the walls, the drapes striped maroon and yellow and a blue that was bright as a king-fisher—nothing of the fluorescent tubing and bleached furniture that drove many old timers of Turtle Shell district to the barns and bunkhouses.

The two Martins were up beside the radio, to catch the good news, and Penny too, her Red Cross work put aside and knitting a skating cap for Kathie, blue and white as her school stipulated. The Miltons were off in a corner, with pipe leg room for the old man, young Milton hunched forward, hands clasped between his knees, looking up only once, as the election returns picked up and Iron Leg roared out, "Had enough? By God, the old mare'll learn to keep her tail down—when it's too late!"

Hazel was away, off at the state headquarters at Cheyenne. Early that morning she had asked Milton if he wanted to come with her to the victory party.

"Plow the snowbanks down that way just to watch those buzzards strut and preen for 1948 and after, if there's anything left on the bones?" Milton demanded, and felt mean as a stinkfoot about it. But Hazel hesitated as she buttoned her gray coat at the door and came back, concern in her oval face, in her golden brown eyes. "Oh, Milton, what's happened to you?" she asked, meaning that people were saying: "How well your husband looks!" and sitting around on his 52-20, not even helping to stuff campaign envelopes. Then there was the abortion she felt she had to have, with the future so uncertain, and since then more formality, more chicken between them.

But Milton still had to smooth things over, pretend she was talking about today. "Nothing's happened, darling, I just thought maybe I'd find a last mess of mallards snowed in up at Seep reservoir, if anybody drives out that way."

"Take the car; I'll go with the Ridges. I don't like to have you in the snow thumbing rides," she said soberly. "It looks bad, like a professional vet, a bum."

"That's what I am, a house-broke, woman-kept bum," he answered, "me and a couple million like me."

With a sigh Hazel went out to the car, the sun breaking through now and then, bright on the snow about her as she waved to Milton in the windowed front. It gave him the trembles to watch her, like a sixteen-year-old with his first beautiful woman, for tomorrow she was going away. He had known about it since the last of August, when she finally showed him the worn letter from Potter offering her a job with his office. "In recognition and appreciation. . . ." The pay was triple that for the summer and included rates in a good school for Kathie, close enough for week-end visits, and a Washington apartment rent-free.

Yes, and all the plays and concerts, and the capital crowd for a pretty young woman. Against these what did Dunhill, Wyoming, have to offer, Milton thought angrily, knowing then why Hazel had come home that time and consented to start on the fishing trip, the letter already in her pocket. But he held himself together while she argued that the Senator had influence. "You can get something through him. I'm doubtful about engineering, but surely something organizing——"

"American Action?" Milton demanded.

She laughed scornfully. "Something much more important is coming up."

"By God, I guess there's no way to keep a monkey like Potter from showing his ass when he gets up high, but I don't have to be there and fan it," Milton had shouted, and slammed the door, hurrying down to the telephone company. But although he put in the afternoon checking up on all his applications, there was nothing, not in reclamation or the MVA or anything. Nothing a man could keep a family on.

So Kathie was sent ahead by train in charge of a woman from the summer camp. The small girl cried a little when she had to go, looking fearfully over to her father, although she hadn't seen him half a dozen times. Finally she broke from the woman and ran to him, her arms around his knees, her face against him. "Oh, daddy, I don't want you to run away while I'm gone," she whispered. "Oh, daddy . . ." and so Milton squatted down to her height and made a circle about her with his arms, looking into her worrying eyes. "I won't run away, baby," he promised. "I'll be right here when you come back. I wouldn't ever leave you; don't you know that?"

But her eyes were doubtful and so he started his sleight of hand, rolling up his sleeves, making the all-over motions swiftly, talking in a high, faker's voice: "Ladies and gentlemen! With your kind permission I will endeavor to demonstrate my colossal, world-shaking, great invention for the atomic age, the Portable, Extra-dimensional Hole! Just a hole," making dimensional motions, "to set up anywhere, a place to throw your old razor blades, park your car or put your dolly. You don't see anything? That's because it's a hole without anything around it, no shell. Put it into something, like, say, this," pulling an old wadded-up sock out of the air, flopping it, holding its top open with his fingers while, like the children from France to China, Kathie's eyes grew round, her lips parting, "the hole is like this old khaki sock, a top, sides, a bottom. Pushed down a little like this, you have a fox hole, a little deeper a well ready for the bucket, or the windmill. Pulled out real long an oil well. Pushed upside down, like this, it's an igloo, and with a chimney," poking a finger up, "and a stoop," pushing out a knuckle, "you have a quonset for the GI and his wife and little girl. Pulled out like this a telegraph pole, and taller, the Empire State building.

"But for this atomic age I recommend the special super-duper, extradimensional qualities of this portable hole," Milton announced in the grand talk children liked, pulling the carved figure of a man long as a little finger out of the air, and a woman and a small girl. These he placed carefully inside the puffed-out sock, just so. Then he began his spiel again, rolling from the bottom and the sides and back, folding in all the dimensions until there was only a little ball in his hand and suddenly it was gone too, and he held his palms out, empty. "Extradimensional! Safe!"

And then, to Kathie's big eyes, he looked into her pocket and there was the man, and woman and the little girl too, right in her pocket, and so, clutching them in safety, she went into the railroad car, looking back.

For a few hours, back in August, Milton had been happy over the battle the GI's put up at Athens, Tennessee, to get a decent election.

But violence was not the way, and September brought even darker times—more labor troubles, with the large corporations getting paid for shutdowns through their tax refunds. The stock market slid farther, with little comfort to Marty in Iron Leg's remark: "New fat fries out easy. . . ." Then there was the ballooning inflation and the general strike of the meat producers against OPA, jamming storage and pasture with beef while butcher shops closed, chicken went to a dollar a pound.

"Meat-starve the citizen into voting with them, like the privilege boys in Spain starved the countryside into revolting against the Republic," Milton complained.

"Yeh, an' with every good man fired from the papers and the radio," old Iron Leg agreed, "it's head with the belly—" Instead the public got sensationalism and war scares to justify the reports of bombers carrying a stock of A-bombs from Wichita to Alaska and stashed away from England around to Greece. Finally Wallace spoke out on foreign policy, clearing the air a little, and next Stalin, and while the newspapers and the commentators howled, it seemed to Milton they both tried to talk past them to the people like those in Wyoming, in all the Wyomings. "There's been a vacuum there, since Roosevelt——"

The election returns moved westward like the migrations into the remoter regions, the House lost, the Senate too, even without the coalition of monopoly Republicans and Southern reactionaries—all government blocked like the last two years under Hoover and Wilson. Now at last controls would come off: with no housing for the vets, labor's power to strike against the inflated dollar going, and prospects good for young Marty, highest tariff of all time to hold his prices where they were.

"First farmer I ever seen who can't understand there won't be nobody to buy his stuff—with no foreign trade, an' all the gold down to Ft. Knox!" his grandfather scolded.

But there it was, and so old Martin brought out a victory drink, and a farewell. With Hazel leaving tomorrow if the Senator's plane could get off the ground, Milton was heading to Denver the day after, for his hospital checkup, and to get some kind of a job. But he felt heavy as under full pack, with the reclamation service curtailed and the MVA too, as though there were no barren, denuded regions as reminders: China, the Near East, even the canyon-deep gullies of

Oklahoma, the eroded hills he saw in the South, like tear-ravished, sorrowful faces. "The earth is not a private chattel but a public trust, a trust held for posterity," Milton's professor used to remind his class.

At the airport Milton kissed his wife's cold lips and handed her into the plane and then stood back to watch it rise into the raw wind and circle away to the east until it was not even a lonesome speck against the gray sky—a wandering goose caught by winter. The Senator's cars, and Hazel's too, had started toward Washington, the airport deserted by shivering patronage hound and jobhunter. So Milton started off to buck the windy snow to Seep for a last night, but he drove around past the house on the terrace, the curtains drawn across the front of plastic that was like the nose of a bomber carrying death and devastation, and so, somehow, he ended up with Agnes. But it didn't turn out as it might have. Agnes was alone all right, but sick, torn in pain. "Mother mustn't get mixed up in this, with all her old trouble around here, so I can't even call a doctor."

Afterward the girl cried a long time, silently, hopelessly. "I knew he was a stinker, but I tried to believe him. You have to believe in something."

4 — Wyoming Regatta

Milton wasn't a tame cat very long after he got off the home doorstep, with his name in the papers twice the first month, once because he was in jail. But the plans for another summer at a girls' camp for Kathie had been completed last year and so Hazel finally let her come anyway and Milton had his daughter for a few hours—between the morning train and the supper bell from the gabled Alpine chalet.

The morning was a fine one, the first sun on the ring of mountains picking out the snowy peaks, floating them bright and golden above a nest of shadowed mist when Milton went out to the Capitol grounds to wait. Mary Barlow was taking him down to meet the Zephyr—not for hours, only he couldn't sleep.

By mid-morning they were in the deep granite canyon of the Big Thompson. At first Kathie was shy of the father she had not seen in almost a year, and the strange woman at the wheel, sitting quiet and awed between them as the canyon walls rose ominously toward the sky, seeming all the steeper for the occasional blue drift of larkspur between the sheer rock. But when the river boiled up white against the highway, shouldering it into the canyon wall, she moved a little closer to Milton, although it was Mary's face her eyes sought out to know if she must be afraid—turning to a stranger before the father, to a woman she had never seen before.

"They're like great high buildings," she said hopefully. "They won't fall down."

At the first gentle slope they stopped for a color shot of Kathie, tall in her pink dress, her arms full of flag and golden banner, with flowers and sun all around her. It would make a fine picture for her mother, only Kathie was suddenly stubborn and sullen as none of the Stone children had ever been, and not until Milton folded his camera and turned back to the car would she look up pleasantly, and then with wet, disturbed eyes.

Afterward they threw a couple of stones into the foaming stream, hurried a fat marmot into his rocky hole, and counted a dozen bluebirds sitting on a fence. Then up near Estes several deer and a spotted fawn crossed the road in their easy way, turning their shy delicate faces to look back before they vanished into the pines. Kathie watched them at the open car window, her eyes excited, her fingers grasping the car door, and when they were gone she put a hand out to Milton's knee as for reassurance. But later they saw other things too: beaver dams, an eagle like a far plane against a cloud, Longs Peak a giant mouse reaching for a chunk of cheese, and at a turnout they stopped to look down over a glacier, and a bull elk standing among the twisted timberline trees below.

But it was in feeding the ground squirrels and chipmunks with chocolate bars from Mary's pocket that Kathie finally forgot her shyness, laughing, chasing from boulder to boulder, until she was out of breath. Then one of the squirrels came to scratch boldly at her shoe, looking up into her face like a fat old Rhine woman begging.

At the ranger station Milton bought Kathie a cowboy on a horse woven of rushes—almost as big as she, and a silver ring with a bird on it, the Zuni knife-wing bird that never lights, the girl sober and attentive, making secret childhood interpretations of his words as she clutched her rush man.

"Like Gran'pa's stories," she finally said, matter-of-factly.

Mary Barlow squeezed her shoulder, laughing, and finally Milton laughed too. Plainly it was time to eat now, and afterward they went around Grand Lake in a speedboat, skimming along on the water, watching the white sailboats swoop and run before the chill, snow wind.

On the way back Kathie settled down, and with an arm around her rush doll, her face against Milton's shirt, she slept. He held himself very still, breathing as quietly as he could, and looked off into the blue shadows of the afternoon mountains, the weight and warmth of his daughter a sweetness and nostalgia. This was how he had seen her all those nights thousands of miles away, working under enemy flares, squatting in the water and mud of slit trenches, or on the jogging litter, the fog of morphine in his brain and the pain in his breast.

But he had her for just this little time, and the woman beside him wasn't her mother, although her face was as concerned when the girl whimpered in her sleep.

Yet it was a good day, one Milton Stone would carry a long, long time.

Mary dropped him off at the old Windsor Hotel and he went into the smoky bar to talk to Iron Leg. The old man was spread out in a booth like a setting hen in a feed box, talking over the Wall Street squeeze of last fall with an old miner cleaned out by the silver demonetization back in '93, and now making a new start in uranium. Old Iron Leg had come down from Seep right after Milton got himself into jail, and stayed. What with stinkbugs in every berry dish, and only a slat fence against the wind nowadays, the two real Stones ought to stick together.

Milton was glad. When he first came to Denver he had pushed the hospital checkup aside and gone straight to the reclamation offices—through snow-piled streets as deserted as after a mine bust without the mobs of war-time soldiers. But the ring of the mountains was the same, and the sturdy white Federal Building where he was told that, confidentially, prospects were bad and actualities worse. With the administration lukewarm and the reactionary congress full of power company tools, reclamation appropriations would shrink further, and with the army grabbing everything up around the Missouri, the TVA endangered, and the Little TVA, all hydros and REA hamstrung by legislatures. "Your record's fine, and with your interest in irrigation and soil rehabilitation, why not get into the foreign field? Some of our best men. . . . It seems everybody's to profit by our excellent know-how except the Americans."

Milton nodded soberly and went out into the cold. Yes, he had applied for foreign clearance when he saw how rugged things were, but he couldn't get through, physically. Men from his outfit who had sprung a gut to get out were re-enlisting; even his captain, demonstrating roofing at $32.50 before deductions, had gone back as a private. Jim Becker in New York too, writing:

"With my FTT running out, it's get in some of the rackets sprouting up here and ending in the East River in a sack, or take on another hitch. Winnie's put in four years with the bloodbucket in the ETO and isn't liking it, but I can't take up married life a parasitic male. Anyway, with that State War Disaster Military Corps that Dewey's cooked up, and training to handle 'grave domestic disturbances' like maybe the working man resisting the crack-down coming, a feisty Joe like me'll be in less trouble with Hitler's old outfits than around Dewey's new SS boys. . . ."

Yet Milton knew of many vets who had got jobs as good as any "defers" or 4F's, so he had to make one last try before the hospital, going down to Nebraska to see Dr. Jolle. The old physicist ran his fingers through his gray uprush of hair and answered deliberately. "Prospects are not good. With the great technical advances, production can treble while employment goes down, taking the consumer's purchasing power with it. It's a greased slide, and little likelihood of a real public works program to brake, or even sand the slope."

"I used to think you were a State's Righter."

"The outs always are, you know," the old man said ruefully. "But now, with nuclear fission, there's no place for the smaller rights, only World Rights."

So Milton got his permission to add that to his Portable, Extradimensional Hole routine, pulling the khaki sock from his pocket. It tickled the old professor and he took Milton to Sigma Xi with him, and after the chancellor's talk, got him to give a demonstration. It felt good to be around the old place, even though most of the students were GI's, without the horseplay.

Back in Denver there was no news, except the unseasonal, man-high snow banks, and talk of storm-bound ranchers, and cattle that had been held off the market to break OPA dying by the tens of thousands. At the hospital there was a handful of calls and telegrams from Washington. When Milton got to Hazel, her voice was so anxious he had to clamp his hand on the receiver and take a long, slow breath. She had been worried, with him not even registered there, afraid of something foolish, desperate. "Why must you worry me so? All summer you've been strange . . ." and Milton couldn't say he hadn't expected her to call; that such hopes were of a time long done, and so he stammered like old Plew, while Hazel, still uneasy, promised to make reservations immediately. She would spend Thanksgiving in Denver.

Milton had left the phone booth happier than any time since he saw the mushrooming cloud over New York, so he went back to town and walked along the old brownstone rooming houses, past the little colored glass window of Hazel's cubbyhole room there, made of beaverboard set across a stair landing—space for nothing beside a cot, where she slept and lived the two months he was stationed at the chemical plant. Then, from the Capitol grounds he looked off toward the mountains, blue-white in winter snows, and forgot the poor Joe he was, the tame cat of old Iron Leg's predictions. Standing there, with such happiness in him, he saw the snow of the mountains as he would have a year ago, the snows of all the mountains of the world a promise of water for the parched earth, relief for the weary backs, and light for far, dark huts, so those who labored by day could read by night, hear music —read and hear the things that belonged to all the scattered people of the earth, make them a whole.

But it turned out wind pudding and graveyard sauce. Hazel didn't come. The weight of organizing the new congress fell heavily on Senator Potter, and with the strikes, and the necessary curbs for the labor monopoly . . .

By then Milton had sweat out his hospital checkup—nothing new except a nurse called Mary Barlow, who pretended that his bullet was just a piece of rustler decoying—the old dodge of a dime under the skin of an unbranded calf. No news to interest a young woman in the political swim of Washington, her employer the front for the next president.

This time Milton Stone did not leave the hospital into bright June, with home and family and the easy belief in a job ahead, but into chill, thawing November. So he wandered over to the Capitol grounds, to that stone bench where so many came to sit, in joy and in loss.

After awhile he remembered little Eddie Mack, the boy he saw that day Hazel told him she was coming. The boy was making little coaxing whistlings around the snowy bushes, gently stalking a small, dusty bird. Once he had sneaked off to a little two-wheeled trailer covered with low bows and canvas, and then hurried back with a slice of bread and jelly on his palm, sharing bits with the bird. Then a woman slipped off the walk into the trailer, like a hen stealing out her nest, the boy watching sideways. So Milton took out his Portable Hole sock and shaking it, mumbled some mysterious words and made it disappear, come back and disappear again. Soon the boy was beside him, his thin little face eager, even talking some, until the woman came by and he had to follow, but looking back once.

Today Milton found the boy over in the Museum, keeping his thin little britches close to the heat and watching out for the guard. They were still in the trailer, having to sleep in it too, he admitted over a cup of hot chocolate, since the night worker whose bed they used got changed to a day job. Parked near public buildings, filling stations doing for restrooms over Sundays. The mother clerked in a dime store; the father run off with a woman at maneuvers. "It's getting pretty cold now, but some people are trying for us . . ." Eddie said hopefully.

At the AVC they knew about the Macks and hundreds of others living in chicken coops, holes in banks, or in cars right through the long blizzard that killed so much fat stock. ". . . We'd oughta raise hell! If somebody was just willin' to go 'head, like over in the UK, movin' in on them earl and duke palaces," a man waiting around said. Yes, Milton agreed, with hundreds of empty places right here, and the building material going for roadhouses, thirty-room homes, and tourist camps that closed all winter.

He thought about this as he went down Sixteenth Street, taking the curb edge from the Thanksgiving rush, feeling low-down as on burial detail. Suddenly a man in an old battle jacket jumped out before the roar of a bus plowing the traffic like a charging Mark IV. Milton went for him, took him out, and then crumpled down himself.

When he came to he was stretched on the pavement, legs all around him—people, a flashbulb exploding, a reporter copying from his wallet in a cop's hand. So it was back to the hospital for Milton, sore and skinned with a knot on his forehead. In the morning Mary Barlow brought him a paper: DESPONDENT VET IN SUICIDE TRIES. A waist-gunner with 50 missions attempted death a second time after a lead-bearing vet saved him from bus. Broke from police to plunge under car. With the story was a spread of pictures: the man crumpled in the street; Milton down too, and an inset of his x-print with the bullet dark and smudged, and of Kathie and Hazel, identified as secretary to Senator Boyd Potter. There was little more about Walter Cooke, except that he had used up his GI schooling and couldn't get a job in New London, so he came to Denver because he remembered it as the city of sunshine. Now he had a broken back.

But the city of sunshine had five successful suicide tries that week —one a liberal radio commentator who lost his job in the purge, the others vets. The holdup at the Rookery, with a $100,000 take from the gambling crowd, was blamed on vets too. "Anybody strong enough to hold up a powder room at the YW's bound to be a vet, maybe twice over," Milton complained. So far nobody was laying the town's rocket scare on them, the Reds getting the credit from everybody except the meteor man.

The day Milton was out again, the wind blew wet and raw as he went down to the Chamber of Commerce to give his Portable Hole routine at a luncheon. He got a lot of laughing and applause, and an offer of a job, nothing heavy, clerical work over at one of the shallow coal mines around town when the army took over. Milton nodded his understanding. He had seen heavy equipment moved in, ready. "Taking over from the strikers."

"Yes. Look good to have some 'disabs' on the job when the shooting starts."

Shooting. . . .

Finally he got away, hurrying out to find Eddie Mack, with the snow beginning to run gray through the streets again. The little trailer was pulled up in front of a church below Capitol hill, Eddie sick and coughing, Liza Mack huddled beside him, trying to keep the boy warm without asphyxiating him or burning him up with the kerosene heater in the cot-sized interior that was barely high enough to sit up in. The stench of the heater and the boy's gas-reddened eyes, coming on top of the threat to use soldiers against the miners, made Milton go like his grandfather the day he stomped out of the blacksmith shop on a new pipe leg. Running to a telephone in the Capitol annex, he called hotels, agencies. Nothing could be done today; no room, nothing. So he hurried to the drug store, bought a heater and a lamp, and stuffing them into the trailer, dragged it around to the delivery entrance of the annex and pushed it straight in, got it clear back to the farthest loading platform, one side of the canvas rolled up and the heater and lamp plugged in before some men came to look, to run over. He put up a little fight, ducking and dodging down the dark corners, whooping, sticking a foot out, and finally landing in jail.

The morning paper had the story: VET GOES BERSERK. Set up housekeeping in state Capitol with strange woman and boy; the opposition paper saying VET HERO JAILED SHELTERING SICK WAR ORPHAN. This time Milton hit the wires, with a good picture of Hazel and the morgue cut of the Senator over a quote on the importance of restoring housing to private enterprise.

That was when old Iron Leg came down from Seep. To go to the hospital, Penny wrote, adding her mortification over a son in jail; one of her children a lawbreaker, a common brawler and worse. It was the army, and those undesirable influences around the Stockmen's Cafe.

Old Iron Leg came roaring that he wasn't a sick man, just having a little trouble with the stump, an old malahack job. "No better'n a hole in a sock tied 'round with string, Charley Powell says to me eighty years ago." But he was hobbling slowly on two canes, his sagging old face white as an emptied flour sack, and nowhere a sign of the whirlwind that used to camp in his coattails. At the hospital they managed the time to make a little fuss over him, shot him full of vitamins and stuff and soon had his leg healing, for all his years, his bed a gathering place for story tellers, the nurses pretending to scurry out of reach of his long arms.

Hazel wrote too. Stiffly. She trusted Milton would not embarrass them further. "If you must conduct yourself so, please remove my name and picture from your identification. . . ." Perhaps it would be best not to send Kathie to the Colorado summer camp.

But she had come, and long before then, Eddie and his mother got a little room on Grant Street out of the jailings, and Milton a new mustache. Although the offer of the mine job was withdrawn even before Lewis capitulated, Milton got another one, clerk of parts at a garage, twenty-four dollars a week, including an unheated attic room up on the hill, so his government money could go to Kathie. Besides, things looked almost good for the UN, in spite of the stink of oil that hung over it, even over the gift of the home site from a Rockefeller. So with Iron Leg beside him, Milton called Washington Christmas morning, talked to Hazel and to Kathie too, steadying himself a moment when he heard the girl's shy voice.

Afterward he signed up to teach a night class in engineering at DU with a big Sunday morning field turnout, mostly "quon-seteers," and was excited by the idea of millions of such young Americans going to college as vets instead of loafing adolescents, or not at all. Given the time, these might be the margin for a good world.

Given the time. . . .

Milton had registered for a little work himself, a class in nuclear physics and a series of lectures on world affairs under Hugo Dean, the red-headed professor of history he met at Mary Barlow's little apartment. Hugo had been on war leave to the government, got his nose mashed by a Royalist pistol in Greece, long before Truman's shouts of the guyascutus to be fattened and harnessed in the Greco-Turkish hills for the conference circus at Moscow. At the peace conference at Paris Hugo had seen the terror of American A-bombers nesting like jet-powered gorgons in the heart of Europe, rising to circle the earth and spreading their shadow. Disgusted, he returned to the university and talked hopelessly for a world federation in his old room at the Windsor. He got Milton and his grandfather in there too, so the tall, diamond-dusted mirrors that once reflected the beauty and magnificence of Baby Doe Tabor, and then the old-age pensioners, now reflected an iron-legged old tom-walker.

The doctors had cut out the growth in his ear, so he could hear almost like a shirt-tail young 'un again. His white hair washed to a cloud of silk around his head, in a new GAR suit and showing off a new wolf tooth pushing through, he was a year 'round tourist attraction at the old mine boom hotel, autographing his Iron Leg stories published in a book. With pictures of Jim Bridger, Kit Carson and Packer, the mountain cannibal, around him, he told stories of the ghost on the Devil's Stairway and how Colorado got her gold and silver—the linings melted out of the devil's pots and kettles when a Kansas cyclone came busting through and fanned up the hell fire. He bragged about his grandson too, with a left that could smash a granite boulder, or a New York publicity man.

Nights they sometimes went to Mammoth Garden to see the Angel or maybe Cowboy Shank, Iron Leg recalling the old Indian wrestling and the knuckle fights. They went to the A-power display too, the old man looking at the little gray lump big enough to drive an engine for months, heat a hundred houses.

"Godamighty!" he roared. "An' no bigger'n a throwin' donnick!"

"Yes, looks like man's really ready to step out as boss of this old puffball we live on," Hugo Dean agreed. "We think we've won the fight to keep nuclear power out of private, monopolistic hands and the complete control of the strong arm boys, but almost nobody seems to sense the danger in making and storing A-bombs, not only to international relations but as an immediate menace here. With even one of the bombs in existence, any Hitler-minded little man might manage to get his hands on it, with a little scheming and a few promises. Any man, even that Carl Weigert. . . ."

"I know; it's a constant nightmare to me," Milton said.

"Yes, so we're all like a lot of hens on a cold night, moving onto the warm pole any thief sticks through the henhouse window, without even waking up."

But there were troubled dreamings in that henhouse, with every blast or explosion followed by a wildfire of A-bomb scares. And who was to say how it was abroad, with the growing exclusion of foreign news, a sort of journalistic Ellis Island growing up?

"Keeps us from protesting each imperialistic tom-walking move in time," Milton told his grandfather. "Letting Russia take on the role of defender of the downtrodden, making ourselves out to be, every poor Joe of us, an iron-heeled oppressor, a cartel tool and a bomb maker to fatten the exploiters' pockets, when so recently we were the hope and defender of every hungry, terrorized man."

In other ways Milton's second year out of dog tags had not been good. Fearing a belated "Dear John" letter, he looked at Mary Barlow and wished it would come. Then, the day after he did his Portable Hole routine for St. Joseph's orphans, looking into the faces of the children watching, he wrote Hazel he wanted to get his family together, forget the bullet. It wasn't only for himself but for Kathie too. He was afraid for her, without her parents.

"But there *is* a bullet," Hazel answered, and with the future so precarious, she could not risk her daughter's security or expose an emotional child to a home shadowed by imminent death. Besides, her duty, like the soldier's in the war, lay beyond the call of her family in this crucial election year that would determine the survival of the American way of life, usher in the era of American Destiny.

Giving him that bushwa. . . .

So Milton went down to the Ship's Tavern, to the table near the side door, and at the first crack like that, he rose up, struck out with his left and as the stranger went down, turned and walked out before anybody could stop him. Only afterward he recalled why the man had looked familiar. He was one of the hunters who took old Iron Leg up to shoot an elk, at ninety-nine.

Election time, Milton borrowed Mary's car and drove the old man home, roaring out that it was like after his war, the same rascals waving the bloody shirt, only now they didn't even pretend it was against any enemy except the little fellow. He talked about the hopeful times of the past too, the Farmers' Alliance, Populism, even the Coxey uprising, while here for the third time in his life he had to watch a lot of skyugling postwar grafters take over the White House.

"Grant, Harding and Fauncy-Dauncy . . ." he shouted by habit to Milton. "Not even a skunk kin stand skinnin' that many times."

By nine that night the drift toward the general was clear, a landslide for Daunce of *The Senator from Yahooia,* old Milt's hoarse voice singing:

> "We're Dauncy and Daft and Wry
> 'Down with FDR!' still is our cry!
> We handed the pap
> To Nazzi and Jap;
> We may not do good,
> We don't try,
> We're the dauncy, the daft and the wry."

Yes, there it was, another postwar president, this one drafted out of skypiloting back in '17 to drive the brass building the training camps, finally marrying the daughter of a lumberman he saw get rich from army contracts. So Daunce had dropped his exhorting and went into army contracting too, getting in with the old Van Horn Moseley gang in Hoover's war department that burned out the bonus marchers and little Benny. Later he was appointed to the Senate, whooping it up for Hitler isolationism, called Pearl Harbor a Roosevelt trick with camouflaged American bombers, and demanded immediate invasion of Canada and Mexico. Offering him a star got him out of Military Affairs to build the posts and bases he had sold to the government with Boyd Potter. But he was good at it, Milton had to admit, his high exhorter's voice screaming against any obstacle that could not be bought up with public money at a good rake-off, whether prairie dogs claiming the ground, a snowstorm chilling the dedicatory ceremonies, or a committee investigating profits.

But Daunce had done what FDR tried; he had broken party lines like a bulldozer tearing through Normandy hedges. Headed for the White House with the coalition of reactionaries behind him, Daunce had taken up piety, leaving the racism, the labor and Red baiting to his followers. It worked, well dry and the barn afire, old Milt growling that the vets' money and the oil lands they stole last time would be just sheep turds on a hillside compared to this. Milton watched him stomp slowly off to bed, and then left too, for Dunhill, to hunt up Agnes, and did not return until dawn.

By summer the newspapers left still with mailing permits were optimistic about the era of American Destiny, now that the country was free of such foreignisms as the Wagner Act, the SEC, and Social Security, and the UN confined on an island, and to debating a Disraelian world. "Godamighty, we're back to '66 and the old Hound's Tooth down in Cincinnati, markets shot, no money in circulation, and this time no free land for the poor man, not even a medicine wagon, or a iron leg," old Milt complained. "Instead we got American Destiny and the A-bomb. . . ."

Now and then a hint of something unfavorable slipped out, the serious leveling off in trade, domestic and foreign, with home prices kept up by curtailment and foreign dumping. Jim Becker wrote about violence against American troops everywhere, and at his last checkup, Milton ran into Sam Alton at the hospital, with a back wound he got from some Norskies. He saw tractors selling up there for half what they cost a man at Detroit. Afterward Milton got drunk with a Kansas wheat grower who said his state was blackened by farmers burning grain to keep up the market. "My gran'pap shucked and burned ten-cent corn but we won't harvest enough to glut the market."

Wall Street was shivering again, only a seasonal chill, of course, now that the labor uncertainties were over. If the rumors of fifteen million unemployed were true, they were quiet, quieter than Milton, who had spent his twenty-sixth birthday in jail for tripping a cop who was breaking up the lines at the relief offices. This time he got no publicity or pictures. By now most of the young men were gone from the lines, either in military suntans or in the new steel gray of the Industrial Guards, the government-authorized answer to the sabotage strikes. Reclamation, except in favored spots, was stopped, the deserted Missouri dam sites like the blasted landscapes of the moon, the Forestry Service cut two-thirds under Secretary Walper, once charged with lumber black-marketeering. ". . . The Cabinet was not selected with an eye to restored confidence," a great daily had said stiffly, and nothing since.

In August a great radioactive cloud was reported high over Alaska, drifting downward, with tremendous excitement and real concern over damage to life, and a run on white materials and white paint for protection. Sifting the radio experting and alarms, it seemed an A-bomb or several, more powerful together than all the five from New Mexico to Bikini, had been exploded somewhere. "Somewhere beyond the polar regions."

The blast was reconstructed in a nation-wide, Wellesian broadcast, a scale model blown up for television and shown free all over the country by the new Industrial Information Bureau, sending people shaking out into the thunder-resounding summer night, with radio and sound cars blaring, "Bomb Moscow!" Then some scientists working in Alaska reported by short wave, denying the whole story, saying it was cooked up by the Nazi scientists with the IIB. But nobody could tell, and nothing more was heard from the Alaskan station, and nothing from the Atomic Commission, about this or anything else.

The next week Hazel wired that the Senator planned a few days of rest at the Mountain States Grand Encampment and Regatta at Turtle Shell over V-J Day, where he was the main speaker. Once more Milton planned. Among the Laramer street scroungers he found an air corps man who had lost his gas station, his house going too. It was small, but close to school for Kathie, and close to the bears in the park, with a snowball bush in the corner and a stoop that looked toward the evening mountains.

The great, man-made lake at Turtle Shell stretched smooth and blue between the far wall of the Big Horns and the rolling sagebrush plains, pale morning clouds and a couple of bombers reflected serene. The tourist lodge was a rambling two stories of native stone, the deep verandas overlooking the sandy beach, with cabins scattered back around a timbered inlet that used to be a sickle box canyon, the floats of the regatta half-hidden at the far end. Off up the lake was a smudging that Milton had learned to recognize as a distant tent encampment.

As the sun warmed, a double-decked ferryboat moved out against a gentle curl of water; motorboats scattered in practice runs like frightened waterbugs, or lay like insect eggs in rows along the piers, while beyond, a dozen thin-masted little craft waited, one white sail running up as the water began to streak. Then the sail blossomed full and Milton knew it would be a fine, windy Wyoming day in his home country, and with Hazel near, even a regatta so close to the stomping grounds of old Chuck Sherman seemed all right. Chuck was dead now; with nothing left but a couple of bullets after they took him off WPA he shot his invalid wife and himself—His T-Square brand had once been known clear to the Chugwater in the old free range days.

But now the sun was shining and an eagle soared lazily over Monument buttes, so high he looked like a slim-winged reconn plane, with points of ack-ack soon to break around him, and over there in the lodge was Hazel, perhaps in a dusty green dress that brought out the lights in her eyes. Only when Milton asked for her, the desk man gave him the hardnose. "She's out—you kin find her to the Senator's headquarters, if you got business, bud," and Milton remembered what an old ranger had told him: "Barely half a dozen trained men left in the whole Rocky Mountain service."

It was the same on the telephone, so Milton sent a note to Hazel and finally caught a ride up to the encampment, laid out with wartime efficiency, from flagstaff through HQ, quonsets and the farthest shelter halves, conspicuous against the hodge-podge of the civvie camp scattered over the ridge beyond—trailers, tents, cars, children running, smoke rising from the late cooking, and that cluster of trailers off in a little draw already tolling Joes out that way. There were jeeps everywhere, and staff cars, with a Sherman and a couple of anti-tanks near the entrance, and at the water's edge squatted a couple of ducks and an alligator, the underparts wet from a demonstration, small boys hanging around thick as in Italy, or China.

At the registration booth the bulletin board listed the grand total attendance—28,116—with the biggest day just beginning, a pleasant-faced girl in a WAC uniform asking not only for Milton's discharge but evidence of employment. "Screening the troublemakers," she said, and Milton remembered that some of the vets down in Denver had talked sour about the get-together. Even Dr. Jimms of Christ Church. "I do not like the looks of it . . ." others talking more direct: "Ass lickers, just pension hounds and ass lickers!"

Most of the men and many of the women were in uniform, with all their trimmings, and Milton felt like a fence-crawling 4F in his slacks and gray and yellow shirt. But there was something good about the smell of a new camp, the worn grass, the fine dust underfoot, the Joes he had known one place or another. At chapel he heard the Reverend Hiley from Cheyenne, and from Normandy, where he had bellied along with his tail down like the rest on D-Day, hunting out the wounded and the dying. But somehow today his sermon was like a fist hitting a sack of kapok. ". . . Let us never forget the heroic sons of America!" Afterward Milton ran into a pretty yellow-haired WAC from Baltimore he knew in the UK. She pulled his head down, kissed his brown cheek and asked how he was, and after some fried chicken at a booth they went to see her boy at the camp nursery. He was a fine, pale-haired buster, and Sue Pillard as proud as she used to be of getting a staff car through the muddy, blacked-out byroads. But when she asked about Hazel he had to say she was up at the Potter headquarters.

Sue looked concerned. "Potter? My Dick's so worried about things in Washington, with the United Nations doing KP for the war boys, and Joes stationed at every crossroads, and all those Industrial Guards. Something's coming up, but he can't put his finger on it."

There were many who would agree.

Once more Milton tried to get to Hazel, but the telephone was closed; the milling around the Senator's cabin like hogs at a leaky corncrib. So he went back to watch the parade—fine brassy bands flashing in the sun, a few long-haired old soldiers of the Indian wars; a couple of Rough Riders on horses, the rest in cars; the vets of the first World War still stepping out with their drum corps, even a few of the nurses, and thousands of new vets, with their disabled—all the services. The army made a good showing, Milton thought loyally, particularly the armor and the amphib engineers; the rangers and the airborne still looking sharp, too. And overhead moved blimps, cubs, helicopters, seaplanes, troop carriers, gliders, and so on, with fighters and bombers roaring and whooshing, dipping to the reviewing stand. Everything except a GAR. They had offered to come for old Iron Leg, but he wouldn't go. Asking him to sit and listen to dead-beat Potter speechifying! ". . . Foogling a basket full a knotholes—a turd-beetle letting wind of a hot day!"

As the floats began to move for the regatta, Milton went back and was told Hazel was out—after his night trip on the bus, and five hours scouting the terrain here! Disgusted, he went to take a nap but he couldn't sleep, uneasy about what Sue Pillard had said, on top of the cooked-up A-bomb scare, the strong-arm talk around the encampment here, with men like Carl Weigert, out of the mental hospital, big-bugging it around; the brass all men Milton hadn't seen anywhere in the war. Besides, a loudspeaker outside the window was blaring off the winners in the regatta and announcing the pageant to follow: "The Battle of the World! Ladies and gentlemen, from Stone Age man to the A-bomb, and the era of American Destiny!"

Once more Milton got the surly "Nothin' fer ya, bud," at the desk, so he went over to the amphitheater and sat on what was once a cowpath along a slope, to watch the pageant. It reached from young Larp Miller, a Stone Age man in a wolf hide swinging a rock in his hand, to the star-marked bombers and directed missiles attacking Objective X, a miniature city enclosed in barbed wire—canvas and cardboard with onion-topped spires that collapsed and roared into flame and heat, leaving only a fringe of slow-burning shacks along the near edge, the upwind side. The cheering was loud with an unnatural unison, suddenly broken by a woman's shriek as a small toddler broke from the edge of the burning shacks, his clothing and hair bursting into flame in a puff of turning wind. As he fell, the shacks around him blazed up and crumpled; men running in, Milton, the closest, vaulting the wire barrier, pushing into the smoke, his shirttail up over his head as he rolled the child on the ground to smother the flames. But the delicate skin slipped as he lifted the boy, blackened, dead, while overhead the bombers came circling back in formation, dropping streamers of the American flag to float over

the encampment, seeming to cover the whole sky as the mother
and her son were taken away.

It was evening when Milton was cleaned up, his burnt brows and
hair evened off, his hands dressed, and now he hung at the telephone
until he got to Hazel, her voice almost lost in a roar of talk like a
regiment of GI's headed stateside. "Oh, Milton! Where have you
been? We wanted you to sit with us at the regatta. Now come right
over for cocktails and a snack before the Senator speaks."

Crossly he went to the big cabin on the point, with a banner
draping the front: HEADQUARTERS OF SENATOR POTTER. Inside, Milton
was directed across the wide living room to the sun porch, overlooking the evening inlet. He saw the Senator out there, the top of
his bald head showing now and then between the shoulders around
him. And at the archway, like an intercepter, stood Hazel—impersonal in a frosty white wool suit, distant as some painting, a
Sargent, perhaps. Old Nat Ridges was on one side of her, and a
couple of mountain politicians on the other, the men attentive,
watchful; the crowd over to her somehow divided down the middle
of the long room, little knots eyeing each other cautiously: several
governors, senators from Idaho to Nebraska, including the current
hired hands of Eastern utilities, and the army officers from the encampment, besides the oil, mine, copper and sugar men, and some
like Nat Ridges' brother-in-law from Denver, an America Firster,
who was so afraid of Communism under Roosevelt he had put all
his money into Norwegian banks, where the Nazis got it. But he
seemed to be doing all right now, laughing with a few of the women
who must be wives, and some who certainly weren't.

Hazel started toward Milton, the crowd coming together around
her, getting greetings and smiles. "Everybody a voter," Milton remembered, and was ashamed, but there were whisperings too, a
loud: "Got her eyes on the White House, that bitch has," Milton
snapping his head around, seeing only a back getting away through
the crowd.

As Hazel came closer there was tightening like a toggle in his
breast. She was really beautiful now, with a studied perfection he
had seen a time or two in Paris, and in Lisbon, perhaps at a sailing
in New York, and suddenly he wanted to take himself and his
singed face out of the sight and way of his wife, crawl off into the

sagebrush like the dying Bruno dog. But she was holding out her slim, ringed hands to his bandages. "Oh, you're burned! That poor child, the mother so neglectful!"

"Hazel, Hazel . . ." Milton was saying, unable to stop, even before all these people. "Hazel. . . ."

But after a while it was all right, Hazel with her hand through his arm, taking him toward the dining room to cocktails and mounds of food, the Senator's Filipinos busy in their white jackets. Then they picked up old Nat Ridges and took him over to the opposite side of the room where a mining senator puffed up at his coming, like a range bull át another's bellowing approach, the talk in the room waiting. Calmly Hazel stood between the men, introducing Milton. Yes, carried out the burnt child. Look at his hands, and his face, too, his mustache and lashes almost gone. And so modest. Coming here without his uniform or decorations, although the bullet was still in his heart, as the x-ray in the papers showed. "You remember," she said, as though to each one alone, "two, three years ago . . ." the crowd going silent again as word was passed in whisperings; staring.

Expecting me to drop dead for 'em! Milton thought angrily. It was an appalling thing, this showing him off for some political purpose, an incredible thing for a man's wife to do, incredible and hateful.

But the two men plainly agreed on public praise of heroes, the crowd too, pushing up to shake Milton's arm, to spread cordiality, bragging on the sons of the West.

But it didn't last. Almost at once the mine senator was out of hand. "Ah, my young friend, you are a sacrifice to the God of War," he was orating. "I feel bound to repeat it," looking directly at Nat Ridges, but sizing up the alignments around them. "A war spawned by an unholy union of Eastern interventionists—bankers, Wall Street and the Reds!" the crowd dividing once more, as though a fold of ground had lifted between them.

Before Hazel could put in a pretty word, command a pretty compliment, old Nat, now an injured Wall Streeter himself, started in with the ridiculous old goose call, Milton wondering what it covered, what ten-bore load of buckshot waited. "Yes," Nat was shouting, "an unholy union for war, Senator, but it was the Jews and your munition-mongering mine lords!" Then he stopped, perhaps realizing that he was a little drunk and had grabbed the bait: let everyone see how independent a senator from a mountain state dared talk, and so he put his thin, bony fingers together and turned to smile upon the tall young man beside Hazel. "Do not take my old friend's little joke too seriously, my boy. You were great heroes, great and noble heroes!" And because his hands were bandaged, Nat Ridges an old man, and Milton's anger really elsewhere, he held himself and said, "Thank you, sir," and backed away like a good GI.

The evening clouds lay golden upon the lake, Monument buttes black shadows against the west when the Senator's party started to encampment. Frogs croaked, somewhere a shitepoke pumped for rain, and a wind came up to blow into the wall of cloud rising fast in the northeast, bringing the smell of sweet water. Hazel was driving a loan car, a fancy, air-sweep model that gave Milton, beside her, the feeling of sitting in the nose of a bomber. He had kissed his wife at last, after almost three years, until she finally pushed him gently away. "My lipstick, darling . . ." and slid under the wheel.

They got out behind the speakers' stand already flooded with a light that was bluish in the yellow evening. Somebody was testing the public address system, somebody calling back from the crowd waiting on the tiers of folding chairs and benches, and up over the sloping ground, blankets and newspapers spread on the dry, warm earth, a cigarette lighted here and there in the dusky shadows of the storm, while cars still hurried to slide into the wide semicircles around the back.

"Do we have to sit up under those lights while the Senator spouts?"

"Speaks, my dear. A senator speaks," Hazel laughed. "No—you don't; I doubt if there's a seat for you, but I'll have to take notes."

"OK, go sit on the monkey platform and I'll be seeing you afterward."

"Oh, I'm sorry, but—well, the Senator has a lot of conferences after the talk," Hazel apologized, with a regretful shake of her head.

"Then you aren't coming to the lodge with me. . . ."

"Oh, darling, I can't."

Slowly the man straightened, holding himself, guarding his bandaged hands. "Are you coming at all?" he finally asked, quietly enough.

"But the conferences may last all night; they often do."

Now Milton Stone forgot the place, the crowd; everything except Hazel's loveliness and that she was his wife. "You mean you won't," he roared out, his anger suddenly tight within him. "What the hell you think I came up from Denver for—to look at the Senator's pot belly?"

"Please, Milton, remember where you are. . . ."

A long time he looked at the woman, the scorched mustache suddenly dark in the glare. Slowly he drew back a bandaged hand, Hazel crying out, "Oh-h!", her face blank white in the reflection from the speaker's stand. Somebody gasped, laughed, then a few more, the crowd stirring, stretching that way as the woman held her palm to her cheek, reddening from a slap, public and loud as a spank on a baby's bottom.

Foolishly Milton pulled his cuff down, then turning, he slipped away between the cars, heading into the gathering dusk toward the storm and the flicker of lightning that was like the flash of far artillery rising with the night.

A long time Hazel looked after him, the crowd watching, the excitement and talk spreading outward. Then the band started and someone came down for her, to take her to her place.

By the next night Milton Stone was back in Denver, pounding on Mary's door. She was there, and alone, and this time he did not leave. It was late when he awoke himself out of a disturbing dream, and before he could wonder about the empty pillow beside him, the sting of a burnt hand brought him half up, and then he remembered that most of his dream was memory. He had really come down to hitting women, his own wife, and as publicly as though he had put her on a squatting slab.

But there was something more to think about today, and dressing slowly, his fingers stiff and awkward, he went out into the sunlight to hunt up Hugo Dean, to talk over what Sue Pillard's Dick said, and what the split, the foolish talk at the Senator's headquarters, might mean.

5 — Beauteous Lady and a Bobtailed Cow

It had been bobtailed cow in flytime for four years now, and a dozen anxious to be the Hank Lodge of their generation, usher in the age of American Destiny—while the papers and the radio played up A-bombs, poisons and death rays, helped the depression make room in New York and Chicago, even in Denver. Finally a rumbling earthquake in San Francisco sent half a million people scurrying like sheepherder bugs through the fog and night, heading for open country; thousands injured and many killed in the trampling, although barely a dish was broken back in the city, except that a building already burning had fallen in and flared red into the fog of the sky.

Hugo Dean looked up from the story in the paper Milton had brought him. "It seems impossible, after at least a hope at Christmas time only three years ago. But the systematic terrorizing by the AD boys—I wonder how the people in Moscow must feel, or even London."

Yet with all the empty apartments in Denver there were homeless. In the cold snap of late September, Milton sneaked one or two into his room, and when a warm evening turned to sudden, unseasonal snow, the hotel manager sick with the flu, Milton slipped the lock of the Mountain Man Room, big enough for two hundred diners, and rounded up a dozen men from drifting alleys and doorways. But there was coughing, and toward morning a rumpus; someone went to look, let out a yell and called the police. They found a dead man stuffed into the closet. So Milton and Hugo were rooted out of bed and hauled away, with barely time to pull their pants on, along with a couple of flops that hadn't fanned off. The University got Hugo released, with no more than a little blood on his matted red hair. Milton had an eye closed, his head and back bruised, his breast bullet-cramped, and his clothes wet from the water they threw on him. It wasn't over the dead man, who, it seemed, died of natural causes—malnutrition and exposure—but because Milton wouldn't say he was a revolutionary, for taking over private property.

Finally the Portable Hole routine got him out, although he had to do it with a damp handkerchief rolled up like a sock. Pretending to be ready to talk, he started his rigamarole, making the handkerchief disappear with a dozen matches and his cigarette inside, then finding the smoldering butt on one of the cops. The officer laughed, foolish and mystified as a kid, and remembering Milton's picture in the papers, sent to the Windsor for his wallet and identification. Iron Leg came too, looking suddenly very old and tired in the glare of the midday police lights, and Milton had to see how far things had gone with him since the violence of the general strike. So he hired a man to take his grandfather home to Seep. It wasn't only that he hadn't enjoyed being the oldest at the Mountain and Plains Festival this year, or sitting up with the governors and the movie stars, but he had lost interest in autographs, getting Mattie, the chambermaid who signed the old-age pension checks for everybody, to write up a batch ahead. Now winter had come down on the old man, reaching a hundred, with cold and hunger and violence all around.

A long time Milton stood looking after the car that took him away. Then he moved himself up on the Hill again and went to work that night to avoid a docking for the day off.

Two weeks later, while Milton was entering up the mechanic's work he had to do now to hold his job, young Martin suddenly stood there at the counter, grinning sly as a snapping turtle. And that moment some of the numbness in Milton melted, the numbness of that one day of protest striking. Every thorn and burr between the brothers the last few years seemed gone too; everything but a sudden anxiety.

"Kathie's sick, or old Iron Leg!"

No, everybody well enough. So Milton had to wait, although Marty admitted half his beets were still out, with a hard freeze due. Together they went down to the Bearclaw, with trophies to look at and a steak a cowman could accept as fresh enough for something except buzzard bait. But Marty scarcely noticed the smoky walls hung thick with stuffed animals, Kodiak pelts and weapons from tomahawk to bazooka, so Milton led him back to the vets' little room. Over a beer he considered his brother, his stockiness thinned, and his roundish face all lean and sleepless until it was almost like Milton without a mustache looking at himself in a battle mirror—leaned down to bed slats, to hoofs 'n hair.

But there was something sheepish in Marty too, a little like that time, long ago, with Benny Green and the old Flossy mare. The Greens had no stock at all, and Benny came over horny as a tomcat to try out something he'd heard about. So they finally took him down to the barn, watching the door while he was inside. Then he skinned out for home, leaving them to go in to supper alone, and feeling sneak-dirty. But that was when their father was getting so bad, and nobody noticed.

They laughed a little together about that afternoon, like the brothers who were born the same year, but almost at once Milton pushed his empty glass back. "Now cough it up, Marty," he ordered. "The stock market?—or is it the new bride?"

Oh, he'd taken his market loss long ago; twice—took a real plunge when the ban on margin came off, and was cleaned. And Nollie was OK. Everybody fine except old Iron Leg, mostly not even putting on his pants any more. "Says it's up to you now. But Penny was disappointed not to see you Campment time."

"I felt stinkin' as a doggie's socks," Milton admitted, "but with everything blowing up, and Hazel. . . ."

Yeh, well, war marriages. . . . Yet they had fancied Hazel the months she was at Seep for the baby. Penny wasn't believing the story that he slapped her up at the lake, but maybe if Milton were more managing and conniving, not taking it out blind-bucking, bunching off with flophouse bums. . . .

"Yes, a conniving garage clerk, with a chunk of Chicago editorial under my vest."

Uncomfortably Marty stirred up his coffee, hunching forward, with none of the importance of thirty-cent beef that was busting in him that first summer home. It was a damn shame, he said, Milton never getting to try his luck at engineering, when he had that raft of grades and letters and stuff. Ought to be good for something besides papering the privy.

"You didn't come clear down here to feed me trade-lasts."

Slowly Martin cut into his steak. "Looks like a hard pull ahead and the hamestring busted," he admitted. "Prices gone to hell and a lot of phony business going on. Cattlemen eating the national parks and forests into the ground; timber companies chewing their power saws through tracts old Martin claims been closed to's much as a jackknife since TR."

"So when it's his watershed, dad's had enough. . . ."

"Yes." Martin agreed, uncomfortably. "He came home pretty low from that bi-partisan protest meeting up at Boise, not talking, almost like he was that other time. By God!" young Marty roared out, pushing his half-finished plate back, "when I think of damn fools like the Stones of Seep Creek getting important helping the big outfits bust restrictions! Following the big shots like pups after a man with bear grease on his boots, and it turning out croton oil!"

Once more it was like putting a hand out to hold a younger one back. "The truth isn't too easy to come by, nowadays."

"Still pulling slivers out a my ass, ain't you?" Martin demanded. "Seep Creekers used to have the sense to see the papers whooped it up on the side of the advertisers, and that maybe a government that got them land and water could be trusted to decide how much metal could be spared from war guns for hog rings."

Uneasy about this sudden burn in his brother, Milton looked away, around the room filling with vets and re-drafts, some nodding to him, looking curiously at Marty. "War times people get desperately dependent on front-page news when their boys are in it," Milton tried to explain, with the eldest's need to comfort those younger, "so it's hard to remember your skepticism when you turn the page. Anyway, I guess people figure it's legal expropriation whether you lose your property by depression and foreclosure or just have its value destroyed."

"Well, we're getting expropriation, with the big companies working the oil-soaked layers in Black Earth Park, stripping the topsoil off."

That struck through to Milton. So they were stripping the national park now?—The Turtle Shell watershed, making a cancerous wasteland like around Pittsburgh and Hibbing. Maybe that was behind the split he saw at the Senator's headquarters too.

"We let Secretary Walper and Boyd Potter hamstring the hydros and civilian use of A-energy so they can make money tearing off the topsoil for the oil outfits, tearing up Wyoming."

Marty nodded, sloshing his water glass back and forth, not noticing the trio of holy singers or the old gap-mouth exhorter passing tracts and a collection plate around the tables, a couple of re-draft Joes pulling their beers back as he came. There was some of the swift, angry talk that broke out so easily these days, the exhorter repeating his "Come to God, ya sinners! Harken to the warning at 'Frisco an' come to God!" one of the re-drafts booming out, "God, hell; God's a goddamn civilian!"

But when Marty didn't even notice the two pretty girls at the next table, plainly on the make, Milton pushed his pie back. "If you're trying to save me, come clean," he commanded. "You didn't leave your beets half out for something going on all fall."

Well, yesterday Penny did get an airmail note from Hazel, not signed, but in her envelope. Nothing except a warning to keep quiet and sell the place immediately, that day, before it was worthless.

"Sell the home place? Why, if they don't get us into war, we'll roll Daunce and his outfit in a hole like dead Japs before a bull-dozer. And good land comes back."

"Ours won't, not if the water's gone, cut off."

"But that's government—" Milton started to say, and then remembered the national park stripped. Slowly, he put his hand against the edge of his chair, tightening his fingers against the wood, making himself take the realization slowly. The ditches of Seep Creek, they would be drying down, the fine, lush greenness shrinking to a string farm again, the dust and sage moving in on the handsome place until there was only a little creek that a good man could jump across.

Out in the raw fall darkness the brothers walked past a couple of evangelist tents, the light through the canvas like army days but the crowd inside whooping halleluja. "Like buzzards to a kill," Milton complained.

But mostly the brothers walked in silence across Cherry Creek bridge and up the long slope to the Hill, Milton dull as from wound-shock, much as he had been since the Saturday after Potter got back to Washington from his swing around the country and almost every pay envelope in the country held the General Wage

Adjustment Slip. A general wage cut twenty per cent effective immediately.

With their tails already dragging, an estimated thirteen million went out that morning, from coal to radio, enough to paralyze the country, silence it for a few hours. But by noon it was plain why so many hungry vets had been tolled into six months' re-enlistment by the "Give a Service Man a Furlough" campaign. In addition there were the half a million Industrial Guards from every trade, ready to take over, and the State Emergency Corps, and nobody caring where the wage cuts would lead, with mechanization throwing men out like the 300 shoemakers replaced by one machine in Iron Leg's time, with less and less in the pay envelopes to buy beef and auto parts. The few scabs at the radio stations called it a Red uprising and reported the movements of the army like armor going against an invader. Instead of the pistols and gatlings against the Pullman strikers, or the tanks and gas against Benny Green and the bonus marchers, it was spitting BAR's and flame-throwers this time, with the Chief of Staff hitting the coal country from the air, strafing the fleeing thousands, his publicity corps and the head of the Industrial Guards along.

"Hell, we knew all about that. Eastern Reds and Jews taking over," Martin said impatiently. "Ridges went on the radio. . . ."

Now Milton was aroused. "Old Nat Ridges, yelling the guyascutus is loose!" he said angrily, stopping under a street light to pull out his GWA slip from his wallet. "Here's proof the strike was over pay cuts, mine from $24 to $19.20."

Martin pushed the slip aside. "Hell, I cut my help twenty per cent, and put them on fifty-four hours. This is AD," American Destiny.

Now Milton had to hold himself from striking out, hitting his own brother; made himself walk away, then cover it up in talk. Hazel had sent him a wire, first he had heard since Encampment, just saying he ought to take old Iron Leg home, stay and visit a while. Probably hoped to keep Milton out of trouble, jail. But he was here when the cut came, went out, helping with the rescue work at the railroad tracks, stumbling around on the blood-slippery rails to get the injured and dead away as the streamliner came plowing in where the railroaders had stood against the BAR's.

". . . The damned strikers had it coming a long, long time," Martin said, talking big as that first summer again, forgetting that he was in on the meat strike. Surely a general strike, not against an employer but against the nation.

The pup back at the bear grease.

At Mary Barlow's little apartment there were half a dozen sitting around with more drifting in and out, casually, as through a hotel lobby. Martin gave up his topcoat and settled on the sofa, sizing up this Mary, not jeep-nosed and bench-legged as he always expected a service woman to be, but a looker—mighty well set-up. Yes, by God, Milton sure picked 'em with good frames. Hazel was OK, even with that beautiful face, and Nancy's Agnes had enough sticking out at you to make your crotch bind in a Gandhi sheet. But this number—just a look set a man to sweating.

Mary Barlow was around thirty, with a swirling of curly red-brown hair, freckles like a splatter of bran across her short nose, and an easy, intimate smile that helped make something light and temporary of every man's handicap—a great fraud they were putting over on Uncle Sam together—and in addition those far-off, gray-green eyes against wolfing hands.

At first her accent had reminded Milton too much of Andreas, one of the two killed when he got his bullet. It seemed her frail, Swiss-schooled mother had run away with a cowboy on her American tour, and settled on a Colorado homestead, the clumsy-handed Jack Barlow helpless before his wife's slow dying that ended during a dust storm. Some said he shot himself after the funeral; instead of going to her aunts in England, Mary became a nurse, was on Bataan, the maroons claimed, but nobody heard her say so.

Milton and his brother had walked into a discussion of the evening paper: a bloody snow reported down in Kansas, a sure omen of war; a monster crashing through the winter breaks of the Ohio; and a long, flying stick like a rocket over Seattle, swinging off and away, a fiery streak in the night that let something black fall into the city, the radios roaring out: "Keep away from all windows! Keep away . . ." while the State Emergency Corps was called out. But so far there was no explosion.

Milton grinned over to his brother. Old Iron Leg stories. Yes, Hugo Dean agreed, "Keep your mind off the dead in the alleys and the armed guards in the groceriterias. Off America's final absorption of the World Bank, with the Secretary of State head of a financial cartel—a tom-walker vaulting all boundaries like Iron Leg's boy on stilts swinging over a privet hedge. So we're getting one world, a cartel world not so different from I. G. Farben's."

But Elsa, the violinist with Dachau hands cried out, "No, no!— that I cannot bear to hear!" Father Brian beside her making a sorrowful sound, lighting a cigarette for her, the useless hands unstill in her lap.

Martin looked away, embarrassed to have seen, and uneasy, too. These might all be Reds, with their talk about such things as handy as he gassed about beets or beef. So it was Milton who told what Hazel had written about selling the place.

"Oh, Marty!—that sounds like a big game. . . ."

"Either somebody's scaring you into selling, or Daunce really is outdoing Harding," Hugo decided.

"It may be the sand in the eye for some bigger knifing," Milton said anxiously, remembering the division he saw at Encampment. Mary admitted that she was afraid. It was like the old '41 rumors they got of Jap spies and Jap attacks coming, with senators at home blatting about "our good friends in the Orient." But the scare talk had seemed silly, looking out over Corregidor of a warm evening with a Japanese servant putting long, cold drinks into your hands. Now there were new rumors that they would be working for a private concern out at the hospital one of these days.

For a moment Milton sat, withdrawn, but gradually the words penetrated. "The vets' hospital?" he asked. "Why, that plant cost millions; it's our only refuge. Godamighty—even at Anzio or Bastogne you had some chance, and an ending. Here the attacks are continuous, and nothing in our hands. . . ."

Yes, and there was more, too big to tell, and perhaps get Marty a bullet in the back up there in the open country, if he let something slip.

Relieved, Martin settled back, laughing. It was a line, a razzing they were giving the country boy. "Oh, hell, nobody's going to get killed."

Mary looked to Milton, shaking her head. "Your brother doesn't know the people he's up against," she said slowly. "I guess none of us do, but I can tell you about a patient at the hospital, Billy, nineteen. He can't sleep; says he's shell-shocked like his dad at Chateau-Thierry, although the boy was no farther than Chicago, and not a shot fired. Late in September, a couple of months after he enlisted, they were sent against a woman's hunger march through the Loop. The soldiers scattered them with tear gas but the next time the marchers picked a bleak, windy day, making gas pretty useless. The soldiers watched them come again; rows and rows of ragged and gaunt women, some old, some so weak they had to be helped along, the rows close together, so silent Billy could hear the worn shoes, the bare red feet soft on the pavement. It was bayonets, the CO telling the boys the women would break at the steel. But they came right on and went down, the doggies having to step over them to charge the next row, and the next, until young Billy found himself trying to get his bloody bayonet free from a screaming woman, the man beside him yelling, 'Put yer foot on 'er, goddamn it! Put yer foot on 'er an' give a yank!' as he bashed her head in with his gunstock."

A long time there was silence in the little apartment, then Martin let his breath go, saying, "God, God . . ." as though to himself.

"Yeh, looks like hell's blew a boiler, and a break-bone grade ahead," old Martin admitted grudgingly when his sons came in. Then he hunched into himself, his face gray and wrinkled as cooling oatmeal; silent, pulled away as in those days before the old buckskin had to be shot.

Penny, too, looked more her age than even the winter with the foreclosure notice in her trunk, and yet Milton was glad he had driven up with Marty before his next check-in at the hospital. He felt closer to his folks now, and without the embarrassment of a man with the stink of battle still on him, sitting lean among war-fattened civilians.

Marty's young wife Nollie was up from the lower place for supper; a pretty, brown-haired girl, talking in the capitals Rita used. But Rita was turning out all right, off in Alaska with her two children since the ranch where Al worked gave up cattle for dudes. Like Penny and Ma Liz, she would keep her man's backside covered.

But old Milton was missing from the fireside tonight, bedfast in his downstairs room; wearing out, the doctor said. There was cussedness in it too, Penny thought. He could keep writing postcards with his stubby pencil to all those people who asked about his book, and the way he let wind and stomped off to bed when Ed Biggle, raised over near old Plew's, came bragging about the places he managed for Ridges. "Yeh, stole 'em by tricks, like they tried on Penny here!" Iron Leg roared. But not like in the old days, for Ed just laughed. "I got the families with school kids down to two per cent," he bragged, "an' gettin' red a some more a the careless ones come March first. Forty-five per cent of the places is in districts without no school, no school taxes. The landowners really been gettin' together."

"Like goddamn flies gatherin' to a bobtail cow!" the old man had shouted, not making sense, Penny complained, and letting his powerful wind while she tried to cover up by asking about young Benny Green, said to be losing the place he was running. "Yeh, good farmer," Ed admitted, "but shoots off his mouth, an' his kid's goin' on three already. There's thousands a good farmers without no need fer school that's huntin' ground to work."

"Suppose the government had turned your folks off their homestead because they had children?"

"Hell, the government wasn't payin' no school taxes."

After supper Nollie brought the coffee and the squash pie in before the fire, the radio soft on a symphonic record program. Penny had no hired girl now, with farm prices so low, and the uneasiness. . . . But Nollie was good about coming up wash days and butchering time, easing the loss of Rita and her boys, and maybe next summer there would be a granddaughter. Penny didn't speak of Kathie, but Milton knew what was in her mind. It was over two years since any of them had seen the girl, from five to seven, a great and exciting time in the life of a child. Even the notes in Milton's pocket were disappointing. Simple, three, four lines, thanking him for a doll or bracelet, in printing, at seven, when he was reading newspapers at that age, and writing to Washington for his own bulletins on irrigation and electrification. So he was an engineer at nineteen, and a $19.20 a week parts-clerk at twenty-six.

Over the music and the coffee, Marty was telling what he found around Denver: plenty of irrigated places for sale, so many that he knew the same stink was on the wind there. And the rumors at Mary Barlow's. But she had called the morning they left to say the head of the hospital was flying to Washington. Maybe something would be breaking.

Maybe they were scaring too easy anyhow, flighty as hens at the shadow of a hawk. The country was in sound hands; the papers all said so.

When Marty and Nollie were gone home, old Martin went out too, looking around the barns, Penny said, often not coming back all night now—her hands worrying in her lap as she spoke. She wished he got out more, giving Milton the impression she meant even if it was to Nancy's.

But in a moment she was asking about the nurse, Mary. ". . . From what Marty says she's sharp as a corn knife, and as straight out. Just the kind of a woman you might fall in love with, rebound from Hazel."

"Love?" Milton wanted to shout against her, his uneasiness and his helplessness fastening upon his mother's words. "What is love in these times except a man waking up to a dent in the pillow beside him?" But already Penny was on something else, something she had held back so's not to spoil Marty's first night home. The electricity bill had come today, the rate quadrupled, and on a private company's billhead. They had driven right down to Dunhill, found the gold lettering going on the new office windows, everybody of the Turtle Shell district people gone.

Milton looked at the bill a long time, realizing that somehow he had been banking on the rift in the Daunce-Potter forces, but they had got together, as Hazel had planned. "Used me, my bullet, to get the patriotic sob stuff going, bridge the split," he wanted to yell out. But his mother was standing before him, waiting, suddenly tired and gray in his hesitating.

"I'm afraid they can force you out now, cut off the water. Why didn't you all get together with the officials before this, make a protest?"

Slowly she folded the bill into the envelope, smoothing the flap. "Hughie Saul and his father tried it. They're in jail."

"For objecting to the steal?"

"Nobody knows, but they claim Hughie's been talking Jew-radical."

Wearily Milton went in to old Iron Leg's room to sit in the duskiness of the night lamp, the cone of light from the top shining against the old crazy quilt his Lucinda pieced on the long road West. It hung on the wall beside the bed, a background for the old fiddle sack and the faded spray of wild roses embroidered at Miss Farnsworth's, and an enlargement of the wedding tintype, faded too, but still the picture of a handsome boy with his mutilation hidden behind the skirts of his young bride. Beside the light lay a pile of fan mail and on the chair, handy, the iron leg gleamed bright.

Silently Milton let himself down into the rocker, watching the man on the bed, a hundred now, and almost as colorless as the pillow—hair, skin, even his brows that were black tufts for so long, his lips slack and gray. In this time of disintegration, Milton felt close to the old man, and to the two others who had been a little like him. There was Andreas, who stopped that first bullet up in Shensi, the Swiss who talked like Mary Barlow, perhaps because he got away to England soon after the rise of the Hitler shadow. Andreas' grandfather had been a crank on power from ocean tides, wanted to harness them, to pump out the Mediterranean, leach the earth of salt with the great waters of the Dnieper, the Danube and the Nile, and make a new land big as Australia of it, a land free of all the old hatreds and tyrannies. "Ah, if he could have lived to see the nuclear fission harnessed," Andreas cried the day they heard, spinning himself around on one foot, like a boy, like old Iron Leg, and blowing his palm-sized doodlesack.

So Milton told him about an American dream that was like a panoramic picture in his mind: the Missouri region to the mountains, two hundred million acres of arable, irrigable land, sloping, stream-laddered, ready for canal and gridironing by power lines, with great inland storage seas to reflect the kingfisher blue of the sky. Here cheap and clean power and fruitful lands would be brought together in a new society centered around a farm-factory unit: labor free of the blight of the old factory community, with its smoke and fumes and poverty and the dread of layoffs and shutdowns; agriculture free from the gamble of hot winds, drouth and floods—a dovetailing of farm and factory.

". . . An industrialized society," Milton had explained, "with the best in education and the arts, set up in a healthful, pleasant, semirural environment; the interests of the farmer and the laborer at last plainly one, because they are the same man."

It had been easy to say these things to Andreas, who saw water as a power to free man of ugliness and drudgery, an end he followed with the joyous pursuit of a GI out wolfing, until a Chinese patriot with an American weapon came across an American newspaper.

The other man was Jesse Gray, the Anzac who cut paths for armies and civilians through mountains and jungle and sand, and had a stubborn conception of mankind as one great living stone, as the core of the earth is living. "Let the people know: they will do right, whatever it costs them, they will do right." He would argue this, even without opposition, chewing his vowels with Anzac positiveness, and then hum off into his bawdy little song about Alf and the amorous ewe.

People liked his broad red face, and even in remote settlements of China, where dogs and camel calves and children gathered around Milton and his Portable Hole, or Andreas and his little doodlesack, the stranger-shy eyes of the women followed Jesse Gray, while the grandfathers, the decrepit and miserable, the wise and learned, hurried to gather around him, squatting close to his path, touched by the dust of his boots as he passed.

Awkwardly Milton fumbled for his handkerchief, and pulled out the old sock. He looked at it, and over to the ancient man on the bed, white, unmoving, but apparently awake, and so Milton laid out a few matches on the arm of the rocker and began his Portable Hole routine, going through it like a coaxing bedtime story. ". . . So we'll put everybody, Kathie and all of us, into it like this, and this," picking up one match after another, "and this big double one, the old tom-walker with his iron leg," folding the sock close from the top, the sides and the bottom, "all in the Portable, Extradimensional Hole, safe from the A-bombs, the microscopic dusts and poisons, the dreadful power of the cosmic, and the schemes and plotting of all the evil men."

Then he made his passes, the roll disappeared, the matches safely palmed, ready to pick out of Iron Leg's beard, but there was no response, and Milton sat, empty and alone, beside the old, old man, until suddenly he could not bear it and he buried his face in his hands.

But there was a tapping at the door, Penny calling softly, "Something important on the radio, Milton," and as he got up stiffly, the old man on the bed mumbled a little. Milton leaned close. He was talking as to himself. "We fit hard, Johnny an' Clyde an' Andy an' all a us, but we're down to ridin' the double-trees just the same, our butts a fannin'. . . ."

Outside the door Penny was calling louder, so Milton straightened the covers and went out. By the time he had his father up from the barns there were fussy, excited whisperings on the radio, a loud curse cut off in the middle, and then President Daunce, starting slowly, his voice even more nasal, higher. Without the confident puff and blow of the army dedications, he stumbled over the unfamiliar ghost-written words: "A state of great and extreme national emergency exists," he was saying. Penny and Milton looked to each other, and to old Martin, head down, unmoving, as so often sixteen, seventeen years ago.

". . . Deplorable conditions of fraud and thievery within your government . . . great irregularities and graft in the Departments of War and the Interior . . . members of the Congress implicated, with plottings of violence against man and the peace among nations. I have requested resignations within the Cabinet and have been refused. As a consequence I am calling a special session of Congress and demanding a thorough investigation and impeachments."

Still old Martin had nothing to say, Penny pushing her gray hair back uneasily. "Looks like this thievery out here is only a sideshow."

"Probably all the speech and threats're a sideshow, a sort of Reichstag fire, the old cry of the guyascutus loose, to distract the yokels!" Milton said bitterly, but he started to the telephone, Penny nodding her approval after him. "Hazel is so loyal to her boss; she'll feel awful. But she'll get over it, home here," Milton stopping to look back over his shoulder, knowing he should feel something tremendous, but there was only a numbness. So he went, but called Denver. Mary Barlow wasn't at the hospital, not there nor expected any certain time. Away indefinitely.

And when he came back to the living room he had to see Penny's aging face remote and set, the way she looked when, as boys, they did something they couldn't be punished for because their father must not know. And Martin hunched there again, with that blank, unhoping stare under his gray brows, his knotted hands clasped, out between his knees. There was no one to hit for this and so Milton had to get out, going down to Dunhill, to Agnes at the Stockmen's. That was how he got into the cooler. The town was full of soldiers as in war time, and after a few beers, he took a notion to go to the jail and demand Hughie Saul. "Godamighty, you can't lock up a man for trying to defend his home, and everybody else's in the Turtle Shell district! Why, it's built up this goddamn tuckhole of creation—and Hughie with a leg back on Formosa!"

But the sheriff looked up to Agnes, leaned to spit, and told Milton to go sleep it off, and so he struck out that bony left and the men around rushed him as the sheriff went over backward with his chair. From the bullpen Milton was dumped on a Denver bus by some of Ridges' outfit. "Get out and stay out!"

But the alcohol of little sorrows was no escape in this one more crisis in an attenuated nightmare from which Milton couldn't will himself awake.

All week Mary Barlow's apartment remained as empty as the evening Milton first came back from Seep. He had gone over with a chunk of deep-frozen tenderloin of elk he shot on the way up through the mountains, a lucky hit with the automatic Marty carried in his car pocket these days. Penny sent some chokecherry and wild grape jam in the box, the jars packed in old newspapers that would get no lead into the heart of any man of the army. The superintendent had let Milton in, stood around while he put the meat into the ice compartment, but had nothing to say of Mary.

All the week since then, men at plastic-topped desks, at hog pens and mine shafts, or fighting at the city dumps, were busy explaining the President's announcement in their own terms, their own coin. At last the newspapers and radio opened a little. Daunce was denounced as a Red by the Walper and Harrol sheets—loud denunciations both ways, but no information and no mention of Senator Potter. The stock market started to slide still lower and was closed, with uneasy knots of people along Denver's chilly Seventeenth Street. Early mornings Milton saw troops wrinkled from coach jumps march up the hill, around the Capitol and back down to the depot like in the darkest times of '42—the same large troop movements, and not a word in the papers.

Off work for his checkup, Milton just wandered around town, waiting to get a call through to Hazel or Kathie, or a reply to his telegrams. But everybody seemed to have vanished, like Joes before a screaming meemie, even the reclamation offices empty except the mail department. "I guess it's reorganization," the girl said vaguely.

So Milton wired Jim Becker in care of Winnie in New York and then to the Old Man, the old trouble shooter he had followed clear around to China. The colonel's daughter replied that her father was out of service and out of the country, as so many others, on a project he wished Sergeant Stone might have been in condition to join. Winnie wrote too. Jim was in Leavenworth, courtmartialed for something about Red-Day.

So it went, the old man driven out, and a right Joe like Jim in hock.

Low-down, Milton took one of the other nurses to hear Father Brian read his dramatic poem, "The Flame in the Buffalo Horn," to the Poetry Fellowship, the priest pale and worried, whispering to Milton afterward that Hugo must be out of town, missing his classes, and Mary gone too, and now Elsa disappeared. What could it mean?

Late that night Milton picked up a girl in a bar and then ran out on her while she was stripping down. Toward morning he came back from off around the chemical plant, past Mary's dark apartment. When a man hit him for a quarter, he remembered he hadn't been eating lately either, so they went for wheat cakes together. Turned out the man was old as Martin, a double vet, a retread Joe, and talkative when he got thawed out, even about the political situation. "I got nothing to lose, bud," he said, blowing his saucer "not with two jobs tossed away going overseas, and two women. Workin' or marryin' before goin' in sure is just wearin' the doorstep down for a damn civvie. Way I figger, Daunce's still puttin' out the patronage, whole damn civil service open terrain, and come worse, he's got the army agin the rest. No sense us blamin' nobody, Mack, not you ner me. Sure, we was sold out before we come back, both times, but there's been couple elections since V-J, and 'round fifteen million of us vets—greasers 'n all. If we was to get together. . . ."

"Hey, there, pop, ya better quit beatin' yer gums to that tune, er somebody'll be smashin' you in the smooch," the waiter warned.

The next afternoon was warm as summer, the sun bright against the mountains, the air still: a weather-breeder. Milton had to get out, so he went down to the AVC, only a few around, talking about the shoutin' preacher who wrestled with the devil in his mother all night and garroted her in the morning. But when Milton asked about the special session only four days off, they clammed up, even the milk-face just out of dog tags. No talk about a march on Congress for a bonus any more, and no griping about jobs, even by those in sleeping bags or Dauncyvilles. It was like back when Milton was a boy, only now people were really flat, flat as a toad under a half track.

So he went to sit on the gravel at city park lake, looking off to the little island in the middle, the bare yellow branches of the willows dipping to the water that was slanted with the gold of evening. To his soft callings a few of the mallards moved up hopefully, looking back to those hovering around where the great carp fought and churned the water for the feed the children were throwing to the ducks. The Canada geese came too, but more aloof, their feet working as they backed water, and Milton remembered the reservoir at home; sneaking quietly up there with little Rita, a pie pan of corn along to coax the wild mallards and their rows of striped little ducklings bobbing along behind until they grew into such pets, Rita cried when they flew away in the fall. Now suddenly the homesickness for those poor, uneasy days hit him like a physical hurt, and a longing for his Kathie. It looked like a man could manage to have his own daughter part of the time, if he was a man.

But as Milton stirred to leave, there was a mother's anxious calling, and a small boy running down the bank, his face flushed and shining in the reflected light from the water, holding out his mittened hands, crying, "Ducky, ducky!"

Suddenly Milton was up, the mallards chattering back in alarm. He would have his daughter. If Hazel wouldn't leave that rattlers' den in Washington he would steal the girl, take her away: Alaska, maybe farther.

When Milton had his plane reservations he went to his room, dragging his tail as from a long march under pack and instruments. Someone had been there, pushed a clipping under his door, a syndicated gossip column, one section heavily outlined in pencil:

What beauteous lady running a house of assignation for what notorious capital gang keeps hubby with a bullet in his ticker hid away in the vets hospital in a mtn. metrop?

He looked at it a long time, numb, and stuffing it into his pocket, packed his bag for tomorrow. Afterward he tried to look through the papers: another feature story about cosmic rays harnessed by the Russians, said to make the A-bomb just popcorn on a hot stove lid; another spy scare; a royal scandal; and three more traffic deaths, making 524 so far in the state for the year. And Hitler discovered again.

Milton wished Hugo were home, Elsa in her little room, or Liza Mack just around the block instead of set up over at Zeb's Bar-B-Q, her little Eddie out at the t. b. hospital. Although clouding over outside, and chilly, Milton went out again, over toward Mary's place and this time there was a light, two big bags with airline stubs at the door, and inside she was making herself a cup of tea and trying Penny's wild plum preserve with crackers. "M-mm," was the first thing she said, handing the jar to Milton, passing off her absence as a little business trip. It was nice to find a chunk of elk in the icebox, and wasn't his brother Marty a handsome wolf?

The aloofness, the strangeness that gathers around the traveler was still upon her, and something more, something too glib and talky. She looked different too, in a new silvery green suit, like the clump of velvet-soft wormwood that grew beside the old stoop on Seep Creek, her blouse the dusty pinkish brown of pine bark, and the short rose mink coat over a chair. Her hair was smooth and shining, her brows brushed outward like petrel wings, her eyes darker, and suddenly all the misery in Milton was forgotten, and there was only Mary with the sheen on her cheek, and her calm.

But immediately she was the scoffing nurse again, and so Milton took his anger out on the company that grabbed the Turtle Shell. She nodded. The big ones were in private hands, too: TVA, Boulder, Grand Coulee. . . .

"A life and death monopoly like that in the hands of a private ownership rapacious enough to steal it!" Milton protested.

Mary picked up the teapot and napkins. There was a test coming up, she said casually, and turned quickly to the personal. Wasn't he due for a checkup? So Milton told her about the plane reservation to Washington, just that. Mary stopped to look at him. "Good! Dr. Dilten's to be at Walter Reed another week, at least until the showdown. Go there at once; you'll get the best . . ." she said and took over, calling Washington for the appointment, speaking to Milton over the waiting mouthpiece. "You are wise to be near your family now. It's true most women are attracted by success; those who aren't, the Antigones and Jeanne D'Arcs, don't boost the population much. But sometimes just being on hand . . ." letting her voice trail off, not bringing up the beauteous lady gossip she must know. While she waited, she idly lined up the scattered pile of letters and documents on the desk beside her, the passport arranged neatly on top. "Maybe Hugo was right. Postwar society does seem to act like a petulant invalid, a wealthy old woman who bravely fought off a long and dangerous illness, and now is suddenly unwilling to give up the excitement and importance of the gathering about the deathbed, the melodrama and emotionalism of it. Instead, she turns against everybody who helped pull her through, and all the convalescent disciplines. Anybody crude enough to speak of the responsibilities of life, even learning to go to the bathroom again, gets hysteria and abuse and dismissal. The fawning, flattering, business-as-usual gigolos get her approval and rewards, even when the relapse is already on."

Yes, Milton agreed, wearily. In old Iron Leg's day it was plain as that leg cut off, the great region devastated and the many young men gone, but instead of facing this, the country turned itself over to graft and corruption and general irresponsibility. The common man's resources, his markets, even his currency were destroyed—skinned bare even with his hide sticking to his starved carcass like a frozen wolf's. And the same thing in Martin's day, except that the burnt lung was less plain to see, the damage a sickness fooling even old Iron Leg for a while. Now all the world was sick, the danger terrible and immediate and complete, but nobody caring what happened the other times—domestic rape, the great international economic and industrial combines tom-walking, with hunger and the A-bomb used like a club everywhere, and the people blinded, refusing to see, moving in an uneasy dream.

Slowly Mary restacked the papers under her hand, tapping the top with her strong fingers. "Yes, and this time it's like the spot on your x-ray, the bullet in the heart, calling for calm, balance, the utmost caution because the slightest excess or displacement. . . ."

The sky was dark and starless when Milton went out into the night, a spattering of wet hitting his cheek: the beginning of snow. He looked back to Mary's window just as the light snapped off. She had said nothing, but he knew she was leaving when he saw her passport on the desk, felt her already gone—one more bereavement. For some secret, perhaps military reason, she would not be there any more, going as the others, as Hugo and Elsa, must have gone.

Around him all the houses were dark, everything still—with the tangible stillness he had known before—far away, the lonesome stillness when the battle had moved on, or before the night broke into war.

He walked a long time, until he was white as the blue spruce with the soft, clinging snow.

6 — The Guyascutus Loosed

The autumn fog hung low over the Potomac, hiding all but the foot of the Washington Monument, and of Capitol Hill as Milton plodded up Connecticut Avenue. Its grayness lay over the city like the dawn of that morning before Normandy: the cars and trucks of soldiers passing Milton, the lines of ships moving out of nowhere and vanishing before him—headed toward some unknown landfall, with water and beach mined, obstructed, trapped; surely raked by gun emplacements, by rockets and dive bombers; the earth shaking; men falling, and blown into the sky. But today the cars went steadily on into the fog toward the Capitol and the special session gathering to hear a President of the United States trot out the sky hooks.

Milton's overcoat was rasping his neck, like wet GI stuff, his shoes soggy as from a week of foxholes. Yet this day should have been one of Wyoming sunshine for Milton Stone, his step sharp, with high, clear air tingling through his lungs. For the first time in his maturity he would be a free man, free to come and go as he wished, to breathe until his chest was a drum, to lift burdens until flares broke before his eyes with the straining, to sing and make love and give no thought or care to a dark patch on an x-ray film.

Yesterday, for a little while, he felt like that. It came to him while he stood before a neat and orderly desk at the hospital and a man said that if he would come in tomorrow evening, in a couple of days the bullet could be removed. As simple as that. Of course there was always an element of chance in a delicate operation, but nothing to concern a combat man who had carried a slug like that around for four years. Nature had done well by him, built a fine retaining wall against the danger in the best tradition of the Hairy Ears. With the new techniques the excavation should be easy enough, simple as scooping a rock out of a hole with a power shovel, or picking a peanut out of a pocket.

Picking a peanut out. . . .

A moment Milton had stood there, afraid to let himself take it in fast. "Will I be good enough to get cleared for engineering in foreign parts, sir?" he asked, speaking stiffly, as though the machinery of hope had set, rusted.

Soberly the doctor pooched his mouth, tapping the card with his finger. "Yes—oh, yes, and if you get into the more remote regions you may encounter some of us. . . ."

The next thing Milton was running down a strange street, jumping little hedges as though he were a boy leaping the sagebrush of Seep Creek. But finally he noticed people stopping to look after him, a policeman start his way, so he tucked his tie back properly and went to the Senate offices to send in another note for Hazel, promising terrific news this time. He had spent much of the last three days trying to get through to her some way, even by dry runs—faking a leaving and then slipping back to catch her. He had to; the school told him Kathie was not there, taken out a week ago, and no information.

But now he would be a whole man, with the right to his wife and his daughter, and so he went to tell Hazel. They still treated him fine at Potter's offices, made out one of the Senator's special passes. "This'll get you anywhere," Milton nodding, wondering if that included the place beyond Rock Creek.

But Hazel didn't come out to hear his news, and, disappointed and more, Milton left another note, saying he would see her if he had to go to the place that was known as the Little White House in all the bars and smoking cars of the country.

As Milton hoped, that brought her to his shabby hotel. Inside the door of the little bedroom, in a handsome, willow-slender suit of black and a sable scarf, she busied her hands throwing the veil back over her turban and then clasped them safe and tight on the large black handbag. "Well, here I am, Milton," she said, "but I should have appreciated a little patience just now."

Patience! Patience after giving him a three day run-around when he had seen her only once in three years and then provoked him to a slapping! After letting her name be rolled on the lip like a soggy cigar—hidden his daughter away!

But it was no use. Milton couldn't work up an anger against her this wonderful day, or even defend himself, and when she understood the whiteness in his face, not even daring to offer her his hand, she sighed and waited, refusing to sit down. So he tried to tell his plans for an engineering future to a handsome young woman standing against the knob of the door, and with more money on her back than he might make for her the next six months.

But his prospects with the colonel were good, and in other foreign work—building, work he loved, and in it they would get rolling, leave all this unhappiness behind. He said it confidently, but when Hazel made no acknowledgement at all nor brought up the bullet, he had to go on, turning the edge of his defeat against her as he had seen Martin turn against Penny, and as old Iron Leg must have. . . .

Yes, it was time she cut loose from the Potter gang, their grab at graft and power while they whipped up mass emotionalism and hysteria, like a nation of vagrant, irresponsible camp followers, discarding one human value after another as the women dropped their belongings from post to post, grasping at the selfish excitement of the moment.

"Yet you suggest that I start it all over again, from one remote construction camp to another, and with even less security," Hazel said scornfully, "or have you some trick for that too, in the old sock, your Portable Extradimensional Hole?"

But the man was not to be stopped now. It was time sensible people like Hazel Stone and her husband were settling down into their proper work, giving some solidarity to the world, ". . . If it's not already too late. . . ."

"Oh, Milton!" Hazel scoffed. Then suddenly her face became alarmed, "Or—what do you mean?"

"But in that case our daughter will be safer in some far spot, Rita's Alaska, or farther."

So Milton bulled on, knowing it was a footslogger against armor and the terrain rising, and when he was done Hazel had composed herself, not taunting his preaching, or asking about the sudden plans, so he had to tell the good news that deserved a happier moment; tell it to a woman standing with her hand impatient on the door.

Soon he would be free of the bullet. "As free as the afternoon we rolled our gowns around the diplomas and ran to the courthouse," and when there was no response, he found himself going over the words again, in foolish, embarrassed repetitions until the telephone bell finally stopped him.

"Oh!—don't say I'm here!"

It was for Hazel all right, a reporter downstairs, his voice clearly audible through the little room, and when Milton claimed he was alone the man whistled casually. "OK, bud—I appreciate your fix. My wife played handy-pandy with the chairborne while I was sweating it out between decks in the Pacific, but just ask the lady one question: Where is the body of Harrol, the Secretary of War?— No comment? OK," and the receiver clicked. Milton left holding the dead telephone, looking from it to Hazel. She had dropped to the edge of the bed, the streak of late sunlight from the window bright on the velvet squash blossom of her turban, on her hair, her smooth cheek. "Oh, those horrible men!" she cried. "They hound me night and day since the Daunce speech—and after the Senator did so much for him. . . ."

Watching his wife, Milton thought bitterly how much alike people were, women were, *fraulein* and all, when the williwaw struck.

But Hazel never hesitated. "There'll be more calling here; they follow us everywhere," she complained, her gloved palm flat against the bag in her lap. "It's so bad now the Senator makes us all carry guns."

"Guns, against reporters?" Then it soaked in. "You mean you have a gun here?—like a goddamn gun moll?" Hazel snapping the clasp of her bag nervously, "Oh, I must get to the phone!"

Phone! So his wasn't safe enough for talk about Secretary Harrol's body! "What I want to know is, have they got you involved?"

"No—at least I don't think so," she said, looking down, her face stricken as it was the day the notice that meant his embarkation came, leaving her alone with the baby on the way. All the smooth beauty of a few moments ago was gone; in its place an unhappy, frightened little girl.

But Milton was not to be softened, and with him standing over her, Hazel had to make explanations, excuses. "Daunce has been pushing the investigations at the War Department hard, particularly since they brought in that dreadful nurse with a lot of garbled dictograph recordings and stolen files from the mountain regions, Hot Springs, Denver. . . ."

Denver! Then the nurse might be from there.

"—Made the case look pretty bad. The secretary came demanding

* 362 *

that Daunce be stopped, but the Senator said he couldn't do that just then; he'd take care of Daunce later."

"Take care of Daunce?" Milton demanded.

But Hazel barely hesitated. "Oh, it was just a promise, putting Harrol off. Only he was breaking, so he had to—so he shot himself."

"Shot himself! Then there is a body! And how was that kept out of the Daunce papers?"

But Hazel was watching herself now. "Nobody's supposed to know until—until later. I don't see how that reporter—unless Harrol was found or somebody sold out." Then her calm broke. "Oh, I must go!"

Now Milton Stone had enough. "The murdering bastards!" he roared. "And my wife flat in the middle of it! By God, I could kill that Potter for this; I could take his thick bullneck between my two hands and give it a twist like a fat hen's!"

Slowly Hazel raised her face, her disturbed eyes golden in the sunlight. "You?—You could kill him?" she asked, low. "But it's too late. . . ."

"Oh, don't get excited," he said angrily, "I—you helped make— I've been a tame cat on the doorstep too long, a barra hog, without the fight left to kill even a son of a bitch like that."

So Hazel pulled her veil down and rose, hesitating a little at the door to look back to the man standing beside the bed, his brows suddenly very black, his mouth harsh and war-stiff under the growing mustache—the face of an angry, revolted stranger. Then the telephone rang again and closing the door softly she ran to hunt for the back stairway. When she was probably past any watcher, Milton went down to the dingy lobby and picked out at least a couple of men who seemed to be waiting around, casually looking after anyone who left, then turning their faces back.

And outside Milton tried to think that it was another dream from that long litter carry—this killing of Harrol, Hazel carrying a gun. But there was no easy awakening and in this he had forgotten all the joy of his news from the hospital, even to ask about Kathie, almost forgotten his daughter.

Toward midnight Milton went out into the deepening fog to look over the morning papers and to call Mary Barlow, to warn her of the gang that didn't hesitate to put a cabinet member out of the way, threatened to take care of the President. But her phone was disconnected, discontinued. So now he was alone, like a match in the sock in his pocket, in the Portable Extradimensional Hole that was all a hoax.

The papers seemed a dry run too, the Daunce press headlining the President's charges, promising great exposures today, the others demanding his impeachment again, carrying pictures of Walper and Harrol and Potter across the front, or perhaps on the second page, along with an item about the resignation of the Secretary of State for ill health, and others rumored stepping out too—while something called the Seven Bead sex murder was spread across the front.

Milton bought half a dozen papers and went through them carefully in his room. Suicides, hold ups, knifings and a few scattered lines about people found dead of exposure, cold and alone, making death in battle seem warm and remembering. There was a small item about the Secretary of War, gone South, vacationing, with an extended unofficial tour of overseas bases before his return.

Milton looked down on the papers scattered around him like a collapsed parachute, and rubbed a hand over his stubbly chin. Yesterday, for a little while, he had thought he was freed by the words of a kindly man behind a hospital desk, but that was foolish as a mirage over a mine field.

Yet he must make one more attempt to see Hazel before he checked in at the hospital tomorrow night. Try one last time.

Now, his shoes wet and clumpy, Milton was at the fog-shrouded Capitol for the Daunce speech, perhaps a last glimpse of Hazel and a word to pass on to Kathie with the big globe he had sent to Hazel for the girl's Christmas—all the places he had seen in the war circled in orange. Then this evening to the hardstand of the hospital. Beyond that it was like the fog of a new landing, the beaches hidden and unknown.

Milton's pass from Potter got him through all the guarding of troops to the door, and finally inside, although thousands were turned back, here and there one forcibly taken away, perhaps shouting: "This is a free country!" But he was hustled away to the locked army trucks just the same.

Looking over those passed around him, Milton couldn't tell if the guards were favoring one side or the other, or just tough MP's.

Some of those around him were familiar: little men from the American Action, some old Coughlinites, Bundists and Klansmen, including a preacher in a white cowboy hat, even old Fred Carter from Detroit, who had tried to push Martin around that first night on the homestead, when Penny slipped him the old shotgun. Inside the guards were heavy with ammo too, and gas bombs, as though to butter an uprising—nothing like the casual ushering Milton saw here during the war; more like Chungking—government by graft and arms.

He was herded off into a bunch of everyday people, mostly women, probably happy enough over a free afternoon of sitting in the warm. The guards seemed to know them. "No tricks now, Sadie," one warned, when a woman whispered at Milton's pass: "Isn't he a fine, upstanding young Galahad!" smiling her false teeth his way, blowing her gin breath around. Milton's fog-chilled face began to burn. By God, he wouldn't have these hairy-eyed hellcats classing him with their moth-eaten heroes. But the guard of the front benches motioned to him. "I'll try to keep the Moanin' Mollies off a yer neck," he whispered. "Couple throwed theirselves over the rail last time Boyd Potter gets goin' an' today looks like a heller, so if them biddies starts comin' at you, duck, bud—duck an' let 'em jump!"

Slipping out of his wet overcoat, Milton looked around the hall of representatives, surprised that it was even gloomier than with all the steel work in for the roof repair the time he was up from Belvoir, back in '42. Perhaps it was the weather he knew was outside the lighted, glass-set ceiling, the falling fog.

Down on the floor the joint session was gathering early, especially the senators, the kept-cats, the ganymedes of privilege, as Hugo called them—poking their bellies out like chairborne brass at this attack on one of their outfit. The Senate that had used the bloody shirt, the cry of "no entangling alliances" and "beat Russia" to defeat three victories honestly won by the Stones and their kind.

But today the fight was within the exclusive circle, with Daunce from the Senate too. Perhaps it was all only a smoke screen, more sand in the eye, like the Red baiting that covered all the maneuvering for outposts and spheres of influence—outposts with A-headed rockets, spheres of influence when cartels vaulted every boundary. But if today's probable charges of selling the great national properties into private hands, perhaps even the Capitol—why not the Capitol?—and a possible threat to peace were only the sand, then what was the knife? War? The combination of A-bombs with the great world monopolies to paralyze man—the final enslavement by the creature that man conceived when he learned to use a stone to lengthen his striking arm, to extend his trade of cocoanuts and clam shells—a creature he created and never tried to control?

Or was it something swifter, bloodier, a quick slash to the throat?

Anyway, there were none of the usual congressional guests, not a wife or a daughter in the visitors' section, not one of the Daunce family. And in the waiting it all seemed so hopeless, and with the galleries warm, the weight of the sleepless night and the hours of walking, Milton Stone laid his arm on the marble ledge before him and dropped his head. So his wet feet, the hidden body of Secretary Harrol, even Kathie, and all his uneasiness receded, and he slept.

Milton Stone awoke to the stirring among the women behind him. There were little knots gathering on the floor below, the doors fanning. Once Hazel looked in, dressed in a greenish gold suit, a sheaf of papers in her hand, sizing up the galleries, stopping to consider the one Milton was in.

"Oh, yes!" he wanted to cry down to her, "your claque's in place all right, everything set. . . ." And cry out, too, like Iron Leg, that planes might circle the globe with no lime droppings to mark their path, and a market break without sunspots, but a fancy woman falls on her prat.

And an old man must die. The old tom-walker was failing fast, Penny said, when Milton called yesterday to tell her the news of the bullet to be picked from his breast like a peanut from a pocket. The old Iron Leg who once turned cartwheels on a shining piece of pipe, nested cyclones in his coattails, was dying.

On the floor below Milton, Hazel was gone, everybody very quiet, as slowly, dramatically, Senator Potter came in, flanked by a dozen men, probably from the House and the Senate, although Nat Ridges was among them, and his brother-in-law who had lost his money to the Nazis in Norway.

Potter seemed even blockier, more bullnecked from above, his bald head shining in the ceiling lights, his belly pushing out of his open vest, a large red necktie spilling over it. As he stopped and looked up the women began to screech louder, some jerking themselves about, their mouths falling open, private moanings sweeping them, until Milton had to run up the gallery steps, his palm against his mouth and the bitter rising. With the guard's help he made it to the can, retching hard as the first time he saw a bulldozer uncover a trenchful of the murdered men and women, had to help lay them out, see all their private mutilations.

Milton came back to another stirring, everybody standing, the floor below too—all turning toward the roped-off center section of the galleries. But it wasn't brass arriving as might be expected, with the Commander-in-Chief trying to force out a Secretary of War already dead, although the men were imposing enough as they moved into the section opposite the white marble rostrum, and fronted by microphones too, and television equipment. Some Milton recognized, and the whisperings told him the rest: Western interests, sugar, packing, mine and oil; Eastern too, Wall Street, power, railroad, automotive, steel, coal, chemicals, even a sold-out labor lord— perhaps the most powerful two dozen men in the nation, and with their tie-ups, in the world. Men, Hugo Dean called the Thyssens, Krupps and Schachts of American Destiny.

When they were settled, Potter waved to them, and began to talk as though to those standing around him, but with the microphone at his desk open. The women, spent, began to cheer again as the Senator lifted his hands, the soft, thick-padded palms toward them, moving like an eccentric juggler beginning his act: up and down, slowly, easily, the pink palms seeming to glisten with moisture. As those around him stopped their feeder questions, he warmed to his speaking, this panhandler of ten, twelve years ago, a panhandler who had happened to check in the lumber Daunce's company delivered to a WPA project. From the first little graft he had swelled to this challenge of the man who made him, but certainly the men in the center gallery were here for something beyond a fight between two grafters, even a fight within the United States government, particularly the foreign contingent beside them, the new Von Papen, surrounded by his stooges from South America around to Japan—a wattled old buzzard with his hungry brood.

A couple of times somebody tried to brake Potter's irregular harangue to the session not yet called; a woman representative grabbed at the microphone and was pushed away, the galleries booing, shouting "Throw the bitch out!" the women around Milton calling "God bless you, Senator!" and "Amen! Amen!" as he roared that Daunce was the tool of the Commies, who had maneuvered the poor, sick-minded President into slanderous charges against patriotic Americans, throwing up a smoke screen to get the drop on the country, to pull a super Pearl Harbor.

". . . But this is not the day of the crackpot New Deal! This time America will move first!" he cried in a high, almost womanish scream.

The crowd cheered and whistled, the foreigners bowing formally to each other, shaking hands, although there were disturbances on the floor, a fist flying, the guards running in, a circle forming around the Senator. But to Milton it was all talk for the papers to plaster over the country, to be read into the *Congressional Record*.

Then suddenly somebody stood beside him, and, looking up, he saw Hazel as he had so often imagined her, the perfume of her there, the cloth of her skirt touching his arm. But her eyes were dark and miserable.

"I—I saw you and I wondered if——Did you mean it yesterday, when you said you could kill him?" She whispered the words and when he didn't answer she had to go on. "I know it's a lot, but no more than the war asked of you—and for Kathie and all the others . . ." she begged, holding her barrel-shaped handbag open close to Milton's eyes. He drew back, for inside was an automatic, black and ugly against the white satin lining.

A moment Milton Stone looked up into the pale face, into the eyes that were tear-filled as for a moment yesterday. But this time nothing stood between them, and when he put his hand over hers, it was like the coming together in a new wonder and sweetness.

And down there where Hazel looked, like on a pistol range, or an elk standing in the mountains, was the target. A flip of the gun and he would drop, yet Milton couldn't shoot even a blowhard pot-gut like that in peace, not if Potter himself had killed Harrol—not even for all his war-making talk. Milton Stone was not a killer, and a man didn't change his direction like one of those little tanks spinning on its axis. He had to make slow, reasonable turnings. Besides, all Hazel had to do was walk out with him, her husband. Take Kathie and go away with him while there was time, let the people here at home find Potter out. As Jesse Gray said, when the people knew. . . .

So Milton held the bag up to Hazel, but she was already going, the approving words of the women following her, and the eyes of the men. "Isn't she lovely?" and "She's invaluable, invaluable . . ." and underneath it somewhere a bitter hissing, "—bitch, a goddamn bitch!"

For a long time Milton looked down at the black bag in his hand, like something from a morphia dream, something with a desperate, troubling urgency that he could not grasp. He brushed at his eyes, trying slowly, methodically to force himself awake, but the heaviness of the gun was still there in his hand, and from below came the imperative poundings of a gavel.

Lifting his head guiltily, he saw that the joint session had begun, everybody standing around him, all up as from an invocation. Then there was a movement of heads as the President of the United States came in. He walked straight and steady, with his military aides beside him, the wings of plainclothes men settling each way as he took his place before the battery of microphones and television equipment.

At first his nasal voice was almost too faint to hear, and uncertain, his loose face, dirt-white, bowed over the pages in his shaking hands, a distressing twitch in one cheek, and Milton remembered Iron Leg's old saying: "the high monkey shows his ass." But as Daunce enumerated the reasons for the session—graft, bribery, the wholesale debauch of public properties, the maneuvering for war and the resignations denied him, he lifted his head and looked straight to Potter's desk. The Senator, suddenly a gobbler red, clutched the microphone in one hand, the other on something that looked like a signal board with trailing wires that he had just lifted from the drawer, seeming to wait as the President went on: ". . . It grieves me to include a member of this, the world's greatest legislative body —Senator P——"

But the galleries broke into an instant cover of booing, settling into a united roar of "Shame! Shame!" drowning out the name of Potter, drowning out Daunce entirely, ignoring his face gone bleak as an old deserted beachhead, his signal for silence, and the other protesting hands from the floor, even a few from the powerful men in the center gallery. Instead, the roar went on and on, swelling; someone near Milton seeming to lead it—a tall guard in a field coat.

Then the Senator stretched, rose, and held up a thick hand and a "Sh-h-h!" like wind over a rye field swept the galleries. Into the silence his stepped-up mike blared out: "Frederick Daunce, I call on you for a reckoning up. I demand your resignation as President of the United States of America!"

Resignation? There were a few boos to that, and a skeptical laugh or two, but cheers as well, many from the galleries, and plainly the request was no real surprise, not to the three cabinet members, Walper in the center, to the joint presiders behind the President, or even Daunce himself. Quick as a cornered ferret, he looked around the floor and the galleries, then to his aides and plainclothes men. But the faces of those around him all seemed closed, unhearing.

"Resign! Get out!" the Senator repeated.

So the President had to go on. "What infernal arrogance is this?" he shouted, and motioned to the presiding officers, the sergeant-at-arms. Not an arm unfolded, nobody moved, except that the uniformed guards were suddenly thick in all the doors to the floor, and the galleries, pushing in closer, solid all around the back.

"I warn you, I'll have your resignation!" Potter roared. "This is your last chance. For the safety of America I demand your resignation while I count three. One. . . ."

Now at last Milton was driven out of his numbness, wanting to strike out hard with his left, get both hands on that thick neck. Then he remembered Hazel's handbag with the gun on his lap, her words: "For Kathie." He could lift the bag, look into it as though hunting for something, flip the gun up.

But already the Senator had finished his counting, made a couple of little moves over the wired board, as for a bridge opening or a World's Fair. There was a brilliant, blinding flash, a sheet of orange flame overhead that seemed to melt the glass-paneled ceiling, and then Milton's arm was up over his eyes.

"God! God!" ran in a gasp around the great hall, Milton and the others trying to stumble up, to run. But the guards pushed them back as the building rocked under a great blasting push of air, a ground-shaking thunder that rolled in until the galleries seemed to weave, the lights shivered, and pale, open-mouthed faces stared blankly from one to another.

Then, on their first breath, a sound of horror broke from them, "My God, the Russians!" "No, no! Potter!" and in the center section one of the key men was up, shouting, "Murderer! Traitor!" to go down from a shot, the others swaying away from him in every direction. And the silence came as an echo, the dust rolled in little clouds downward from the glass-set ceiling and the ruffled folds of the flag behind the speakers' chairs settled back.

By now the galleries were thick with guards, the protesters hustled away, while on the floor the Senator was surrounded by men, armed men so tall that Milton could no longer see even the bald head.

God—it had come! making real that moment Milton felt over New York, but this was a mushroom cloud that he could have prevented with the weapon here under his hand, Hazel providing it, and the warning, plenty of warning. But he had been too much of a meathead, a self-centered meathead, instead of a man.

By now Boyd Potter was at his microphone again. "I got four . . . more . . . A-bombs," he was saying, speaking slowly, distinctly, each word alone. "And not out to sea like that one was—in New York, 'Frisco; scattered out. I'm taking over, Fred Daunce, but I'm doing it legal. Appoint me Secretary of State, then resign, you and your vice president, and I'll save millions of women and kids. . . ."

In the flat, tense silence, the President of the nation looked down on the armed men, strange men in an armed wall around him, then to the floor beyond, with Potter at his wired board, and to the blank galleries—old, with the stunned face of the wound-shocked. Suddenly Milton couldn't take any more, and with his arm up he stumbled out of his seat into the drawn guns of the guards.

But he got clear up the stairs before anyone shot, and then they only grabbed his arms instead, somebody crying hard, sobbing like a child, and Milton finding nothing in his pocket except the colonel's old sock.

When he had quieted a little, two men came to take him away, Milton looking back from the door. Potter was at the rostrum, being sworn in, people crowding around. A woman, Hazel, in the golden suit, was standing off, her white face turned a moment toward the empty seat where Milton had been. Then she, too, joined the congratulators, separating for her, sweeping her up beside Potter.

Outside Milton saw that the gray fog was ripped and torn by the blast and by the harsh wind that pushed against the rows of guards, blew around the armor and steel surrounding the Capitol, and swept the empty streets beyond. There were a few scattered shots somewhere, far off, and the low, terrorized sound of fleeing people, and then the wind again.

Slowly Milton Stone pulled himself out of a fog that was like that of the long litter carry, the same clockwork of pain awakening in his breast. He opened his eyes to a vague, blurred hospital room, and slowly it came to him: the doctor at the desk saying, "Simple —as picking a peanut out of a pocket."

So it was gone, the bullet was gone, and he was a free man; the horror and violence that seemed to converge upon a glass-ceilinged room at the Capitol was only a drugged dreaming that took so long to awaken. But it was all gone now, and happiness flooded over him and excitement, until the pain in his breast was sliver-sharp, tearing his breath. So Milton relaxed his arms and tried to quiet himself, make himself a vacuum. Gradually the pain slowed to a steady beat again, and as his eyes began to focus, he moved them idly over the tops of the beds, along the bare wall, stopping at a large gilt-framed color print of a man, like the cheap official pictures he saw blowing around the bombed-out streets of Berlin, or found hidden in good Nazi beds.

Idly Milton wondered what such a picture was doing on a government hospital wall. Then he saw that there was something familiar about this too. It was Boyd Potter.